BATTLE FOR KONTUM, 1972

UNDAUNTED VALOR
BOOK 6

MATT JACKSON

I have attempted to recount the events of this battle from a primary and secondary sources. Names of individuals in the events are actual names except in a few cases. Conversations are what was said or would have been said under those combat conditions.

- Matt Jackson

INTRODUCTION

This book, *Battle for Kontum*, 1972, is historical fiction. The battle itself was real, one of three key battles executed by the North Vietnamese Army in 1972 in an effort to defeat the South Vietnamese forces at a time when US and allied forces were withdrawing from Southeast Asia. In March of 1972, North Vietnam launched three major attacks into South Vietnam and one (what I consider) minor attack in the VI Corps region, or Delta as it was commonly called. The North Vietnamese launched the first and probably the largest assault across the DMZ south, seizing Quang Tri and attempting to seize the ancient capital of Hue. The second assault commenced a few days later in the III Corps region north of Saigon in an attempt to capture the town of An Loc and open the way for continued attacks to seize Saigon. The third attack was launched in the Central Highlands in an effort to capture Kontum and drive east to the coast, thus splitting South Vietnam in half. This story is about the drive to Kontum.

In writing *Battle for Kontum*, I have researched the events that occurred and have attempted to stay as close as I could to those events on the timeline that they transpired. I have attempted to utilize the names of key players during the battle, finding them in publicly available sources. Some, especially those in the South Vietnamese Army below the rank of colonel, were difficult to find, and in one case I had to employ a fictitious name. In the case of US personnel, pseudonyms have been employed in a couple of cases. Surprisingly, North Vietnamese commanders were much easier to identify, probably because in the end, three years later, they defeated the South Vietnamese.

What this novel is not is a condemnation of the North Vietnamese or the South Vietnamese forces, it is also not a prowar or antiwar novel. I do, however, praise the actions of the US advisors, Army helicopter crews and US Air Force assets that endured through this battle, staying with and supporting the Vietnamese forces to the end—and the end, for several, was imprisonment or even death. This novel is a presentation of the events that occurred in a format that attempts not to bore the reader with a history lesson. If you want a documentary, I suggest you look at YouTube or the History Channel. In the back, I have referenced the sources that I used, and I strongly suggest *Trial by Fire: The 1972 Easter Offensive, America's Last Vietnam Battle* by Dale Andradé; *Kontum: The Battle to Save South Vietnam* by Thomas P. McKenna; and *A Bright Shining Lie: John Paul Vann and America in Vietnam* by Neil Sheehan, a Pulitzer Prize winner.

This is the third novel about the Easter Offensive and the final in the Undaunted Valor series. I sincerely hope you find it interesting and enjoyable.

'By strengthening the capability of the South Vietnamese to defend themselves rather than depending on American troops, we provide an additional incentive to Hanoi to negotiate. If, on the other hand, Paris continues stalemated, Vietnamization provides the means for the orderly disinvolvement of American troops from combat without having to sacrifice our objective—the right of self-determination for the people of Vietnam.'

— SECRETARY OF DEFENSE MELVIN
LAIRD, 1969

PRELUDE

President Nixon and General Creighton W. Abrams initially enjoyed a fine relationship. General Abrams took command of Military Assistance Command, Vietnam in June of 1968, when the strength of US forces was 543,000 personnel and President Lyndon Johnson was in office. Nixon often said, "What Abrams says, we do." That changed by the spring of 1971, when the South Vietnamese attempted an incursion into Laos, code name Lam Son 719. To outsiders, it appeared to be a disaster for the United States, with high losses in American helicopter crews. Unbeknownst to the free world, however, the North Vietnamese considered it a disaster for themselves as well. They feared that they would appear weak going into the Paris Peace Talks that October. In addition, Nixon was improving relations with Peking and Moscow. That, combined with their poor performance during Lam Son 719, enhanced the pressure on Hanoi to do something that would show they were winning this war and the US was losing. With the withdrawal of American forces underway and considering they felt they needed to show strength, the Nguyen Hue Offensive was conceived. To the free world, this was known as the Easter Offensive of 1972.

The efforts by the United States to expand the armed forces of South Vietnam were mostly realized by the beginning of 1972. This increase saw eleven infantry divisions consisting of one hundred and twenty infantry battalions. In addition, there were fifty-eight artillery battalions, nineteen armored battalions with a mix of vehicles, M48 and M41 tanks, and numerous signal, engineer and logistic support units. In reserve were the 1st ARVN Airborne Division, twenty-one Ranger battalions and a Marine division. Supplementing the army were thirty-seven Border Ranger battalions. Surprisingly, the bulk of the ground forces came from the Regional and Popular Forces, consisting of over five hundred thousand men in arms providing local security throughout the provinces. The navy had been increased as well, along with the air force. The process was thought to have gone so well that William Colby, who had been chief of the CIA's Far East Division in Saigon for many years as well as head of the Civil Operations and Rural Development program known as the Phoenix Program and was currently the executive director of the CIA, later stated that by 1972, "the pacification program had successfully eliminated the guerrilla problem in most of the country."[1]

This success could be attributed to several factors, the biggest being Tet of '68, when the guerrilla forces mobilized and attempted major attacks throughout the country. They were soundly defeated and destroyed. By 1972, they still hadn't recovered, and since 1970, more of the fighting in the South had been carried out by the North Vietnamese Army. The defeat of the guerrilla movement forced the North Vietnamese leadership to make some tough decisions—in particular, whether to continue the effort to overthrow the South Vietnamese government through the guerrilla movement, which was going nowhere at the present time, or mount a major offensive with conventional forces. Lam Son 719 hadn't helped the North's position at the Paris Peace Talks, and they needed a stronger position and quickly. China and Russia were both warming up to President Nixon, and the North feared that their supply line of military hardware would be reduced if relations improved between the three powers. It was decided that a strong showing on the battlefield would carry considerable weight at the Paris Peace Talks and convince the Russians and Chinese that they were a viable force. The decision was made to change tactics and launch a major conventional attack into South Vietnam. The result was that large portions of South Vietnam fell under the control of the North and set the stage for the eventual defeat of the South Vietnamese forces.

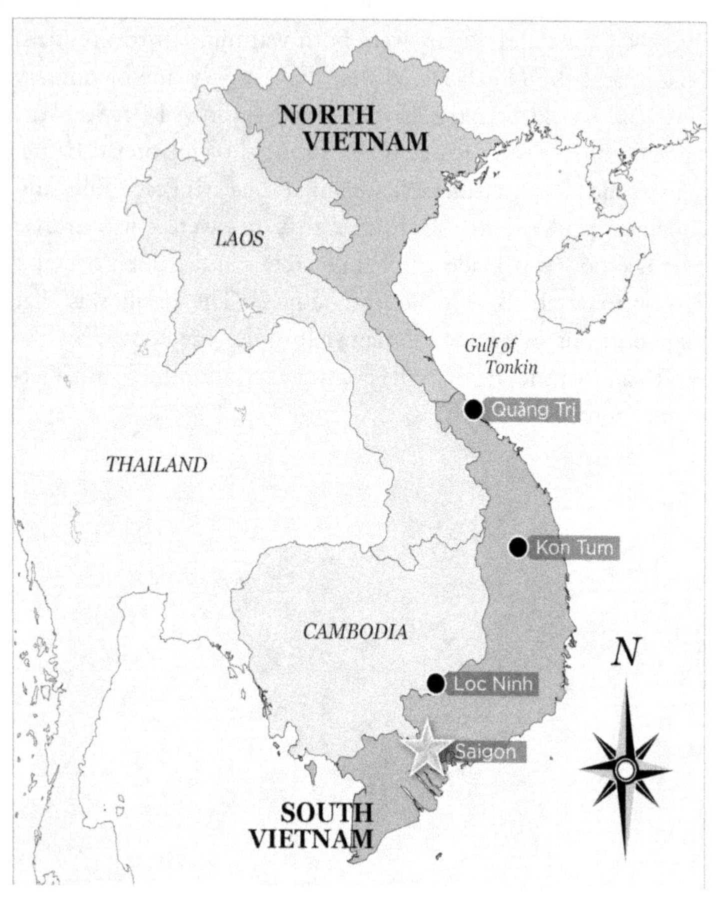

NORTH VIETNAM
LAOS
THAILAND
CAMBODIA
SOUTH VIETNAM
Gulf of Tonkin
Quảng Trị
Kon Tum
Loc Ninh
Saigon
N

1

ANOTHER CUT

Major General John Carley, MACV G-3, found himself being the bearer of bad news more frequently these past six months. Since Lam Son 719, the operation carried out by the South Vietnamese in April of '71, the tone in Washington had changed. MACV, or Military Assistance Command, Vietnam, was under growing pressure to draw down American involvement and accelerate the Vietnamization Program. This message Carley had just handed General Abrams contained the latest changes to the plan. Abrams had read it once and said nothing but puffed harder on his cigar. The second reading increased his blood pressure, Carley was sure.

"Sir, you recall that the president promised in the 1968 campaign that he would end our participation in the war and end the draft," Carley said.

"I do recall all the promises, and I also recall that OPLAN J208A was approved by him and Laird, and that was the plan for the drawdown. What happens? Almost immediately, Laird starts telling us to screw the plan and start drawing down faster. We were supposed to draw down one division in '69—one division, and what happened? Six months into the plan and he says we need to have two divisions out by the end of '69—regardless of the threat or the pace of getting the South Vietnamese Air Force up to speed. Why did we waste our time developing a withdrawal plan if they're just going to arbitrarily dictate the cuts?" Abrams still held the message in his hand and reread it for the third time. Carley could tell he was about to explode.

"The plan supported the Vietnamization Program perfectly as it would transfer the equipment and fighting to the South Vietnamese forces, allowing for a gradual withdrawal of US and allied forces. It had to be a gradual withdrawal, providing time to train the South Vietnamese forces on how to fight and how to use the new equipment they're receiving in their fight against the North. This phased withdrawal was outlined in OPLAN J208A. Someone should have read it to Laird," Abrams said with an angry tone.

OPLAN J208A, implemented on January 29, 1969, specified what the US troop strength in Vietnam would be on targeted dates based on certain criteria concerning the threat, pacification progress, and rate of improvement of the South Vietnamese Air Force. Since the plan had been initiated, monthly reports were sent to the Pentagon and the White House on the strength in manpower, equipment and units remaining in Vietnam and how much equipment had been transferred. MACV was charged with seeing that those target dates were met with the indicated reduction in US personnel.

Although the original plan specified criteria and withdrawal dates, Secretary of Defense Melvin Laird had his own timetable, and almost immediately he had ordered the acceleration of withdrawals. This was just the latest change that was going to cause a knee-jerk reaction in the headquarters.

"Sir, I took the liberty of scheduling a staff meeting for 1600 to brief them on this and get them working on changes. Your calendar was open...," Carley pointed out.

"Fine, you're right. We best get the bad news out early. Let me work up some guidance for them—this one's really going to hurt," Abrams said, withdrawing his cigar and waving for Carley to leave him.

These unplanned changes were seriously disrupting the orderly flow of equipment, personnel and unit redeployments back to the United States.

When Abrams walked into the conference room at 1600 hours, it was immediately obvious he wasn't happy. As he entered, everyone stood.

"Sit down," Abrams bellowed. "Let's get this dog show on the road, General."

General Carley did not take this growling personally.

"The purpose of this brief is to bring the staff up to date on the message we received yesterday on an unplanned reduction in the end strengths as outlined in OPLAN J208A and to receive your guidance on priorities for the force structure as we move to attain these new end strength figures, which are for 1 May 1972. The president announced yesterday that there would be seventy thousand more troops out of Vietnam by that date," Carley said. The air in the room was almost sucked completely out by the staff in exasperation, replaced by murmurs that did not help General Abrams's mood. More than one pencil dropped on the conference table.

"I don't like it either, gentlemen, but we have our marching orders, so you all need to start getting out some meat cleavers and looking at what we're going to be cutting in the next five months in addition to what we've already planned to cut," Abrams said, making it obvious to Carley that Abrams had just taken over the briefing. Abrams surveyed those seated around the table as well as the "horse holder" junior officers seated along the wall in the cheap seats. No one looked happy. He knew those junior officers were the ones that would be doing the work, with those at the conference table putting their heads on the chopping block if the numbers didn't come out right.

"Alright, let me give you some guidance. Plan on a force structure of sixty-nine thousand on 1 May," he started off and watched notes being taken. He could almost hear the unspoken cuss words as the original target of eighty-four thousand was out the window. A lot of work had gone into planning the cuts to get to that number, and now more was going to be needed. These additional cuts were going to strain the personnel side as well as the logistical side as they attempted to figure out which people needed to be removed versus who needed to stay in-country. This was going to create a morale issue, and morale was bad enough in the ranks now, as demonstrated by increased drug use in the lower ranks and higher alcohol use in the noncommissioned officer ranks. More racial issues were being reported as well, along with the fragging of officers and senior noncommissioned officers.[1] Maintenance yards were already full to capacity as equipment was being handed in for turnover to the Vietnamese Armed Forces, which were insisting the equipment be in like-new condition.

"To reach this new goal, I want to maintain the following priorities for manning and equipping, in this order. Command and control of American operations must be maintained as well as installation protection. That's our number one consideration. We will continue to protect US forces and personnel as well as support and administer to our needs. To do this, I want us to keep two infantry brigades, with an artillery battalion with each brigade. These will be for installation security and not active combat operations. Make that clear to those brigade commanders and their chain of command. We will provide minimal support in the area of intelligence gathering and analysis and minimal support in communications. The South Vietnamese can start picking up the ball in those two areas. We've transferred a significant number of helicopters and fighter as well as transport aircraft. They can now expect minimal helicopter and air support from us. I want us to keep three fighter squadrons in-country to be responsive to those two brigades if the need arises. We will continue to provide advisor support to the South Vietnamese forces but cut Army advisors back to one advisor at the brigade and higher levels except in the Ranger and Airborne units. They're the best that Vietnam has to offer, so we can keep a two-man advisor team at the battalion levels in those units. I understand the Marines want to keep an advisor at the battalion level as well. So be it, for now. They can also keep two at the brigade and higher level. We will keep an advisor at the district level as well if that's okay with you, Mr. Colby," Abrams said.

"Yes, sir, thank you," William Colby responded. Colby headed up the Civil Operations and Rural Development Support program, or CORDS as it was known. They were tasked with "winning the hearts and minds" of the rural villages and had Army personnel in the districts across Vietnam serving as advisors to the district chiefs.

"Alright, gentlemen, you know what has to be done, so let's get to it. General Carley, set a date to get back with me on the proposed cuts. That's all," Abrams concluded and departed.

* * *

HOURS LATER, Colonel Irving Pahl, the intelligence officer for Second Regional Assistance Group, sat with his MACV counterpart at MACV headquarters, Major General William Potts.

The two were discussing the previous meeting over a glass of scotch—imported.

"Sir, I heard what he said about intelligence operations, and it's going to hurt. We've already scaled back on assets, and now we're scaling back on more at a time when every indication is that the North is going to make a major push. The question 'is the North going to undertake a major offensive?' has been asked and answered. Yes, they are, in '72. But no one is asking the follow-on questions—where, when and how much?" Pahl said with frustration dripping from every word.

"I hear you, and I've voiced the same frustrations, but right now Melvin Laird is calling the shots in Washington, and we can do nothing about it. Nixon promised to get us out of Vietnam and that's the Holy Grail to Laird. He thinks we have enough intel through the NSA to provide the early warning and picture that we need," Potts explained.

"Sir, we used to have the CIA here with their human intelligence networks, which have been reduced as most see the handwriting on the wall and have left the country. We had the various services reporting through the Defense Intelligence Agency, but as everyone is cutting back assets, the intel picture is minimal. The Air Force is providing stuff, but it's one over the world for us on the front lines.[2] The YO-3 Quiet Star was providing good intel, but those were packed up and shipped home in December, so we have nothing except Air Force photo reconnaissance, which is too broad,"[3] Pahl said, standing to pour another drink. He motioned to Potts with the bottle, asking if he wanted a refill.

"Sure, what the hell?" Potts said. As Pahl poured, Potts continued, "You know, the guys in Ops responsible for identifying the initial units to be sent home identified shipping all the air cavalry units home by next April."

"What!" Pahl said. "Sir, we can't let that happen. They're the last of our eyes and ears in addition to providing some attack helicopter support. Hell, the damn Vietnamese Air Force is not going to conduct those missions. We can't even get them to conduct normal helicopter missions, resupply and combat assaults. Damn cowards and thieves," Pahl said before he slugged down that drink and reached for another. Potts said nothing, thinking it best to let Pahl fume and vent. They had known each other for many years and frequently served together. A good deal of respect for each other was present.

"Sir, back in November, the Air Force spotted that large tank farm up in the vicinity of Base Camp 609, right next to Kontum Province, my area. The YO-3 flights confirmed the information. Sensors along the Ho Chi Minh Trail are indicating increased traffic coming south. What was once a footpath from Hanoi to southern Laos is now just short of being a paved road. And with YO-3 gone, the cav is the only thing we have to keep tabs on the possibility of tanks moving into our sector. Hell, I can't convince Vann that tanks are up there or in our sector. He wants two sets of eyes on the tank from two different sources at the same time before he'll accept the fact that tanks are operating in our AO," Pahl said. Mr. John Paul Vann was the Director, Second Regional Assistance Group, with the equivalent rank of a major general even though he was a State Department employee and not Department of Defense.

"What? What about the photos from the YO-3 and the Air Force? Didn't that convince him?" Potts asked, taking a sip of his scotch.

"No. He said two separate times...he wants two different sources, at the same time, confirming tanks. I think he's putting his head in the sand on this one. Don't get me wrong, I like and respect him, but I think he's wrong on this," Pahl added.

"Well, he was the first to say we could expect a major offensive coming. Even sticking his neck out and predicting it would be after Tet and not during Tet," Potts said. "Argued that they would wait until the weather favors them and not our TACAIR.

Says that would be sometime in late March or early April. Pretty gutsy call," Potts indicated.

Beginning to feel the effects of his drinks, and having released his frustrations, Pahl sat back in the overstuffed chair. Looking up at the ceiling in resignation, he said, "Well, sir, the best we can hope for is that we're wrong and will be out of here before the North does decide to launch an attack."

* * *

Le Tien Kien and his two companions had been in training for eight months since being drafted. Kien had always wanted to be a soldier and a good citizen, believing in the ideology taught in school. He had excelled in his basic training and was soon identified as a natural leader. This had brought him a promotion to squad leader, and he had trained his squad vigorously. At last, the long-awaited march to the south had commenced down the Ho Chi Minh Trail. Visions of glory passed the hours for him as they moved down the dirt road. As they marched, he saw hundreds of construction workers along the road, repairing and widening it. Some were working with shovels, some on bulldozers sporting such names as Mitsubishi, Caterpillar and Kubota. In the darkness, he noticed tiny candlelight markers on the trail. The candles were placed inside notches that had been hacked into the sides of trees, so the flame wasn't exposed outside of the tree but only the light emanated from the notch.

As they continued south on their one-month march, they would move off the trail to established rest camps. In the camps, they found warm food already prepared, latrine facilities, and tentage to sleep under. They could exchange worn-out clothing and sandals as well. Occasionally, an entertainment troupe would be present and sing to them. At each, a political officer praised them for their courage and loyalty to the cause. Kien was proud that he was supporting the effort of ejecting the Americans from South Vietnam, freeing the oppressed people from the corrupt government of the South and joining the two Vietnams into one.

As they continued to walk, Kien's thoughts of glory were interrupted when, without warning, the first explosion ignited, followed by a thunderous rolling sound, growing louder as it came towards him.

2

PAVN PLANNING GUIDANCE FOR MR-II

15 January 1972
B-3 Front HQ
Base Camp 609

GENERAL HOANG MINH THAO, Commander PAVN Forces, B-3 Front, had fought against the Americans since their arrival in Vietnam. Before that, as a young officer, he'd fought the French at Dien Bien Phu. He had been the commander of the B-3 Front since 1967 and had been in the military almost his entire life. At fifty-one years old, he still maintained a trim build and was noted for his energy.[1]

He had attended the 5 January command brief in Hanoi, which outlined the entire Easter Offensive operation. The commanders for the 320th NVA Division, 2nd NVA Division and 3rd NVA Division had also been in attendance with him, along with the separate regimental commanders of the B-3 Front, 203rd Armored Regiment, 66th Independent Regiment. Returning to Base Camp 609 after the briefing, General Thao had set today to issue planning guidance to his staff and subordinate commanders. When Thao walked into the briefing room, which was a partially submerged large bunker, a staff officer announced, "*Chuy*," bringing everyone to attention.

"Please, gentlemen, be seated," General Thao instructed. He was very familiar with the Central Highlands as he had been in command of the B-3 Front since 1967. Under his command he had ten regiments consisting of twenty-eight thousand soldiers. "Gentlemen, we heard the overall plan for the upcoming offensive. I am prepared now to issue some planning guidance, but please feel free to offer your ideas as well," he said as he looked at the faces of his staff and commanders. What he saw was excitement and commitment as well as determination.

"Overall, our objective is to split the South in half by seizing Kontum and driving to the coast. In order to accomplish that, we must first control this ridge that the Americans refer to as Rocket Ridge. There are six firebases on this ridgeline, four of which are occupied—Firebase Camps 5, 6, Delta and Charlie, which must be eliminated before we can proceed towards Kontum. These firebases control movement on Highway 14 and Highway 512. If we cannot eliminate these firebases, then we cannot adequately move forces towards Kontum," Thao said and paused, observing the notes being taken by those present. "Once we control this ridgeline, then we can move along Highway 512 and take Ben Het, Dak To II, Dak To and Tan Canh, which will give us a clear road south on Highway 14 to Kontum. To isolate Tan Canh, we should cut the passes on Highway 14 and Highway 19. Any questions?" Thao asked.

"Sir, what about the border camps?" asked Colonel Tien, commander of the 64th Regiment.

"The three border camps that concern me are the camps at Dak Pek, Ben Het and Polei Kleng. Dak Pek is the northernmost camp in the Kontum Province, and our supply lines must come down the road which it is astride. The same for Ben Het. Polei Kleng sits at the southern end of this Rocket Ridge and could impede our movement towards Kontum." Looking at the engineer regiment commander, Thao stated, "You must complete the road to Polei Kleng by the end of March." The engineer commander acknowledged with a slight bow and nod. Turning to his intelligence officer, Thao continued, "Colonel, what is the current disposition of the ARVN forces?"

Colonel Minh quickly stood and pointed at a map hanging from a timber beam. "Sir, the current disposition of the ARVN forces is as follows. The 42nd Regiment of the 22nd Division is located at Kontum along with the division headquarters. The 47th Regiment is located in Pleiku; the 40th and 41st Regiments are at LZ English on the coast and LZ Pony. There is an airborne battalion, the 9th, we believe, that is located at Dak To II with one company at a firebase on Rocket Ridge. There is a Ranger company and elements of the 47th Regiment on the two northern firebases. The 19th Armored Cavalry Squadron is also at Kontum," he indicated, pausing to check his notes before looking up again. "Sir, the 23rd Division is located to the south with the headquarters in Ban Me Thuot and the 45th Regiment. The 44th Regiment is located in Song Mao and the 51st Regiment is in Dalat. The ARVN II Corps headquarters is in Pleiku. The Border Ranger battalions are located at Dak Pek with the 88th Battalion, the 71st and 95th Battalions are at Ben Het, the 90th Battalion is located at Dak Seang and the 65th Battalion is at Polei Kleng," Colonel Minh summarized. "I should also mention that the Korean Division is located in the vicinity of Mang Yang Pass and An Khe," he concluded.

"We must also be considerate of the American forces operating in the area. The Americans are pulling ground forces out. American airpower, however, is going to be a problem that we must account for. Besides the American Air Force, what aviation units are located at Pleiku?" Thao asked.

"Sir, the Americans have an air cavalry unit, an aerial weapons company and two companies of UH-1 aircraft at

Pleiku. There are also some of the CH-47 aircraft there at this time. One aviation company that call themselves the Chickenmen are due to depart and return to the United States this month. Our sources tell us that the air cavalry unit will be leaving in the later part of March or first week of April," Colonel Minh replied.

"Good, we need to employ our air-defense systems to reduce the effectiveness of the American aviation units. The greatest ally we have is the weather, which will prevent the employment of American fighter planes in the support of the ARVNs," Thao stated. "I have spoken with General Giap, and his guidance is to allow the attack to commence in the Quang Tri area of operations first. This may draw the ARVN leadership to concentrate on that area initially. A few days later, the attack in the Loc Ninh/An Loc area will commence and further capture the attention of the ARVN leadership. Our attack will commence days later, when the enemy has committed all its attention, and all its assets, to those two fights. Deception is our ally, and we must use it. Our initial attacks will be executed by the 3rd Division along the coast. This will appear to be in support of the invasion in the Quang Tri area and may panic the II Corps headquarters to shift one of the regiments of either the 22nd or 23rd Division to the coast to support the two regiments that are there, thus weakening the defense of Kontum. Are there any questions?" Thao concluded. There were none.

"Good. Now you have my guidance, and the staff can begin to develop our operational plan. They will coordinate with each of your staffs and work out the details. Let us come together in two months and go over the final plan," Thao said as he stood to leave.

3

DISCUSSIONS

22 January 1972
MACV HQ
Saigon

Abrams walked back to his office from the morning intelligence update. *I hope to hell Laird has the same intel picture as I do*, he was thinking as he entered the outer office, where Colonel Purdom, his executive assistant, was waiting for him.

"Sir, Ambassador Bunker is on his way over to talk to you. He has some concerns he wanted to discuss," Colonel Purdom said almost apologetically. "I tried to explain that you had a conference call with the SecDef, but he said he wouldn't be long."

"Okay, how much time do I have before SecDef calls?"

"Sir, you have two hours," Purdom said without looking at his watch. He had already known the question would be coming and he had the answer.

"Well, there goes that one-hour nap. Okay, send him in as soon as he shows up," Abrams said, walking into his office.

Tossing his briefing papers on his desk, he took the time to extract a cigar, a Cohiba, from his humidor, and after properly preparing it, he lit it and inhaled deeply. Being that they were Cuban and all Cuban products had been banned in the US, he couldn't obtain his favorite cigar in the States. But, this being Vietnam, no such ban existed here, and his aide was easily able to purchase them for him in the open markets. *One small enjoyment of the day*, he thought as he rolled out his desk chair and sat down. *Ah, a few minutes of peace and quiet to myself.* While he was enjoying his cigar, the intercom buzzed.

"Sir, Ambassador Bunker has arrived," the voice announced.

"Send him in," Abrams said, rising to his feet and moving around the desk. He left his cigar in the ashtray.

"Mr. Ambassador." He extended his hand and approached Bunker.

"General, I apologize for the short notice, but I just came from President Thieu's office and wanted to discuss his concerns with you," Bunker said, accepting the hand and moving to an overstuffed chair that Abrams was pointing towards.

"Mr. Ambassador, excuse me, but I just lit up a very fine Cohiba cigar, and I hate to waste them. Would you join me?" Abrams asked.

"General, I smelled it when I came through the door, and truthfully, I would be delighted to join you," Bunker said, and Abrams quickly returned to his ashtray and retrieved another cigar from the humidor. Preparing it, he handed it to the ambassador and held a lighter for him to light the cigar. Drawing in his first drag, Mr. Bunker allowed the smoke to slowly escape.

"Damn Cubans do know how to make a good cigar, I'll grant them that," Bunker said. Leaning forward in this chair, he became very serious. "But smoking your cigars isn't why I came. President Thieu's concerned about the intelligence picture his people are giving him. He believes that there's a major fight coming and coming soon. He's smart enough to know that US troops aren't coming back but is hoping that he can get air support, a lot of air support, from us," Bunker said.

"I've had a similar concern for the past month," Abrams said, standing and moving to his desk to rifle through his hold box. "I had Colonel Wollenberg, who drafts daily messages that express the 'Personal Assessment of the COMUSMACV,' prepare this message on 20 January and send it to the JCS. Let me read it to you.

"'The stakes in this battle will be great. If it is skillfully fought by the Republic of Vietnam, supported by all available US air, the outcome will be a major defeat for the enemy, leaving him in a weakened condition and gaining decisive time for the consolidation of the Vietnamization effort. We are running out of time in which to apply the full weight of airpower against the buildup. The additional authorities requested are urgently needed. In the final analysis, when this is all over, specific targets hit in the southern part of North Vietnam will not be a major issue. The issue will be whether Vietnamization has been a success or a failure.'"[1]

For a moment the ambassador said nothing but drew another breath on his cigar as Abrams laid the message on his desk and returned to his seat in the adjacent overstuffed chair.

"Let me ask, General, what additional authorities did you ask for?" the ambassador asked with some concern in his voice, thinking, *The man has all the authority in the world. What additional authority could he be asking for?*

"I have in previous discussions with Laird asked for additional aircraft, the lifting of budgetary restrictions on aircraft sorties, and the authority to attack targets in the DMZ and the southern part of North Vietnam," Abrams said as he curled a finger on his open hand with each point. "It seems the cone of silence has descended on Washington, and I have had no answers. I was hoping that this message would have opened some eyes."

"Well, if it helps to move the ball any, I told Kissinger that the situation is evolving into the maximum military effort the North is capable of making in the next few months," Bunker said, drawing on his cigar with a smile. The knock on the door interrupted the moment of contemplation both men were sharing.

"Excuse me, sir," Colonel Purdom said, opening the door slightly.

"Yes," Abrams acknowledged.

"Sir, the SecDef is on the line for you," Purdom said.

"Very good." Abrams stood and walked over to his desk. "This should be interesting."

Picking up the receiver, he placed it in the cradle. "Mr. Secretary, good morning to you. I have Ambassador Bunker in my office, and I have us on speakerphone if that's alright," Abrams said, knowing that unless the SecDef wanted to discuss something very classified, it would be permissible to have the ambassador there.

"Good afternoon, General. By all means it's okay. Ambassador, I hope he's sharing one of those cigars with you," Secretary Laird said.

"He most certainly is, Mr. Secretary," Bunker responded with a smile on his face and a chuckle in his voice.

"Good. General, the reason I'm calling you—and you will get this in a message before the end of the day—is in response to your message of 20 January referencing more assets and authority. We have a concern here, militarily and politically, and I must admit PR-wise as well, that some of what you're asking for could be a hot potato for the administration. Some of this we can accommodate you with. Let's start with that. First, we're sending an additional eighteen F-4 Phantom jets, nine each to Da Nang and Thailand. Second, we've ordered an additional eight B-52s to Guam. Third, we're moving a fourth carrier to

Yankee Station, and lastly, we're lifting the budget band on aircraft sorties," Laird outlined.

"Well, sir, that's all very good and will enhance our capability to help the South Vietnamese, but what—" Abrams didn't get to finish as he smiled and glanced at the ambassador.

"At this time, we're withholding the authority to engage fighter ground facilities with antiradar missiles outside of Hanoi-Haiphong as you asked for. We're studying that request. And your request to strike MIG bases, troop concentrations, and supply depots in the southern portion of North Vietnam is also denied at this time but being considered. No need to argue the point with me right now. I know your thoughts and feelings on these points, but there are other factors that we must consider," Laird said, cutting off Abrams's arguments.

"I understand, sir," Abrams responded with dejection dripping from every word. His look at Bunker indicated he was not happy.

"Now one more thing. We want you to take maximum advantage of the authority to conduct protective reaction strikes against anti-aircraft units in North Vietnam that fire at US aircraft. Am I clear on this?" Laird asked. Abrams and Bunker exchanged looks of puzzlement.

"Yes, sir, you are, and we will," Abrams responded as a smile slowly crept across his face.

"Good. You gentlemen have a good day, and that message will be arriving sometime today, General. Goodbye," Laird said, ending the call. Abrams hung the phone back up and picked up his cigar. As he moved back to his comfortable seat, the smile was evident on his face.

"Sounds like you got most of what you wanted, General," Ambassador Bunker said.

"Oh, I just may have gotten a lot more, Mr. Ambassador," Abrams said, blowing a smoke ring towards the ceiling.

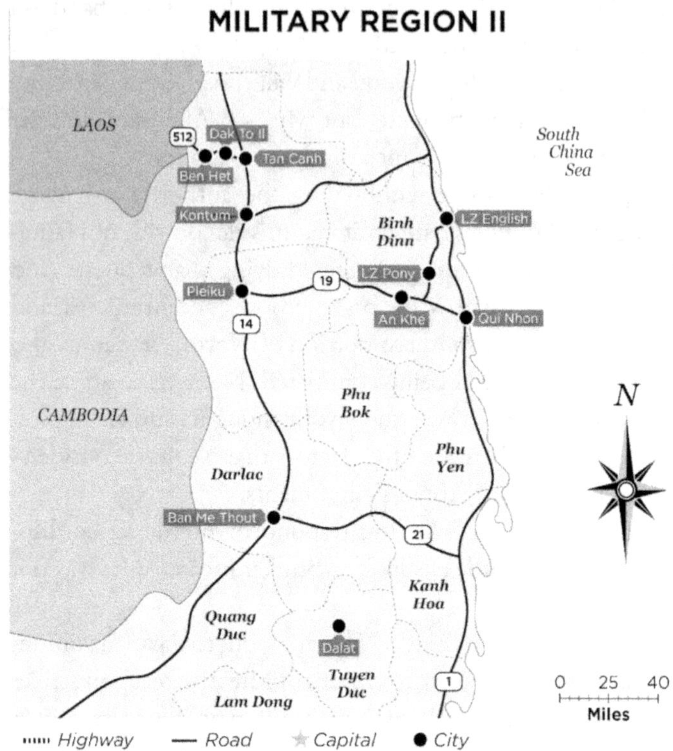

MILITARY REGION II
LAOS
512
Dak To II
Tan Canh
Ben Het
Kontum
Binh Dinh
LZ English
South China Sea
Pleiku
19
LZ Pony
14
An Khe
Qui Nhon
Phu Bok
Phu Yen
CAMBODIA
Darlac
Ban Me Thout
21
Kanh Hoa
Quang Duc
Dalat
Tuyen Duc
Lam Dong
1
N
0   25   40
Miles
Highway
Road
Capital
City

4

———

SHIFTING OF FORCES

23 January 1972
  MR-II Corps HQ
  Pleiku

LIEUTENANT GENERAL NGO DZU was looking at a map of the area when Mr. John Paul Vann arrived. Dzu was politically connected to President Thieu, which had helped him achieve his position as he was not noted for his combat command record. A stocky, pudgy-faced individual, he wasn't the inspirational type of warrior to lead men in battle. Throughout the advisor network, the leadership ability in Military Region II was considered the worst in Vietnam. Dzu had been serving on the Joint Staff when the corps commander for MR-IV was killed in a helicopter crash in 1970 and officers had to be shuffled. Suddenly Dzu was propelled into the Region II corps commander position.

John Paul Vann was head of the Second Regional Assistance Group. Vann had spent several years in Vietnam, first as a US Army officer. He was a lieutenant colonel when he retired after spending a tour in Vietnam as an advisor and joined the State Department. Once there, he quickly returned to Vietnam and began working in the pacification program, winning the hearts and minds of the people. There he met Dzu. Vann was the pacification advisor at that time for MR-IV, so the two worked together. When Dzu was transferred to take the command position for MR-II, Vann asked him to put a good word in for him to be moved to the senior advisor position when the then-current senior advisor departed.

As pacification advisor, Vann had discovered that Dzu was involved in a lucrative drug operation run by his entire family, headed up by Dzu's father. His brother was a Vietnamese Air Force pilot and Vann had proof that Dzu's brother was flying cocaine and heroin out of Laos in Air Force aircraft. Vann found that he could easily manipulate Dzu and some said blackmail him if necessary. Dzu wanted no conflicts with Vann, so he pretty much acquiesced to any suggestions Vann made.

Moving Vann to MR-II to be the head of the Assistance Group was no small task. The three other Assistance Groups were commanded by general officers. Vann couldn't exercise any judicial actions as a civilian, so his title was Director, Second Regional Assistance Group. Brigadier General George Wear was appointed as his deputy who could exercise judicial actions.

"General, you wanted to discuss something with me?" Vann asked as he walked into Dzu's office on a Monday morning. Generally Dzu would be in his Pleiku office on Monday, having spent the night in Pleiku on Sunday. Monday afternoons, he would return to Qui Nhon and not be seen again until the following weekend. His excuse was that he had to take care of business in Qui Nhon, but no one knew exactly what the business was.

"Yes, I have been looking at the intelligence reports and have some concerns. We have had much contact on Rocket Ridge and I fear that there will be a buildup and attack from across the border. I am considering moving some units to reinforce our positions closer to the border. Currently the 22nd Division Headquarters is in Kontum, with one regiment as well as a second regiment in Pleiku. The 23rd Division Headquarters is in Ban Me Thuot with one regiment. One regiment of the 23rd is at Song Mao and one regiment is in Dalat. I think I move the two regiments of the 22nd: the 40th Regiment from LZ English and the 41st Regiment from LZ Pony," Dzu announced.

"General, if you move those two regiments, you'll have no forces in the coastal plains. The only forces to oppose the enemy will be the RF/PF forces and they're not sufficient," Vann countered.

"What do you suggest, then?" Dzu asked.

Referring to the map, Vann thought for a moment. "Why not move the 47th Regiment sitting in Pleiku up closer to the border as well as the 42nd Regiment that's in Kontum? I would also move the 22nd Division Headquarters closer to the border to exercise better control and coordination of the area," he offered. Dzu continued to stare at the map.

"Right now the 2nd Airborne Brigade is on Rocket Ridge with his battalions manning the fire support bases. The 9th Battalion is in Tan Canh with one company on a firebase on Rocket Ridge. The 2nd Airborne Brigade could be pulled out at any time by the JCS and that would leave us wide open," Dzu mumbled as his hand wandered over the map. Then, in a loud, definitive announcement, he said, "Yes, I have decided. We will move the 22nd Division Headquarters to Tan Canh. I want his 42nd Regiment there with him and he can position the 47th Regiment at Dak To II. They can move from Pleiku in two days maybe."

"What about the 19th Armored Squadron? Are you going to leave them behind in Pleiku?" Vann asked.

"I will have them move to Tan Canh as well. They can reinforce the 14th Armored Squadron," Dzu responded.

"Moving the 22nd up to Tan Canh, you should establish a command structure that's announced to everyone so the commanders will know who's supporting and who's supported," Vann said. "Why not do this? Designate the 22nd Division as the command responsible for all the forces in the Dak To region, to include Tan Canh, Dak To II, Ben Het, Dak Pek, Dak Sang, Dak Mot, and FSBs 5 and 6, as well as all the firebases on Rocket Ridge. Place Colonel Nguyen Thinh in charge of Kontum as he's the province chief for Kontum Province. Place Colonel Tuong, your deputy, in command of Pleiku."

"That does appear to make sense. But what about the central plateau? We have forces in the east on the coastal plain and we have responsibility for the west, but we have a gap in the Central Highlands between An Khe and Kontum," Dzu pointed out.

"Expand the AO for the 23rd Division. East of An Khe there's the Korean Division, and the area is fairly quiet. Give An Khe to General Vo Vinh Canh and the 23rd Division," Vann suggested. "The 23rd's sector has always been fairly quiet, so expanding it shouldn't be a problem." As Vann studied the map and the planned moves, his mind was working on a strategy.

"You know, General, if you have a regiment at Dak To II and one at Tan Canh, in that terrain, you'll control Route 512, especially if you hold the firebases on Rocket Ridge. If the NVA do attempt to attack down Route 512, they will be seen from Rocket Ridge and hammered by artillery. We can also send them back to the Stone Age with heavy concentrations of B-52 bomb runs. We can defend right there and stop them if they should attempt to come that way."

"I was thinking we could engage them from those locations and then withdraw back towards Kontum and Pleiku," Dzu said.

"General, an action like that takes coordination, discipline and tight control—three things those regiments don't have. They've never rehearsed a retrograde operation; I've never seen the kind of self-control and discipline needed for such an operation in the officers or the soldiers, and the division headquarters could never keep up with the operation to control it. No, you're better off digging in and holding those towns and positions while we bring in the airpower that's available to us," Vann outlined.

As Dzu studied the map, Vann thought he looked like a deer in the headlights of a car. Finally Dzu turned and proclaimed that he would issue the orders right away and then depart for his duties in Qui Nhon. Vann stayed back, staring at the map. *By God, that's the only way to fight this battle when it comes. To these guys, a retrograde operation would quickly turn into a panicked rout. If they get surrounded and can't run, so much the better. That will force them to fight. We can break the North's back with airpower as we get them to mass for attacks,* Vann thought, smiling to himself as he walked out of General Dzu's office and headed to see the SRAG Operations officer, Colonel Snell.

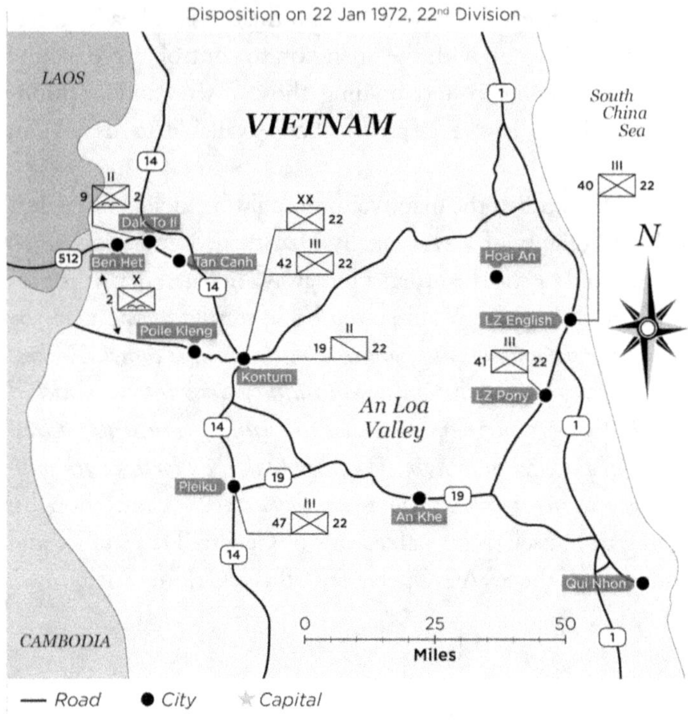

MILITARY REGION II
Disposition on 22 Jan 1972, 22nd Division
LAOS
VIETNAM
South China Sea
LAOS
14
1
II
9 2
Dak To II
512
Ben Het
Tan Canh
XX
22
III
42 22
14
X
2
Poile Kleng
Hoai An
LZ English
40 III 22
N
Kontum
II
19 22
An Loa Valley
III
41 22
LZ Pony
14
1
Pleiku
19
III
47 22
An Khe
19
14
Qui Nhon
1
0 25 50
Miles
CAMBODIA
Road   City   Capital

5

RULES OF ENGAGEMENT

23 JANUARY 1972
MACV HQ
Saigon

"Come in, John," Abrams said to General John D. Lavelle, who stood in the doorway to Abrams's office. Lavelle was a US Air Force four-star general and commander of the 7th Air Force headquarters at Tan San Nhut Airfield in Saigon. He also wore a second hat as Deputy Commander for Air Operations, MACV.

"Morning, sir, I was told you wanted to see me," Lavelle said, entering the office.

"Yeah, sit down. Want some coffee?" Abrams asked as he pointed to one of the overstuffed chairs in his office. He stood and came around his desk to take the other chair.

"No, I'm good. Had enough already today," Lavelle answered.

"How have our aircraft losses been this month?" Abrams asked.

"Well, on the seventeenth we lost two AC-130 gunships over

the Ho Chi Minh Trail with the crews either captured or killed. On the twentieth we lost an RF-4C fighter from the 432nd Tactical Reconnaissance Wing, and the month isn't over yet," Lavelle indicated.

"What's the air-defense coverage along the trail like?" Abrams queried.

"Prior to and during Rolling Thunder, the threat the entire length of the Ho Chi Minh Trail was about one hundred and fifty guns. Once Johnson stopped the Rolling Thunder Campaign in 1968, the North moved all their systems to guard the trail as we shifted all our sorties to the trail. During and before Rolling Thunder, we were running about one hundred and forty sorties a day on the trail. After Rolling Thunder, we were running about six hundred and twenty sorties a day, which is where we're at right now. Today, there are about six hundred and fifty anti-aircraft guns of various calibers from 23mm up to 57mm along the trail, not counting any missile systems that they've moved down. And those guns are moved from one position to another," Lavelle outlined.

"What I want to talk to you about is the buildup of forces across the DMZ in the southern portion of North Vietnam. I requested that we be allowed to hit MIG bases and SAM sites in that area, and the request was denied," Abrams said, telling Lavelle nothing that he didn't already know and fully understand. Lavelle remained quiet and let Abrams continue. "Now under the current rules of engagement, we can exercise protective reaction strikes if fired upon or painted by radar, correct?" Abrams asked, seeking assurance.

"Yes, sir, that's the policy. The rules of engagement are pretty convoluted, but that does stand out. The last time we got the rules of engagement in one neat package was, I believe, in 1968 from President Johnson and McNamara. Those rules are still in effect," Lavelle stated.

"And the rules are...?" Abrams asked.

"North Vietnamese fighter bases are considered sanctuary, whatever that is, as is any fighter aircraft with its landing gear extended, any fighter not showing hostile intent, any SAM site not actively shooting at an aircraft," Lavelle replied. "Back then the North Vietnamese SAMs used high-pulse recurring frequency radars. Our aircraft were equipped with receivers that gave the crews a warning if they were being painted, and they had time to react. In 1971, the North integrated their SA-2 Fan Song fire control radars with their Bar Lock, Whiff and Spoon Rest ground control intercept radars. The ground control radars feed the data to the Fan Song. The radar homing and warning gear in the aircraft doesn't detect the ground control intercept radars, so the first warning the pilots have is when the Fan Song paints them as they launch the missile. Today those rules have been modified through various message traffic, memos and verbal orders from CINCPAC. The pilots joke that we have to have two people in the F-4 jet—one to fly the plane and the other to carry the briefcase with all the rules," Lavelle said.

"Well, I think we need to exercise a rather liberal interpretation of the protective reaction rule when it comes to operations in the southern part of North Vietnam," Abrams indicated.

"At the conference earlier this month, John Vogt told my vice commander, Marshall, that field commanders haven't been nearly as aggressive as they should have in the opinion of Admiral Moorer,"[1] Lavelle said. "He further said that field commanders hadn't been flexible enough in the use of the existing authorities and JCS wouldn't question our aiming points on protective reaction strikes."

"That sounds like they expect a more liberal use of the protective reaction provisions," Abrams said.

"You know, sir, when the SecDef was here back in December, he came to my office and told me, let's see if I can quote him properly... I should 'make a liberal interpretation of the rules of engagement in the field and not come to Washington and ask him, under the political climate, to come out with an interpretation; I should make them in the field and he would back me up,'"[2] Lavelle said with a smile. "I think I should follow that line of guidance, don't you?"

"I think that's some pretty good guidance, but—and this is a big but—we need to be sure that any proactive reaction we undertake can be justified if questions are asked," Abrams replied.

"That shouldn't be difficult. Every reconnaissance flight we fly has an escort now. They turn on the SAM radar, that right there is an immediate proactive reaction to a threat," Lavelle pointed out.

"How big of an escort package?" Abrams asked.

"Probably two aircraft for MIG protection and two for hitting any ground stations."

"Well, I'll leave that up to you. I really don't want to know details. Just provide as much protection to the crews as we can," Abrams directed.

"While we're on the subject, how do you want the B-52s' sorties allocated?" Lavelle asked. "Any changes to the priority?"

"At this point, no. First priority is to MR-I, second to MR-II and MR-III. MR-IV seldom has a target worthy of a B-52 strike, so those if requested will be handled individually for now. The intel picture is such that the Ho Chi Minh Trail is a highway and there are no restrictions on bombing in Laos or Cambodia, so as the intel people find stuff, we hit there if one of the regional groups isn't screaming for a strike," Abrams said in closing.

"Alright, sir, I'll get right on it. I believe we have some strikes later today along the DMZ. Want to make sure they have the proper coverage," Lavelle said before he stood and departed.

An hour later, General Lavelle met with his staff. "Gentlemen, we need to do a better job of protecting the bombers. To do that, we must get better at protective reaction," Lavelle said, moving to a map hanging on the wall that showed all known and suspected enemy air-defense sites. "I suspect that this site here will attempt to engage the bombers before they start their bomb run. They'll see the bombers with their long-range search radar and then turn on the tracking radar just before they launch. The bombers won't have time to react to a missile. I want this SAM site taken out before he has an opportunity to launch. Any questions?"

Looks of wonderment were replaced with smiles.

"Sir, I believe we understand exactly what you want, and we'll get the air tasking order out right away," Major General Alton D. Slay, Lavelle's deputy, responded.

"I want it understood that whenever an aircraft is over North Vietnam, the crew are to assume the air-defense system is activated and they're authorized to fire. We had some really good intelligence reported by our reconnaissance flights. We lost three aircraft back on the eighteenth of December from the 432nd Tactical Reconnaissance Wing. That's three too many in my book. We have a ground control intercept radar here at Moc Chau that controls his MIGs. Take it out before we lose any more aircraft to this site," Lavelle ordered.

"Sir, we have intel about a possible MIG raid on our B-52s," Slay said.

"Oh, what's this about?" Lavelle asked.

"Sir, SIGINT reports that tonight the North intends to launch a flight of their best pilots and make a night attack on a B-52 flight that we'll be sending against a target in Laos.[3] The flight will originate out of Hanoi and fly to Dong Hoi. From there they will launch against our flight," Slay explained.

"This calls for a protective reaction. Send a strike package to knock them out once they get to Dong Hoi," Lavelle ordered. "I want our pilots to know and understand that we will do anything and everything to protect them. Protective reaction must be exercised whenever a threat to the mission is noted," Lavelle said, pausing for a moment. "You know, intel identified the construction of the first SA-2 site in North Vietnam in 1965. We even requested to strike it before it was finished, noting that by taking it out, we would be saving crews. When the request went before Assistant Secretary of Defense for International Affairs John McNaughton, he shot it down. He said they would never use them, and it was a political ploy to get the Russians further on their side. What a dumbass!" Lavelle added. "Alright, let's get air tasking orders out and be sure the wing commanders understand the meaning of protective reaction. I'll be in the command center monitoring this mission. Oh, and, Slay, be sure that the mission debrief reflects that enemy action was reported. We cannot report no action. Our authority is protective reaction, so we have to report there was enemy action."

"Yes, sir. I'll let the wing commander, Colonel Gabriel, know," Slay responded.

6

—————

REPORTS

23 JANUARY 1972
  432nd Tactical Reconnaissance Wing
  Udorn Royal Thai Air Base, Thailand

"Colonel Gabriel, General Slay here," Slay said over the telephone. "Is Colonel O'Malley there with you?"

"Yes, sir, I have you on speakerphone," Gabriel said, glancing at O'Malley, who was the vice wing commander.

"Okay, I want to be sure that you both understand that we must assume from General Lavelle's direction that you'll have reaction to your strike tonight. The crews have got to report and record reaction. Is that understood?" Slay asked.

"Yes, sir. We've already passed the word down and the pilots and crews will be briefed on what to report during the debriefs," Gabriel explained.

"Good, just wanted to close the loop on this. Good hunting tonight. Look forward to reading the report on this one. Talk to you tomorrow," Slay said before he hung up the call.

The 432nd Tactical Reconnaissance Wing had been operating in Southeast Asia since the early days of the 1960s. They also had some of the most experienced reconnaissance and forward air controllers in Southeast Asia and had pioneered the FastFAC technique.

Due to the air-defense threat along the Ho Chi Minh Trail and North Vietnam, the prop-driven aircraft were just too vulnerable, and so F-4 Phantom jets were used, with nose-mounted cameras and a pilot and observer in the back to adjust the attack aircraft. This became the FAC. The second aircraft was an armed F-4 Phantom jet and used the call sign Falcon. His job was to protect the FAC aircraft. The photo aircraft used Atlanta or Whiplash as a call sign.

"Alright, gentlemen, let's get started. Tonight's mission is to take out the airfield at Dong Hoi. Earlier today, a flight of four MIGs left Hanoi and landed there. Their mission for tonight is to intercept and take out a flight of B-52s coming out of Guam. We are not going to let that happen. The 561st Tac Fighter Squadron will precede the strike package and use their Wild Weasels to take out the radars. The strike package is the 562nd and 563rd Tac Fighter Squadrons out of Korat Royal Thai Air Base. All three squadrons are from the 23rd Tactical Fighter Wing and all are flying F-105s. The 555th Tac Fighter squadron will provide MIG cover," the briefing officer said. Pilots with the Triple Nickel Squadron could easily be identified by their wide smiles. They had no desire to get in low and slow like the F-105 aircraft.

"Once the strike package is done, your mission," he continued, looking at the two officers from the 432nd Tactical Reconnaissance Wing, "is to get a photo recon of the airfield so we can make a damage assessment. Your mission sheets have all the information you need, to include routes, checkpoints, call signs and frequencies. I will be followed by Captain Johnson with your weather brief if there are no questions for me," he said, surveying the room for questions. When there were none, he stepped down and Captain Johnson stepped up to the podium.

"Gentlemen, I guarantee that you will have weather as Earth always has weather," he said, making a lame joke. No one laughed but just stared at him with deadpan looks. Recognizing that he shouldn't give up his day job to be a comedian, he continued, "Well, right, ah, forecast calls for low ceilings of one thousand feet broken and fifteen hundred feet overcast with some rain showers in the area. Broken and overcast up to six thousand feet. In the target area you can expect rain showers and low ceilings of one thousand feet. Winds will be out of the southeast, steady at five knots. This pattern will be over the entire portion of Laos and the Ho Chi Minh Trail as well as most of North Vietnam. Any questions?" Captain Johnson asked.

"So basically it's going to be shitty weather for most of the mission is what you're telling us," one of the pilots voiced.

"That sums it up pretty well, I would say," Johnson admitted.

Recognizing that Captain Johnson was done, the Operations officer stepped back up to the podium. "One last point—record any and all enemy action or reaction to your presence. If they painted you with radar, that's a reaction. Alright, if there are no more questions, comments or snide remarks, let's get the birds in the air. Be safe and good luck."

7

FALSIFIED REPORT

25 January 1972
  423rd Tactical Reconnaissance Wing
  Udorn Royal Thai Air Base, Thailand

Sergeant Lonnie D. Franks was an intelligence specialist for the wing. Actually, he was a glorified clerk, debriefing the pilots and observers after missions and filing each report. Others, more senior and experienced, analyzed raw information and turned it into intelligence that was disseminated to the wing and MACV. This was not what Lonnie had thought he was signing up for when he'd joined the Air Force or when he'd come to Thailand. Today he had to debrief the pilot and observer from the strike on Dong Hoi.

"Hey, Sergeant, you want to debrief us today?" Captain Wilcox asked as he walked into the debriefing room.

"Yes, sir. I just need you to give me a quick rundown to supplement the film you brought back," Lonnie said as the two officers pulled out chairs and sat down.

"Pretty routine mission. We watched the strike go in and then we raced in behind them before the gooks could recover. The MIGs never left the airfield because the weather was so bad, and they're shitty pilots in bad weather. Hell, the F-105s blew the crap out of the runways so they couldn't take off. I imagine the little buggers will be patching that runway for the next week or so," Captain Wilcox said.

"So the MIGs never got off the ground?" Lonnie asked.

"Nope, never had a chance to do so," Lieutenant Waldrep said.

"So what engaged you on the strike?" Lonnie asked.

"Nothing engaged us. The Wild Weasel took out their radars so they couldn't launch any missiles, and the weather was so crappy that their gun crews couldn't pick us up soon enough to track us before we were back in the clouds and gone. Wish every mission was like this one," Wilcox said.

"So nothing engaged you and no radar painted you, is that correct?" Lonnie asked.

"That's what we said. Is that a problem?" Wilcox asked.

"No, sir, if that's the way it was. I don't have any more questions. Thank you for stopping by," Lonnie said, finishing the debrief. After the two officers left, he was troubled by the fact that no enemy action had threatened the mission. He approached his supervisor's desk.

"Hey, Sergeant," Lonnie said, gaining Technical Sergeant John Voichita's attention.

"What now?" Voichita was in a foul mood.

"I just debriefed the pilot and observer from the mission the day before yesterday at Dong Hoi and they said there was no hostile action or reaction to the strike," Lonnie said.

"So what's the problem?" Voichita asked.

"Well, strikes are only to be conducted as a protective measure. If there were no hostile actions taken, then there should have been no strike," Lonnie said with some frustration. "How do I write this one up?"

"Damn, boy, just write it up that they were painted by radar and prelaunch warning. No big deal. Everyone got home okay and that's what counts. Just write it up."[1]

8

JOHN PAUL VANN

Major Josh Steinhauer would be leaving in the morning to head to Pleiku and was spending the afternoon in his BOQ room, packing his belongings. He was told that he would have a room waiting for him at the BOQ in Pleiku, so he should clean out his room in Saigon. The knock on the door caught him thinking of other things.

"Sir, I've been directed to bring you to MACV headquarters to meet with Major General Brooks in"—the sergeant paused long enough to check his watch—"twenty minutes." Stan Brooks was the MACV Inspector General.

"What for?" Josh asked, curious about this directive.

"Sir, I wasn't told the reason, just to police you up and get you over there," the young sergeant responded.

"Okay, let's go, then," Josh said, grabbing his hat as he headed out the door with numerous questions running through his head. *Why does he want to see me? The others left already, so why me? Did I do or say something wrong? Are we being recalled to the States?* Lots of questions but no answers.

Josh and three other majors were assigned to the Department of Defense Inspector General's Office in Washington. All four had combat experience in Vietnam on at least two tours. Josh was the only aviator of the four and had spent all his time in MR-II. He had flown in the MR-II area on his first tour to Vietnam, when he was a gunship pilot. An artillery officer by branch, Josh had served as a battery commander in Korea in the early '60s. Returning to the United States, he'd attended the Captain's Advanced Course and then rotary-wing flight school with a follow-on assignment to Vietnam in 1966. He had flown for a year out of Pleiku, so he was very familiar with the area. The four majors had been sent to Vietnam to observe the Vietnamization Program that had started when President Nixon entered the White House. The program involved two parts, the training of Vietnamese forces and the transfer of equipment to the South Vietnamese forces. Their charter was to prepare a report without influence for the MACV Command so the president could hand it to Congress and show the success of the program.

When they arrived at General Brooks's outer office, the female administrative assistant, a sergeant first class, told Josh to go on in. "He's waiting for you now," she said with a look that suggested she would be waiting for Josh when he came out.

Pausing at the doorway, Josh asked, "Sir, you wish to see me?"

Brooks was reading some paper in his hand and looked up with a smile. "Yes, Major, I do. Come in and have a seat," Brooks said, pointing at one of two overstuffed chairs and coming around his desk with his hand extended. Josh accepted the hand and did as directed, with Brooks taking the adjacent seat.

"Major, you're leaving tomorrow to go to Military Region II, correct?" Brooks asked, knowing full well the answer.

"Yes, sir. I have a U-21 flying me up in the morning," Josh responded.

"I want to fill you in on the individual you will be—how do I put this?—dealing with to a certain extent. He's unique and I think you need to understand his background before you get there. His name is John Paul Vann. He's a civilian and the director of the Second Military Region Assistance Group," Brooks stated. "He's a State Department civilian with the equivalent rank of major general. It's his deputy, General Wear, who has the military UCMJ authority—but let me back up and give you the full background so you'll better understand the man and what you may see up there," Brooks said. General George E. Wear was from Colorado. A graduate of the US Military Academy at West Point, New York, he had served in the Battle of the Bulge in 1944 and been wounded. Over the course of his military career he had seen combat in Korea as an infantry officer and had a previous tour in Vietnam as a brigade commander in the 25th Infantry Division.

"I suspect this is going to be interesting, sir," Josh exclaimed, sitting back in the chair.

"John Paul Vann came from the worst of conditions as a kid, I'm told. Poverty, alcoholic and promiscuous mother, several fathers, and many moves from one shithole to another. Finally, he got lucky, and a church pastor took him under his wing and got him into a boarding school, where he excelled. Got into Rutgers and was in his second year when he joined the Army Air Corps to be a pilot. Went through pilot training and just before graduation did some stupid aerial maneuver over the airfield and they pulled him out of the class for pilots and made him a navigator. Retained his commission of a second lieutenant, however.

"When the Air Corps separated from the Army, he saw the handwriting on the wall. He realized that to get ahead in the new US Air Force, one had to be a pilot, so he stayed in the Army and went infantry, airborne infantry. Got assigned to Japan in G-4 logistics and did great work, max efficiency reports. When the North Koreans attacked, he was tireless in moving supplies to the front. An opportunity came along to get command of a Ranger company that was composed of cooks, bakers and candlestick makers recruited from the rear echelon, and in seventy-eight days he had them whipped into shape and conducting reconnaissance missions behind the Chinese lines. Again his performance was excellent," Brooks exclaimed, pausing.

"He then went to Fort Benning for the advanced course and stayed to teach at the newly formed Ranger School. He wasn't even Ranger qualified until he went as a cadre member. When it came time to choose a specialty, he chose logistics and attended college. He got his master's degree and almost finished a doctorate as well. Promoted below the zone to lieutenant colonel. In 1963 he was assigned to MACV and was an advisor for the 7th ARVN division in the Delta and did yeoman work. He left Nam to attend the Industrial College of the Armed Forces but dropped his retirement papers before the course started."

"Sir, he sounds like a fast tracker and combat officer. Why would he retire at twenty years?" Josh asked with some amazement.

"Two reasons. He was a hell of an advisor and was the key advisor in the Battle of Ap Bac. Over the course of his one year as an advisor, he formed some very controversial views on the role of the United States in the execution of this war, views that were counter to those of some very powerful general officers in high places. He had no qualms about telling whoever would listen about his views, which put him at odds with those generals. He spent a few months in the Pentagon between Nam and going to the college. He put together a presentation on his views and was about to make a major presentation when some powerful people got it stopped two hours before it was to be presented.

"It was an excellent paper, strongly endorsed by his immediate supervisor, a Colonel Porter. Maxwell Taylor at that time had just become the ambassador to Vietnam, and the report didn't sit well with him. He must have called powerful friends in the Pentagon, because just two hours before Vann was to brief his findings to the JCS staff, the briefing was canceled. He dropped his papers that afternoon. Between you and me, if he had briefed them and they had adopted some of his ideas, we would not have been as heavily committed for as long as we have been here," Brooks explained.

"And the second reason, sir?" Josh asked tentatively.

"He couldn't keep his dick in his pants. He was charged with statutory rape while attending the Command and General Staff course at Fort Leavenworth. It went to an Article 32 investigation.[1] Both he and the young lady took lie detector tests, and both proved to be telling the truth. So it was he said, she said and the charges were dropped, but it was still in his record," Brooks stated.[2]

"I can understand how that would ruin a career. What was the controversy with what he expounded in his views on the war, may I ask?"

"Vann put it all in writing. After the Battle of Ap Bac, he wrote a ninety-two-page after-action report, very factual, that hit upon all that was wrong with the way we and the South Vietnamese were going about this war, point by point. From indiscriminate bombing of villages, to the Strategic Hamlet Resettlement Program, to the leadership of the South Vietnamese Army, to supply distribution and the aid programs," Brooks outlined.

"So what's the man like, sir?" Josh asked.

"He's arrogant, opinionated, extremely driven, very intelligent and an exceptional leader. He takes care of his people, resulting in their devoted allegiance to him. They know he'll move mountains to protect them. He will, I'm sure—he'll impart his ideas to you but won't insist that you adopt them. And he won't ask to see your final report," Brooks explained.

"Sir, how did he come to be the director of the Second Regional Assistance Group?" Josh asked, intrigued by what he had heard.

"When Mr. Vann left the Army, he went to work for Martin Marietta and got involved in supporting Lodge's attempt for the presidency. He found civilian work boring and began looking at government jobs. At that time, State was looking to fill positions in Vietnam and found that the best people to fill them with were retired officers. John got hired at a low level as a district pacification advisor and was placed in III Corps, up by Tay Ninh. From there he worked his way up and was noted for the success of several programs that he put in place. He was refining his beliefs that the war was being prosecuted all wrong and continued to make those beliefs known. But people were starting to listen. His beliefs ran counter to Westmoreland's, which kept him in trouble, but not down.

"Westmoreland believed that the Viet Cong and the North would be brought to the negotiations after they were beaten down and attrited. Vann believed the way to win the war was to win the hearts and minds of the peasantry and that you didn't do that by forced relocation, bombing and destroying their hamlets. Vann feels this is a revolution and it cannot be won with the current government in power in Saigon or the corruption that's rampant in the country.

"Vann eventually worked his way to be the senior pacification advisor in IV Corps, working with General Dzu. When the previous IV Corps commander was killed in a helicopter crash, Dzu was a colonel and was moved to IV Corps to take command. He was in tight with Diem and the Saigon Catholic Mafia. He then got moved to II Corps and asked that Vann be the Second Regional Assistance director. I suspect Vann has something on Dzu. Vann pretty much runs the show up there," Brooks outlined and then paused. "Major, that's about all I have for you. I just wanted you to know the background of the director and what you might expect when you meet with him. Any questions?"

"No, sir. I'm sort of looking forward to meeting the man," Josh said.

Standing, Brooks again extended his hand. "Have a safe flight and get back here in one piece."

"Thank you, sir. I hope to do just that," Josh said as he accepted the extended hand and departed.

9

WELCOME TO MR-II

Second Regional Assistance Group HQ
Pleiku

Major Josh Steinhauer sat in the copilot seat of the U-21. The Army version of the Beechcraft Queen Air normally carried only one passenger and the pilot as this aircraft in particular normally served as a radio relay platform or would monitor NVA communications with a Vietnamese interpreter riding in the back to record them. Josh wasn't a fixed-wing-rated pilot but was a rated helicopter pilot. If you can fly a helicopter, you can fly a fixed-wing aircraft, most helicopter pilots believed.

"Have you ever flown in this part of Nam, Major?" asked the pilot, an old crusty senior warrant officer.

"Yeah, I flew out of Pleiku a couple of years ago, gunships. Always loved the scenery up this way. This is really a beautiful country," Josh said.

Not much had changed, he thought now as he looked down ten thousand feet to the green carpet below. Off to the east, he could see the white sand beaches being assaulted by crystal-clear green waves from the Gulf of Tonkin. Due to the weather, a straight flight from Saigon to Pleiku was not in the interest of their longevity. The pilot had followed the coast to Qui Nhon and then turned west towards Pleiku. From the flat coastal plain with rice paddy fields to the hills of the Highland plateau to the mountains around Pleiku, Josh was taking it all in.

"Did you ever fly over Dalat?" the chief asked.

"Only one time, and that had to be the resort spot of Vietnam in my opinion. I had to use two blankets to keep warm at night. The mountains, the lush forests, the waterfalls and clear streams. I just loved it up there," Josh said, reminiscing.

"How did you like Pleiku?" the chief asked, slightly adjusting the power on the left engine.

"Pleiku was okay. Not a great place for the old Charlie-model gunships. Some of those mountains up there are eight thousand feet and the density altitude was high. We couldn't take off with a full load of fuel and ammo in the summer months. Crew chief and gunner would have to run alongside the aircraft as we slid along, trying to build up speed to hit translational lift and get off the ground, then they would jump on board," Josh explained. "Have you been up there for any length of time?"

"Nope. I came here in '63, supporting advisors and flying the OH-13. Flew mostly liaison runs but did some recon as well and medevac," the chief replied. "It was interesting times back then. No one to really come and get you if you went down, but we didn't see the intense ground fire that you see today either. Only had to contend with the VC and they couldn't shoot at a moving helicopter to save their souls."

As they continued flying to Pleiku, Josh mentally revisited landmarks from his previous tour. The passes along Route 14; the places he had taken fire from. It was all coming back as if it was only yesterday.

The U-21 aircraft touched down on the runway and taxied to the terminal.

"Thanks for the lift," Josh said as he climbed down the stairs from the back of the cabin and the pilot handed him his bag.

As Josh headed for the Quonset hut that served as a terminal, a jeep approached and stopped between him and the building.

"Excuse me, sir, are you Major Steinhauer?" the driver, a buck sergeant, asked as he came to a halt. His name tape read Howard.

"Yes, that's me," Josh said, stopping in his tracks.

"Sir, sorry I wasn't here to meet you. I've been directed to take you to your quarters and then to headquarters. General Wear wants to see you. Can I take your bag?" the sergeant asked, getting out of the jeep and reaching for Josh's bag, which he surrendered. The sergeant tossed it in the back, none too gently.

Walking around the front of the jeep to the passenger side, Josh asked, "And who is General Wear?"

"Sir, General Wear is the deputy commander of Second Regional Assistance Group. He's a brigadier general. Not sure how much longer he's going to be here, though," the sergeant stated.

"Why's that?" Josh inquired.

"He has some stomach issues that have been nagging him for some time now. Has flown down to Saigon a couple of times to see the doctors down there. Man is a workaholic, as is the director," the sergeant added.

Driving across the compound, Josh took in the sights. Camp Holloway was the military installation outside the town of Pleiku and was still a very active installation. The airfield area, known as the Golf Course, was the original home for the 1st Air Cavalry Division when it had arrived in Vietnam. Rolling up his shirt-sleeves and donning a bandanna, the assistant division commander picked up a machete and had everyone start clearing the low brush.

When they were done, the only thing standing was the grass, hence the name "Golf Course." He could have cleared it quicker using a bulldozer, but with all the helicopters that the division was bringing, he didn't want to kick up a bunch of dust. Most of the buildings were permanent structures, some of wood, some of concrete block. Electricity and running water, both hot and cold, were available in the showers. There was now a paved runway for C-130 support, long enough to accommodate a C-141 if the need arose.

Pulling up to a two-story building, the driver parked the jeep and hopped out, grabbing Josh's bag. "Sir, this is the BOQ, and I have a room for you already," Sergeant Howard said, leading the way through the door and walking down the hall. Stopping at a door, the sergeant produced a key and unlocked it. Entering, Josh found a simple room with a single bed, dresser, mirror and chair. In the corner were a rucksack and load-bearing equipment as well as a .45-caliber pistol with two ammo clips, both loaded, and a flak jacket.

"Sir, General Wear had me draw the field gear from supply for you. When you're done with it, just leave it in the room and I'll police it up and return it to supply. Hooch maids come around each morning and clean your room and make up the beds. Any boots that are left on the chair will be shined for you. Any laundry you need done, leave on the floor next to the chair. They'll have it back to you the next day. Goes without saying, don't leave money or valuables out. They're pretty honest, but why take the chance?" Sergeant Howard said as he placed Josh's bag on the foot of the bed. "They charge ten dollars a week, which you just leave on the dresser on Fridays." He paused. "If you're ready, sir, we can head over to see General Wear," Sergeant Howard said, turning to leave.

"Let's go," Josh said, pointing at the doorway. He was anxious to begin his assignment of evaluating the South Vietnamese Army. He knew that MACV headquarters had twenty-two officers from the MACV Inspector General's Office out doing the same thing, but their assessments would be delivered directly to General Abrams. Josh suspected this was to counter any unfavorable conclusions that he and his three compadres presented.

Arriving at the headquarters building, Sergeant Howard escorted Josh to General Wear's outer office and introduced him to General Wear's secretary, a sergeant first class.

"General Wear is waiting for you, sir. Go right in," the sergeant directed. Josh stopped in the open doorway and knocked. General George E. Wear was standing with his back to the door, studying a wall map of Kontum and Binh Dinh Provinces.[1] "Come in, Major, I've been expecting you," Wear said, turning. Josh came to attention and saluted.

Returning the salute, Wear pointed at an Army-issue metal armchair in front of his desk. He walked around and pulled out his desk chair. "Would you like some coffee?" he asked. "I'm having some."

"Yes, sir, I'll join you. I didn't get a chance to fill up before we took off this morning," Josh said. Truth be told, Josh, like most pilots, had a two-hour bladder and didn't want to have to pee in the Queen Air. The sergeant must have overheard the conversation because no sooner had Josh responded than in came a pot with two cups, a container of milk and sugar. General Wear filled his cup and poured a second for Josh. He then sat and took his first sip.

"Okay, Major Steinhauer, Stan Brooks called me this morning and told me you were on your way and briefed me on what you would be doing up here. Told me to give you all the support you want and not to ask questions or attempt to influence you in any way," Wear said.

"Sir, that's correct. My report will be combined with three other reports to present an overall picture of what we've seen and our assessment of the Vietnamization Program," Josh replied.

"Will people be named in the reports?" Wear asked.

"I can't speak for the others, but my intent is to name those worthy of note for outstanding efforts. Give credit where credit is due. Also if someone is totally incompetent, corrupt or ineffective, that will be noted as well if it's truly necessary—but I suspect that will be an exception," Josh added.

"Fair enough, Major. I can live with that. We will give you all the support we can. I just ask to be kept informed of where you are is all. I can also tell you that Mr. Vann is not happy about not being able to see your report before it goes to the president. He's been back in the States getting re-blued at the State Department for the past month and only arrived back in Saigon yesterday.[2] He'll be coming back here sometime this week. Don't worry about him, I'll run interference for you."

"Thank you, sir," Josh said.

"Well, I can tell you Vann is full of bluster but has the interest of everyone forefront. He will scream and shout and then give you the shirt off his back. He's a workaholic, keeping late-night hours and then sleeping in until 1000 hours. I have to remind him that he's no longer an infantry platoon leader charging into battle. He takes too many damn risks for one thing. Wants to be at the tip of the spear to make the decisions. Has his own helicopter that he had his pilot teach him how to fly. He can handle it as well as his pilot almost. Definitely leads from the front. Wish I could say that about his counterpart," Wear stated.

"His counterpart, sir?" Josh asked.

"Yeah, General Dzu. A man of unlimited indecision. He pretty much lets Vann run the show. Dzu commands the forces here in Military Region II but does whatever Vann tells him to do. The junior Vietnamese officers refer to him as 'Vann's man.' Dzu spends Sunday nights here and the rest of the week he's down in Qui Nhon, where First Field Force headquarters is located and where he has a house, on the beach. First Field Force Headquarters is his main headquarters. Vann also has a house there but he spends a lot more time up here," Wear explained and took another sip of his coffee.[3]

"Sir, what forces do you have up here?" Josh asked, hoping to move the conversation to what he was going to be looking at. Just then, Wear began to cough, a hard rasping cough.

"Excuse me, Major...picked up something and haven't been able to shake it," he exclaimed. The coughing continued for another minute. When he stopped, he poured a glass of water and drank.

"Ah, better now. Where were we?"

"I just asked what forces you have up here, sir."

"Good question, and I can see you want to get into the weeds. Good for you. My G-2, Colonel Irv Pahl, has prepared a briefing for you on the enemy situation up here. When he's done with you, he'll turn you over to the G-3, who's prepared to go over things with you. I'm sure you got a few briefings one over the world when you were down in Saigon," Wear said.

"Sir, we've been in briefings for almost a month in Saigon. Between you and me, I think General Abrams wanted to be positive that we understood the conditions here and what was occurring. I think every member of the MACV staff briefed us, then the Marine staff, then Air Force staff and then the Naval staff. When they were done with us, they had us briefed by the Vietnamese Joint Staff. That tried the limits of our Vietnamese skills," Josh explained.

"You speak Vietnamese, Major?" Wear asked.

"Sir, I studied it on my own when I went to flight school as I figured I would be coming over here. And when I was here on my last assignment, I practiced it as much as I could, having long conversations with my hooch maids," Josh stated. "Since I've been here this time, I haven't let on that I speak it so I can easily eavesdrop on Vietnamese conversations. Everyone on the team speaks it and that's part of the reason we were selected for this assignment."

"Well, I'll keep that between you and me," Wear said. "How familiar are you with the history of the advisor program?"

"Not very, sir."

"Well, let me enlighten you just a bit. Advisors started coming here in 1950 to assist the French, who were receiving US equipment. When they got their asses kicked, we then started providing equipment directly to the South Vietnamese. In 1960, President Kennedy increased the role of the advisors as several advisors had been killed in the late 1950s in attacks on ARVN compounds. Over the years, the number of advisors increased, but that led to problems. First, most advisors are junior in rank to those they're advising, which doesn't sit well with the Vietnamese. Second, most of the Vietnamese have more combat experience than the advisors. Third, advisors have only one-year tours, so over the course of a couple of years, a Vietnamese officer may have six or more advisors. Fourth, the language issue. Most advisors don't speak the lingo and have to have an interpreter, who may not have a great command of the language. And we have cultural differences. Asians are reluctant to deliver bad news. It's that face-saving thing. Because of face-saving, they're reluctant to be aggressive or take risks. That makes them overreliant on airpower and artillery. Lastly, there's a psychological handicap for the ARVN leadership. They're of the opinion that the North Vietnamese soldier is a better soldier, tougher and better trained. Their leadership is probably better, I'll grant them that, but not the soldier," Wear stated.

"Why say that about their leadership, sir?" Josh asked, puzzled.

"The North Vietnamese officer corps is promoted on merit and ability. After the rank of captain, the South Vietnamese officer corps is promoted not so much on ability as on political position. It's not uncommon for an officer to become a province chief because his wife 'lost' fifty thousand dollars to his superior's wife in a card game. Most of the corps and division commanders are in those positions because they're in tight with the president or someone in the president's family. After the coup that took Diem out, the subsequent leadership started surrounding themselves with people they could trust, supposedly. Okay, enough of the cultural and political enlightenment," Wear said, reaching for the intercom button on his phone. Promptly, the sergeant appeared.

"Would you call Colonel Pahl and ask him to join me? Tell him the inspector guy is here," Wear directed and gave Josh a wink.

"Yes, sir" was all the sergeant said before exiting the doorway.

"Damn good NCO. Been here for five years now. Used to do SOG missions over in Laos and other places. I felt it was time to get him out of the bush. He was going native too much. I think he resents it, but I hope to have him go home sane," Wear said as he sipped his coffee.

"Sir, may I ask how long you've been here?"

"I'm closing in on my second year, eighteen months now. And I'm sane," he added with a smile. "I try to get out each day that Vann isn't out or isn't in the AO. One of us attempts to visit every advisor at least once every three weeks, some more often depending on what's going on. Don't want them to feel they're alone in their assignments."

"Sir, you wanted to see me," Colonel Irv Pahl said, coming through the doorway.

"Yes, Major Steinhauer, this is Colonel Pahl, our G-2. Irv, this is the major I was telling you about. He has carte blanche when it comes to anything and everything," Wear announced.

"Sir, we'll give him anything he wants. Glad to meet you, Major," Pahl said as he extended his hand. "Let's head down to my office and get you up to speed on the situation here."

"Major, if you need anything, and I mean anything, you ask, and if you don't get it, Sergeant Howard knows how to get a hold of me. I'd like to detail that young sergeant to you to assist you in getting around, arranging transportation as well as serving as a bodyguard. Don't care to have a single individual wandering around by himself. Deal?" Wear asked.

"As long as he understands he's working for me and not spying for this headquarters, you have a deal, sir. No disrespect meant," Josh said tactfully.

"Understood and none taken," Wear said with a chuckle. "Stop by and see me before you leave Pleiku if you would, please," Wear asked.

"Yes, sir," Josh said and turned to Colonel Pahl.

"Follow me, Major. My staff is waiting for you. So I understand you're here to evaluate the Vietnamization Program," Colonel Pahl said, changing the subject.

"That's correct, sir. The president wants an independent assessment of the program," Josh explained, giving his pat explanation for the hundredth time, it seemed to him.

"Good. Maybe some people in high places will believe what we're telling them then," Colonel Pahl said as he led the way to his area.

"And what's that, sir?" Josh asked.

"When you're done and before you leave the AO, come see me and I'll give you my assessment. Right now I don't want to influence you," he said, turning slightly with a grin. *Two can play this game, Major*, he was thinking.

10

INTELLIGENCE BRIEF

1 FEBRUARY 1972
  SRAG G-2 Office
  Pleiku

REACHING THE G-2 SECTION, Colonel Pahl made the introductions. "Gentlemen, this is Major Josh Steinhauer. I will let you each introduce yourselves. Whatever he wants to know, tell him. Nothing is off-limits with him, understood?" No one responded as it was obvious that he had already briefed the staff. "Josh, I'll turn you over to them. See me when they're done," Pahl directed.

"Yes, sir, and thank you, sir," Josh replied, watching Pahl depart.

"Take a seat, Major, and we'll get started," a Lieutenant Colonel Bodine said, pointing at a chair at the conference table. The table had eight chairs around the perimeter with an additional eight chairs along the wall. At one end of the room was a wall map of Military Region II and a projector screen with a

VGT projector. The three other officers, ranging from a captain to two majors, also took seats at the table. Lieutenant Colonel Bodine moved to the front of the room and picked up a pointer.

"How familiar are you with the AO, Josh?"

"Sir, I flew out of Pleiku on my last tour but worked mostly in the southern part of the AO," he explained.

"Okay, let's do a bit of a refresher, then," Bodine said as he began pointing at the map. "Here we have sixty-five miles of border on the northwest side with Laos and then it's one hundred and seventy-five miles of border with Cambodia. That's our western border. The area is thirty thousand square miles with three hundred and twenty miles of coastline in the east. In the northwestern portion of our AO and lapping over into Laos is Base Camp 609, where most of the supplies coming down the Ho Chi Minh Trail flow into and from there support their operations in Military Regions I and II. From the northwest and coming south, then east, is Highway 14, which passes through Dak Seng in the northwest corner of our AO and comes down to Dak To, Pleiku and Ban Me Thuot. Route 512 comes out of Cambodia and passes south of Ben Het and Dak To II, continues on between Dak To I and Tan Canh and then connects with Highway 14 at Dak To," Bodine explained.

"Excuse me, sir, but I don't recall a Dak To I and a Dak To II," Josh said with a curious look.

"Ah, there's the town of Dak To here on Highway 14. Then on Route 512 there's an airfield at Dak To I and a second airstrip at Dak To II, with Route 512 running between Dak To I and the compound at Tan Canh. It will make sense once we get you out in the AO," Bodine clarified. Moving his pointer down Highway 14, he came to a road junction. "At this junction, Highway 19 intersects Highway 14, and that goes to An Khe and Highway 1 on the coast and Qui Nhon. Moving south on Highway 14 is Pleiku and ninety-six kilometers further down is Ban Me Thuot.

Those are the major roads in the AO, except for Highway 1, which is on the coast and you can drive from the Chinese border all the way to the southern end of the Mekong Delta down south on that road. Any questions?" Bodine asked. "Wait, let me back up for a second. Out of Kontum is Route 511, which goes west to a camp at Polei Kleng. There's an airstrip there as well. Five klicks east of Polei Kleng along Route 511, there's a major river, the Dak Bia River, with a bridge. There's also a bridge on 512 between Ben Het and Dak To II, the Dak Seng River."

"What are the choke points on the major roads, sir?" Josh asked.

"There's one on Highway 14 here north of Kontum and one here on Highway 19 at An Khe," Bodine said. "This is where French Mobile Force 100 was taken out by the Viet Minh back June of '54. We refer to it as An Khe Pass, but the proper name is Mang Yang Pass." Pausing for a moment, he went on, "Between Pleiku and Ban Me Thuot there's the Chu Drew Pass, another place that Mobile Force 100 got badly torn up. I wouldn't call it a choke point, but this stretch between Ben Het and Tan Canh is narrow with the mountains coming down to within a klick of the road and the river on the other side. The river is too deep and wide to be forded. The two major rivers are the Dak Seng, which flows south, and the Dak Bia, which starts in the valley area west of Rocket Ridge and flows south to Polei Kleng and on to Kontum. Questions?" Bodine asked again.

"No, sir, I'm tracking," Josh said.

"Okay, this ridgeline to the west that starts at a point four klicks south of Ben Het and runs southeast towards Kontum is known as Rocket Ridge. It deserves the name as this is where they launch their 122-millimeter rockets from to hit almost anywhere in the western part of the AO. We control the peaks, most of the time, and they control the base, most of the time," Bodine added. "This low area is the Plei Trap Valley. From the border we've discovered a four-meter-wide road being built under the jungle canopy coming into this valley," Bodine pointed out and turned to face his audience. "I leave anything out on this geography lesson, guys?" he asked his staff.

"No, sir," the captain responded.

"Now let's talk bad guys. This entire area is under the command of the B-3 Front. Lieutenant General Hoang Minh Thao commands and he's very familiar with the area, having been in command since the late 1960s. MACV G-2 has told us that he will hit us with the 320th NVA Division and the 2nd NVA Division in the west and the 3rd Division in the east out of Binh Dinh Province. The 2nd NVA Division has always operated out of Base Camp 609 and had forays into either MR-I or us. We anticipate he'll come down Highway 14, unless he's operating in MR-I," Bodine briefed.

"Do you know his strength, sir?" Josh asked.

"He maintains his divisions at about ten thousand troops," Bodine replied. "The 320th has always been a pain and maintains pressure on Rocket Ridge over the years. He has two regiments that operate in the valley that we know of, and we suspect there's a third. They frequently probe or outright attack the fire support bases on the top. Over the years those bases have changed hands frequently, with each attack preceded by sappers, so he must have a sapper battalion as well. Fortunately, the fire support bases are mutually supporting with indirect fire and he's never attacked two adjacent firebases at the same time. Dak To II and Ben Het also provide artillery support," Bodine added.

"And the 2nd Division...?"

"The 2nd Division has two regiments that we know of. He probably has an artillery unit, but we haven't seen any 130mm stuff coming from him as his contacts are almost always hit and run."

"What reconnaissance assets do you have to keep track of them?" Josh asked.

"With the drawdowns, that's become a problem. The ARVNs have a few long-range patrols, but since the SOG mission is over, we've had to rely pretty much on their reports, and they're subject to exaggeration or contain no information. MACV now depends mostly on aerial photos, which for the big picture may be fine but really does nothing for us. We did have a full air cav squadron operating in the area and they provided us with reconnaissance, but one troop has already been sent back to the States, a second troop is scheduled to rotate back shortly and the last one will be going home sometime in April. The FAC provided good support at one time, but they've been cut back as well. We're beginning to run blind, so to speak," Bodine said almost apologetically.

"What was some of the information the cav and FAC were providing?" Josh asked, his curiosity piqued.

"Well, the FAC was reporting in January that the Ho Chi Minh Trail looked like a superhighway. Said they weren't even bothering to camouflage their trucks moving south. Activity in the vicinity of 609 appeared too high. We did have a report from an aerial scout recon of what appeared to be tank tracks in the valley, and a Cobra in January reported—unconfirmed, mind you—that he engaged a tank," Bodine said with a smile.

"A tank! Have there been any other reports of tanks?" Josh asked.

"No, and this report was unconfirmed. Mr. Vann doesn't believe that it was a tank and will not accept any discussion about tanks until we have confirmation. Two sets of eyes at the same time identifying the tank, and not in the same aircraft. Pilot was pretty pissed when Vann simply dismissed it. Told him he would go back out and drive the damn thing to the headquarters. Vann told him that until that happens, we don't believe it," Bodine said.

Damn, they're really sticking their heads in the sand on this news, Josh was thinking.

"What kind of artillery support do they have?" Josh asked.

"The standard stuff—82mm mortars, 122mm rockets and some 130mm artillery. Mostly he fires the rockets at Pleiku, occasionally at Kontum, and he saves the mortars for the district compounds and Rocket Ridge. Haven't seen him use his one-thirties very often, and when he does, they're firing from inside Cambodia to Rocket Ridge. It's always the same, a few rounds a day, and if it's an attack on one of the FSBs, then it may be a hundred mortar rounds following the assault," Bodine added.

"In the east, what about the 3rd NVA Division—the Yellow Star Division, I believe it's called?" Josh asked.

"The 3rd has operated for years in northern Binh Dinh Province with a strong cadre base and a lot of support from the local VC. About half of the division is NVA, and VC make up the rest. Binh Dinh has always been a hotbed for the VC. Last year the government considered pacification a success with only seven districts in the country not under the government's total control, and all seven are in the northern portion of Binh Dinh Province. Back in January, the district chief, Colonel Nguyen Van Chuc, was giving a speech at a celebration when the VC blew up a building near him. He came through okay, but a lot of people listening to the speech didn't. Pretty brazen attack," Bodine injected.

"You said the SOG mission is ending...?"

"Yeah, the drawdown has hit that as well. They're currently out of the areas they usually operated in and are transferring everything to the Strategic Technical Assistance Team 158, which will stand up on May first and support the Strategic Technical Directorate of the Army of the Republic of Vietnam, part of the Vietnamization Program," Bodine answered, then asked, "Didn't they brief you about this at MACV?"

"No, sir, seems they forgot that little tidbit," Josh answered as he pulled out a notebook. Once he was done writing, Bodine put his pointer down.

"Major, that's about it for the intel side of our brief. I'll take you down to Colonel Snell's office and he'll bring you up to speed on our forces and the plan for defending this place if and when it ever happens," Bodine concluded.

"One last question, sir, if I may. At MACV the major question seemed to be not how big the attack would be but when. No one seemed concerned about the North having thirteen to fifteen divisions and all of them either in the southern part of North Vietnam or in Cambodia and Laos, or the fact that the Soviets and Chinese have been offloading tanks, artillery, aircraft and supplies in the harbors, or that the Ho Chi Minh Trail only needs a stoplight. The concern all focused on when it was going to start, not even where but when," Josh explained.

"That's because they're sitting in Saigon and not on the front line. We, on the other hand, are concerned not only with the timing but also the size of the force coming at us. We think we understand his approach in our area. His ultimate goal would be to split the country in half. To do that, he has to take Kontum and drive to the sea and take Qui Nhon. To take Kontum, he must take Dak To and Tan Canh, and to do that he must first take Rocket Ridge. He'll hit Rocket Ridge hard and each of the firebases simultaneously. Probably have the 320th do that and follow up with the 2nd Division coming right behind him. In the east he'll push the 3rd Division eastward towards Highway 1 with the hope of reaching Qui Nhon so he could link up with the forces coming from the west through Kontum. But when is the question, and what other forces he has that we don't know about. Those are our concerns," Bodine concluded.

"I heard rumors of possible Soviet advisors with the NVA forces. I recall seeing a captured Chinese advisor on my previous tour. Have you seen any indication of Soviet or Chinese advisors?" Josh asked.

"We've heard the same rumors but nothing confirmed. The few times he's fired his 130mm guns, they've been accurate, which leads us to believe that Soviet or Chinese advisors may be with their artillery units. Any other questions?" Bodine asked. Josh had none.

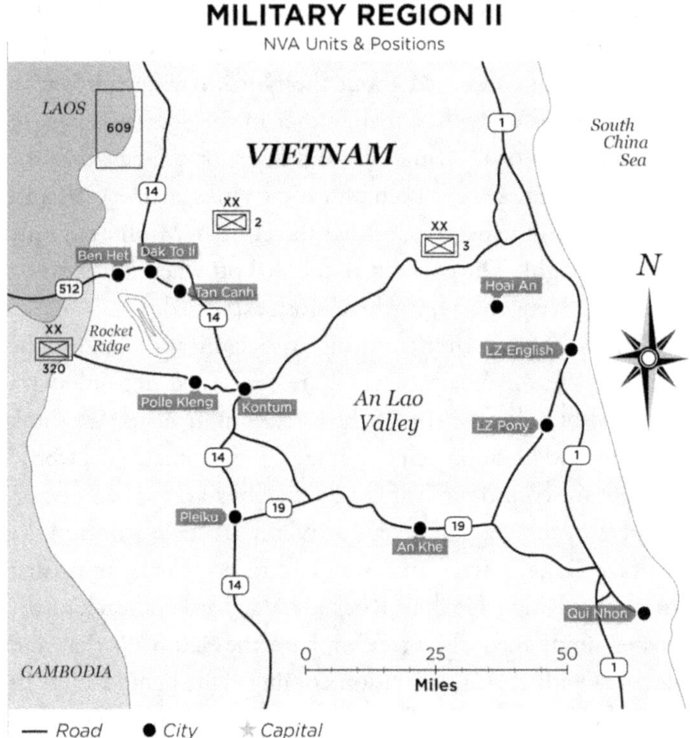

11

OPERATIONS BRIEF

1 FEB 1972
  SRAG G-3
  Pleiku

"MAJOR STEINHAUER, Colonel Snell, our G-3, is waiting to brief you in his conference room. Captain Harvey will escort you down there. If you have any other questions, please feel free to come back and ask," Colonel Pahl said, extending his hand.

"Thank you, sir, and I will," Josh replied, accepting the handshake.

"If you'll come with me, Major," Captain Harvey said as he held the door open. The short walk down the hall was quiet, with neither officer saying anything. The door to the G-3 section was open, so Captain Harvey led the way and walked in, approaching a staff sergeant seated behind a desk reading the latest copy of the *Stars and Stripes* newspaper.

"Sergeant, this is Major Steinhauer. I believe Colonel Snell is going to give him a briefing this afternoon," Harvey announced.

The staff sergeant looked up and closed the paper, finally standing. "Major, if you'll follow me, I'll take you to the colonel. He's in his office," he said in an almost bored tone.

"Thank you, Staff Sergeant, but if you just point the way, I'm sure I can find his office and you can get back to reading your paper," Josh said, sending a clear message in a polite manner to the sergeant. When a senior officer approaches you, get off your ass promptly. Josh had been told there were discipline problems, and he was beginning to see them.

To Josh's surprise, the staff sergeant simply pointed towards an office door in the back of the section, stating, "He's in there, *sir*." The last word was dripping with attitude. Josh said nothing and walked to where the sergeant was pointing. He knocked on the office door and was told to enter.

Colonel Snell was seated behind his desk, shuffling papers. He looked up, but recognition didn't register on his face. "What can I do for you, Major...and who are you?"

"Sir, I'm Major Steinhauer from the DOD Inspector General's Office. I believe you're expecting me," Josh said.

Colonel Snell immediately stood and muttered under his breath, "That fucking sergeant." Coming around the desk, he said, "My apologies, Major, I have been expecting you. How was your brief with Colonel Pahl?"

"Sir, it was good. Gave me a good appreciation for what you might be up against shortly," Josh stated.

"Yeah, I just hope Pahl has it right. If not, we could be in a world of hurt around here. Let's go into the conference room. Want some coffee?" the colonel asked.

"Would love some, sir," Josh replied. The colonel turned and in a booming voice said, "Staff Sergeant, two cups and a pot of coffee, now!" Everyone in the section heard him and understood the situation.

"The staff sergeant is a royal screwup. Was a good soldier, but his attitude and morale went downhill when he got a Dear

John letter from his wife. We've done everything to turn him around, even tried to get him reassigned back to the States, but he shot himself in the foot, getting into a fight with a sergeant major, who pressed charges. Not much we could do then. He's under charges for insubordination along with intoxication on duty," the colonel explained as they entered the conference room. Another officer was already there, seated and working on a map.

"Morning, sir," the officer said.

"Morning, Tom. Whatcha working on?"

"Just plotting out some of the latest locations on the map. I can do this someplace else…"

"No, keep your seat. In fact, stick around and you may be able to fill in a blank or two. This is Major Steinhauer from the DOD IG office. Major, this is Major Billings, our assistant Ops officer," the colonel said. The two officers exchanged handshakes as the staff sergeant walked in with a tray containing two cups and a pot of coffee. Tom took the tray and poured out two cups, handing one to the colonel and one to Josh.

"Do I need to bring you a cup, Major Billings?" the staff sergeant asked with no enthusiasm.

"No, Staff Sergeant, I've had my fill for the day, thank you," Billings replied.

"Take a seat and I'll get started," stated Colonel Snell as he moved in front of a wall map of the AO.

"Sir, is it okay if I take some notes?" Josh asked, pulling out his notebook. Most officers carried a small green softcover note-book with the word *Memoranda* on the cover. Measuring three and a quarter inches by five and a half inches, they fit nicely in shirt or cargo pants pockets.[1]

"Nah, please do. Okay, Military Region II covers twelve provinces, with Kontum and Binh Dinh Provinces in the north and Binh Thuan and Lam Dong in the south. Most of our hot spots are in the northern provinces, so that's where the bulk of our forces are located. Along the western border with Cambodia and Laos starting in the north are Kontum Province, Pleiku Province, and Darlac and Quang Duc Provinces. Military Region II falls under the Second ARVN Corps, which is commanded by General Dzu. I'm sure you've heard about him," Colonel Snell commented.

"General Wear gave me a rundown on him, yes, sir," Josh replied.

"Okay, under his command we have the 22nd ARVN Infantry Division and the 23rd ARVN Infantry Division here in Military Region II. The headquarters for the 23rd is located at Ban Me Thuot and the headquarters for the 22nd was here in Pleiku, but it moved or is in the process of moving to Tan Canh. There are two armored cavalry squadrons as well. The 22nd Division armored unit is the 14th, and the 19th Armored Cav Squadron is attached. There are eleven Border Ranger battalions scattered throughout the region in addition to the Regional Forces and the Popular Forces. We got word this morning that the ARVN 2nd Airborne Brigade is arriving this week. Their headquarters will go to Vo Dinh, which is sixteen kilometers west of Kontum, and they'll man FSB Delta and Charlie on Rocket Ridge. One battalion, the 9th, will go to Tan Canh and have a company up on Five or Six," Snell stated and paused. "The 22nd Division, as I said, is moving its headquarters to Tan Canh. In addition, one regiment, the 47th, is moving to Dak To II and one regiment, the 42nd, is moving into Tan Canh with the division headquarters. The 47th has troops on FSB 5 and FSB 6. The 40th Regiment is located in the east at LZ English and the 41st Regiment is south of there. The 23rd has one regiment in Ban Me Thuot, the 45th Regiment, and the 44th Regiment in Song Mao way down south. Damn, where the hell is his 53rd Regiment located?" he asked, turning to Captain Billings.

Billings quickly scanned his notes. "Sir, the 53rd Regiment is in Dalat," he said.

"Thank you, Captain," the colonel said with a hint of embarrassment in his tone. "We have eleven Border Ranger battalions throughout the region, located in key district centers and along the border. They're our trip wires for detecting any NVA movement across the border. Truthfully, they mix it up pretty good, a lot of times better than the ARVNs. Most of the Border Ranger battalions are Montagnards or other ethnic minorities. Any questions?" the colonel asked.

"What's the difference between the Regional Forces and the Popular Forces? I recall hearing the term Ruff-Puffs but never understood what it meant aside from the fact that they weren't part of the regular army," Josh asked.

"Okay, the Regional Forces are organized much like the army, with their own artillery, even. They work for the province chief and he can and does move them around within the province, but seldom do they go out of the province. For the most part they're as good as the ARVN soldiers," Snell explained. "The Popular Forces are the home guard. They pretty much stay around their respective villages and protect them, guard infrastructure such as bridges and government buildings. They're equipped with just light weapons, although they're getting M16s that we're leaving behind. Any other questions?" Snell asked.

"No, sir, I'm good," Josh replied.

"Aviation units at our disposal include the 361st Aerial Weapons Company, call sign Pink Panthers; the 344 Aviation Detachment; and the 57th Assault Helicopter Company, call sign Gladiators for the slicks and Cougars for the guns. Troop H, 7th of the 17th Air Cavalry Squadron, as well as the 180th Assault Support Helicopter Company," the colonel outlined. "The Pink Panthers have twelve AH-1G gunships and the cav have nine AH-1G, eight UH-1H and ten OH-6 Loach aircraft. The 57th has eight AH-G gunships for escort and twenty UH-

1H for lifts. The 52nd Combat Aviation Battalion here in Pleiku is the parent organization," the colonel explained.

"For two divisions over this large of an area, that's not a whole lot of aviation support, is it, sir? You have, what, twenty-nine gunships in the whole region and at best thirty slicks for lifts," Josh noted with some concern.

"Well, no, but the bulk of the support must come from the South Vietnamese Air Force, which controls all helicopter support on an as-needed-and-willing-to-pay-for support basis," the colonel stated.

"Sir?" Josh replied, caught off guard by the comment.

"Truth is the VNAF has all the helicopters and are as crooked as they come. They cancel missions at the last minute with no explanation. They will not enter a hot landing zone to insert troops, or extract them. They won't land to load wounded troops. They sell blade hours to anyone that has the money to buy a ride for anything. Hell, I wouldn't be surprised if they were hauling for the enemy even—oh, did I just say that? I didn't mean it," the colonel said with no embarrassment.

"So I take it you're not impressed with the VNAF and their helicopters," Josh said, attempting to lighten the mood.

"Years ago we made a mistake and put US Air Force advisors with the helicopters in the VNAF. Good pilots and instructors, but lacking a knowledge of combat assaults. We should have put experienced Army pilots in with them and that would have made a world of difference," the colonel explained. "I need to clarify that their fixed-wing air support is good. It's just the helicopter support that's horrible. Okay, let's talk artillery," he added, quickly changing the subject. "We have artillery batteries of at least four guns located at Ben Het, Dak To I and Dak To II, and Tan Canh. Pleiku has a battalion of artillery, as does Kontum. The 23rd Division has their organic artillery at Ban Me Thuot. LZ English is with one battalion. Questions?"

"You indicated that there are some armored units," Josh pointed out.

"Yes, the 1st of the 19th Armored Squadron is here at Ben Het along with one company of the 71st Border Rangers and the 95th Border Rangers Battalion.[2] The 71st is pretty much a Montagnard unit with Vietnamese officers. Truthfully, the total strength is about reinforced company size, one hundred and fifty to two hundred men. There are two advisors up there. There are Ruff-Puffs at Dak To and Tan Canh as well. Most of them are Montagnards," Colonel Snell said and stood, moving to the map. He motioned for Josh to join him.

"Let me show you where everyone is located. Over here on the coast in Binh Dinh Province, we have the 40th Regiment. The 40th is commanded by Colonel Tran Hieu Duc and the senior advisor is Lieutenant Colonel David Schorr. Part of the regiment is at LZ English and part is at LZ Orange, which sits at the mouth of An Lao Valley," Snell pointed out. Josh got a slight shiver at the mention of An Lao Valley as he was very familiar with the tactical situation there from his previous tour. Snell continued, "Part of the 41st Battalion is located south of English at LZ Pony at this time with LZ Crystal north of Qui Nhon their home base. Lieutenant Colonel Don Stovall is the senior advisor to the 41st."

"I'm familiar with FSB English, sir, but not LZ Orange or Pony," Josh said.

"Well, if you get to English and talk to Schorr I'm sure he'll be glad to take you out there," Snell offered. "He can introduce you to the district advisors over the area as well. You'll want to talk to them. They probably have a tougher job than those that are assigned to ARVN units," Snell added.

"Sir, you mentioned fire support bases. Where are those and this Rocket Ridge?" Josh asked, looking at the map.

"Here south of Ben Het begins this ridgeline. It runs north-west to southeast. Ben Het sits just north of the northwestern end and Polei Kleng sits just to the southeast of the southeastern end," Snell said as he dragged his finger along the map. The 1:50,000 map clearly showed the ridgeline, with its steep slopes depicted by the closeness of the topographic contour lines. Snell continued, "Here at the northwestern end is Firebase 6, then 5, followed by Yankee, Charlie, Delta, and Hotel. Each is manned by elements of the 2nd Airborne Brigade or the 47th Regiment. There's an American advisor with each ARVN element on those firebases. Over the years those firebases have changed hands several times. Firebase 6 had a couple of choppers shot down there last year. Two on the firebase in April. The firebase was overrun that night. The unit with some of the advisors and the downed helicopter crews E&E'd out of there. A couple of days later, the ARVNs went and took it back. A month later another aircraft is shot down and the crew chief is the only survivor. Another aircraft got in to rescue him but was shot down coming out and everyone was lost.[3] That place has always been bad news," Snell said, moving back to his chair and picking up his coffee. Josh resumed his seat.

"Sir, back at MACV there appears to be some concern about a major offensive kicking off in the near term," Josh stated.

"We do have our concerns, Major," Snell said, standing and moving back to the map. As he spoke, he dragged his finger along the route he was outlining. "We think that they'll launch an attack across the border towards Ben Het and Tan Canh, then on to Kontum and Pleiku. We believe that General Thao will put his main force on Route 14 down to Pleiku and then attempt to continue on Route 9 to the coast and split the country."

"May I ask what General Dzu's plan is to defend against such an attack?" Josh questioned.

"Right now we have two courses of action that we're debating. One course is for us to establish a strong defense at Tan Canh and Dak To II, causing the enemy to bunch up while we pound him into the Stone Age with B-52 strikes," Snell said, pausing to cough.

"The second course of action, sir?"

"Oh yeah, the second course of action is an initial delaying action and retrograde all along Route 14 back to Kontum. Force the enemy to fight for every mile as we delay him and pound him with B-52 strikes and TACAIR."

"When will there be a decision made on which way to go?"

"Mr. Vann will be back tomorrow and we'll get him and Dzu together and have a decision made. There are already forces positioned at Ben Het, Dak To I and Dak To II, and Tan Canh as well as Rocket Ridge. It'll just be a matter of moving the 23rd Division up from Ban Me Thuot," Snell explained.

"May I ask which course of action you favor, sir?" Josh asked tactfully.

"I'm willing to trade space for time. I think a delaying action wearing his ass down before he gets to Kontum, where he hits a strong defense, is the best course of action."

"And General Dzu...?"

"We've talked and he agrees with me. We'll discuss it with Vann tomorrow."

"Well, sir, how about I start in the south at the 44th Regiment and work my way back this way?" Josh suggested.

"Good. The sergeant already has a vehicle assigned to him with radios. He got you some field gear, so you're ready to roll anytime you want. If you're heading to the 44th tomorrow, it isn't a bad drive, and in daylight the roads are pretty secure. I can call ahead and give Colonel McKenna a heads-up that you're coming," Snell offered.

"Thank you, sir, but I'd prefer that you didn't. Don't want people cleaning up their acts because I'm coming. I'd like to see things as they are," Josh stated.

"I don't blame you, Major. Again, if you need anything, you

call us," Snell said as he stood, indicating this meeting was over, and extended his hand.

Josh accepted the hand and departed to find the young sergeant sitting in the outer office.

"Let's go, Sergeant, we have a trip to plan out," Josh said as he walked past the young man.

"Yes, sir," the sergeant replied with a bit too much enthusiasm for Josh.

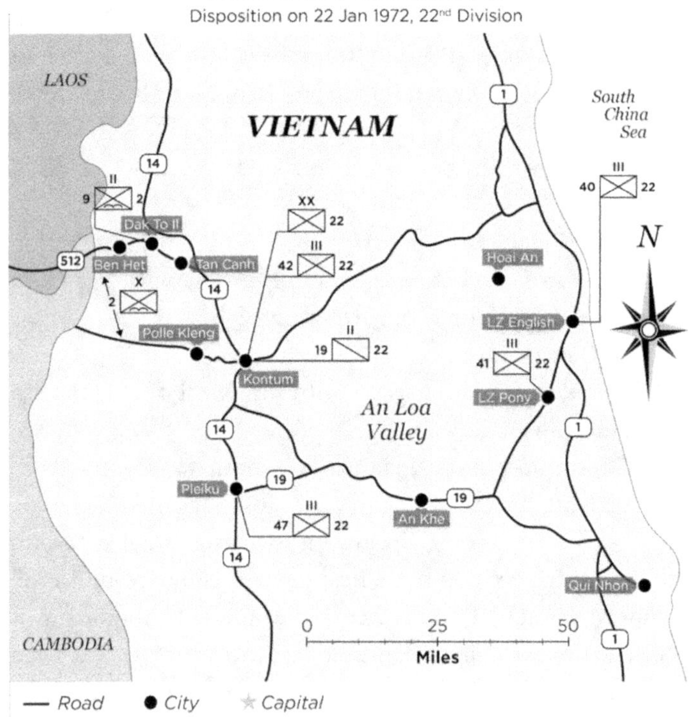

12

RECAP

14 Feb 1972
   SRAG II HQ
   Pleiku

Mr. John Paul Vann had assembled the entire advisor group in Pleiku for a meeting. He did this about every three or four months, partly to inform the advisors of what was going on throughout the region as well as the country and partly to impart some of his ideas to them as well as receive feedback. The advisors liked to attend as it got them away from their counterparts and allowed them to eat more palatable food, drink freely, and blow off steam about anything and everything. Some of the advisors felt that these sessions were Vann's opportunity to play division commander as he had never commanded anything above a company level.[1] Some felt that Vann's ego drove the train in many decisions, but one thing they all knew, he supported them one hundred percent and would do anything to get an advisor out of danger. They were all loyal to the man. Josh had been in Song Mao when the meeting was announced and got on the chopper with Lieutenant Colonel McKenna for the ride up to Pleiku. Colonel McKenna was the senior advisor to the 44th Regiment.

Walking into the conference room, General Wear announced, "Okay, gents, get a seat and we'll get started. Mr. Vann will be here in a minute. He's just wrapping up a few things with our new 22nd Division commander, Colonel Le Du Dat."

"Oh, lucky me," could be heard in the middle of the room.

"Comment there, Colonel Kaplan?" Wear asked.

"Oh, sir, I was just commenting on how fortunate I feel to be the senior advisor for such a distinguished indecisive Vietnamese officer," Lieutenant Colonel Phillip Kaplan said with sarcasm dripping off each word. Kaplan knew Dat well and didn't think much of him. Those feelings had been expressed to Vann on several occasions and the feeling was mutual. Further discussion stopped when Vann walked into the room.

Before anyone could react, Vann said, "Keep your seats, gentlemen," moving to the podium that stood off to one side of the low stage. On the wall next to the podium was a map of MR-II. "I thought this was a good time for all of us to get together. Things are going to be heating up, I believe, and we won't have the time nor the ability to do so in the near future. I want to go over the intel picture as MACV understands it and talk a bit about how we're going to respond to how I think the North is going to come at us," he said, pausing and surveying the room. The unspoken words were, *Get comfortable because we're going to be here for a time.* Vann noticed some getting comfortable in their seats.

"First the intel picture, Irv," Vann said, turning to the SRAG intelligence officer, Colonel Irv Pahl.

"Gentlemen, MACV is reporting a large buildup along the DMZ with movement of troops and equipment. Reports from the outposts along the border are that they're hearing construction and increased air-defense actions across the border," Pahl said, indicating on a map projected on a screen in the front of the room.

"MACV also reports a large buildup of the enemy forces in the vicinity of Tchepone in Base Camp 611. It's expected that the attack will come from Tchepone down Highway 9."

"Question," Lieutenant Colonel McKenna said. "Any chance he would attack across the DMZ?"

"No chance as that isn't allowed by the Geneva Convention that divided the two Vietnams," Pahl said, then quickly added, "At least that's what MACV says."

"Do you think that piece of paper will deter the North Vietnamese if they really want to take this place?" Kaplan said, mocking the comment. "Hell, Tet '68 killed the Viet Cong and this has been an NVA fight for the past three years. I wouldn't be a bit surprised if those guys have had a bellyful of this and have decided it's time to get this over with one final push of all-out conventional forces, and what could be done about it? Nothing. We have nothing but airpower left. They'll roll right through the South Vietnamese Army and we won't do a damn thing about it," Kaplan complained. Kaplan's attitude was not appreciated even if most of the advisors in the room felt the same way for the most part. Josh had witnessed the quality of the South Vietnamese leadership and so far was not impressed.

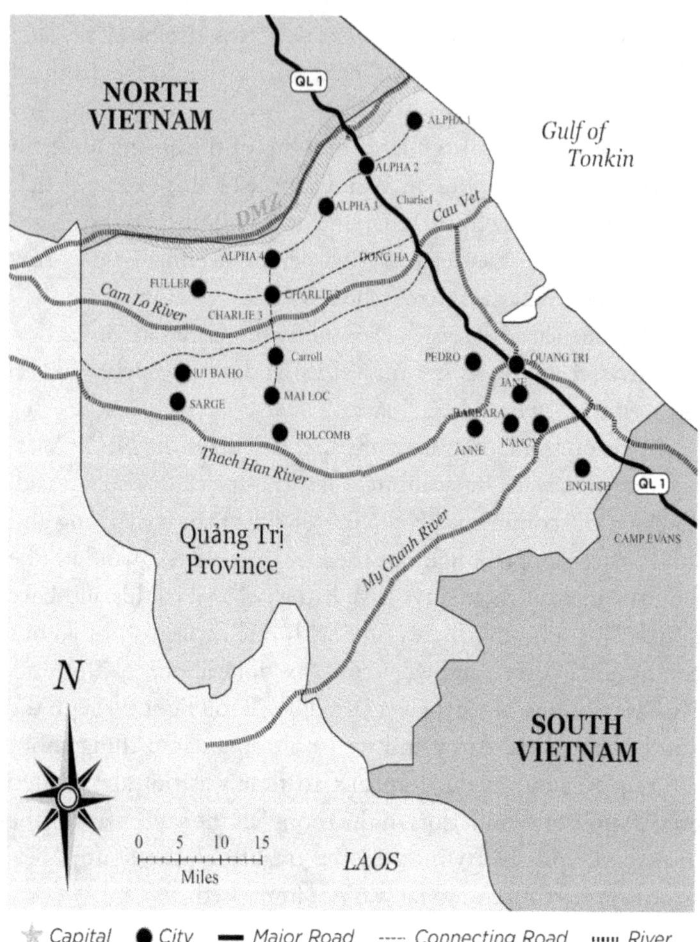

Vietnam I Corps Area of Operations

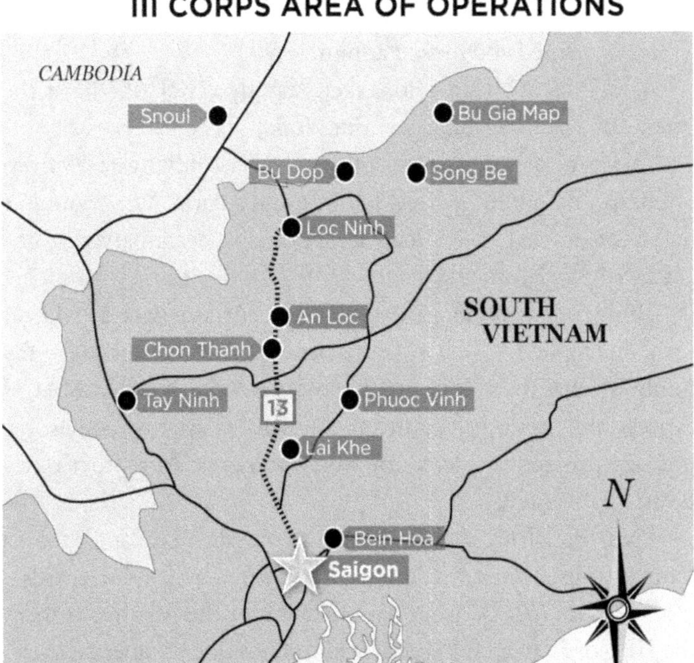

Pahl paused long enough to change the slide, bringing up a map of the III Corps sector without responding to Kaplan's comments. However, Mr. Vann made a note of them. Continuing, Pahl referred to the new map of the III Corps area of operations.

"In the III Corps area there have been reports of a buildup of forces around Snoul and in the base camp areas north of Bu Dop and Bu Gia Map. Also just northwest of Tay Ninh. Traditionally, the North has attacked through Tay Ninh and that's the anticipated route again. They—" Pahl didn't finish before he was interrupted.

"Excuse me, sir, if I may," Major Steinhauer said, looking around, a bit embarrassed that he'd blurted out the interruption. Everyone turned and looked at him.

"Yes, Major," Pahl said, taken slightly aback. "What's the question? I assume you have a question."

"Yes, sir. Sir, coming out of Cambodia is Highway 13 from Snoul to Loc Ninh, An Loc, Lai Khe and Saigon. Why wouldn't he attack on that major road as opposed to secondary roads to get to Saigon?" Josh asked.

Pahl turned and looked at the map. Turning back to address Josh, he replied, "Well, Major, because coming through Tay Ninh is what he's done in the past and that's what MACV expects him to do in the future. Whichever way he comes, it's not our problem, so let's not worry about it. Any other questions?" Pahl asked.

"No, sir," Josh replied. "Thank you, sir." No one noticed Vann jotting down a note on one of his three-by-five-inch cards.

"The 5th VC Division has operated for the past five years in the III Corps area and is expected to continue to operate there. Two other divisions have been identified in the area of Snoul, the 7th and the 9th NVA Divisions," Pahl said, turning to an NCO standing next to a second projector. "Bring up the organizational chart, please." Almost immediately, the enemy organization for battle came up.

"In our sector, the forces in Base Camp 609 are forces of the B-3 Front under the command of Lieutenant General Hoang Minh Thao. He has been the commander since 1967. The B-3 Front is organized as indicated on this slide."

B-3 Front Organization

<u>320th NVA Division, Colonel Kim Tuan</u>
48th Regiment
52nd Regiment

<u>64th Regiment, Colonel Khuat Duy Tien</u>
K-7, K-8, K-9 Battalions
54th Artillery Regiment
2nd NVA Artillery Regiment
7th Engineer Regiment

<u>3rd Division, Colonel Giap Van Curong</u>
2nd Regiment
12th Regiment
21st Regiment

<u>2nd Division, Colonel Nguyen Chon</u>
1st Regiment
141st Regiment

"Under the B-3 Front is the 320 NVA Division, and we believe the 2nd Division. The 3rd Division is also under the B-3 but is located in Binh Dinh Province. It's believed but unconfirmed that the 203rd Tank Regiment is in Base Camp 609 as well. The 320th and the 3rd Division both have three regiments of infantry. Aside from that, the organization of the B-3 is sketchy. There's been increased traffic on the Ho Chi Minh Trail for the past six months, and aerial reconnaissance has confirmed seismic sensor readings. Master Sergeant Stevens, would you like to comment on this?" Pahl asked, looking at a US Army master sergeant seated in the back.

Standing, Master Sergeant Lowell Stevens responded, "I went up with a Covey pilot in January. As we were flying over the Ho Chi Minh Trail looking for enemy activity, they weren't even interested in covering up what they were doing. Driving down the road like it was Sunday on the Long Island Expressway. Nothing was camouflaged, no one was pulling off the road. They weren't demonstrating any fear of an air strike. I've been up several times over the past two months and have found a couple of new roads being pushed across the border into the region," Stevens said, flashing a look at Lieutenant Colonel Stephen Bachinski, the senior district advisor for Kontum District, who returned the look. *What is this about?* Vann thought, catching the inaudible expressions.

"Where are these new roads?" Vann asked, flashing a glance at Colonel Bachinski. Bachinski caught the look and decided it was best to speak up.

"Sir, if I may. These sightings were not confirmed and therefore not reported up the chain. Once I have confirmation, then we'll forward their locations to your headquarters," Bachinski said, glaring daggers at Master Sergeant Stevens. They didn't penetrate Stevens's hide. He just returned them.

After deadly silence hung in the air for a moment, Mr. Vann picked up the brief. "Anything else, Irv?"

"Only that it's the 320th that's been beating up on the firebases up on Rocket Ridge. We aren't sure where the 2nd Division is located, just that he is or was in Base Camp 609. When we lose the cav, intel is going to become a problem as the ARVNs aren't very active in patrolling away from their base camps. The Border Rangers do a better job for the most part. Once the cav leaves, our best source for intel will be the FACs. That's all I have, sir," Pahl concluded.

"Thanks, Irv," Vann said and turned to face the audience. "Our own sector, I believe, however, is the most critical to support of a major offensive by the North. They'll come down Highway 14, seize Dak To, Tan Canh, Vo Dinh, Kontum, and An Khe, and push right to the coast, effectively cutting South Vietnam in half. Divide and conquer. Classic," Vann pointed out. "There has been anticipation for some time about a major attack coming this year. The questions have always been where, when and how big. Tet will be here in a few days, but I doubt it'll be much. They tried that once and it failed. I think the main attack is going to hit us and I've told General Abrams as much, that we can expect to see it around 1 April," he indicated.

MILITARY REGION II

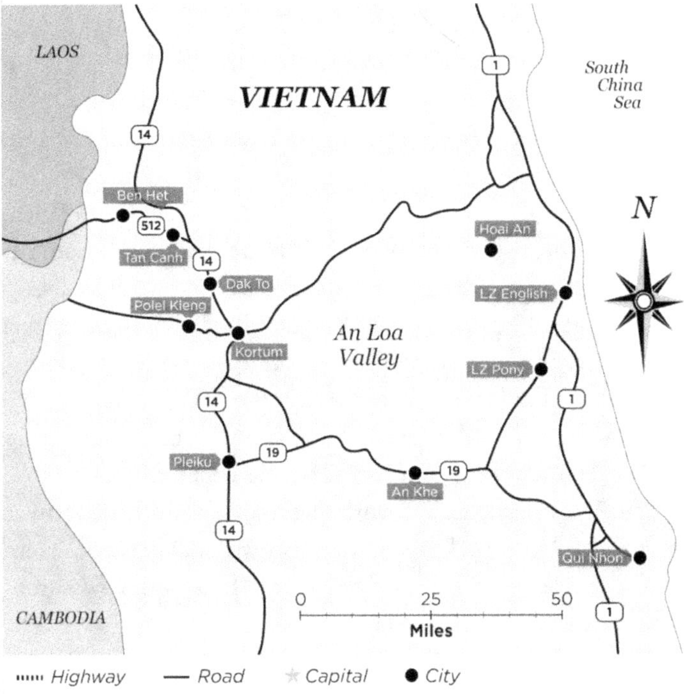

"The weather will be in their favor at that time as well as a few other things. The 7th of the 17th Cav Squadron is in the process of going home. Alpha Troop has already departed. Bravo Troop is scheduled to depart on 27 April and C Troop is due to leave on 6 April. Right now, C Troop is scattered to the four winds with elements in An Khe, Tuy Hoa, and An Son. We lose the cav, we lose our eyes. Vietnamese Air Force sure as hell isn't going to fly reconnaissance missions the way our guys do. Once we lose the cav, we're going to have to put more pressure on your counterparts to aggressively patrol," Vann directed and paused to check his notes, which were written on three-by-five-inch cards that he carried everywhere.

"General Abrams has been asking Washington for increased authority to bomb just across the DMZ border but is making no headway. Okay, Major Duffy, would you give us a quick rundown of what you're seeing up on Rocket Ridge?" Vann asked.

Major John Duffy was the senior advisor for the ARVN 11th Battalion, 2nd Brigade of the 1st ARVN Airborne Division, located at FSB Charlie. Seated next to him was Captain O'Brien, senior advisor to the ARVN 6th Airborne Battalion, located at FSB Delta, and Lieutenant Colonel Peter Kama, senior advisor, 2nd Airborne Brigade. The ARVN 2nd Brigade was occupying most of the firebases on a hill mass located between the border and Dak To/Tan Canh. There was also the ARVN 9th Airborne Battalion, which was located in Tan Canh with one company up on Rocket Ridge. Major Duffy and the other advisors of the ARVN 2nd Brigade didn't work directly for John Paul Vann as the ARVN Airborne Division had its own advisor team, Team 162. But since they'd been located in MR-II, a working relationship with SRAG II had been put in place.

"Yes, sir," Duffy said, standing. Duffy was prior service and had enlisted in the Army in 1955 as a private from New York City. He'd attained the rank of sergeant prior to attending Officer Candidate School at Fort Benning and receiving his commission. He was now on his fourth tour in Vietnam as an advisor. His home unit had been the Seventh Special Forces Group for most of his Army career. "The situation on Rocket Ridge has remained fairly stable. We hold FSBs 5, 6, Charlie, Delta and Kilo. He wants them and daily probes them or hits us with indirect fire. Last year, in March, he overran FSB 5, but we took it back the following day. Lost two helicopters from an outfit with the call sign Chickenman back then and another two in May. These firebases are all ringed with anti-aircraft weapons. We have sufficient artillery up there for mutual support to each other, but if he decided to hit us all at the same time, we'd be in trouble. As long as Rocket Ridge stays in our hands, it's doubtful he'll be able to attack down Route 512 or Highway 14 as we control the area from up there. Any questions?" Duffy asked. There were none.

"Thank you, Major," Vann said as Duffy sat down. "I wanted to have you all hear his remarks. Colonel Kaplan is the senior advisor for the 22nd Division, which has recently moved into the Dak To II area. Colonel, how about giving us a rundown of your AO?" Vann suggested, and Kaplan knew better than to say no.

"Yes, sir," Kaplan said, standing. "Now we've only been in the area for a month, so I'm still making my initial assessment, understand. When we moved in, General Trien had the 42nd Regiment move to Tan Canh and the 47th move from Pleiku to Dak To II. He decided to leave the 40th and 41st Regiments on the coast. The 40th is at LZ English and occasionally gets into it with the 3rd NVA Division. The 41st is south of there, at Crystal now," Kaplan explained, pausing when he noticed Vann pulling out one of his index cards and jotting down a quick note. "Within the 22nd's AO are the camps at Ben Het, Dak Sek and Dak To, which is north of Tan Canh up Highway 14."

The two advisors from Ben Het, Captain Sparks and Captain Heslin, exchanged looks as Kaplan went on to discuss the outlying camps, which he hadn't yet been to visit. "The 19th Armored Cav Squadron is located at Ben Het along with elements of the 71st reinforcing the 95th Battalion. In the rest of the border camps, we have only the local Montagnard RF/PF units. The 19th, although designated a squadron, is really only the size of a US company, and he's supporting the division's own 14th Cav Squadron, also a company-size force," Kaplan said.

"Why are the armored units all up at Ben Het?" General

Wear asked. He understood the awesome power of tanks that were properly employed, and employing them in a fixed position was not the proper way.

"Sir, that question has been asked and discussed several times...as recently as yesterday. Lieutenant Colonel Tuong got into it with Colonel Dat. Tuong is our senior armor officer and he attempted to convince Dat to hold them in reserve and use them for a counterattack force, capitalizing on the speed and shock effect that tanks have. Dat didn't buy it and so our tanks all sit as mobile pillboxes."

"How's your reconnaissance efforts?" Vann asked.

"Sir, we're finding them, and with the help of the forces on Rocket Ridge we're finding them fairly easily. I believe at last count we've had eighty B-52 strikes since the first of the year," Kaplan said.

"Now I know why I can't get more" was heard from the back of the room. Vann knew who'd said it.

"Care to comment, Colonel Schorr?" Vann asked. Schorr was the senior advisor for the 40th Regiment, located at LZ English.

"No, sir," Schorr said, slinking down in his chair. He and Vann had already had this discussion when Vann had last visited LZ English.

"Anything else, Colonel Kaplan?" Vann questioned.

"No, sir" was Kaplan's response.

"Okay, then. Colonel Kellar, you're up," Vann indicated, and the acting senior advisor for the 23rd Division stood. Sitting beside Kellar was Lieutenant Colonel J.W. "Bill" Bricker, the G-3 advisor for the 23rd Division and in Vann's opinion a very capable officer. Lieutenant Colonel Mike McKenna was seated on the other side of Kellar.

"Sir, our AO is fairly quiet, with the division headquarters along with the 45th Regiment located at Ban Me Thuot. The division commander, BG Vo Vanh Canh, is ready to give up the command, and Colonel Ly Tong Ba is slated to be the new commander. Personally, between us ladies, I'll be glad to see Canh gone. Worthless in my opinion. Colonel Ba, on the other hand, has a good reputation as a fighter and a commander. The 53rd Regiment is located in Dalat and the 44th Regiment is located at Song Mao. The 8th Armored Squadron is also located at Ban Me Thuot. As I said, things are fairly quiet, with just VC activity," Kellar said, indicating that this was all he had to offer.

"Good," Vann said, retaking the discussion. "Last month we met with General Abrams at MACV headquarters and he put out some guidance that I want to be sure you all understand. He sees, as I do, that we have a major battle approaching. He requested and is receiving more air support. Yesterday, a major bombing campaign commenced with eighty B-52 strikes being carried out over a forty-eight-hour period on Base Camps 609 and 611. He still couldn't get authority to bomb north of the DMZ, but hitting those two base camps will certainly take some fight out of the enemy. Eighteen additional F-4s have arrived in Da Nang, and eight additional B-52 aircraft have been repositioned to Guam. The number of aircraft carriers on Yankee Station is being increased from three to four. He received approval to plant sensors in the DMZ, and budgeting restrictions on sorties have been lifted. All good news for us," Vann said, taking a pause.

"Now for the bad news. Nixon has announced troop reduction, which surprised Abrams as it's counter to OPLAN J208A timelines. Another seventy thousand more bodies by 1 May. OPLAN J208A called for an end strength on 1 May of eighty-four thousand. Now it will be sixty-nine thousand and a promise of another reduction by April. That means, gentlemen, that we are getting smaller and smaller. So, what is the impact on us? Abrams's priorities will focus as follows. Command and control of American operations is first priority. In that case, I will be the last to leave," Vann added to lighten the mood.

"Second priority is installation protection, which means we can expect to keep the cav and infantry that remains guarding Pleiku and Da Nang here for a bit longer." You could almost hear the sighs of relief. "Third priority is support and administration elements for US personnel, but...minimal intelligence support and minimal commo support." A groan could be heard. "The telephone switchboard and landlines will be turned over to the Vietnamese in the coming weeks. We will continue to provide advice to the South Vietnamese forces, but with reduced capability. And that reduced capability means we're going to have to rely on the Vietnamese Air Force a lot more for helicopter support because the remaining two infantry brigades in-country and the remaining cav squadron in our sector are going home. We lose the 7th of the 17th in April, although the one troop is already stateside-bound," Vann stated. "Any questions?" There were none.

"So, with no cav or reconnaissance, how should we fight this fight?" Vann asked, allowing the question to hang in the air for a moment. "Colonel Snell."

Colonel Dillon Snell was the SRAG G-3 Operations officer. Snell and Vann had discussed the upcoming fight and how it might be fought. General Wear had participated in these skull sessions, presenting an opposing view to Vann's.

"Sir," Snell said as he stood and walked to the front of the room. "I see two ways we could go at this. Course of action one is to build up large forces at Ben Het, Dak To II and Tan Canh. Force him to mass his forces and then, when he's prepared to attack, hit him with B-52 and TACAIR. Course of action two is to conduct a delaying action at Ben Het, Dak To II, and Tan Canh, wearing his forces down as he attacks, causing him to waste time and resources while we fold our forces into Kontum, building a strong defensive position—then hit him with B-52 strikes, massed artillery and TACAIR," Snell stated. On a paper pad mounted on an easel, he wrote

COA 1 on the left side and COA 2 on the right, underlining each.

"Okay, gentlemen, here's where you get to give us your pros and cons of each plan."

General Wear was the first to speak up.

"I like course of action two, delay back to Kontum. It will drain him and allow us time to consolidate forces and supplies. It brings us closer to our support. Course of action one could put the ARVNs in encircled positions and that would panic them, I think."

Vann quickly responded.

"But if they're encircled, they have no place to run to and will fight better, I bet."

"Or quickly surrender," Wear shot back. "Colonel Kaplan, what do you think?"

Oh damn, this is one dogfight I don't want to get in the middle of, Kaplan thought. "Sir, both are valid courses of action with pros and cons. The 22nd Division is in the forward position and could be a blocking force initially. If the situation became such, then they could revert to a delaying strategy. As long as we control Rocket Ridge, I don't think the enemy could push us out of Dak To II or Tan Canh," Kaplan said, attempting to play both sides.

"Kellar, what's your opinion?" Vann asked.

"Sir, if it appeared that the 22nd was going to go into a delaying action, the 23rd could move north and reinforce Kontum. We would need two days for the move, however, and that's if the enemy hasn't closed the roads coming north," Kellar stated, also attempting to avoid the argument. As he spoke, Colonel Snell was writing down the pros and cons.

"Well, gentlemen, it appears to be a draw between the two courses of action. I'll discuss this further with General Wear and General Dzu and let you know what the plan will be as well as the Vietnamese commanders. Any questions?"

"Sir, I have two," Lieutenant Colonel McKenna said. Vann nodded in acknowledgment.

"Sir, do you have any more good news for us, and what time does the bar open?"

"No, there's no more good news, Colonel, and the bar opens right now. Gentlemen...," Vann said, heading for the door and waving everyone to follow. He paused for a moment and looked around the room. Everyone froze in place.

"Major Steinhauer," Vann called out.

"Yes, sir," Josh responded.

"Major, before you leave in the morning, stop by my office, please," Vann requested. Everyone turned to Josh, who was now the center of attention. Murmurs of "you screwed up now" and "it sucks to be you" could be heard as Vann turned and led everyone to the bar.

13

THE INTERVIEW

15 FEBRUARY 1972
SRAG HQ
Pleiku

BEFORE THE PREVIOUS evening's festivities had ended, General Wear told Josh that his appointment with Vann would be at 1000 hours as Vann wasn't noted for being an early riser. When Josh arrived at Vann's office, the old sergeant first class aide told him to go on in. Entering, he found Vann sitting on one side of a couch with coffee and two cups sitting on a coffee table.

"Come in, Major," Vann said, pointing at the pot of coffee. "Have a cup."

"Thank you, sir...I will," Josh responded and, picking up the pot, began to pour. "Can I top you off, sir?"

"Sure, I haven't even gotten through the first cup yet. Need two just to start my heart. Sit, sit," Vann indicated, pointing at the opposite end of the couch.

Once Josh was seated and in the middle of his first sip of

coffee, Vann started the conversation. "Wear has given me a basic overview of your being here, and that was in line with what General Brooks said back in December. Now I want to hear it from you."

"Well, sir, I've been directed by the DOD IG to come to Vietnam and observe the training and conduct of the South Vietnamese forces. I and three other officers are to report back to the DOD IG with our findings in a report that the president intends to hand to Congress. We've been directed not to share our findings with anyone outside of the DOD IG office. General Brooks assigned me to MR-II as I had flown in this area on my last assignment to Vietnam and am familiar with the area," Josh concluded, bracing for what he was sure was going to be a tirade about not sharing the report despite what General Brooks had told him prior to flying up to Pleiku.

Vann sipped his coffee for a moment and said nothing. Placing his coffee cup down, he turned and looked at Josh. "Very good, and I hope you do exactly that. I won't ask to see the report, and if anyone in this command asks, I want to know about it right away. Fair enough?" Vann asked.

Josh was caught off guard. "Yes, sir, fair enough."

"Good. What do you know about me?" Vann asked.

"That you're a retired lieutenant colonel with a tour as an advisor and now hold the equivalent rank of major general," Josh answered.

"Well, let me fill you in a bit more and then you might understand some of the things that I do and say," Vann said, pausing to pick up his coffee cup and take another sip. "I was an advisor in 1963 to the 7th Division in the Delta. I worked for a General Harkins, who was the senior Army officer here back then for the eleven thousand US personnel in-country. At that time there were only about three thousand advisors scattered over the country. Harkins emphasized that we were advisors only and couldn't command the Vietnamese forces.

"When I arrived, I enjoyed working with my Vietnamese counterparts—that is, until I got to know them. I advised a Colonel Cao, who was the division commander, and a General Tho, who was the Corps or Military Region IV commander. Colonel Porter was his advisor and my boss. Damn fine officer and boss. We were engaging hard-core VC, which were really left over Viet Minh from the French occupation. They had old weapons—bolt-actions, .30-caliber machine guns and not much more, maybe a 60mm mortar. Our initial engagements were partially successful against the local VC, but the hard-core always seemed to slip out of a firefight. That's when I discovered that Cao would always leave an escape route open for the hard-core to retreat out. As my time continued, I saw that he was filing false reports on number of casualties, number of enemy killed, even false operations. I started to wonder why.

"The South Vietnamese leadership of the early 1960s was steeped in Vietnamese tradition and culture as one would expect, and which Americans didn't understand. First, in 1960, the airborne attempted a coup to overthrow President Diem. It failed, but the result was that after that, Diem promoted officers not for their military ability but for their loyalty to him. Second, Diem was a Catholic and the majority religion was Buddhist. Buddhist officers didn't fare well under Diem's government. Third, the Vietnamese culture is one in which face-saving is an overriding consideration. No one wants to report bad news up the flagpole for fear that they'll be relieved, and they'll go so far as to conceal failure from higher headquarters in many cases," Vann said.

"Sir, has any of this been reported to higher headquarters or Washington?" Josh asked. Vann gave him a "you really asked that question" look.

"Back in 1963 when I was an advisor to the 7th Division, I reported this and a lot more. I reported falsified reports outlining combat actions that didn't happen. I reported incompetence bordering on treason. It was all reported and sent to Saigon, General Harkins. We—and I mean all the advisors in the 7th Division—prepared an after-action report after the Battle of Ap Bac, ninety-two pages, specifically outlining exactly what happened, which Colonel Porter endorsed.[1] And where did it get us? What did I get for those reports? Almost relieved," Vann said with some disgust in his voice.

"Did Washington ever hear about this?" Josh asked.

"Do you think you're the first investigative team to come to Vietnam? In 1963 a team of seven generals from all branches came out here on a fact-finding mission. They spent time traveling the countryside but didn't come to the hotbed of activity. Harkins steered them away from the Delta. No, they had one general come to the Delta, which was the area with the most activity, and he spent one day here. We told him everything. Did that get back to Washington? I doubt it as we're still in Vietnam after ten years," Vann indicated.

"Who was filtering the reports that you were sending up?" Josh asked, more interested in hearing the details of this history lesson.

"Our reports were sent to Military Advisor Group Vietnam, headed up by General Harkins. He never once came to the field, and I never saw him in a set of fatigues and boots. He would fly in his Beechcraft airplane over the countryside but always landed at major headquarters. He heard what the Vietnamese wanted him to hear and ignored his own advisors because what we were telling him was that the Vietnamese Army wasn't able to defeat the Viet Cong, and in those days, prior to 1968, it was mostly Viet Cong they were fighting. Harkins was feeding Washington a line of bullshit about the success here in Vietnam," Vann said, reaching for the coffeepot to refill his cup.

"Sir, why do you say that the Vietnamese Army wasn't capable of winning, besides the poor leadership?" Josh asked, making mental notes.

"Two reasons...first, the Strategic Hamlet Program, and second, our arming the Viet Cong," Vann said, staring at Josh to see his reaction. It was as expected.

"Sir, we were arming the Viet Cong!" Josh repeated Vann's words.

"Indirectly, yes. Prior to 1962, the Viet Cong were operating with homemade shotguns that were deadlier to the shooter than the target—weapons from the Japanese and from the French, which were US weapons left over from World War II. Scattered all over the Delta were hamlets with a Civil Guard force. They were supposed to defend the hamlet. We supplied the South Vietnamese government with modern weapons, and they in turn gave them to the Civil Guard, who would leave them behind after an engagement and not retrieve the wounded soldiers' weapons or were Viet Cong sympathizers and would claim they lost a weapon in a canal and couldn't find it. Some even joined the Viet Cong on their nightly attacks as long as it was against the South Vietnamese forces and not the people or another hamlet. After the Battle of Ap Bac, the North realized that the Viet Cong could stand up to the South Vietnamese and began regular supply runs down the coast in fishing trawlers. They brought more modern weapons and heavier weapons like 12.7mm machine guns and 82mm mortars as well as recoilless rifles. We told Saigon to stop supplying weapons to the Civil Guard, but it fell on deaf ears," Vann said.

"And what about the Strategic Hamlet Program...?" Josh asked.

"That was the second act that really pissed off the people. The decision was made to move people out of areas where it was thought that the Viet Cong were getting aid or intimidating the population, so one of two courses of action was taken. One was to physically move the people out of their comfortable homes where they could walk to their fields easily and transplant them to an area where they could walk a few miles to their fields and rebuild a hamlet and new house...at their expense, of course. To build the new house, which was going to be a lot smaller as the people were packed into a compound circled by barbed wire, locked in at night and guarded by the Civil Guard, they had to purchase the material from the province or district chief, who was given the material free by the US government. In addition to working their fields, they had to dig and prepare the defensive positions around the hamlet too. The final act of humiliation was that, as the people left their hamlet for the new place, aircraft would come in with napalm and destroy what had been their homes," Vann explained.

"I'm beginning to understand why the Viet Cong became so strong," Josh offered. "I always felt the Vietnamese people didn't care who the government was. They just wanted to be left alone to raise a family, grow their crops and live in peace. You said there were two courses of action with the Strategic Hamlet Program. What was the second one?"

"If the decision wasn't to move the village, then in order to enclose the hamlet and properly guard it, it had to be reduced. So the homes and families living on the outskirts were moved to open space in the interior of the hamlet. People were packed in closely so the Civil Guard could monitor and, quote, 'protect' them better. A hamlet might have been over a mile long in some cases and was pushed together to cover an area half its original size. Wire was then emplaced to encircle the hamlet, a berm and ditch constructed, and punji stakes prepared and put in the berm and ditch. This was almost as bad as the relocation option," Vann acknowledged.

"Sir, this has been very interesting. The fact that you reported the problems ten years ago and it never was acknowledged, I find baffling," Josh said, shaking his head.

"You have to remember the times, Major. We had just come out of the Korean War. The French had just been kicked out of Southeast Asia. The Brits had just concluded a ten-year war fighting the ethnic Chinese in Malaysia. Cuba was in the process of being turned into a communist country on our doorstep. The Cold War was threatening to go nuclear, and we had the Cuban missile crisis in October of '62. The threat of communist expansion scared the administration. And now South Vietnam was in danger of falling to the communists as well. The problem was that the original architect for US support of South Vietnam was wrong, starting with leaving Diem in power as president. If they had removed him and replaced him with someone with credibility and integrity, things may have been different. Unfortunately, we didn't do that until after it was too late. With Diem as the president and his cronies in command, the counterinsurgency effort in the Delta was approximately ten or twenty percent of what could reasonably be expected in view of the personnel and resources available,"[2] Vann explained.

"Why so long to remove Diem?" Josh asked, totally engrossed in the history lesson he was receiving.

"Diem was like a tick burrowed into the Vietnamese society. Put in power by the French, his brother was the senior Catholic cleric in Vietnam. Everyone in the military in any position of importance was beholden to him or his wife, who was a powerful figure in her own right. Things started to unravel for him in 1963 with the Buddhist Crisis and the monk that set himself on fire in Saigon. Diem wasn't fazed a bit and came down harshly on the Buddhist population, driving them to the side of the Viet Cong. The administration recognized that it all could have been avoided, but Diem only scoffed at the threat of further violence and encouraged it against the Buddhists. The administration couldn't decide who to replace him with or how to go about replacing him, so Diem stayed in office and we became more involved," Vann explained.

"May I ask, did you ever get a chance to brief anyone in Washington back then?" Josh asked, curious to see if Vann's story would be the same as what Josh had previously been told as well as whether it would reveal who Vann had spoken to in Washington.

"I left here and went to D.C. to attend the Industrial College of the Armed Forces, but I arrived in Washington before the course started and was assigned to the Directorate for Special Operations in the Pentagon for a few months. I prepared a presentation that was supposed to go to the entire Joint Chiefs, but an hour before the presentation, it was canceled," Vann said.

"How come?" Josh asked.

"If I'd given that presentation, several general officers would have been seriously embarrassed, those at the pinnacle of the general officer corps. They weren't about to have their reputations destroyed by a lieutenant colonel," Vann said.

"So what happened, if I may ask?" Josh inquired.

"About five weeks after my failed attempt, an article came out in the *New York Times* that was almost identical to my presentation. That started a firestorm throughout the administration. Around the same time, the Buddhist Crisis was building steam and riots were breaking out across the country. Diem was being a hard-ass and really cracking down on the Buddhists. Kennedy replaced the ambassador with Henry Cabot Lodge Jr. I'm told he was of a similar opinion as I was. Shortly after his arrival, Diem was overthrown and assassinated."

"I have to ask—did you release your presentation to the *New York Times*?" Josh asked with some hesitation.

Mr. Vann smiled and stood. "Major, I wish you the best in your time here. If you need anything, just ask. If anyone roadblocks you, you come to me. Now, if you will excuse me, I have a meeting to attend with General Dzu," he said and extended his hand. This meeting was over.

14

DEFENSIVE PLAN, MR-II

General Abrams left the conference feeling drained. *I absolutely hate these all-day marathon briefings*, he was thinking as he walked the short distance to his office. He could hear the footsteps of those following him down the hall. Each would want their "five minutes" to privately discuss something with him that for some reason couldn't be discussed in the briefing. Most of it was bullshit. People had all sorts of excuses to get "face time" with him and it just pissed him off. A few of the people he did want to pass something to, but most would be blocked by his admin assistant in the outer office and told to make an appointment. It was so much easier and more pleasant being a tank battalion commander in Germany those many years ago, he reminisced.

His aide was waiting by his office door when he entered the outer office. "Give me a few minutes before you start the procession," Abrams directed as he handed the young major the briefing book he had just received in the conference. Entering his office, he made a beeline to the walnut box sitting on the sideboard. He was in need of a fix as he hadn't had one yet this day. Opening it slowly, he reached in and extracted a Cohiba cigar. Clipping the end, he slowly placed the flame below it and twirled the cigar to obtain an even burn. Once the end glowed, he took a long drag and relished the aroma. His entire demeanor began to relax, and he closed his eyes just to enjoy the moment that he knew would end shortly. And it did.

"Excuse me, sir, but General Carley is outside and says he needs to talk to you. Rather important, he says," the aide stated.

"Okay, Bob. Send the general in. I'm ready for him," Abrams said as he moved behind his desk and pulled out his chair. *Might as well get comfortable for this marathon now*, he was thinking when the MACV J-3 Operations officer walked in.

"Sir," General Carley said, entering the inner sanctum. Carley had been on the MACV staff for the past six months, fresh out of the five-sided puzzle palace, as the Pentagon was called by those who had served there or avoided having to serve there. As a rising star in the Army, he had had all the right jobs and command positions so essential for promotion and had avoided the career-ending assignments such as recruiting duty, ROTC instructor or National Guard advisor. He cherished his infantry time with the 82nd Airborne Division the most of all his assignments.

"Your aide gave me today's briefing book with your notes and I'll get back to you with some answers later this evening," Carley said.

"No rush. Nothing earth-shattering in there today," Abrams said, taking a long drag on his cigar. "So what's up now?"

"Sir, I got a call from John Paul Vann. He's flying down as we speak and wants to come in and see you right away. I think you should hear him out. As he expressed in the December and subsequent meetings, he thinks the North is about to launch a major assault towards Kontum," Carley said.

"What's he want this time... more B-52s allocated to MR-II?" Abrams asked. Vann was always asking for more B-52s to support ARVN operations along the border with Cambodia. He was even known to have diverted B-52s that were inbound to support operations in MR-III, which caused more than one confrontation with Brigadier General Hollingsworth, Commander, Regional Assistance Command, MR-II.

"He wants to run the defensive plan for Military Region II by you. Thinks there may be some pushback from the Vietnamese JCS," Carley explained.

"Did Dzu approve it and submit it up to JCS?" Abrams asked. He didn't want to get drawn into a pissing contest between the regional commander and the Vietnamese JCS. Too often, American advisors were accused of "meddling" in Vietnamese affairs.

"I don't know, sir," Carley answered.

"I was afraid you were going to say he wanted me to see that Dzu was relieved. Now if that was the case, I would personally walk over to JCS and recommend it. Except for General Truong down in MR-IV, the rest are worthless. All political flunkies of President Thieu. Hell, General Lam up in I Corps does nothing significant except play tennis every afternoon. General Minh in MR-III can't make a decision to save his soul, and Dzu...he's a damn drug smuggler in business with his brother, who's an air force pilot flying the drugs out of Cambodia. Dzu has to be the worst of the four. Wear was telling me that Dzu comes to Pleiku on Sunday afternoons and spends the night. Has a room in the Bachelor Officers' Quarters right above Wear. Spends Sunday afternoons with Wear, drinking Wear's scotch, and then they go to dinner together. Monday mornings he has breakfast, attends a staff brief, spends an hour beating up on the staff and leaves around 1000 hours, not to be seen again until the following

Sunday. He says he has important things to attend to in Qui Nhon. Has a house on the beach, just down the street from Vann's place," Abrams fussed.

"Sir, if Dzu is as incompetent as Vann makes him out to be, how did he wind up as a military region commander?" Carley asked.

"Dzu's family is politically connected. He worked on the JCS staff up until 1970, when Brigadier General Nguyen Viet Thanh was killed in a helicopter crash. JCS sent him to MR-IV. Vann was his senior advisor down there. In August of that year, Dzu got promoted for some unknown reason and moved to MR-II. He brought Vann with him. As I said, he's suspected of being involved in the drug trade and Vann probably blackmailed him to bring him up to MR-II," Abrams went on to explain.

"Interesting" was all Carley said. "If there's nothing else, sir, I'll get you some answers for the questions of today," he added before he turned and headed for the door.

The aide beat him to it, opening the door from the outer office and announcing, "Sir, Mr. Vann is here."

"Send him in...oh, you might as well stay and hear this. Should be interesting," Abrams said, pointing at a seat for Carley.

The aide held the door, which was set to close automatically whenever opened and could be remotely locked from Abrams's desk, while Mr. John Paul Vann strode into the room. The air of confidence followed him like a ghost.

John Paul Vann was not a physically impressive individual but did project an air of confidence and energy that couldn't be denied. Some thought him arrogant, egotistical, abrasive, and blunt. Subordinates recognized him as a person who had their best interests at heart. He was considered by all as an energetic competitor. He expected and insisted that the proper protocols be extended to him, as his State Department position was the equivalent rank of a major general. He generally dressed in the typical State Department bureaucrat attire of slacks, short-sleeved white shirt and tie. The only thing outside the bureaucrat uniform was the cowboy boots he wore.

"General Abrams, thank you for seeing me on such short notice. I have a couple of items I'd like to discuss with you and ask for your support," Vann said as he rolled through the doorway and approached General Abrams's desk. "General Carley," he added; this was all the acknowledgment that Carley rated.

"Mr. Vann, General Carley said I should hear you out on this short notice, so let's get to it. What exactly do you wish to discuss?" Abrams asked as Vann immediately rolled out a map on Abrams's desk.

"General, you're aware of the threat that we have coming down the Ho Chi Minh Trail at this time. Back in November at the intel brief, General Potts said we were looking at fifty thousand enemy troops, with tanks and artillery and being poised to cross into Kontum in early January. It was also expected that the attack would kick off in the dry season. At the last look, we now estimate that the fifty thousand is probably accurate. Our reconnaissance shows that the Ho Chi Minh Trail has so much traffic on it, all flowing towards the west of Kontum Province, that they probably need to put in a stoplight or two. North of Ben Het, we've found tank tracks, and on January twenty-fifth, two Cobra gunships from the Pink Panthers engaged two tanks and spotted four more just west of Rocket Ridge, they claimed," Vann outlined.

"Has Potts received this information?" Abrams asked, glancing at Carley.

"I don't know, sir" was all Carley could say.

Not missing a beat, Vann boasted, "Sir, we've captured some documents that indicate that the NVA will make the same mistake they did in Tet of '68."

"And what was that, Mr. Vann?" Abrams asked.

"Sir, he dispersed his forces and didn't concentrate them," Vann explained with a look of surprise. "Sir, his plan, from what we found in the documents, is to have his main attack against Tan Canh and Dak To II and the firebases on Rocket Ridge. The second phase of the attack will be continuing towards Pleiku and Kontum. This is when he'll launch his attack into Binh Dinh Province and the coastal plain. If he can manage it, these two attacks will cut the country in half."

"So, have you been able to identify which units are going to conduct this operation?" Carley asked.

"Yes. The B-3 Front, led by General Hoang Minh Thao, will have overall command. He'll have the 2nd NVA Division, which has operated in the Central Highlands since 1967, and the 320 NVA Division, which is made up of the 48th, 52nd, and 64th Infantry Regiments and the 54th Artillery Regiment. We've also identified the 2nd Artillery Regiment and the 203rd Armored Regiment. The 3rd Division is just north of Binh Dinh Province on the coast and supports the local VC. The 7th Engineer Regiment is currently building a road that's four meters wide and pointed towards Kontum. At their current pace, this road will be completed by the end of March."

"Well, it sounds like you have a good picture of what you're up against," Abrams commented. "What's Dzu's plan to defend?"

"Dzu's plan is to reinforce Tan Canh and Dak To II and stop the advance there and then pound him back into the Stone Age with B-52s," Vann offered.

"Suppose the NVA get around these two towns, what then?" Carley asked.

"Then Dzu has them right where he wants them and we just continue pounding them. The forces in these two locations are more than adequate to hold the enemy at bay. He's requested reinforcements from the Airborne Division, and they're en route as we speak—and the 2nd Airborne Brigade has joined us," Vann stated.

"So with the airborne brigade, what does that give Dzu?" Abrams asked. He posed his question to indicate that Dzu was the commander in MR-II and not John Paul Vann. Though he was well known for attempting to emulate a commander, and unofficially he was the commander in MR-II, Vann didn't command anyone, officially.

"Sir, currently we have the 22nd and 23rd Infantry Divisions, the 2nd Airborne Brigade and two armored cavalry squadrons. I could really use two more infantry battalions to be located in Kontum to defend the city against local VC attacks. Another airborne brigade would be nice if we could get it—but, sir, I'm asking that you see if JCS will break loose those two more infantry battalions for Kontum," Vann explained.

Ah, so now comes the begging for more troops, Abrams thought. "Well, I can certainly ask the JCS to provide those, but has Dzu asked for them?" Abrams asked.

"No, sir, he feels that they're not needed," Vann reluctantly offered.

"Well, I think he should ask for them first before we do. If he asks for them, I will support him on this one. Don't want to be accused of meddling in Vietnamese affairs," Abrams said, glancing over at Carley.

"Okay, sir, I'll go back to him and talk to him again," Vann said, pausing for just a moment. "On another subject, sir, the 361st Aerial Weapons Company is slated to redeploy on 7 April. Can we stop that redeployment and extend them until we're sure they're not going to be needed?"

"John, do you have any idea the pressure I'm under from the president to cut troop strength here? Laird sets one time schedule and then, with the next demonstration on the Mall, changes the schedule and cuts us some more," Abrams said in frustration, looking at Vann.

"Sir, I'm sure you are, but the 361st is the last gun company we have in the II Corps area. The 17th Aviation Group has been reduced from twenty-seven companies to only nine. It's gone from five aviation battalions to one. If the 361st departs, that leaves only the cav troop with attack helicopters besides a platoon in one lift company. The VNAF have no Cobra gunships, and the Charlie-model Huey is almost useless in the Central Highlands. On top of all that, we have no antitank-capable helicopters in-country except a few Charlie models equipped with the SS-11 antitank systems," Vann explained.

Abrams looked surprised and turned to Carley. "I thought the SS-11 systems were pulled out of country in 1970," he exclaimed.

"Sir, they were, but because of Lam Son 719 last year, six were returned. They're available," Carley said. "We have had a request from Aviation Systems Command to send over here two Charlie-model aircraft that are equipped with the new TOW system. Hughes Aircraft wants to test the aircraft over here. As this is a civilian venture and doesn't count against our end strength, we approved it. They should be arriving in-country shortly and we can locate them in Pleiku for the moment—unless, of course, we find a greater need in I Corps or III Corps."
[1]

"I will consider your request about the 361st," Abrams said. He looked at Carley, who was jotting down a note. "Tet kicks off today, doesn't it? How has Dzu laid out his forces since the 2nd Airborne Brigade is arriving in your AO now?" Abrams asked.

"Sir, the 2nd Airborne Brigade headquarters is setting up in Vo Dinh, which is sixteen kilometers north of Kontum along Highway 14. The battalions will be occupying the firebases on Rocket Ridge. Command-wise, he's placed Colonel Tuong in command of Pleiku. He's the deputy II Corps commander. He has Kontum under the command of Colonel Nguyen Ba Thinh, the province chief. The 22nd Division commander is responsible for all the rest—Ben Het, Tan Canh, Dak Mot, Dak Pek and Dak Seang and Fire Support Base 5 and 6 on Rocket Ridge," Vann outlined.

"What's at those hamlets?" Abrams asked with a furrowed brow.

"Sir, those are occupied by Border Ranger camps."

"I understand that General Wear thinks that Dzu should set up a series of blocking positions to wear the enemy down with a strong defense concentrated at Kontum," Abrams said. This caught Vann by surprise. He didn't know that General Wear had spoken to Abrams about Vann's plan for the defense. Vann had presented the plan as if Dzu had developed it.

"Well, yes, sir, but Dzu decided that this would be better, cost less ground. I was also afraid that the soldiers don't understand nor have ever done a retrograde operation and that it would turn into a route back to Kontum and not stop a thing," Vann stated. Abrams absorbed this last comment but said nothing for a long time.

"Okay, John," he finally said, "I'll consider your request to extend the 361st until we see what's going to happen. If there's nothing else, I believe I have others waiting to come in. You have a safe flight going back," Abrams said, indicating the meeting was over.

15

MOVE THE 44TH REGIMENT

12 FEB 1972
44th Regiment
Song Mao, Binh Thuan Province

THE 44TH REGIMENT was commanded by Colonel Tran Quang Tien. Lieutenant Colonel Thomas McKenna thought him to be a competent officer and commander, and they got along. Tien had been in command since 1971. His English was fair. Tien would consider the advice McKenna gave him and make a decision. McKenna was part of Advisor Team 33. His deputy was Major Tony Swachek; Captain Jack Martin was the temporary third member of his team. The team motto was "Nunc Imus," Latin for "We Go Now," which was a common phrase for the Vietnamese. The advisor accommodations at Song Mao were pretty good. At one time there had been over fifty advisors with the 44th. Advisors were with each company and battalion as well as regimental headquarters. Now it was just three advisors and an interpreter, Sergeant Hao, and while the advisor compound hadn't changed, it had become hollow.

"What do you have planned for today?" McKenna asked his deputy, Major Swachek, as he sat down with a paper plate of eggs and bacon. They had a Vietnamese cook who did alright if they could get her the ingredients. Coffee was one ingredient they could always get.

"Well, I'm going to go over to 1st Battalion and talk to the commander about the training exercise he ran yesterday on attacking a trench line. He was employing old French tactics left over from the First World War. I didn't want to say anything in front of his soldiers—face-saving—but thought I would take him aside today and go over some stuff," Swachek said before he swallowed another sip of coffee.

"And you?" McKenna asked Captain Martin, who was just finishing his breakfast.

"Sir, I thought I would talk to some of the company commanders in 2nd Battalion about artillery adjustment. We built a sand table yesterday with some cotton balls for rounds and string for grid lines. It represents the area north of here. I'll act as the unit in contact and drop the balls for them to adjust. Seems like every time we try to get the artillery to shoot for real, they say they can't as they don't have enough ammo," Martin explained.

"They don't. It isn't like when we were with US line units and we had all the ammo we wanted to shoot. They're limited to twenty rounds per day per gun unless it's in contact. That doesn't give much room for training. I know for a fact that during Lam Son 719 last year, the artillery units from the Delta that were brought north had difficulty shooting high-angle trajectory over the mountains. Got to the point that the ground commanders didn't trust the artillery and wouldn't bring it in closer than a klick. That sand table exercise is probably the next best thing," McKenna said, indirectly complimenting the young captain for his initiative. "Why don't you ask Major Steinhauer if he wants to join you and observe?"

"Good idea, sir. I will," Martin responded.

"Whatcha got going for you today, sir?" Swachek asked.

"Colonel Tien wants to see me this morning to discuss something. He sent a runner to my room around 0700 and asked if I could come by at 0900. The runner didn't know what it was about," McKenna explained.

"Sir, can I take Sergeant Hao with me?" asked Captain Martin.

"Yeah, Colonel Tien speaks pretty good English, so I shouldn't need Hao," McKenna agreed.

After breakfast, McKenna grabbed his soft cap and strolled over to Colonel Tien's office. Tien was a short man standing next to an American, but not an ounce of fat was on his body.

"Good morning, Colonel. You wanted to see me?" McKenna asked, walking into the colonel's office.

"Yes, come in. Sit. You need coffee?" Tien asked.

"No, sir, I'm good," McKenna responded, taking a seat in one of the overstuffed chairs that Vietnamese officers always had in their offices. Tien took the adjacent chair.

"We have new orders. We move. We go An Khe. Unit at An Khe let sappers get to ammo dump and blow it up. They are being moved someplace else and we take their place. We leave in two days. Go by trucks. Two-day trip, five hundred kilometers. We take Highway 1 up the coast, then Highway 19 west to An Khe," Tien outlined.

Leaning forward in his seat, McKenna asked, "How bad was the damage?"

"Very bad. Ammo dump gone; bunkers gone. We have much work rebuilding bunkers and secure An Khe," Tien explained.

"Do we know how they got in?"

"They have spy. He recon perimeter and ammo dump days before. He watch guards change. He find dead space both day and night. Sappers come at night and disconnect trip wires in front of bunkers. Quietly they slip through wire while mortar fire is hitting interior. They move fast inside with satchel charges, grenades. Some had AK-47. Commander said they killed some, some got away. He not happy. He be relieved," Tien said.

"Well, sir, I'll try to get some attack helicopters to provide cover for us as we move up there, although I wouldn't expect any trouble on Highway 1. The only trouble spot is on Highway 19 at the An Khe pass between Qui Nhon and An Khe. We probably need to have attack helicopters and scouts to cover us on the patch. I'll get a request in for them. Anything else you want me to get?" McKenna asked.

"No. That be good. I have staff brief tomorrow morning with plan. You be there," Tien requested, but in his English, it sounded like an order.

Chuckling to himself, McKenna said, "Yes, sir, I will be there."

The briefing went very smoothly, and the staff had the details all worked out. Vehicles began lining up for the road march late in the afternoon so they could get away early without any delays. Tien had his commanders back-brief him that evening with McKenna sitting in. While he did that, Martin and Swachek got their stuff packed up and loaded the M-151 Jeep and quarter-ton trailer with their gear. They made sure there was room for the small refrigerator in the trailer. That was a priority item, right after the radios and R-292 antenna. Sleep was fitful as they slept on their air mattresses on the floor, and they enjoyed a C ration breakfast. The cook had already departed with all the rations she could carry right after dinner.

The convoy began to roll out onto Highway 1 at 0600 hours. McKenna and team were in the middle of the pack, but since Highway 1 was a paved road, there was little dust. Major Steinhauer and Sergeant Howard were following in their jeep. McKenna noted a lot of traffic moving south on the road, more than he would have expected, but nothing too unusual. Catching a glimpse of the ocean and the sea breeze made for a pretty nice drive. Captain Martin was doing the driving, so McKenna allowed his mind to wander. *Crystal-clear water, white sand beaches, forested hills a mile from the beach. I should be looking at high-rise hotels, golf courses and resorts. Give this place a chance and it'll flourish*, he was thinking. *The jobs these people could have and the prosperity it would bring them—why in the hell can't they just get along?* Along the side of the road, young girls were selling soda to any car that would stop, and mamasans were selling vegetables at roadside stands. Sales for the sodas were down since American forces had for the most part departed the country.

Tien had decided and coordinated for the convoy to spend the night in Qui Nhon. Qui Nhon was a thriving city, but things had slowed down since the US forces had left. The nightlife was more subdued now that GIs weren't filling the barstools.

"Who wants to take a dip in the ocean?" McKenna asked as they pulled into the compound that would hold them for the night. It was previously a US base camp, now abandoned, and right on the water.

"I'm up for it," Captain Martin announced. "Never swam in the South China Sea before."

"Well, you'll be in for a treat," Swachek said with a grin.

"Why, are there a lot of jellyfish?" Martin asked with some alarm.

"No, don't think so. Never saw one when I went in for a dip," Swachek said, putting the young captain at ease.

"Do we need bathing suits? I don't have one," Martin said, looking at the inviting water as they came to a stop.

"Suits are optional. Wear your skivvies if you get embarrassed being butt-naked," McKenna said, pulling off his shirt. "You joining us, Major?" McKenna asked Josh as he exited his jeep.

"Sir, I think I'll pass at this time. Got a few things I need to take care of, but thanks for the offer. Enjoy," Josh said, declining the opportunity. Moments later the three naked officers were scampering across the sand. Martin had built up a head of steam and at a full run dove into the water. He quickly surfaced and stood.

"Damn, that's salty water," he exclaimed.

"Try floating," Swachek said as he rolled over onto his back. He was almost overbuoyant and had trouble remaining on his back. Martin fared no better and the three officers resorted to just swimming and wading in the refreshing waters. They noticed a group of children beginning to form on the beach, pointing and laughing.

"What's this all about?" Martin asked, looking perplexed.

"I suspect they don't see that many naked round-eyes swimming off this beach," McKenna explained. "Let's get dried off and go find some dinner. I know of a good restaurant in town," he added as he began to wade ashore.

The next morning after a satisfying dinner and some sleep, they loaded up and moved out with the convoy for the trip to An Khe. As on the previous day, Josh followed in his jeep. Clear skies with a slow buildup of clouds forecast a good day for the trip up into the mountains of the Central Highlands.

The convoy departed on time, and again the advisors took a position in the middle of the convoy and were prepared for a leisurely drive. That was until they reached the An Khe Pass. McKenna was half-asleep when the vehicle came to a halt.

"Why are we stopping?" he asked, looking at Martin.

"Not sure—" Martin began when the sounds of automatic weapons and explosions were heard from the front of the convoy.

"Crap! They've driven right into an ambush," McKenna said as he got out of the vehicle. Looking at Martin and Scheck, he added, "You two stay here. I'll take Sergeant Hao with me and see what we can do." With that, Sergeant Hao grabbed a radio backpack and followed McKenna up the road. Josh's vehicle stopped and he walked up to join Martin and Scheck.

"Where is the colonel going?" Josh asked.

"He said for us to stay here while he sees what's going on. Think the lead vehicles hit an ambush," Martin said.

Watching them move up the line of vehicles, Martin turned to Swachek and asked, "Isn't this the same place where the Viet Minh massacred that French force back in the 1950s? Mang Yang Pass, it was called, I think."

"Yeah, Mobile Force 100 was the designation of the French force, and it was pretty badly mauled. When it finally reached its destination at Pleiku, only about one hundred soldiers were left out of a force of over five hundred."

16

GENERAL HOANG MINH THAO

1 MARCH 1972
  Base Camp 609
  Laos

LIEUTENANT GENERAL HOANG MINH THAO had studied both his Vietnamese and American opponents in detail, attempting to understand their thought processes, fears, and attributes. He was noted for saying, "To defeat one's enemy, one must know one's enemy."

Today he had called a meeting at his headquarters in Base Camp 609. Before him sat his division and regimental commanders who would be involved in the upcoming offensive. They had their orders and had time to review them, prepare their soldiers and ensure they had the logistics to support the operation.

"Gentlemen, I thought we would get together and review our plans and the intent of this operation," General Minh said. Seated before him were the commanders of the 320th, 3rd and 2nd NVA Divisions as well as the commander of the 203rd Tank

Regiment and the 7th Engineer Regiment, plus the division infantry regimental commanders, the commander of the 66th Independent Regiment and the artillery commanders. The artillery regiments had been equipped recently with the 130mm Soviet artillery piece, which outranged anything the ARVN forces had. With the Soviet artillery came Soviet advisors too. The tanks, Soviet T-54s, were considered superior to the ARVN M41 tanks. Thao could only hope.

"You all were briefed by General Dung and know the intent of this upcoming fight is twofold: show the Soviets and Chinese that we can defeat the Americans and the South Vietnamese and strengthen our position at the Paris Peace Talks. To accomplish this, we must do two things: destroy the South Vietnamese Army as much as possible, and seize and hold as much ground as we can. This is not about winning the hearts and minds of the people. That approach failed in the Tet Offensive of 1968, and we will not repeat that mistake. Am I clear?" he asked. All acknowledged that he was.

"Good. Colonel Curong, will you brief us on your plan, please?" Thao directed. Colonel Giap Van Curong was the commander of the 3rd Division, referred to as the Yellow Star Division.[1] He had been in command since 1965 and was one of the longest-serving commanders. His division was located in the northwest corner of Binh Dinh Province along the coast and had fought for years against American forces. Standing, he moved to a map that was on a sheet of plywood, compliments of left-behind material from the American withdrawal.

"Sir, my mission is to destroy the 40th and 41st Regiments of the 22nd ARVN Division and move south along Highway 1. The 40th Regiment is located at LZ English and LZ Orange. LZ English is a well-established firebase, having been used by the Americans for many years. It has an airfield capable of landing the C-130 cargo plane. I will initiate the attack employing the 303rd, 306th and 20th Sapper Battalions, which have already been conducting reconnaissance of the firebase for the past month. Once we have destroyed the 40th Regiment, I will move down Highway 1 and engage the 41st Regiment, which is located at LZ Crystal," Colonel Curong briefed.

"Colonel, you must move rapidly to drive deep and seize as much terrain as possible. The local VC should be a major help to you as these districts have our strongest supporters, I'm told. Let the local VC police up any potential troublemakers. I want you to move out of your position in the An Lao Valley and sweep south and east to the coast on 4 April," Thao directed.

"Sir, why am I to wait if my orders say the offensive will start on 30 March?" Colonel Curong asked with a puzzled look. The others were wanting an answer to that question as well.

"Colonel, I want you to delay the attack in your sector so that General Dzu, who will recognize a major offensive is commencing, will withdraw forces in front of you and shift them to the west. He will receive reports of the major offensive on Route 9 up north towards Dong Ha and Quang Tri and anticipate that we will attack on Route 14 or from the north with the 2nd Division. His 23rd Division is located in the south around Ban Me Thuot, and it will take time to move that division north if he moves it at all," Thao explained. Those seated exchanged smiles.

"Thank you, Colonel. Are there any questions?" Minh asked the group. There were none.

"Colonel Chon, let us hear from the 2nd Division," Thao directed. The 2nd Division had been operating north of Dak To for many years in small groups. Now it was slipping across the border and taking up positions west and north of Dak To. Colonel Nguyen Chon rose and moved to the map board.

"Sir, my mission is to destroy the ARVN forces at Dak To I and Tan Canh. We have been engaging the 42nd and 47th Regiments north of Dak To for the past month when they venture from their base camps, which is not often. This is the 42nd Regiment plus one battalion from the 41st Regiment and the 22nd Division command post located at Tan Canh," Chon said, pointing at Tan Canh. "Once we destroy the forces in Tan Canh, we will continue the attack to Dak To II, where the 47th Regiment is located. Once we commence the attack, the 66th Independent Regiment will attack from north of Tan Canh in coordination with our attack from the west. The 203rd Armored Regiment will accompany our attack on Dak To II. If the enemy moves tanks against us, I am confident that the T-54 tanks of the 203rd Armored Regiment can handle them. Any questions, sir?"

"No. Do not become decisively engaged in the Ben Het or Dak Pek camps. Bypass those camps if possible, along with the camp at Dak To. You cannot allow these camps to delay your attacks on Dak To II and Tan Canh. Understood?" Thao asked.

"Yes, sir. I planned on rapidly bypassing these camps and will allow follow-on forces to mop them up later," Chon explained.

"Good. Okay, Colonel Tuan, please brief us on the 320th Division," Thao requested.

Colonel Kim Tuan commanded the 320th Infantry Division and had for the past two years been engaging forces on the hill mass known by the Americans as Rocket Ridge. Moving to the map board as Colonel Chon passed him a pointer, Tuan started his presentation.

"Sir, as you know, there are four occupied positions on this hill mass—Firebases 5 and 6 on the north end and Firebases Charlie and Delta on the southern end. We will continue to harass all these firebases until the time of our major assault. Then we will attack Firebases Delta and Charlie as our main effort as they are mutually supporting. Firebases 5 and 6 are the same in the north, but I believe that Charlie and Delta hold the key to our advance towards Kontum and Pleiku. There is one company from the 71st Battalion with a platoon from the 42nd Regiment at Firebase 6 and the 71st Ranger Battalion minus with the company minus from the 42nd Regiment at Firebase 5. There is currently a Ranger company at Firebase Charlie and one at Delta, so they would be the easiest to seize. Once we have seized these two positions, we will then converge our forces on Polei Kleng, which is occupied by the 62nd Border Ranger Battalion. Questions, sir?" Tuan asked.

"Where is the rest of the 71st Battalion located?" Thao asked.

"Sir, the remainder of the 71st, one company, is located at Ben Het."

"Colonel, it is imperative that you quickly take out Firebases Delta and Charlie. The firebases control the highways, and until they are eliminated, we cannot successfully move our supplies on Highway 14 towards Kontum and Pleiku. Understood?" Thao asked.

"Yes, sir, I understand my responsibility," Tuan said.

"Good. Now I can tell you gentlemen—but I do not want this disseminated further—that the attack in Quang Tri will commence on 30 March. We must be ready to launch our attack shortly after that. The B-2 Front will commence their attack just days after the attack in the north and will concentrate on An Loc down Highway 13. Our attack will follow that attack for the most part, except the 3rd Division, which will launch at the same time as the B-2 Front. We are to seize as much terrain as possible. Do not care about winning the hearts and minds of the people. In Tet of '68, they showed where their allegiances were, and now, they will pay for that betrayal."

17

CANARY SINGS

15 MARCH 1972
SRAG HQ
Pleiku

COLONEL PAHL WAS SEATED at his desk when a smiling Colonel Kaplan walked in unannounced.

"Have I got some news for you," Kaplan said with a grin stretching from ear to ear, "right after you offer me a cup of coffee."

"Sergeant!" Pahl yelled, and the misfit sergeant eventually came through the door.

"Yes, sir," he said with all the enthusiasm of a schoolboy going to the principal's office.

"Two coffees, please, with cream...no, make it a pot, Sergeant," Pahl ordered.

"Yes, sir," the sergeant responded and sulked off.

"I just heard the major tell the sergeant to make a fresh pot and we should be able to snag the whole thing before the major gets his cup. Great opportunity for the major to fly off the handle at the sergeant," Pahl said with a smile.

"You people really don't like that sergeant, do you?" Kaplan asked.

"Truthfully, no. He's worthless. Ever since he got a Dear John letter from his old lady, he's moped around and done nothing except get drunk and not come into work. Once he's here, he shows no initiative. Hell, a private is more productive than him. He's only waiting on his administrative discharge to come through so he can get out of here. He's lucky he isn't leaving with a bad conduct discharge or worse," Pahl explained. "So what do I owe this meeting to?" Before Kaplan could explain, the sergeant returned with a pot and two cups.

"You both take it black, right, sir?" the sergeant asked, with the *sir* sounding like a snake hissing.

"Black is fine, Sergeant. Close the door on the way out," Pahl directed, which the sergeant did not do gently. Kaplan poured two cups and sat back down, handing one cup to Pahl.

"We picked up a prisoner yesterday. Actually, he's a chu hoi," Kaplan said, pulling out his notebook.[1] "A Master Sergeant Nguyen Trong Huy. He's from the Second Platoon, C-25th Transportation Company, 64th Regiment, 320th NVA Infantry Division. The commander of the regiment is Colonel Khuat Duy Tien. He said there are three battalions in the 64th, each with three hundred men. In addition, they have a reconnaissance company, anti-aircraft company, recoilless rifle company, mortar company with 82s, and engineer, signal, medical and transportation companies," Kaplan outlined.

"Where did you find this guy?" Pahl asked as he frantically wrote some notes.

"Captured him nineteen kilometers north of Kontum," Kaplan said, again referring to his own notes. "But that's not the best of the information."

Pahl stopped writing and looked up.

"Well!" he said.

"He said that the K-7 battalion was hit on the twelfth by an air strike that caused a lot of casualties. Then, the next day they lost another sixty-five in a firefight with the ARVNs that took him prisoner. The transportation company had been briefed that a major fight was coming that would be awesome and be an attack to seize Kontum by the 64th Regiment, supported by a sapper battalion with tanks."

"I've got to get this to Snell and MACV. Vann isn't convinced that tanks are in the area despite what the attack heli-copter pilots are telling us. I had another POW report that the 2nd NVA Division is going to attack the airfield at Dak To II as well as seize the regimental CP at Tan Canh. They know the layout of Tan Canh as they've already done a recon of the place," Pahl said.

"What! When the hell were you going to give me that piece of information?" Kaplan said, almost coming out of his seat. "Does the 22nd Division staff know about this? Because I haven't heard a word about it. Did he provide a date?"

"No date given, and we just got this today. I was fixing a message to send over to Dzu for dissemination to the commands. Do you want to brief Colonel Dat?" Pahl asked.

"Don't know what good it will do. He's convinced that the NVA are better soldiers and his soldiers can't defeat them. He keeps hoping that the US will send forces back, and I keep telling him he might as well whistle Dixie out his ass because it's not going to happen," Kaplan explained.

"He may be right. The NVA soldiers are better trained and led. NVA soldiers have twelve weeks of basic training. They're placed in three-man teams that eat, sleep, train for the duration of their hitches. This instills comradery, cuts down on deser-tions, and if one of the team begins to question too much, the others eat cheese on him. Officers are all promoted through merit and not political pull. Now compare their officer corps to the ARVNs, who are politically promoted. Most are corrupt, keeping deserters on the rolls so they can collect the pay. Soldiers are allowed to go work a civilian job as long as they split their civilian pay with their officers. The whole system is crooked as hell. Truthfully, the best thing that could happen is that the NVA surround the ARVN in Tan Canh so they can't run, and then they'll fight. Same for Kontum. Trapped like rats, the ARVN will fight, but if the door is open, he'll run like a rabbit," Pahl said with some disgust in his voice.

"Hey, just remember, I'm going to be at Tan Canh when it gets hit. Thanks for the coffee," Kaplan said as he stood and headed for the door.

"I'll be sure they send a chopper to get you" were Pahl's parting words.

18

―――

MISSING BUT NOT FORGOTTEN

27 MARCH 1972
57th Assault Helicopter Company
FSB Charlie

CW2 LARRY J. Woods had been summoned to Flight Operations. He was standby for the day and already at 0800 he was being called. He wouldn't be standby for long today. His copilot was Second Lieutenant Ngo Binh Quan, Vietnamese Air Force. For the past several months, US and Vietnamese pilots had been flying together as more equipment was turned over to the South Vietnamese Air Force. It was also thought that by training with US Army pilots, the Vietnamese Air Force pilots might become better.

Woods was met by the unit flight operations officer, Captain Harrimon. "Mr. Woods, sorry to have to call you out, but we need you for a recovery mission."

"Whatcha got, sir?" Woods asked, pulling his map out.

"There's a VNAF aircraft down at this location," Harrimon said, pointing at Woods's map. "Need you to go get them. The

Cougars will provide two escort aircraft to go with you, and they've just been briefed and are preflighting their aircraft. Call sign is Cougar Two-Six. Any questions?" Harrimon asked.

"No, sir. We'll get out and contact Cougar and be off. I preflighted early today and the crew is out there right now," Woods said and turned to his Vietnamese copilot. "Any questions, Quan?"

"I good," Quan said—his standard answer.

Turning back to Harrimon, Woods said, "I'll call when we lift off."

"Oh, one other thing...you'll have a couple of passengers with you on this. They're getting their stuff together and I'll send them out to the aircraft. Captain Lyle Rhoads, an advisor, and Captain Nguyen Duc Phuc, the commander of the 3rd Battalion, 47th Infantry Regiment," Captain Harrimon added.[1]

"No problem, sir," Woods said as he turned to walk out the door.

"Sounds good. Be safe," Harrimon responded, thinking nothing more of this mission.

Thirty minutes later, Gladiator Three-Six was airborne and had Cougar Two-Six in tow. While Quan flew, Woods started examining the location of the supposed down aircraft. The point was about two kilometers east of FSB Charlie.

"Wong, Hannon, listen up. We're looking for a downed VNAF helicopter. It was shot down about two hours ago. Once we spot it, I'll decide how I want to approach it. I'm told that it's down on the side of a hill, but there's an open clearing where it's resting. Since it was shot down, be on your toes as I suspect there will be a welcoming committee standing by to greet us," Woods said with sarcasm dripping off every word.

"Understood," Hannon said. Hannon was the crew chief for aircraft number 67-17841, and Wong had been the door gunner on the aircraft for four months. He was an infantryman who had volunteered for door gunner duty. The combination of

Woods, Hannon and Wong made for a good team. Quan was a recent graduate from the US Army Rotary Wing Flight course at Fort Rucker, Alabama. This was his second flight with Woods as new pilots were rotated amongst the aircraft commanders.

As they approached the location of the down aircraft, a smoke grenade ignited.

"Sir, I have a red smoke at three o'clock," Wong reported, raising his gun. Hannon raised his at the same time and began scanning the forest canopy.

"Hey, Chief," Captain Rhoads said over the intercom, getting Woods's attention.

"Yeah, Captain?"

"Captain Phuc is in contact with the folks on the ground and they say that there's no contact now," Rhoads reported.

"Cap'n, if there's no contact, how the hell did he get shot down? And don't you think if you were the enemy and had an aircraft down in your area, bets are good that another aircraft would come to get the survivors? No, the Indians just aren't showing themselves yet. Have Phuc notify the guys on the ground that we're coming in hot and they need to get down. When I land, they have three seconds to get their asses in the aircraft or they'll be left behind. Understood?" Woods announced. Rhoads immediately began talking to Phuc, and he in turn was on his AN/PRC-77 radio in a conversation with the folks on the ground. Finally he looked at Rhoads and nodded, affirming that they understood. While Phuc was talking to his people, Woods announced his intentions to Cougar Two-Six.

"Cougar Two-Six, Gladiator Three-Six, over."

"Go ahead, Three-Six."

"Two-Six, I'm going to make my approach from the east to the west and low level. I told them they have three seconds to load. They're in a crater next to their aircraft, but it's on the side of that hill, so I'm probably going to have to hold a hover while they climb aboard. Over."

"Roger, Three-Six, we'll hit the tree line with minigun and hold off with the rockets until we have definitive targets, over."

"Well, let's hope you have no definitive targets, over."

"Roger," Cougar Two-Six came back with a chuckle in his voice.

Moving away from the landing site, Woods put the collective down and began losing altitude until he was fifty feet above the forest canopy, at which point he turned back onto his final approach, heading to the crash site. Flying at ninety knots, he closed quickly on the landing spot, and just as he went into a rapid deceleration, automatic weapons opened fire at his aircraft from the tree line. Cougar was laying down a stream of minigun fire that was effective, but the damage had already been done. Woods was committed to a low-speed, low-altitude autorotation to a slope. This situation was commonly referred to as the "dead man zone." The aircraft landed hard and began to roll on the slope. Before Woods could say anything, the main rotor smashed into the ground, sending pieces flying in every direction. The body twisted and the tail boom broke off.

With the dying engine winding down, Woods reached over and cut the fuel off and then reached out to turn the battery off. The last thing he wanted was a fire. Once the aircraft stopped, Woods found himself hanging upside down, held in only by his seat belt and shoulder harness. Others were not so lucky. Captain Rhoads and Captain Duc Phuc were lying on the roof of the cabin as it was now the floor. Wong had been tossed out of the aircraft when the roll started. Hannon was on the ground and dazed. Looking up, Hannon saw Wong half running and half walking up the hill. It appeared that Wong was bleeding from his head and his legs. Hannon's attention then turned to helping Mr. Woods.

"Mr. Woods, let me hold you when you release your seat belt," Hannon said as he attempted to hold Woods's shoulders. Hanging upside down in the pilot's seat is an uncomfortable feeling because you know when you release the seat belt, your head is going to smash into the greenhouse window above you—now below you.

Once everyone was outside the aircraft, Mr. Woods took a head count. "Where's Wong?" Woods asked.

"Sir, he ran up the hill to the friendly forces' location," Hannon said, pointing to where the people from the first aircraft were slowly moving towards them. The group approaching consisted of an American pilot, crew chief, and gunner and four Vietnamese soldiers, one being a pilot. They were carrying a stretcher with an individual covered with a poncho. His hand wasn't covered and a class ring was on his finger.

Rhoads asked Hannon, "Is that your gunner?"

"Yeah, I recognize the ring," Hannon said, slowly shaking his head. "We'll take him with us to Firebase Charlie. There's a relief force coming to us from there." Charlie was only two klicks away. When the relief force of fifty soldiers arrived, everyone was accounted for and the entire group moved out. It was 1600 hours when they crossed the perimeter of Fire Support Base Charlie. In moving up the trail to the firebase, Hannon turned at one point and noticed the litter bearers and the litter sitting down and resting.

"Hey, Mr. Woods," Captain Rhoads called out. "We have two VNAF medevac aircraft inbound and one US aircraft will be here in about an hour. We'll get you guys out on the American aircraft. Why don't you and your crew chief wait in my bunker until it arrives? I'll come and get you. There are a couple of cold beers in the ice chest under my cot if you like."

"Thank you, sir. I'll take you up on that," Woods replied, motioning for Hannon to follow him. The bunker was nothing elaborate. A simple bunker, six feet by six feet with a cot on one side and a table and one chair on the other. On the table was an AN/PRC-77 radio connected to an R-292 radio antenna outside, providing the distance for Rhoads to talk to his support in Pleiku. The ceiling was PSP metal planks covered in four layers of sandbags. The ice chest was quickly located and two beers extracted. There was no ice. As they sat and unwound, they could hear the two VNAF aircraft land and depart with Vietnamese wounded. An hour later, Captain Rhoads stuck his head in the doorway.

"You two ready to go home?" he said jokingly.

"Yes, sir," Hannon replied. "Not that we don't like your hospitality, but..."

"Can't say I blame you, Specialist," Rhoads said, leading the way to the helipad.

Arriving at the pad, Hannon started looking around.

"Hey, where's Wong?" he asked. Both Rhoads and Woods now began scanning the area for a body on a stretcher.

"I'll be right back," Rhoads said, and he took off in a run towards the aid station. A few minutes later he returned.

"They said that he was placed on one of the VNAF aircraft and taken to the Vietnamese hospital in Kontum," Rhoads said almost apologetically. "I'll call back to the rear and have someone go over and retrieve him. Here comes your aircraft now." The approaching UH-1H medevac aircraft looked very good to Woods and Hannon, and they quickly boarded for their flight back to Pleiku.

The next morning, Mr. Woods and Specialist Hannon were called to the commander's office.

"Sir, you wanted to see us?" Woods asked, entering.

"Yeah, what's the story about Wong? When was the last time you saw him?" the major asked.

"Sir, the last time I saw him was when he was on the stretcher covered with a poncho," Mr. Woods responded.

"And you, Specialist?"

"Sir, when we were on the trail back to Charlie, I looked back and saw the litter bearers taking a break with the stretcher on the ground," Hannon replied.

"Did either of you see him loaded on a chopper at the firebase?"

Both Woods and Hannon exchanged puzzled looks.

"No, sir. We were in a bunker when the VNAF aircraft arrived. The advisor told us afterwards that he was flown to the Vietnamese military hospital in Kontum. Why, what's going on?" Mr. Woods asked.

"Well, someone from SRAG went over to the Vietnamese hospital and they couldn't find him. According to some of the wounded that came in from Charlie, there was no stretcher or American on the aircraft. Wong is MIA at this time!" the commander said with anger dripping off each word.[2]

19

BIG WINDY GOES DOWN

31 MARCH 1972
  180th Assault Support Helicopter Company
  Pleiku

CW2 WALTER ZUTTER expected the day to be like any other. Flying from Pleiku to Dak To and picking up supplies to take to one of the firebases on Rocket Ridge or possibly one of the outlying camps was a routine day for Mr. Zutter. Even having a Vietnamese Air Force captain for a copilot wasn't unusual. Zutter's unit was the 180th Assault Support Helicopter Company, part of the 17th Aviation Group, 1st Aviation Brigade, which controlled all the helicopters in Vietnam at the time.

His CH-47 Chinook helicopter was loaded and the flight engineer and two door gunners gave him the up. From Dak To, he could look west and clearly see Firebase Delta. Delta was occupied by a company from the ARVN 2nd Airborne Battalion, 2nd Airborne Brigade, and a company from the 6th Ranger Battalion. Zutter was delivering the supplies and all appeared quiet around this lonely bald spot on one of the peaks along the ridge. The only thing out of the ordinary for most pilots was the fact that Zutter's copilot was a Vietnamese pilot as aircraft were being turned over to the Vietnamese Air Force and US pilots were transitioning the Vietnamese pilots in the aircraft. Passing over the firebase, Firebase Delta, Zutter made contact with the advisor on the ground.

"Six-Five-Bravo, Big Windy Four-One, over," Zutter transmitted.

Moments later, a voice with a southern Alabama accent came on the air. "Big Windy Four-One, Six-Five-Bravo, go ahead," Captain O'Brien, the senior advisor on FSB Delta, transmitted.

"Six-Five-Bravo, Big Windy Four-One inbound to your location with resupply, over."

"Big Windy, roger. Winds are light from the north at five. Negative enemy contact at this time, over."

That was music to Zutter's ears—light wind and no enemy. This was his second tour in Vietnam, and he had been in this same region on his first tour. As he looked down at the firebase, he could see the helipad that was on the north side of the perimeter. What he was looking for wasn't the helipad, which he was familiar with, but confirmation of the wind velocity and direction. Not that he didn't trust the advisor on the ground, but smoke from burn barrels was the best indicator.

To his crew, Zutter directed, "Okay, guys, I'm going to make my approach north to south. Supposedly no enemy contact, but stay on your toes." He had been around long enough to know that things could turn very quickly anywhere on Rocket Ridge. As he completed his orbit, he turned to make the downwind leg of his approach and began losing altitude rapidly. He wanted to make his base leg of the approach in close to the firebase with only a short final approach—techniques not taught at Mother

Rucker but learned while combat flying on earlier tours in Vietnam.

"We're taking fire!" blared over his headset at the same time as a sledgehammer blow was repeatedly heard in the back of the aircraft, both sides. Turning into his final approach, he considered aborting the approach when the master caution light began flashing and the master caution horn sounded.

"We're losing hydraulics!" his copilot, Captain Nguyen Binh, informed him with a high level of anxiety in his voice.

"Shit, we're going in. Brace—" Zutter couldn't finish his statement before the aircraft landed hard on the helipad with all four wheels. Binh was immediately releasing his shoulder harness and jettisoning his door. SSG George, the flight engineer, who had been standing between Zutter and Binh, was now on the floor, in pain. Zutter reached up and called out, "Fuel off, battery off!" He heard the engines winding down, and the engine instruments confirmed it, but something wasn't right.

"Everyone out," Zutter ordered as he jettisoned his door. He noticed that the aircraft was slowly rolling backwards. Binh, in his panicked attempt to exit the aircraft, had not put the brakes on. The aircraft was on a slight downslope and was now moving downhill. Before Zutter could go through his jettisoned door, he looked back to see George trying to stand. He was barely able. Zutter noticed Binh going out his door, but he realized George was going to need help. Climbing out of his seat, Zutter began to move through the interior of the aircraft as Specialist Thompson, the crew chief, grabbed George under one arm and helped him. Zutter was now under the other arm and they moved to the side door to exit the aircraft, which was still slowly moving backwards. Specialist Cantrel, the door gunner, had gotten the door open and was already outside, covering their exit with his M16. The door was only wide enough for one person at a time to exit, so Thompson went first while Zutter held George, then George went but stumbled on his first step into the arms of Thompson, both falling to the ground. Then Zutter exited.

Smoke was beginning to fill the cargo bay as the aircraft continued on its way, rolling backwards downhill with increasing speed. Thompson and Zutter helped George up on his one leg.

"Sir, let me carry him," Thompson said, picking George up in a fireman's carry over his shoulder. George was in obvious pain as the bone protruded through the side of his trousers. Captain Binh was nowhere to be found.

As the crew moved away from the burning aircraft, an American advisor with captain's bars approached Zutter. He had four Vietnamese soldiers with him, one of which was carrying a stretcher.

"Chief, let's get him up to the aid station," Captain O'Brien said, leading the way. "Welcome to Firebase Delta. I'll call down and see if we can get you out of here. Things have always been brisk up here but had been quiet this morning. I heard three .51-caliber machine guns firing at you when you turned to final."

"I never heard the guns, but I sure as hell felt them hit. Knocked out the hydraulics, and that bird doesn't fly without them," Zutter said, turning to look at his aircraft, which was now engulfed in flames but no longer rolling downhill. Turning back to O'Brien, he said, "Captain, can I get a call to my unit and bring them up to speed?"

"Yeah, let's get him settled in the aid station and then you and I will go over to my bunker and make the call," O'Brien said. "We only have medics here and we need to get him out on a medevac bird as quickly as possible." Once George was settled in the aid station and a shot of morphine relieved his pain, Zutter and O'Brien made their way to O'Brien's bunker to make the call. Zutter notified Flight Operations that the aircraft was a loss and they needed a medevac aircraft to come and get George as well as the rest of the crew. He was told medevac would be there in thirty minutes.

"You want some coffee while we wait?" O'Brien asked, holding a pot in his hand that was on a Coleman camp stove. "It's only about two hours old," he added.

"Why not?" Zutter said, accepting the coffee, which resembled mud. "Oh yeah, first sergeant coffee. I can stand the spoon up in this. Thanks."

"It'll keep you awake for the rest of the day," O'Brien replied with a smile. "It's the best I can do. Ran out of beer yesterday. My resupply was on your aircraft."

"Sorry about that, Cap'n," Zutter joked as he took another sip of the thick, dark coffee. "Oh yeah, that's going to keep me awake," he announced, faking a chewing motion. Moments later, the radio crackled.

"Six-Five-Bravo, Dustoff Two-Six, over."

O'Brien reached for the hand mike.

"Dustoff Two-Six, Six-Five-Bravo, go ahead, over."

"Six-Five-Bravo, Dustoff Two-Six is five minutes out for landing and pax pickup, over."

"Dustoff Two-Six, wind is out of the north at five. Be advised, enemy contact on the north side. Recommend a south-to-north approach to our pad. How copy? Over."

"Six-Five-Bravo, I have good copy and will comply. Commencing my approach—"

Before Dustoff Two-Six could finish his transmission, the sound of several heavy machine guns could be heard from around the perimeter.

"Six-Five-Bravo, Dustoff, taking heavy fire. We're hit, returning to base!"

O'Brien flashed a look a Zutter that said, "Ah shit."

"Dustoff, Six-Five-Bravo, are you going to make it back?"

"Six-Five, I have one wounded crewmember and my caution panel looks like a Christmas tree. We're heading for Dak To II as it's the closest. Over." In the background, Zutter heard the telltale noise of the master caution warning horn.

"Roger, Dustoff, keep me posted on your location," O'Brien said but received no response. Looking at Zutter, he said, "Shit, I hope he makes it back."

"It's a seven-minute flight from here to Dak To II, maybe ten. Depending on what's been hit, he should make it—if it wasn't the engine, transmission, or main rotor hub," Zutter said.

"Hell, what's left?" O'Brien asked with a shocked look.

"Plenty. Hydraulics, electrical, fuel cells," Zutter ticked off until he was interrupted by the radio.

"Six-Five-Bravo, Dustoff Two-One, over."

"Dustoff Two-One, go ahead," O'Brien transmitted.

"Dustoff Two-One is at Dak To II. I'll see if they can get another aircraft out to you. I counted six, I say again, six heavy guns around you, over."

"Dustoff Two-One, can you give me locations? Over."

"Six-Five-Bravo, I was a bit busy at the time. I can tell you they have you surrounded. Over."

O'Brien and Zutter exchanged looks.

"Dustoff Two-One, roger. Thanks, Six-Five-Bravo out." As O'Brien laid the hand mike on the field table, he said, "I don't think you're leaving here anytime soon."

20

PREPARE FOR INSERTION

I April 1972

1 **April 1972**
  2nd ARVN Airborne Brigade HQ
  Vo Dinh

"Sir, you wanted to see me?" Major Duffy asked. He and his counterpart, Lieutenant Colonel Bao, had been called to the 2nd Airborne Brigade TOC for a meeting with the senior advisor, Lieutenant Colonel Pete Kama, and the airborne brigade commander, General Lich. Major Terry Griswold, the deputy senior advisor to the 2nd ARVN Airborne Brigade, was also present.

"Come in, Major. Let me show you tomorrow's operation," Lieutenant Colonel Kama said, pointing at the map. Lieutenant Colonel Bao had already received his briefing from the brigade operations officer, so he was more of an observer for this conversation, just confirming that what he had been told matched what Duffy was being told. "Tomorrow we're inserting the 11th Battalion here on this location on Rocket Ridge, X-ray Delta zero-zero-niner-one-zero-eight, which is Fire Support Base Charlie." As he spoke, Duffy began writing down notes. "The landing zone is a four-ship with a fifteen-minute flight time. Once you've landed, you'll reinforce the company of Rangers that currently occupy the position and Lieutenant Colonel Bao will take command of the firebase and prevent any movement towards Kontum or down Highway 512. Your pickup zone will be at Dak To II airstrip. PZ time is 0900. Any questions?" Kama asked.

"Do we have any idea on the enemy strength or disposition up there?" Duffy asked as he continued to take notes.

"Not really. We believe the NVA are going to attempt to take Kontum by punching through the pass at Hill 1015. They've rebuilt the old French road, which will allow them to move troops and resupply forces. We know there are bad guys in that area as they've been harassing all the fire support bases with platoon-size probes. You can expect they're going to harass you as well," Kama said. "There was a CH-47 shot down the day before yesterday at Firebase Delta, and we still haven't gotten the crew out because of the air-defense .51-cals around the firebase. We believe this is elements of the 320th NVA Division, which has been operating in the area for a couple of years now, coming out of Laos just across the border. ARVN intelligence is reporting NVA forces moving into a staging area west of Rocket Ridge," Kama concluded.

"Okay, sir, I got it, and we'll get it done," Duffy said, with Lieutenant Colonel Bao nodding in agreement.

"How many men do you have going in up there with you?" Kama asked. Duffy flashed a look at Bao.

"We take four hundred seventy men," Bao said in his pidgin English.

"Colonel Bao, I'll make sure we have enough aircraft to get you in quickly and keep you resupplied," Kama said. He had already coordinated with US aviation assets to take the troops in on UH-1H aircraft. He knew that the VNAF helicopters were unreliable when it came to inserting troops in potentially hot landing zones.

"Major, that's all I have for you. Good luck and be safe," Kama said, extending his hand, which Duffy accepted with a "Will do, sir."

That evening Duffy and Bao went over the mission with the battalion Operations officer, Captain Hai Doan, and Major Me Le, the battalion executive officer. Utilizing a reverse planning sequence, they developed the ground plan upon landing so they could quickly move to the established perimeter. Based on the ground tactical plan, a landing plan and load plan were developed. Included in the plan were fire support target reference points and flight route plans. Consideration was also given to the use of VNAF fighter planes, the A-1 Skyraiders, as well as the use of attack helicopters on suspected potential targets if it became necessary. When the plan was developed to their satisfaction, company commanders were brought in and briefed on the plan. The battalion had done so many airmobile insertions that it was almost done by standard operating procedures and the briefing was quickly concluded.

At 0800 hours, the battalion was assembled on the airstrip, waiting for the UH-1H aircraft that would carry them to the intended landing zone. From where they stood, they could clearly see Rocket Ridge and the intended landing zone location. When the aircraft arrived, they were quickly loaded. The artillery prep on surrounding and suspected enemy air-defense positions commenced at H minus six and lasted for four minutes, concluding as the aircraft began to land on the firebase. A few rounds found the sides of aircraft, but none caused serious enough damage to halt the assault. Troops immediately exited all aircraft and moved to reinforce the perimeter while the aircraft returned to Dak To II and picked up the second lift. By 1000 hours, the entire battalion of four hundred and seventy men was on the ground and digging in. Only light small-arms fire was noted, which made Duffy and Bao both very nervous.

"Colonel Bao, what do you think? I was expecting a lot more contact than what we've received so far," Duffy asked as he and the Ranger company commander walked the perimeter, inspecting the bunkers and fighting positions.

"I think he is patient. He is moving into positions to attack and he is observing our preparations to determine where to attack. Tomorrow he will come and contact us," Colonel Bao said. The Ranger company commander nodded in agreement.

As they moved around, Bao designated three locations for a command bunker, and work began immediately to improve those locations. The work was interrupted at times due to small-arms fire that was intended to harass. There was no doubt in Bao's or Duffy's mind that more than harassment fire would begin soon. Throughout the night, fifty percent manning was the order. Sporadic gunfire was heard around the perimeter. Duffy slept with relative ease as he was on his third combat tour in Vietnam and the gunfire wasn't the least bit intense. That changed at first light.

Standard procedure in the battalion was for everyone to be awake and in their fighting positions, ready to engage the enemy at 0500 and some days 0430. When Duffy entered the TOC at 0400 hours, he asked about the sporadic shooting.

"Sappers try to get through wire. They no get through. We kill six," Captain Hai Doan, the Operations officer, said with some pride.

"Good job. When I walk the perimeter this morning, I'll congratulate the troops," Duffy said, pouring a cup of coffee resembling mud. "Have we heard from the OP/LPs this morning?"

"LP One reported in a few minutes ago, all quiet. He on south side. LP Two on east side say all quiet too. No hear from LP Three on west side," Major Doan said. Duffy's head snapped up from his coffee cup.

"How long has it been since LP Three checked in?" Duffy asked.

"It be maybe three hours," Doan answered with a look of a lightbulb suddenly illuminating.

"LP Three is in front of 111 Company, right?" Duffy said, glancing at the map on the wall with the unit positions. "Call him and give him a heads-up. He's going to be hit. I'm going over there," Duffy exclaimed as he grabbed a PRC-77 radio and headed for the door. Arriving at the 111 Company commander's position, Duffy jumped into the foxhole with the commander.

"You're going to be hit shortly, I think, with a ground attack. LP Three hasn't reported in and may have been taken out. Did you have any sappers last night?" Duffy asked.

"No, no sappers. We alert," the captain said.

"I'm sure you were, but they didn't put sappers here because they want us to look elsewhere. Be sure everyone is up, awake and has plenty of ammo," Duffy instructed.

The company commander immediately began moving to each platoon position and briefing the platoon leaders. Unlike American platoon leaders, who for the most part were on their first tour in-country, ARVN platoon leaders had been in combat for four or five years already. They knew the score without being told, especially the airborne platoon leaders. Duffy continued to move from fighting position to fighting position, encouraging the young paratroopers with words of praise for their vigilance. These were the best of the ARVN soldiers, and their determined looks and smiling responses assured Duffy that they were going to make a fight of it if the NVA came.

Returning to the command bunker, Duffy found Colonel

Bao on the radio, talking to an ARVN artillery unit. He eaves-dropped on the conversation as Bao sent the location of potential targets to the artillery for them to designate as preplanned targets. As the night turned to morning twilight, the NVA commenced their assault. The first indication was sporadic small-arms fire on the west side of the perimeter, followed by incoming mortar rounds as well as outgoing mortar rounds from the firebase. Reports began to come into the command bunker that it appeared to be a battalion-size force hitting the western perimeter. Bao's previously artillery-designated locations were now being hit with 105mm howitzers from Dak To II.

Duffy was on the radio. "Dusty Cyanide, Rogues Gallery, over." Mr. Vann was in the air.

"Rogues Gallery, Dusty Cyanide, over."

"Dusty Cyanide, Rogues Gallery, sitrep, over."

"Rogues Gallery, we have what appears to be a battalion-size force hitting our western perimeter currently. We're receiving some incoming mortar fire as well, over."

"Roger, Dusty Cyanide. I'm going to divert a BUFF strike to support you on your western side. Strike is fifteen minutes out, how copy?"[1]

"Rogues Gallery, I have good copy and will get my people ready, over."

"Rogues Gallery out." Duffy turned to Colonel Bao. "Sir, we're going to have a B-52 strike hitting on the western perimeter in fifteen minutes. Notify everyone to be ready and open their mouths and hold their helmets when the first bomb goes off." Bao smiled and made the call, notifying everyone. Right on time, the first bomb exploded, and for the next minute rolling thunder could be heard and shock waves felt as the three B-52 bombers flying at thirty thousand feet dropped their loads of seven-hundred-and-fifty-pound bombs eight hundred meters from the perimeter. NVA soldiers hadn't gotten the word to open their mouths, so those not in the direct blast were hit with the shock wave and had their eardrums broken. Those closest to the blasts that survived had eyeballs protruding from sockets as well as busted eardrums. These were the fortunate ones. By noon the attack was over, but Bao and Duffy knew this was just the beginning.

21

PINK PANTHER TO THE FIGHT

2 APRIL 1972
 361st Aerial Weapons Company
 Pleiku

"FIRST, I want to thank you all for volunteering for this mission. Tomorrow's mission is to cover the extraction of a CH-47 crew that were shot down on FSB Delta on the thirty-first, in addition to getting supplies in as well. A couple of attempts to get them out have been unsuccessful due to the ADA threat up there. One of the crew members has a broken leg. We're going to attempt to get some of the wounded ARVNs out as well," Lieutenant Colonel Ron Merritt announced to the assembled audience of volunteers.

In the back of the room sat John Paul Vann and Brigadier General Wear. The volunteers included pilots from the 57th Assault Helicopter Company gun and lift platoons and pilots from the 361st Aerial Weapons Company, known as the Pink Panthers. The gun platoon for the 57th was known as the Cougars, and the lift aircraft used the call sign Gladiator. Gladiator Six, the commander of the 57th, would be the flight leader for the assault helicopters, and Panther Two-Zero, flown by Captain Lynn Carlson, would be flight leader for the aerial weapons aircraft. Overall air mission commander would be Lieutenant Colonel Merritt.

"Tomorrow morning, we launch at 0500. The enemy situation up there is intense, as reported by those who made previous attempts to rescue the crew. The concentration of enemy appears to be on the northeast and northwest sides for the perimeter, but the advisor reports that 51.-caliber machine guns have encircled the firebase. We will approach the firebase from the southeast side as it appears that the ground forces on that side aren't as thick as on the north and west sides. When we're six minutes out, Captain O'Brien is calling in an artillery prep on the southeast side of the firebase that will be from H minus six to H minus two. At H minus two, Captain Carlson, you'll take the Pink Panthers and clear a path for the assault helicopters and initiate a racetrack with the Cougars to support the lift ships as the landing zone can only handle one aircraft at a time. The Big Windy crew will be on the first bird coming out. If we can, we'll get the other lift birds in to drop supplies and extract wounded. Any questions?"

"What's the frequency for the mission, sir?" Carlson asked.

"I'll run the operation on VHF one-two-eight. The frequency for the advisor is four-five-five-oh Fox Mike and his call sign is Six-Five-Bravo. I want you all to be hearing my conversations with him so I won't have to be relaying info to you. My call sign is Dragon Six. Mr. Vann will be in the air and his call sign is Rogues Gallery. Captain Carlson, what is your call sign?" Merritt asked.

"Sir, my call sign is Panther Two-Zero. I have Panther One-Five and Panther One-Three with me. Call sign for the lift flight leader?" Carlson asked.

"Gladiator Six" was heard from the side of the room, courtesy of a major. "Gladiator Two-Six will be Chalk Two." Again, everyone was jotting down call signs.

"Okay, the weather for tomorrow is scattered clouds at five thousand, winds light as five knots from the south," Merritt said and looked at his watch. "I have 1925 hours. If there are no questions, I will see you on the flight line and cranked at 0500."

The next morning, standing beside his aircraft, Captain Carlson watched the fireflies moving around the aircraft next to his. These fireflies were flashlight beams carried by the pilots and crew members conducting preflight inspections on their respective aircraft. Flying around the area was dangerous enough without something breaking on the aircraft. Fortunately, maintenance was excellent, so mechanical failures were infrequent, but they did happen.

"Morning, Lynn," Captain Robert Gamber said, approaching. "Looks like we'll have some decent weather this morning." Carlson glanced up to confirm the weather. Although he couldn't see the scattered clouds, he noticed large patches of the night sky with no stars and assumed that it was cloud cover. He pulled the zipper on his jacket a bit higher to ward off the cold.

"I don't think I'll ever get used to the cold mornings up here. We're in Southeast Asia, flying over jungles. It's supposed to be warm," Carlson moaned.

"At least we don't have to worry about not getting off the ground with a full load because of the high temperatures. I heard that when they were flying Bravo- and Charlie-model gunships up here, the crew would run alongside the aircraft until it broke ground and then jump in because with a load they couldn't get off the ground," Gamber said, tossing his flight helmet in the front seat.

"Let's hope we never have that problem with these aircraft," Carlson responded with a bit of a chuckle. "I'll get the rotor head, why don't you look at the undercarriage?" And he commenced to climb up the aircraft to examine the rotor head, holding his small flashlight in his teeth. The first item on his mental checklist was the Jesus Nut. It was tight and the slippage marks were aligned. From there it was a matter of looking at slippage marks on other nuts and bolts as well as inspecting safety wires and making sure there were no holes in the top of the rotor blades.

As he was finishing up, Gamber had completed his walkaround and was donning his chicken plate. He had untied the blade already. As they climbed in, Gamber in the front and Carlson in the back, they could see the other two crews doing likewise. Across the tarmac, they could hear a turbine engine aircraft, possibly a UH-1H, starting up as well.

Again, Carlson resorted to his mental checklist for starting the aircraft, and when all was ready, he yelled, "Clear," and pulled the starter trigger. Slowly the engine began to turn, building quickly to full RPM. Meanwhile, Gamber was running through his armament checklist.

"Panther One-Five, One-Three, you guys up?" Carlson transmitted, observing the lights on his two wingmen.

"One-Five is up," First Lieutenant Michael Sheuerman responded.

"One-Three is with you," CW2 Dan Jones announced.

"Roger, Panther flight. Stand by," Carlson told them as he switched radios. When he had the right frequency, he listened for a moment to hear anyone talking. No one was.

"Dragon Six, Pink Panther Two-Oh."

"Pink Panther Two-Oh, Dragon Six, over."

"Dragon Six, Pink Panther Two-Oh, flight of three is up, over."

"Roger, wait one. Break, Gladiator Six, Dragon Six, over."

"Dragon Six, Gladiator Six, flight of two-plus is up." Hearing that, Carlson looked across the tarmac and could see the red flashing lights on seven aircraft. Then an eighth light came on. Moments later, he learned why.

"Dragon Six, Rogues Gallery is up and will be in the AO," John Paul Vann transmitted.

"Did I just hear that right?" Gamber asked. "Mr. Vann is on this operation too?"

"Yeah, I guess he's interested in getting those guys out of there. I'll give the man credit. He does look out for everyone," Carlson applauded.

As he did so, on the mission frequency he heard Dragon Six say, "Flight, we have clearance to take the active. Order of march is Pink Panthers followed by Gladiators and Cougars. I'll be tail-end Charlie."

Immediately Carlson transmitted, "Pink Panther Two-Oh is taking the active," then to Gamber, "Coming up."

"You're clear," Gamber replied, looking to the left and right of the aircraft as it rose to a two-foot hover and began to move forward. Gamber noticed Panther One-Five and One-Three were also rising up and positioning behind them, and the three aircraft slowly moved to the active runway.

When they reached the active, Carlson turned slightly at a hover and could see the Gladiators and Dragon Six lining up behind his flight of three on the active, with the Cougars bringing up the rear. A slight pedal turn and Dragon Six announced, "Flight, we are cleared for departure."

"Panther Two-Oh is on the go," Carlson reported as he increased his collective and moved the cyclic slightly forward, resulting in the aircraft slowly climbing and increasing speed into the night sky. To Carlson, this was the best time to be flying. The very early hours of the morning were generally quiet on the radios, and there was generally no turbulence caused by up/down drafts. Best of all, seldom did anyone shoot at you at this time of day as most were still asleep or couldn't see you and didn't want to give their positions away. The only bad thing was finding a landing spot if you had an engine failure and had to autorotate. In flight school, they taught the theory that you should turn on your landing light. Once you turned the light on, if you didn't like what you saw for the landing spot, just turn the light off and it would go away. He had no desire to test the theory.

Taking a western heading, Carlson glanced over his right shoulder to see Panther One-Three and Panther One-Five flying in a right echelon. The sky behind was beginning to show signs of a new day to his rear when a sudden flash grabbed his attention up front.

"Did you see that?" Gamber asked over the intercom.

"Panther Two-Oh, Panther One-Five, over." Before Carlson could answer, he distinctly saw a second flash to his front in the night sky, but these weren't lightning flashes. These appeared to be explosions in the sky. When he saw the rocket flame rise up from the darkness and arch to the location of the other explosions, it registered in his mind. FSB Delta was under attack!

"Dragon Six, Dragon Six, Six-Five-Bravo, over," a calm but elevated voice could be heard on the radio.

"Six-Five-Bravo, Dragon Six, over."

"Dragon Six, Six-Five-Bravo, we have a full-blown ground assault on our northwest and northeaster perimeter, over." Carlson could now see a significant number of explosions, all concentrated on one spot in the darkness as they approached what appeared to be a ridgeline forming in the early-morning light.

"Roger, Six-Five-Bravo, understood. Wait one," Dragon Six directed. *Where do you think he's going to go?* Carlson was thinking.

"Gladiator Six, Dragon Six, over."

"Dragon Six, Gladiator Six, go ahead."

"Gladiator Six, take up a holding pattern southeast of Rocket Ridge until we sort this out, over."

"Roger, Gladiator Six. Do you want Cougar to join Pink Panther? Over."

"Negative, over."

"Roger."

"Panther Two-Oh, Dragon Six, over."

"Dragon Six, Panther Two-Oh, over."

"Panther Two-Oh, proceed to vicinity of FSB Delta and hold for additional instructions, over."

"Roger, understood, Dragon Six."

Switching to the Panther flight frequency, he asked if the others had heard the change in mission. They responded that they had. As they closed on the location of Firebase Delta, they began to clearly see the tracers of small-arms fire, green tracers moving up the hill and red tracers firing down the hill. The origin of the green tracers appeared to be moving up the hill. It was clear that this was a major ground attack on the northwest and northeast sides of the base and very close to the perimeter of the firebase.

"Six-Five-Bravo, Rogues Gallery, over," Carlson heard over the FM radio.

"Rogues Gallery, Six-Five-Bravo, over" came a reply. The sound of gunfire almost drowned out Six-Five-Bravo's voice.

"Six-Five-Bravo, what is your situation? Over."

"Rogues Gallery, I have heavy contact on the northwest and northeast sides. It appears to be battalion-level strength on each approach. We're taking heavy indirect fire as well, over." *For a guy up to his ass in alligators, he sure sounds calm*, Carlson was thinking.

"Six-Five-Bravo, can you hold? Over."

"Rogues Gallery, I would appreciate some help if you have it. They're in the wire and we're going to be pushed off the perimeter shortly, I fear. Over."

"Roger, stand by. Break, break, Dragon Six, Rogues Gallery, over."

"Rogues Gallery, Dragon Six, over."

"Dragon Six, put Pink Panther Two-Oh in support of Six-

Five-Bravo. Right now we're not going to get the Gladiators in, so they can return to base. Over."

"Roger, Rogues Gallery. Break, break, Gladiator Six, did you monitor?"

"Roger, Gladiator, returning to base."

"Dragon Six, Pink Panther Two-Oh, I monitored and will contact Six-Five-Bravo now, over," Carlson transmitted. Not waiting for a reply, he switched his radio selector switch to the FM radio and made the call. "Six-Five-Bravo, Pink Panther Two-Oh, I have a flight of three inbound to your location. Where do you want our ordnance? Over."

"Panther Two-Oh, the northwest and northeast perimeter. They're in the wire and almost on the berm, over." Carlson was watching the events unfold below and had a good idea of where Captain O'Brien would want the first rounds.

"Roger." And Carlson switched to his flight's frequency.

"One-Five, One-Three, have you monitored?" Both responded that they had.

"Follow me," Carlson said as he rolled the AH-1G Cobra gunship into a steep dive from twenty-five hundred feet above the approaching firebase. "Lead's in hot!"

His approach was from east to west along the northern end of the firebase. As the sky was sufficiently light now, he could clearly see the enemy in the wire on the north and northeast sides of the firebase. Gamber's canopy in the front seat filled with the firebase as the Cobra plunged towards the ground. Holding the flex sight with his left hand, Gamber reached with his right and moved the weapons selector switch to fire the M129 40-millimeter grenade launcher. In the back, Carlson had already selected to fire his rockets mounted on the wing pylons in pairs, inboard and outboard. He was carrying four pods with nineteen rockets in each pod. The inbound pods had high-explosive rockets, and two outboard pods had flechette rockets. The seventeen-pound high-explosive rocket was the equivalent of one 105mm artillery round. The flechette rockets each released twenty-two hundred six-gram nails and were devastating on troops in the open. Carlson decided in this case to use his high-explosive rockets on the initial pass.

O'Brien was concentrating on the enemy and never saw or heard the approaching Cobra gunships until the first rockets impacted amid the enemy. The enemy hadn't heard or seen them either until Carlson fired. A combination of high-explosive rockets and 40mm grenades were tearing into the enemy formation, causing momentary surprise and a pause in the assault. As Carlson began to pull out of his dive, Gamber switched his control panel and fired a burst of 7.62-millimeter minigun into the enemy formation. That simple burst spat out five hundred rounds instantly. As Pink Panther Two-Oh clawed its way to gain altitude, Gamber switched to the 40mm grenade launcher. The low-velocity 40mm grenades were impacting on the enemy as Pink Panther Two-Oh made his break. Pink Panther One-Five was laying down his rockets and minigun fire into the enemy as soon as Two-Oh was clear, and then One-Three entered the fray with his weapons. This team had done this so many times before that it was a standard tactic that needed no discussions. As one aircraft was breaking off, another was engaging. And now the NVA air-defense guns were able to see the aircraft.

"Panther Two-One, we're hit. I say again, One-Five is hit." At that, Carlson's head snapped around to see One-Five.

"One-Five, how bad? Over."

"Two-One, it appears we took one through the hydraulics. I have a master caution light."

"Roger, break and return to base. One-Three, escort him as far as Highway 19, then return."

"Roger, One-Three returning to base."

Carlson looked back and saw both aircraft turning to head for Kontum. He was alone now.

"Six-Five-Bravo, Pink Panther Two-Oh, over."

"Pink Panther Two-Oh, that helped, but they're through the wire and are in the north bunkers now..."

"Roger, get your people under cover. We're coming back," Carlson replied, reaching for his rocket control switch.

As he did so, Gamber announced, "Lynn, one and two o'clock, there are two .51-cal positions." He was already traversing the M28 nose turret to one of the positions. Lynn began scanning and quickly spotted the positions. He selected the flechette rockets. Anyone under cover would not be injured by these darts, but anyone outside didn't stand much of a chance. Gamber flipped the switch back to 40mm rounds. He had expended half of the three hundred 40mm grenades that the aircraft carried, but he still had thirty-five hundred rounds of 7.62 ammo. Carlson turned the aircraft to the southeast and made a shallow dive as he approached the closest enemy position and punched a pair of flechette rockets. Gamber put a burst of minigun into the second position as Carlson adjusted his approach to unleash two more flechette rockets on it. Both enemy positions were silenced.

Breaking off his approach and regaining altitude, Carlson initiated a reattack on the northeast perimeter of the firebase. His intent was to fire flechette rockets in pairs. Unlike high-explosive rockets, which the pilot could see all the way to the target, the flechette rocket was not visible. The pilot could tell the accuracy of his attack only by watching the enemy bodies being mowed down, and Carlson was pleased with his shots as he saw clusters of enemy troops suddenly stop and drop. Gamber was reinforcing the flechette rockets with accurate minigun fire that was walking through the enemy ranks. As the Cobra flashed past the perimeter, Gamber detected the sounds of light taps somewhere on the aircraft, causing his eyes to quickly scan the master caution panel. All appeared to be okay and in working order.

"Rogues Gallery, Panther Two-Oh, over."

"Panther Two-Oh, go ahead."

"Rogues Gallery, I have enough ordnance for one more good pass over," Carlson informed Vann.

"Roger, make one more pass and return to rearm as quickly as possible. I'll contact higher and request Spectre," Vann transmitted.

"Roger, will be initiating one more pass and expending," Carlson responded.

"Panther Two-One, One-Three, over," Carlson heard on the radio.

"One-Three, Two-One, what is your position? Over."

"Two-One, I'm two mikes from you. One-Five is on his way home, over."

"Roger, join me. I have enough ordnance for one more pass. We expend everything on this one," Carlson said before he switched his radio over to speak with Captain O'Brien.

"Six-Five-Bravo, Panther Two-One."

"Panther Two-One, that helped, but we could use some on the northwest side, over."

"Roger, I have enough ordnance for one more pass. My wingman is almost fully loaded. We will expend everything on this pass on the northwest side and then break to refuel and rearm. Get your people under cover. How copy?"

"Understood, Six-Five out."

Carlson didn't have to wait long before One-Three, flown by CW2 Dan Jones and CW2 Loy Maple, was in position behind him. Everyone understood this would be one pass and all ordnance would be expended. Carlson reached down and set his rockets to ripple-fire pairs of rockets from outboard and inboard pods. Once he pressed the trigger, rockets would depart from the pods until there were no more rockets left. Mr. Jones did the same. When Carlson was satisfied he was in the right position to commence, he rolled into the attack. Almost immediately, rockets began flowing out of the pods. As the AH-1G Cobra gunship closed on the enemy along the perimeter berm, bodies started dropping. Gamber engaged with the minigun as they plunged toward the enemy, and when the last round was fired, he switched to the 40mm and began spraying the area to the front and the side of the aircraft as it broke off target and climbed. Executing his break, Carlson could hear the exploding rockets from Jones below and behind him.

"Six-Five-Bravo, we're expended and heading to base. Will get back as soon as possible. Panther Two-One out." Carlson quickly switched frequencies. "Rogues Gallery, Panther Two-One, over."

"Panther Two-One, Rogues Gallery, over."

"Rogues Gallery, Panthers are expended and returning to base for rearm and refuel. Should be back in one hour, over."

"Roger, Panther Two-One. I have a Spectre en route and he should arrive in three-zero mikes. Contact me when you start back, over."

"Roger, Rogues Gallery, Panther Two-One out."

The return trip to Kontum was uneventful for Two-One and One-Three. Contacting Flight Operations at the 361st Aerial Weapons Company, Carlson was informed that One-Five had executed a successful running landing at Pleiku with no hydraulics and the aircraft was already in maintenance.

Arriving at Kontum, Carlson and Jones maneuvered their aircraft into the refuel point, with Gamber and Maples climbing out of their respective aircraft and refueling them.

"Two-Oh, One-Three, over."

"One-Three, Two-Oh, go ahead."

"Two-Oh, how much fuel you taking on?"

"Just one thousand pounds or else we're going to have to cut back on ammo, over."

"Roger, one thousand it is."

Once the refueling was completed, they repositioned to the rearm point and shut the aircraft down. Much to their surprise and glee, a couple of armament soldiers were at the rearm point and assisted in loading the aircraft. Under ideal conditions, each aircraft would take seventy-six rockets, three hundred rounds of linked 40mm grenades and four thousand rounds of linked 7.62 minigun ammo on a full fuel load. But nothing was ideal in Vietnam. The combination of temperature and high terrain elevations in Pleiku and Kontum limited what the aircraft could carry in ordnance and fuel and still get off the ground. Trade-offs were required.

Climbing out of the cockpit, Carlson turned to the armament specialist. "We'll take sixty rockets total, one hundred fifty rounds of 40mm and fifteen hundred rounds of 7.62. With our fuel load I doubt if I can carry more than that."

Loading all this with just four people would have taken a good hour, but the additional help made things move much faster. In forty minutes both aircraft were back in the air and racing towards Rocket Ridge. Approaching, they could see Spectre working above the firebase.

"Rogues Gallery, Pink Panther Two-One, over."

"Pink Panther Two-One, Rogues Gallery, go ahead."

"Rogues Gallery, Panther Two-One is a flight of two en route to your location. Five minutes out, over."

"Roger. Spectre is working the area at this time. It appears that Six-Five-Bravo has restored the perimeter and the enemy is withdrawing. When Spectre's done, I'm going to take in a resupply of ammo. I want you to escort me on my approach. It'll be a low pass over the firebase and a kickout. How copy?"

"Rogues Gallery, I have good copy. One bird will be on each side of you. Let me know when you're ready to commence your approach. Over."

"Roger" was all Vann responded.

Soon, Spectre broke station as it appeared that the assault on FSB Delta was over and the enemy retreating, although small-arms fire, mortars and rockets did continue to fall upon the defenders.

"Pink Panther Two-One, I'm ready to commence my run," Vann transmitted.

"Roger, Rogues Gallery, we're taking up position at this time," Carlson reported as he slipped to the right side of Vann's OH-58 helicopter and Jones took up position on the left side.

As they came down on final approach to the firebase, some firing was received from the tree line, which both gunships engaged, primarily with minigun fire. As Vann raced across the firebase between impacting mortar rounds, his interpreter in the rear of the aircraft was pushing out boxes of ammo to the troops below. Six more times that day, Vann would return to Kontum, load up with ammo and fly it to the firebase, never being able to land but only make fast passes over the base and kick out ammo. He still couldn't get Zutter and the crew out.

22

DAK TO II GETS HIT

3 April 1972
42nd Regiment
Dak To II

THE NIGHT HAD BEEN DISTURBED as usual with outgoing artillery fire in support of FSBs 5 and 6 as well as base defense at Dak To II with illumination rounds. Most people, unless they were new to the war, slept through the fire outgoing and even through the occasional incoming round. Lieutenant Colonel Robert Brownlee and Captain Charles Carden were old salts to the war and generally slept well through the fire. Tonight had been different.

"Chuck, you asleep?" Brownlee asked.

"No, sir. I guess you aren't either," Carden answered in the dark of their advisor bunker.

"No, I have a strange feeling. I'm going to head to the command post and see what's going on," Brownlee said as he rolled off his cot and started to put his boots on. *Damn, I've got to start working out more,* he was thinking as he bent over.

Brownlee had been a runner to stay in shape, but since he'd been assigned to Dak To II, his jogging days were over.

"Want me to come with you, sir?" Carden asked.

"Nah, I'm just antsy. Try to get some sleep and I'll see you later," Brownlee replied as he laced his boots up. Carden didn't have to be told twice and rolled over, pulling his poncho liner up to his neck.

Standing, Brownlee checked his watch. *Damn, 0430 and another sleepless night,* he was thinking when a loud explosion suddenly bathed the inside of the advisor bunker in light.

Carden immediately rolled off his cot onto the floor. "What the—" He didn't finish when automatic weapons began firing. From the sound, it was an exchange of M16s and AK-47s.

"Let's get out of here!" Brownlee yelled as he started out the door with his weapon. Carden was pulling on his boots as quickly as he could. He didn't bother to lace them up but wrapped the laces around the tops and tied them off as another explosion was heard. The last place they wanted to be when a ground attack was underway was in the advisor bunker. They knew it would be a target for the enemy. Without the advisors, the chance of getting air support was greatly diminished, so advisors were always targets.

As they exited the bunker, another explosion was heard along with more small-arms fire. "They're hitting the airfield," Brownlee said as he led them towards the command bunker. When they entered, mass confusion was evident. Colonel Minh was yelling and the staff was almost in a panic.

"Colonel Minh, what's the situation?" Brownlee asked as he approached Minh, who had his back to him.

Spinning around, Minh cried, "Get air support. We under attack!"

"Okay, sir, what's the situation? Where's the main enemy effort?" Brownlee asked as another explosion was heard.

"We under attack!" Minh yelled again.

"Sir, calm down and let's look at the situation. What are the line units and perimeter reporting?" Brownlee asked, attempting to get some clarity on the situation. Minh turned and started yelling in rapid Vietnamese to his staff, who were scurrying about the command post in every direction.

"Hey, sir," Carden said, tugging on Brownlee's sleeve. "Why don't I head out to the perimeter and see if I can determine what's going on?"

"Good idea. I'll try to calm Minh down. Be careful. Some of these guys may be a bit trigger-happy," Brownlee responded as Carden headed for the door. Once outside, Carden paused for a moment, squatting down next to the command bunker. He could see two fires over at the airstrip, which appeared to be the refuel point with four thousand gallons of aviation fuel. *No one's going to be refueling any aircraft here for a few days*, he was thinking. As he observed the scene, he could hear the small-arms fire along the perimeter of the airstrip, but it appeared that instead of fire from the perimeter going away from the airstrip, it was going across the airstrip.

Crap, this isn't a full-blown attack. Damn sappers have gotten in and are blowing stuff up, he suddenly realized as he saw a burst of green tracers from an AK-47. After a moment, Carden started to jog to the perimeter at the east side of the airfield. Most of the shooting was on the west side, and he didn't want to run into the middle of that fight. As he approached the soldiers on the perimeter, they were as nervous as Brownlee predicted. Only by calling out in his pidgin Vietnamese was he able to identify himself to the soldiers so they wouldn't shoot. He had made it a point to frequently visit the soldiers and attempt to speak in Vietnamese to them. They got a chuckle out of his butchering the language, so it was easy for them to recognize him. Once in the perimeter, he obtained a guide to take him to the west side of the perimeter to observe the actions there and talk to the company commander. Lieutenant Long was directing small-arms fire whenever an AK-47 muzzle flashed but wasn't maneuvering to find the sappers.

"Lieutenant Long, you must maneuver to stop the sappers," Carden said in his best Vietnamese. Long looked at him as a deer looks at the headlights of an oncoming car. "Come on, we'll take a squad and you and I will find them," Carden said, but Long just stared and didn't move.

Finally, a sergeant approached Carden. "My squad, you," he said in his bad English, but Carden got the idea.

"Okay, Sergeant, we go," Carden said and turned back to Long. "Long, tell your men to cease fire. We're going out to find the sappers and I don't want your people shooting at me. Do you understand?" Carden asked in a forceful voice. Long just nodded in acknowledgment.

Once Long's soldiers stopped shooting, Carden led the squad forward. As they did so, the sergeant had his squad exercise good fire team overwatch tactics, which impressed Carden. *Damn, I guess they've learned something that I've been trying to teach them*, he thought as they moved towards the last burst of AK-47 fire.

Suddenly, off to the right, someone jumped up and began to run. He was silhouetted against the burning fuel and it was obvious he was a sapper. He was quickly cut down by the fire team on the flank. Continuing their sweep, the squad killed several other sappers but managed to capture three, which they quickly bound and moved them to the command post. The Vietnamese would interrogate them and Brownlee and Carden wanted nothing to do with the interrogations. They knew the Vietnamese methods could only be described as brutal despite their efforts to convince them to treat prisoners compassionately.

"Let's go get some coffee," Brownlee directed as the prisoners were removed from the command post. As they walked to their bunker, Carden commented on the sun coming up over the mountains to the east. Dak To II sat in the bottom of a valley adjacent to the river and Highway 512. West on Highway 512 was Ben Het, with one bridge between them over the river. East was Tan Canh also along Highway 512.

Inside the advisor bunker, Carden prepared a pot of coffee. The percolator coffeepot was typical of coffeepots in the fifties and sixties, with a basket and glass dome on top. Previous advisors had left a Coleman two-burner camp stove, which was good for heating coffee and water and the occasional C rations that the advisors received. Most of their meals were with the Vietnamese and consisted of rice and some kind of meat, but they were never sure what kind it was. A can of Carnation Evaporated Milk added a bit of flavor to coffee that would have been too strong to drink as Carden made it strong. As they sipped their drinks, home and loved ones were the usual topics of discussion as they seldom got sports news at their location, so outside of work, there wasn't a lot to talk about. The young captain and older lieutenant colonel had developed almost a father-son relationship.

"Do you think they'll get any useful information out of the prisoners?" Carden asked, staring at his coffee.

"They may get something, but those sapper guys are pretty dedicated and tight-lipped. Besides, anything you get from beating the crap out of a guy is usually not the most reliable information," Brownlee replied, pausing and cocking his head. "Do you hear a helicopter?"

"I do. Sounds like an OH-58 and getting louder," Carden said, standing and moving to the doorway. "Hey, sir, it looks like it might be Mr. Vann's aircraft."

Brownlee stood and moved to look. "You're right. Wonder what he's doing here. I best go meet him," Brownlee indicated as he put his coffee down and moved out towards the airfield.

As soon as the aircraft touched down, the door on the right side opened and Mr. Vann stepped out. Wearing a white short-sleeved shirt, dark slacks, and cowboy boots, he could not be misidentified as a military officer. Colonel Kama climbed out of the back of the aircraft.

Approaching the two, Brownlee rendered a proper military salute, which Kama returned. Brownlee had met Kama at some of the advisor meetings, but as Kama was advisor to the airborne brigade, they had never worked together.

"What happened here?" Vann asked, looking over the burning fuel.

"Sir, we had a sapper attack this morning. They hit at about 0430 and got through on the west side of the perimeter. We captured three, who are being interrogated now by Colonel Minh, and killed several others," Brownlee reported.

"If Minh is interrogating them, you know he's beating the crap out of them. Don't know how useful whatever information he gets is going to be," Kama offered.

"I was hoping to use this as a refuel point this morning. We have a situation up on FSB Delta and I need to refuel Cobra gunships and slicks," Vann said, looking around.

"Sir, we won't be much help as they hit the POL area and the rearm point. I suspect—" Brownlee didn't finish his sentence.

"Incoming!" Kama yelled as the first round of artillery came screaming into the base camp. Vann didn't flinch when the round impacted. Everyone else squatted but refrained from throwing themselves on the ground.

"Guess we should be getting out of here. That chopper is just too much of a target," Vann said as his pilot started the engine without any indication from Vann, who began walking towards the aircraft. As they lifted off, a second round impacted on the airfield and Brownlee made his way back up to the advisor bunker. As he did so, he heard a distant explosion north of the perimeter. Changing course, he went into the command bunker.

"Colonel Minh, I just heard an explosion but no incoming

rounds. It was up on the north perimeter," Brownlee said. It was obvious from the confusion in the command post that they knew what was destroyed.

"Recoilless rifle destroy M41 tank on north perimeter. This may be the ground attack," Minh said with fear written all over his face.

I've got to get him under control before he loses it completely, Brownlee was thinking.

"Sir, I'll go up to the perimeter and assess the situation. If it is a ground attack, I'll get some TACAIR on it and call you back," Brownlee assured him. That seemed to calm Minh down. There was no ground attack, but for the rest of the day, Dak To II was under artillery and recoilless rifle fire. Brownlee spent the day just attempting to calm down Minh.

23

———

MACV WAKES UP

6 April 1972
 MACV HQ
 Saigon

MAJOR GENERAL CARLEY had scheduled the commanders' brief for 0800 hours. All night he and General Ivy, MACV G-2, had been gathering information and data on the situation developing. They were ready to brief General Abrams. Ahead of General Abrams came Mr. Vann and BG Hollingsworth as well as MG Kroesen. Upon entering, Carley called the room to attention, and just as quickly, Abrams told everyone to keep their seats. He did not immediately take one, however.

"Two days ago we were fat, dumb, and happy and totally in the dark as to what was happening even though we knew Charlie was going to do something soon. If that Lieutenant Colonel Turley hadn't raised a flag, the damn North Vietnamese would be sitting in Hue before the Vietnamese JCS would have said anything to us. Damn face-saving culture," Abrams said with irritation in his voice. He looked at General Kroesen. "And that senior advisor for the 3rd Division, Colonel Metcalf, does he have a clue what the hell is going on? Let's get him replaced as soon as this mess quiets down," Abrams directed. "Tomorrow President Thieu has called a meeting to discuss the situation in each region. I want to know what we're dealing with before I go into that meeting and hear the bullshit stories the South Vietnamese perfume princess generals are going to tell him. I want to know how we can assist the Vietnamese and the advisors that are on the ground," Abrams added as he took a seat.

"Morning, sir," General Ivy said as he stepped up to the podium. "The enemy situation currently is as follows. In MR-I there are three divisions pushing into the region. Two have come across the DMZ and are attacking south. The firebases along the DMZ have been overrun and the enemy is now along the Cam Lo/Cam Vet River and held up since the bridges at Dong Ha have been blown. A third division is attacking from Laos along Highway 9, and FSBs Sarge, Carroll and Mai Loc as well as Holcomb have been overrun. Ai Tu is under artillery bombardment almost constantly. Pedro at this time is the only fire support base west of Quang Tri. All enemy forces are north of the Thach Han River," the colonel explained. "In each division, there appears to be a tank regiment supporting the division. We're estimating approximately three hundred tanks based on the reports from FACs and our advisors. His artillery is 130mm, which can outrange anything the South Vietnamese have. In addition, he's acquired a large number of our 105 and 155 artillery pieces as he overruns the South Vietnamese firebases," General Ivy went on to explain. "His air defense has been formidable with SA-2 and SA-3 along the DMZ, and 23mm and 37mm moving with his ground forces and engaging our helicopters," General Ivy continued.

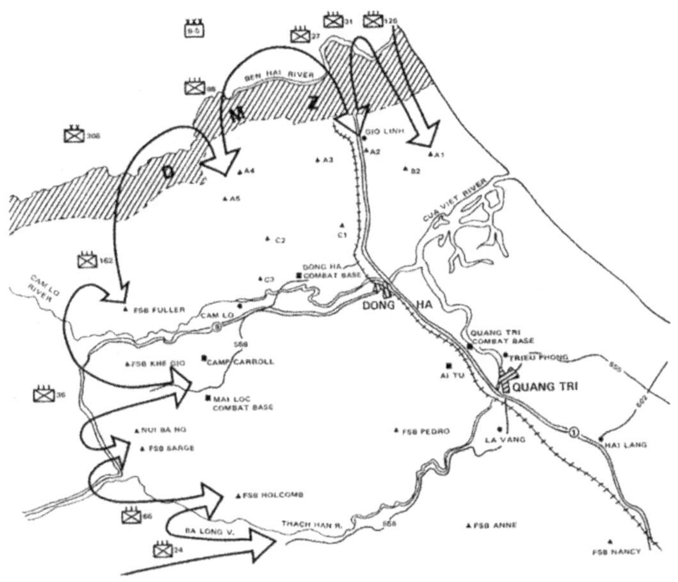

Lieutenant General Quang Truong Ngo, The Easter Offensive 1972,
Washington D.C., U.S. Army Center of Military History, 1980.

"We also lost a B-66E just north of the Cam Lo River, call sign Bat Two-One. We also lost two helicopters attempting to rescue a down crew member."

"So pretty much what Turley told us is the situation up there. What do the ARVNs have holding them back?" Abrams asked.

General Carley, the MACV G-3, spoke up. "Sir, the 3rd ARVN Infantry Division has their forward command post at Ai Tu as Lieutenant Colonel Turley explained. They started out with the 56th Regiment, the 57th Regiment and the 2nd Regiment. In addition they had three Vietnamese Marine brigades under their control, the 147th, the 369th and 258th. Also the 1st

ARVN Armored Brigade and the 20th Tank Battalion, which was undergoing training on the M48s that we've given them."

"Okay, what about MR-III? I understand things have heated up there," Abrams said, looking at BG Hollingsworth. Before Hollingsworth could answer, Colonel Ivy spoke up.

"Sir, the enemy conducted a feint towards Tay Ninh with two regiments and quickly overran a firebase thirty klicks north of Tay Ninh and then pulled back. They withdrew so fast that they didn't take the artillery or trucks, which were all recovered the next day. Yesterday morning it appears that the 5th NVA Division crossed the Cambodian border and attacked the district compound and ARVN compound at Loc Ninh. They're still heavily engaged at this time," General Ivy said.

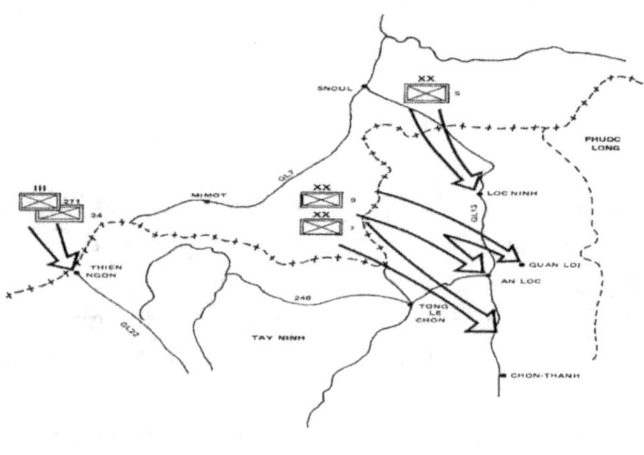

Ngo, Lieutenant General Quang Truong, The Easter Offensive 1972, Washington D.C., U.S. Army Center of Military History 1980.

"So we have just this one division pressing in MR-III, then...," Abrams said.

"Excuse me, but no, sir," General Ivy said quickly. "There are two other divisions also pressing the attack. It appears that the 5th Division is going after Loc Ninh. The 9th VC Division is poised to attack Quan Loi and An Loc and the 7th Division is moving to cut Highway 13 between An Loc and Lai Khe. In doing so, An Loc will be isolated. There's also, it appears, a regiment of tanks supporting this operation but not under the control of the respective divisions."

"Holly, do you think they can hold at Loc Ninh?" Abrams asked.

"I wish I could say yes. There's an advisor captain up there that's making them pay dearly for any gains they're making. He's employing TACAIR and attack helicopters to the fullest. One of the majors from the DOD IG office is up there as well, helping out."

"What do the ARVNs have up there?" Abrams asked.

"Sir, there's a regiment from the 5th Division, but it's getting cut to pieces. Part of the regiment was closer to the border in two locations and they were cut off and ambushed attempting to return to Loc Ninh. An armored unit that was up there surrendered to the NVA without a shot. The captain called an air strike in on them as they moved back to Cambodia. The regimental commander at Loc Ninh is sitting in the command bunker in his underwear ready to surrender and is only being restrained by the threat that our captain will shoot him if he tries," Hollingsworth explained.

"If a regiment is up there, isn't there a senior advisor, lieutenant colonel in charge?" Abrams asked, turning in his chair to get a better look at Hollingsworth.

"Sir, there is, but it appears that he's been severely wounded with a head injury and is pretty much out of the fight," Hollingsworth explained.

"So, Holly, what's the corps commander doing about this?" Abrams asked.

"Sir, General Minh is moving to reinforce An Loc. There's a task force of two battalions with tanks and artillery between An Loc and Loc Ninh. He's having them move back to An Loc. In addition, he's moving the 8th Ranger Group to An Loc along with a request for an airborne brigade from the strategic reserve. The 5th Division has one regiment in An Loc at this time, the 7th Regiment. There are also the local Ruff-Puffs, which have a pretty good commander."

"Are the ARVNs going to be able to stop them from taking An Loc?" Abrams asked.

"I honestly don't know, sir," Hollingsworth said.

There was a long pause as Abrams absorbed all that he had heard. Finally he looked at General Ivy. "What are we looking at in MR-II?"

"Sir, activity in MR-II actually began several weeks ago, or I should say has been a continuation of what we normally see in MR-II except yesterday districts in the northern part of Binh Dinh Province came under attack by elements of the 3rd Division. The 3rd Division has always operated out of the An Lo Valley, and it appears that they've come out in a big way now. LZ Pony and LZ Orange are under pressure at this time. In the west, activity along the border has increased, with concentrated artillery fire on firebases along the border as well as an increase in probes. We have identified the B-3 Front as the commanding headquarters operating out of Base Camp 609. Under their control are the 320th NVA Division, the 2nd Division, and the 3rd Division, as well as some independent unit. The 203 Tank Regiment has also been noted supporting the 320th but hasn't been seen in South Vietnam."

"Unconfirmed reports, sir," Mr. Vann said, catching General Abrams's attention. "Sir, we have had reported sightings of tanks since January and even supposed engagements by attack helicopters, but none of these reports have been confirmed. And besides—" Vann attempted to finish but Abrams cut him off.

"And besides, they weren't confirmed, so you thought it unimportant to report them to us. Am I correct, Mr. Vann?" Abrams asked.

"Well, yes, sir. If he has tanks, sir, they're not going to be much of a problem in our area. Our terrain is very restrictive, keeping the tanks on the few roads. We dominate the high ground and have control of the roads entering MR-II. General Dzu has put two regiments in at Dak To and Tan Canh in restrictive terrain. There are also two armored cavalry squadrons located in sector, starting at Ben Het back to Dak To II. The two bridges along Highway 512 have been rigged for demolitions. Dzu plans to slow the advance down, and when they bunch up west of Dak To and Tan Canh, hit them hard with B-52 and TACAIR and destroy them."

"So why didn't he launch his attack in coordination with the attack across the DMZ?" Abrams asked.

"Sir, I'll bet he was waiting to see if we would pull the forces located along the coast, the 40th and 41st Regiments, and send them north to assist up in MR-I. He would, except that Dzu would then send one regiment from the west to replace those regiments on the coast. With only one regiment then standing in their way, he would attack down Highway 14 to Highway 19 and then eastward through An Khe to Qui Nhon and cut the country in half," Mr. Vann said.

"Well, is Dzu planning on moving anyone?" Abrams asked.

"No, sir. He's considering expanding the 23rd Division area of responsibility northward, to include Kontum and An Khe, however," Vann reported.

"Have the B-52 strikes degraded the enemy forces in your sector?" Abrams asked.

"Sir, in the past two months we have had over one hundred B-52 Arc Lights, and I would say those strikes have crippled the enemy significantly. In keeping with our strategy of blocking the enemy on Highway 14 and Route 512, we intend to hit him hard with Arc Lights when he bunches up for an assault," Vann explained.

"Sir, I would like to comment here," Hollingsworth chimed in.

"Yeah, Holly?" Abrams said, redirecting his attention. He knew what was coming.

"Sir, we've requested B-52 strikes for MR-III, and they've been scheduled. However, within the last four hours of the mission, the aircraft have been diverted. We tracked to see where they were diverted to and found that Mr. Vann's people have been diverting them into their sector in that last four-hour window. I haven't said anything before as we haven't had a situation until these past couple of days, but now, we cannot afford to lose any more B-52 strikes," Hollingsworth said.

Got you with your hand caught in the cookie jar, Mr. Vann, Abrams was thinking. "Care to address General Hollingsworth's accusation, Mr. Vann?" Abrams asked.

"Sir, I'll have to investigate this matter and get back to you and General Hollingsworth about this. If it's true, I will take corrective action. I'll let you know," Vann said. *Damnit, I told Captain Schudder and Snell to be careful and not get caught rerouting those bombers. Shit,* Vann was quietly thinking.

"Sir, we've noticed a problem with some of the Arc Lights," Vann said, attempting to change the subject.

"What is it?" Carley asked.

"We've noticed on some of the strikes, and too often to just be a coincidence, that a targeted unit will move three to four hours before a bomb strike goes in, resulting in seventy thousand pounds of bombs killing a lot of monkeys and nothing more. Is there any way that the enemy could be tracking our scheduled bomb strikes? A leak somewhere?" Vann asked. Looks were exchanged between Abrams, Ivy and Carley.

"Sir, I'll look into this," Carley said, then asked, "Have you noticed this in MR-I, General Kroesen?"

"We have seen similar actions but thought them just to be coincidences," Kroesen stated, but his aide was taking notes.

"Look into this, Carley, and ask General Lavelle to get back to me on this," Abrams said. "Okay, what about MR-IV... anything significant down there?"

"Sir, just the usual stuff. A slight uptick in VC actions but nothing significant compared to the other three regions," Carley indicated.

"Okay, we need to stay on top of this situation. Protect our advisors that are out there. Don't want to lose anyone if we can help it. No unnecessary risks. No heroes or cowboys. Understood?" Abrams ordered as he stood to leave. "Carley, Ivy...my office," he ordered as he left the room.

24

BINH DINH STARTS TO CRUMBLE

LIEUTENANT COLONEL DAVID SCHORR had been the advisor for the 40th Regiment of the 22nd Division since July of 1971. He was the only advisor, so when the resupply helicopter arrived that morning with Major Josh Steinhauer aboard, he was rather pleased to have a friendly face joining him, even if it was only for a short visit. From the air, LZ English was one of the larger named landing zones Josh had seen. The former home of the 1st Air Cavalry Division until 1968 and then the 173rd Airborne Brigade until 1971, it was a well-constructed firebase with three rows of concertina wire over a mixture of claymore mines and fougasse fuel drums. There were clear fields of fire around the entire camp and an adjacent airfield capable of handling C-130 aircraft. The entire perimeter consisted of strong bunkers with connecting trench line providing conceal-ment in moving between bunkers.

"Major, welcome to my humble abode," Schorr said, extending his hand in friendship.

"Thank you, sir," Josh responded, accepting the hand.

"Let's get your gear stowed and them take you over to meet Colonel Doc, our regimental commander. He's getting ready to send two battalions out on an operation, much to my non-advice," Schorr said as he led Josh to a bunker.

"Your non-advice, sir?" Josh asked.

"Yeah. He wants to send two battalions down to LZ Pony and commence an operation in the mouth of the An Lao Valley. The valley is formed by those mountains to the southwest of here and Highway QL1 and the An Lao River. That area and the area west of there has always been the home of the 3rd NVA Division, the Yellow Star Division. For years, units like the 1st Cav Division have fought in that area and it never turned out great for anyone," Schorr said, ducking his head as he entered the bunker. It had originally been built to hold ten advisors and support personnel, but he was the only occupant now.

"Pick a cot and make yourself comfortable," Schorr directed as he leafed through some mail that Josh had delivered. When he was done, he opened a small refrigerator and handed Josh a cold soda. "The other reason I'm against this operation right now is what I'm seeing. You noticed we have a lot of civilians in the camp. Some are the families of the soldiers stationed here. Others, however, are refugees that have come in this past week. They're coming down from the An Lao Valley and quietly telling me 'Beaucoup VC,'" Schorr exclaimed as he took the last of his soda in one long pull. "Let's go see if we can talk him out of this one more time," he added, picking up his steel pot helmet and heading for the door.

Walking across the compound, Josh noticed the large contingent of civilian families. He almost had the sense that he wasn't on a firebase as much as he was walking through a Vietnamese village that had taken over a firebase. Kids were playing and doing chores. Chickens were everywhere and a few goats and pigs were tethered to some post, possibly waiting for the dinner bell—their owners' and not theirs. As they approached one large bunker with an antenna farm on the roof, Josh assumed it was the command post as a guard was at the entrance and the bunker was surrounded with concertina wire as well, triple-strand stacked. There were also several armored personnel carriers, M113s, parked next to the bunker. Upon entering, it took a moment for Josh's eyes to adjust to the darkness of the bunker, lit only by a couple of electric bulbs and kerosene lanterns. Standing around a map board, a short, thin Vietnamese officer was wrapping up a brief with four or five other ARVN officers.

"That's Colonel Duc giving the brief," Schorr pointed out in a low voice. "The two officers on the left are taking their battalions out and the other two are staying here. The fifth guy is the artillery commander here."

"What is Colonel Duc like?" Josh asked.

"He seems okay. Mr. Vann thinks highly of him. He's kept the camp looking fairly military by their standards, and he does have active patrolling around the province. Last week, he had a patrol out that ambushed a group, and come to find they killed the local VC commander in the ambush. That got him brownie points with General Dzu. I guess you could say that Duc is a 'fair-haired boy' of Dzu's."

As Duc was finishing the briefing, he noticed Schorr standing in the rear. "Ah, Colonel Schorr, I see you have company today," Duc said with a wide grin.

"Yes, sir, let me introduce Major Steinhauer. Major, Colonel Duc," Schorr offered.

Steinhauer came to attention and rendered a proper military salute. "Very glad to meet you, sir. I've heard some very good things about you from Mr. Vann," Josh said, lying through his teeth. In his short time serving in this capacity as an inspector, he had learned that senior ARVN officers liked flattery, deserved or not.

"Mr. Vann is too kind. How long you stay?" Duc asked.

"My mission here is to observe the advisors in their roles throughout MR-II and provide a report back to Washington. To do that, I keep moving from unit to unit and just observe the advisors performing their duties," Josh said.

"He no like this operation," Duc said, his openness surprising Josh.

"Sir, I just think splitting your forces at this time isn't a good idea. Intel has indicated some activity in the An Lao Valley. And this morning, reports from refugees indicated that something has happened up north of Quang Tri," Schorr said.

"Quang Tri way up north. Refugees talk too much and not know what they say," Duc said dismissively. "We move down to Pony and hold any trouble in check. You see, all good. I go now. Major, you see," Duc said, picking up his helmet, which appeared to be way too big for him, as was typical of the US steel pot helmet on an ARVN soldier's head.

After Duc left, Schorr motioned Josh over to the map. "Let me give you an orientation of our AO. Here we are at LZ English astride Highway 1, which runs from the North Vietnamese border with China all the way to the southern end of South Vietnam. It's the main north–south highway in the region and runs through Quang Tri, Hue, Da Nang, Phu Cat, Qui Nhon and south to Saigon," Schorr said, dragging his finger down the highway. "Over here to the west are Kontum, An Khe, and Binh Khe, sitting on Highway 9, which intersects Highway 1 right here at An Nhon. The Republic of Korea Tiger Division is located in this area around Binh Khe. We're located here, north." Schorr pointed at their position. "Pony is about ten klicks southwest of us here at the mouth of the An Lao Valley. The 41st Regiment is located here at LZ Crystal north of Qui Nhon."

"So where are your trouble spots, sir?" Josh asked.

"Here," Schorr said, pointing at the town of Hoi An. "But that's not to say we don't have trouble all over the eastern part. In January, the new province chief was giving a speech at an outdoor event when the communists blew up a bomb. A lot of people were killed. Saigon considers Binh Dinh Province to be one of the worst, if not the worst, trouble spot as, of the seven hamlets in the country controlled by the communists, all seven are in Binh Dinh."

"How does that make you feel, sir?" Josh inquired.

"Hey, I advise the Army, not the district chiefs. That's someone else's job, as I'm sure you're aware. You'll have to ask them. I've asked the district advisors to join us for dinner tonight. I got us a pig and a pretty good cook who's going to fix us some rice and pork. Naturally she'll probably take the better cuts for her family, but at least it's not fish heads and rice."

That evening in Schorr's bunker, a couple of field tables were arranged with folding chairs. Paper plates held mounds of steaming rice, and a large platter of pork dominated the center. Cold Carling Black Label beer was sweating, but no one cared. Major Gary Hacker and First Lieutenant Thomas Eisenhower had accepted the invitation to dinner and would be spending the night. Driving the roads at night as a single vehicle was not the safest maneuver. Major Hacker was the district advisor in Hoi An, and Lieutenant Eisenhower served as his deputy.

"So, Gary, I understand this is your second tour as an advisor," Josh commented.

"Yeah, my third tour over here. First was in '65 as a brand-new lieutenant, then back as a captain advisor in this area and back again. Trying to teach this new lieutenant a thing or two before I rotate home. Don't want him to screw up my work," Hacker added with a smile, but then his tone changed. "Truth is I'm not sure he could screw it up any more."

"Why is that?" Josh asked, attempting not to appear over-anxious.

"It seems that we take two steps forward and three steps back every time. You get a program in pacification going and think it's all on track one day and the next, the damn VC have come in and torn it down, blown it up or terrorized the people into shutting us out. There's no strong civilian leadership left, and that which appears to be is in most cases communist sympathizers. The white mice, the police, are all on the take for the most part. I tell you if this whole thing goes under, teachers, police chiefs, loyal politicians, lawyers are all going to be executed. They best be the first to get out of town," Hacker stated as Josh made some mental notes.

25

———

THE DAM BEGINS TO BREAK

8 APRIL 1972
Regional Force Battalion
LZ Pony

THE NIGHT HAD BEEN QUIET, but that wasn't unusual for the area, except that on this night, not even the birds or insects were making noise. This worried the Regional Force battalion commander, Major Chau, and his advisor, Major Gary Hacker. Hacker had left LZ English at dawn and driven to Pony. He had planned on returning to the district headquarters in the afternoon, but it was not to be. At 0300 hours, a soldier woke him and said the battalion commander wanted to see him. Getting his boots on, Hacker made his way to an observation tower in the middle of the base. Climbing the tower, he was handed a night vision starlight scope by the commander.

"Look to west," Major Chau said, and Hacker did. The cautious movement of individuals could not be missed.

Removing the starlight scope, Hacker said, "That's a lot of people."

"Now look north," Chau indicated, pointing in that direction. Again Hacker complied and saw an even larger group moving towards the compound.

"I think we need some air support and need it quick," Hacker said, looking at his counterpart, who only nodded in agreement. Before Hacker could move down the tower, the distant sound of a mortar round leaving the tube could be heard.

"*Incoming!*" Hacker yelled. Every ARVN soldier knew what that word meant. The round impacted in the center of the compound and was quickly followed by several other rounds. ARVN soldiers who weren't manning the perimeter were running to their fighting positions as quickly as they could, seeking overhead cover from the rain of mortar rounds falling on the base. Hacker grabbed the starlight scope and looked to see what the individuals surrounding the camp were doing, but he already knew. In typical North Vietnamese fashion, they were walking in a cluster towards the perimeter, engaging it with small-arms fire. Hacker could never understand this tactic of human wave assaults, as seldom over the course of the war had a prepared base camp been overrun by these human waves. Against modern weapons, it was just not a viable tactic, yet the North Vietnamese forces continued to employ it.

As sunrise came, Hacker observed the enemy withdrawing but still engaging from the protection of the surrounded forest. Pony was located at the mouth of the Hoai An Valley. This valley wound back west into the mountains that had been occupied by the 3rd NVA Division, the Yellow Star Division, for several years and had been a constant thorn in the side of US forces over those years.

"Major, I'm going below to see about air support," Hacker said.

"No, I will get Vietnamese air support," Chau said as he dropped through the hole to climb down the ladder. As he did so, the incoming mortar rounds intensified. For the remainder of the morning it was mortars versus Vietnamese Skyraider airplanes. As Hacker and Chau watched the action and attempted to influence the battle, they began to see an increase in small-arms fire coming into the base.

"Chau, I think we best call for reinforcements," Hacker said, attempting to make it sound like a suggestion as opposed to an order, which he really didn't have any authority to issue.

"I think it is a good idea. I call," Chau said and again disappeared into the command bunker. Moments later he returned to the tower with a smile.

"I call. Hoai An District headquarters. They say 40 Regiment will come," Chau indicated with hope radiating.

"How soon did they say?" Hacker asked.

"Come soon" was Chau's reply. Hacker knew what that meant...anytime between now and when they showed up. As the day wore on, the small-arms fire became sporadic, and finally a battalion from the 40th Regiment arrived with a company of M113 armored personnel carriers. Their arrival lifted spirits around the perimeter.

Vann had received the call that Pony was under attack and decided to fly to Hoai An to confer with the district commander and the commander of the 40th Regiment. When he arrived at Hoai An District, Lieutenant Colonel Schorr and Colonel Nguyen Van Chuc met him and escorted him to the 40th command post, which had been moved from LZ English to the district headquarters. He didn't say much as they walked. Entering the command post, Vann immediately approached Colonel Tran Hieu Duc, the 40th Regiment commander. Vann had been instrumental in getting Duc promoted.

"Colonel Duc, how are you this fine day?" Vann asked, full of enthusiasm. His enthusiasm was not returned by Duc.

"Day not fine. Pony will withdraw in morning."

"What! Why would you withdraw from Pony?" Vann asked in surprise.

"Too big of enemy force. We withdraw to English. I give order."

Vann and Chuc exchanged looks of amazement. For the next hour Vann and Chuc attempted to change Duc's attitude and order. He did not relent. Chuc was the immediate supervisor for the district, to include all forces in the district, even though the 40th was part of the 22nd Division and thus Duc took orders from Chuc. Vann couldn't issue an order, but Chuc could and did so.

"Colonel Duc, there will be no withdrawal from Pony. I will determine when that will be done. Understood?" Chuc said as forcefully as Vann had ever heard an ARVN officer speak. Duc just acknowledged the order and left.

10 April 1972

Lieutenant Colonel Schorr and Major Steinhauer had departed by jeep from LZ English the day before and driven down to Hoai An District headquarters following Colonel Duc in his M113 track vehicles. Trouble had been reported the day before—LZ Pony was receiving intense indirect fire. Arriving at Hoai An, Schorr and Steinhauer went into the advisor bunker. No sooner had they arrived than the mortar fire began.

"Incoming!" Schorr yelled as the first mortar round impacted, followed by two more explosions. He lay on the floor of the bunker until what appeared to be the last round impacted.

"Let's go take a look outside and see what's going on," he said, grabbing his M16 rifle as he headed for the door. It was the first time Josh had seen him carry the weapon outside. Josh had only been issued a pistol that was attached to his load-bearing equipment.

Outside, confusion was absent. The civilians were going about their business as if nothing had happened. "This isn't their first rodeo. They're used to the shelling, although it's been a while since we were hit. Most of the time it's directed at the airfield at LZ English. General Wear is coming in today and I hope he lands up here."

Inside the command post, confusion was present.

"Colonel Duc, what is going on?" Schorr asked.

"Pony under attack. Pony say he has regiment assaulting his position. Hoai An has only one company and he say same. They want TACAIR. You get," Colonel Duc directed.

"Sir, I can call it up, but there's no one at Pony to call it in. Major Hacker has no radio to talk to the air support people. We talked about this and the fact that if they got in trouble I wouldn't be there to direct air strikes for them. Let me see if I can get a scout aircraft in the air to give them some support," Schorr said, and he turned and headed for the advisor bunker with its radios.

Reaching the advisor bunker, Schorr put a call in to request TACAIR support and support from the cav. As he did so, General Wear contacted him to say that he was inbound to his location. While Schorr worked the radio request, Josh moved outside to meet General Wear as his OH-58A aircraft came into view and landed. As the aircraft pilot shut the aircraft down, Wear approached Josh.

"Well, Major Steinhauer, it looks like you're going to have an opportunity to see an advisor in action," Wear said and immediately launched into a coughing fit. "I'm fine. Just got this damn hack and can't seem to kick it," he stated when he was done, as the look on Josh's face showed concern. "Where's Colonel Schorr?"

"Sir, if you'll come with me, he's in the advisors' bunker, attempting to get an air strike. Seems that Colonel Duc sent two battalions south the other day, one to LZ Pony and the other here, and Pony is claiming they're having regimental-size ground attacks," Josh informed him as they reached the entrance.

"Sir, it's good to see you. We seem to be on the short end of getting TACAIR support," Schorr expressed with frustration. "I'm being told that priority for TACAIR is going to MR-I up along Highway 9 and the firebases north of Quang Tri. What the hell is going on?" he asked respectfully.

"That's what I wanted to discuss with you. It appears that there's a major attack underway up there. We've heard that on 2 April, the 56th ARVN Regiment surrendered en masse to an NVA attack, and MACV didn't find out about it until the fourth. Information is sketchy right now as the Vietnamese JCS has been telling Abrams that everything is fine and it's just minor skirmishes in MR-I. Abrams hit the ceiling when he saw some naval traffic sent by a Marine lieutenant colonel requesting a Marine brigade be brought ashore at Quang Tri. I understand he had that Marine lieutenant colonel on the carpet on the fourth and that's when MACV really learned what was going on up there," Wear explained.

"Damn gutsy for a Marine colonel to request that. Are they going to do it?" Schorr asked.

"Knowing Abrams, hell will freeze over before that happens," Wear responded. "In our sector, Firebase Delta started getting probed on the third and the airfield at Dak To II got hit with sappers and recoilless rifle fire. FSB Charlie is under attack, and FSB Delta is now getting pounded. Not sure how much longer they can hold out. We lost two M41 tanks," Wear said as another coughing attack started.

"Sir, let me get you a cold drink," Schorr said, quickly opening a refrigerator and extracting a soda, which General Wear accepted and began to consume. After a few minutes, he regained his composure.

"Thank you, Colonel. This damn cough has really gotten to me. We did get some good intel out of the three POWs that were captured. They confirmed that the 2nd Division is north of Dak To with the 1st Battalion of the 141st Regiment, planning to attack Tan Canh and Dak To II. I haven't heard if that happened as I left Pleiku pretty early today and haven't talked to Vann or Colonel Snell. They also told us that the 17th Signal, 18th and 19th Trans, and 20th Medical as well as the 12th ADA and 14th Heavy Weapons battalions had moved into the area north of Dak To. I can tell you Dzu is shitting bricks and wants to pull you and the 41st out of here and bring you over to Kontum," Wear explained.

"Sir, he does that, then this whole area will only have a few Ruff-Puff garrisons to cover the area. He can kiss off this province as the 3rd will come rolling out of An Lao Valley and those mountains to the west," Schorr pointed out.

"Vann is not going to let that happen. He's convinced that's exactly what the enemy is hoping for, so Dzu will be fighting in two directions and be running back and forth like a chicken with its head cut off. If you get any word that you're moving out of here to anywhere, we want to know about it right away," Wear directed.

"Yes, sir."

"Vann has suggested to Dzu, and I think he'll go for it, that we keep everyone right where they are as far as the 40th and 41st are concerned. He's pushing Dzu to expand the area of responsibility for the 23rd further north to include An Khe and Highway 19," Wear added as he stood. "How is Duc doing?"

"Sir, he seems a bit rattled about his force being at Pony and in contact. Got a bit panicky when the first rounds hit here earlier. Tried to talk him out of splitting his force, but he was hell-bent on doing it," Schorr said.

"Well, let's walk over there and see if I can calm him down. Shall we, gentlemen?" Wear said, leading the three Americans back to the command bunker.

26

CONCERNS EXPRESSED

10 APRIL 1972
SRAG HQ
Pleiku

GENERAL WEAR HAD FLOWN east to LZ English at sunrise to talk to Lieutenant Colonel Schorr, the senior advisor to the 40th Regiment, 22nd Division. The day before, LZ Pony had been hit hard by three battalions from the 3rd NVA Division, and LZ English was on the receiving end of artillery and mortars as they talked. Arriving back at Pleiku, Vann was waiting for Wear in his office.

"I'm worried about Dzu. I don't think he has the fight in him to deal with what's coming," Vann said, which surprised Wear, who had been saying this all along.

"Now what makes you think that?" Wear asked.

"First, he's slow to make a decision, and once he makes it he has a tendency to want to countermand it shortly afterward. Second, he hasn't left the command post in the past two weeks to see what's really going on in the AO. Third, he keeps asking when American forces are returning despite my repeated statements that they are not. He keeps asking for B-52 strikes but doesn't know where his people are and is liable to have us drop a load on his own troops. This fight that's coming is just too much for him," Vann explained.

"I've seen the same with General Dat over at the 22nd Division and Kaplan confirms it as well," Wear offered.

"I think Dzu needs to go," Vann finally said.

"Have you discussed this with General Weyand?" Wear inquired. *Where is this going?* he was thinking.

"I have, but I don't think the guys in Saigon understand the situation here. They're totally focused on the actions along the DMZ and Quang Tri and now An Loc, so we're not getting the attention we deserve. If we don't get the resources and the leadership that's needed, Minh is going to run right straight to Qui Nhon," Vann explained.

"So, what do you want me to do?" Wear asked, thinking, *Stop beating around the bush.*

"I'd like you to fly down to Saigon tomorrow and brief General Weyand on the situation up here and the need for Dzu's replacement. I've already called down and have you on his calendar for tomorrow at 1000 hours. Take Colonel Pahl with you and let him get some face time with Weyand," Vann directed, more confident once Wear didn't object to the trip.

"Okay, let me get with Irv and put together an intel picture so they know what we know and our situation," Wear said as he finished his coffee and stood.

"Good, I'm off and heading over to Kontum. See you when you get back."

The next morning, the flight down from Pleiku was smooth in the early-morning air. Wear didn't care to be bounced around right after breakfast and wanted to study the briefing packet that Colonel Pahl had put together. On their arrival at Tan San Nhut Airport, a car was waiting to take them to the MACV compound, which was adjacent to the airport and the 3rd Field Hospital. *I just might stop there on the way back and see if I can get something for this stomach pain*, Wear was thinking. For the past several months, he had been having gradually worsening stomach trouble. At first he'd thought it was the typical bug that everyone got at some point in their tour, but this was going on for a bit too long.

Once in the MACV headquarters, they quickly made their way to General Weyand's office. General Frederick Weyand was the deputy to Abrams. He was fifty-six years old and had been commissioned through Reserve Officer Training Corps at the University of California in 1938 in the Field Artillery. He never saw frontline action in World War II, however, but he became the assistant chief of staff for intelligence in the China-Burma-India Theater in 1944. His early Army career was predominantly in the intelligence field, and he brought that background with him to his present position. He had come to Vietnam in 1965 as commander of the 25th Infantry Division and pretty much spent the next seven years serving in-theater. He was skeptical of the execution of the war and had been since before Tet of 1968. When Wear reached Weyand's office, to his surprise, General Abrams was waiting to hear what Wear had to say.

"Good morning, sir," Wear said upon entering. Abrams just acknowledged the greeting with a nod.

"Have a seat, gentlemen, and let's get started. General Wear, I understand you have some concerns that you need us to address," Weyand said, motioning for Wear and Colonel Pahl to have a seat. *You can cut the air in here with a carving knife—something's up and they're not happy*, Wear was thinking. *Have I been set up somehow by someone?*

"Yes, sir. First I would like to set the stage with Colonel Pahl bringing you up to speed on the latest developments in our AO, as I believe you'll have a better understanding of our concerns,"

Wear said, acknowledging Colonel Pahl. "Colonel Pahl is our G-2," he added, then turned to Pahl. "Go ahead, Colonel."

"Thank you, sir," Irv replied and then handed a briefing book to General Weyand and General Abrams. *Glad I made up more than one book*, he was thinking as he did so. "Sir, enemy forces since the first of the year have been running supplies, men and equipment down the Ho Chi Minh Trail to Base Camp 609 at never-before-seen rates. Our special operations group recon teams are reporting so much traffic on the trail that there should be stoplights installed," Irv said, attempting to put some levity into the air. The comment didn't appear to succeed. "We've identified that the B-3 Front will continue to operate out of Base Camp 609 and supply their forces, which currently consist of the 320th, 2nd and 3rd NVA Divisions, the 66th Independent Regiment, 203 Tank Regiment and the 7th Engineer Regiment, which we have identified. A captured POW indicated that just north of Dak To II, the 2nd NVA Division has moved into position with the 1st and 141st Regiments as well as the 17th Signal, 18th and 19th Trans, 20th Medical, 12 ADA, and 14th Heavy Weapons Battalions. He indicated that they were going to attack on the fourth but did not.

"We have indications that he has a total of three divisions, four separate regiments, four sapper battalions, two artillery regiments, six air-defense artillery battalions and at least one company of PT-76 amphibious track vehicles, along with supporting ash-and-trash elements. With the renewed bombing campaign, we've been able to hit Base Camp 609 on several occasions. This has diminished his capabilities to some extent, which we are attempting to assess," Colonel Pahl said, pausing for a moment. Weyand and Abrams said nothing. *Now I know what a comedian feels like on a bad night*, Pahl was thinking. *This is a tough audience.*

"Throughout the month of March, we saw the intensity of activity kick up along Rocket Ridge, the ridgeline between the border and Kontum where traditional fighting has occurred over the years. Just recently, however, we've seen an uptick in activity. On 3 April, there was a sapper attack on Dak To II, resulting in an all-day fight. On the fourth, outposts in the northern part of Binh Dinh Province were overrun by elements of the 3rd NVA Division, the Yellow Star Division, and on the ninth, LZ Pony was abandoned and LZ English is under attack. We anticipate that he will be making a major push down Highway 9 shortly to take Ben Het, Dak To I and II, Tan Canh, and on to Kontum. We believe Kontum is the main objective as the 7th NVA Regiment has been building a four-meter-wide road through the jungle and not even attempting to hide it any longer," Irv said and paused. "Sir, that concludes my portion. Do you have any questions?"

"No, Colonel, we are well aware of all this," Weyand said with a bored tone. He then turned to General Wear but didn't speak. Wear sensed that he needed to start talking.

"Sir, our current disposition is the 22nd Division with two regiments at Dak To II, as well as Tan Canh. One regiment is on the FSBs on Rocket Ridge. The 14th and 19th Armored Regiments, which are actually battalion-size, are located between Ben Het and Kontum. The 2nd Airborne Brigade is occupying two of the fire support bases on Rocket Ridge along with elements of one regiment of the 22nd operating around Rocket Ridge, as well as elements of the Ranger Battalion," Wear quickly outlined. *They're probably already aware of this, so need to move this along*, he was thinking. Weyand and Abrams still had not commented but simply listened. "The 23rd Division is currently moving the 44th Regiment to at An Khe, the 45th Regiment at Pleiku, and the 53rd Regiment at Kontum City, along with one battalion of airborne soldiers from the 2nd Airborne Brigade.

"Sir, my concern is the morale of the ARVN forces. In Lam Son 719, we witnessed the ARVNs struggle against a smaller, more disorganized force. They had the backing of US helicopters in large numbers and airpower. This time there's almost no helicopter support and a limited amount of airpower available, especially since there are major campaigns being carried out in the Quang Tri and An Loc areas. I'm concerned that with the plan that Dzu has put in place, he's not going to be able to stop the enemy when they attack. His forces aren't mutually supportive for the most part, with two regiments of the division in the Dak To area and smaller elements around Rocket Ridge. His other regiments are in the east and therefore can't easily reinforce, especially with the passes along Routes 19 and 14 being contested at this time. The 23rd Division AO has been expanded and he has ordered the movement of its regiment to come further north. Due to the situation at the passes, his ability to resupply his forces is greatly reduced to relying on helicopter support, especially for those forces in the Rocket Ridge area. His tanks are scattered along the routes and not in a position to be consolidated for a major attack but being exercised as mobile pillboxes," Wear explained.

Neither Weyand nor Abrams said anything but just sat and stared at Wear. After a moment of silence, General Wear turned to Colonel Pahl. "Irv, will you excuse us, please?"

"Yes, sir," Colonel Pahl said, standing and leaving the room. *What the hell is going on?* he thought as he closed the door. Once Pahl was out of the room, Wear turned to the two stoic officers.

"Sir," he said, addressing his comments to Weyand more than Abrams, "the low morale in the Central Highlands can be directly attributed to the weak leadership of General Dzu and right down through General Dat and some of the regimental commanders. If we maintain the current plan, Dat will collapse at Dak To I and II and Tan Canh. The 22nd cannot hold back the tide, and the road to Kontum will be wide open. The 23rd will not be able to come to the aid of Kontum and it will fall, followed by Pleiku, and the road to the coast will be wide open.

Sir, I believe if we're going to hold in MR-II, we've got to initiate a retrograde operation, bleeding the enemy as he comes forward, trading ground for blood, and make a stand at Kontum after we've pounded him with airpower. The ARVNs didn't fight, as demonstrated in the Plei Trap or on Fire Support Base 6, and I doubt if they will fight at Tan Canh. We need to reinforce or readjust our defensive plan or the enemy is going to get to Kontum," Wear concluded. Both officers sat in silence for a moment. Finally General Weyand stood, as did General Wear.

"We're not going to let that happen. Thank you, General, for your assessment," General Weyand said.

"General, is that all?" General Abrams asked as he stood.

"Yes, sir" was all that General Wear could say.

"Well, thank you," Abrams responded as he walked back into his office with Weyand in tow. Wear moved out of Weyand's office into the outer foyer and Colonel Pahl stood.

"How did it go?" Pahl asked.

"I have no idea. Let's head back to Pleiku."

27

—————

WE NEED HELP

12 APRIL 1972
MACV HQ
Saigon

ABRAMS HAD CALLED a meeting of the three regional commanders. Brigadier Hollingsworth was the first to arrive and really didn't want to be away from Lai Khe too long as things were heating up at An Loc. Vann arrived next and within minutes of Hollingsworth. General Kroesen arrived last. Hollingsworth and Kroesen looked tired as they had been in the fight now for almost two weeks and in neither case was it going well. Vann hadn't experienced heavy fighting like the other two but was getting pressure along Rocket Ridge. When all three were present, General Weyand escorted them to Abrams's office.

"Come in and take a seat," Abrams said, motioning to the four chairs across from his desk. One was already occupied by an Army colonel who stood when the others entered. "Gentlemen, this is Colonel Todd, deputy commander of the 1st Aviation Brigade." Colonel Todd nodded as the others took their seats and he followed suit. "I understand the situation and that right now the only thing keeping the tanks off your backs is TACAIR." Kroesen and Hollingsworth nodded in agreement. "Vann, have you had any tanks in your sector?" Abrams asked.

"No, sir. We have rumors of tanks just across the border, but nothing confirmed, and to tell the truth I'm skeptical that he'll commit tanks in my AO as it isn't good tank country. Better suited for their terrain," Vann replied.

"Sir, right now about the only thing we have to fight tanks is what's left of the 20th Tank Battalion as they have the M48s. The older M41s are just not a match for the T-54 tanks that we've seen," General Kroesen said.

"In my sector it's the grunt with a LAW that's killing them," Hollingsworth added.

"Well, I'm going to request some help. Colonel John Todd is the deputy commander of the 1st Aviation Brigade. He came and told me yesterday of an experiment that's being conducted by the Development Experimentation Command. They've put a TOW weapon system on a helicopter with a sight system to kill tanks."

"Who dreamed this one up?" Kroesen asked with some sarcasm.

"Some crazy aviator, I suspect. How did we come to have gunships and AH-1G attack helicopters? Hell, from the first pencil drawing to roll-off production for the first Cobra helicopter it was eighteen months, that fast," Colonel Todd stated.

"Are they mounting it on a Cobra?" Hollingsworth asked.

"Unfortunately, no. The XM-26 TOW system carries two launch pods with three missiles, fifty pounds each, one on each side of the aircraft for a total of six missiles. The aircraft is currently a UH-1B aircraft," Todd explained.

"A Bravo model. Hell, I'll be surprised if it can get off the ground. Why in the hell didn't they put it on a Cobra?" Kroesen asked.

"Sir, right now the whole thing belongs to Hughes Aircraft, to include the aircraft. No one foresaw that it would be committed to combat so fast as it's only experimental at this stage, but the results have been excellent," Todd offered.

"So you're saying that this XM-26 system has never been fired in combat and only on a test range? Well, it's going to get a test now and we're putting a lot of faith in this," Hollingsworth said in frustration. After a moment of silence, General Abrams picked up the conversation.

"I've put in a call to Washington and told them to send their experiment here and now. I based our request on three reasons. First, they wanted to test this system on Soviet tanks in real conditions. We have that for them. Second, if the system does as well as they think it will, then that'll give them the data they need to go before Congress and request funding. Third, if tanks do materialize in MR-II, we have nothing to send except more LAW weapons. If they don't, then we can use them in MR-I or III. What do you think?" Abrams asked, looking at the three. He already knew that Vann wanted anything and everything he could get. He really wanted to see the reaction from Hollingsworth and Kroesen.

"Sir, may I suggest we get the experiment in-country before we decide where you're going to allocate them?" Hollingsworth offered.

"I'm in agreement with Holly on this. Let's look at the tactical situation once this experiment is operational and decide then where they can best be employed," Kroesen added. Vann decided it was best not to argue the point right now, so he said nothing.

"Okay, good point. We'll send a message out today requesting the experiment be sent. In addition, I'm requesting that a ground-mounted unit with TOWs be sent over, which we'll position around Da Nang and Saigon. They'll be manned by US forces and not given to the Vietnamese. Can't afford to turn them over and have the ARVN take off and leave the system behind. Last thing we want is for the system to fall into the hands of the enemy," Abrams stated.

14 APRIL 1972
0600 Hours

Why in the hell did the Army pick Fort Lewis for this test? We haven't seen the sun in four weeks and it looks like it isn't coming out today, thought Captain Roy Sudeck, the Operations officer for Experiment 43.6 (Attack Helicopter, Daylight Defense), Phase 111.2, as he stood holding a cup of coffee and looking out the window. They had been conducting tests of the XM-26 TOW Sight System and since March had made eighty-five exploratory and record trials. He was supposed to fly this morning and had arrived early to get some paperwork out of the way before going out. In the parking lot, a car was just pulling in, and he recognized Lieutenant Colonel Patrick Feore Jr. getting out. Immediately Feore was sprinting to the office. *Never seen the colonel move that fast*, Sudeck thought, taking another sip. *Must have to use the bathroom really bad.* As Feore came through the door, the phone rang.

"Grab that phone!" Feore yelled, practically diving for it as Sudeck picked it up. Feore yanked it out of his hand before he could speak.

"Yes, sir, I'm here and ready to copy," Feore said, motioning Sudeck to hand him a pen and paper. As soon as he had the pen, he began to write. Sudeck couldn't hear the other side of the conversation but observed some of the notes Feore was writing.

"No, sir, no questions right now. I'll assemble the team on this end and get things started," Feore said. "Yes, sir, I'll give you an update at 1700. If we have to, we'll work through the night, but it'll be on a plane before morning." He hung up.

"What's up, sir?" Sudeck asked.

"Get on the phones. Call everyone and tell them to get in here ASAP. No ifs, ands, or buts—all leaves are canceled. Call the Hughes contractors and tell them to get in here as well."

"Sir, what the hell is going on?" Sudeck asked.

"What's going on is we're going to war. We have seven days to get to Nam," Feore said, scratching out more notes. An hour later, the entire team was assembled.

"Okay, listen up. We received a JCS warning order this morning alerting us to prepare to deploy to Vietnam by 21 April," Feore explained. Shocked looks were exchanged and a low "Holy shit" could be heard. "That includes you guys from Hughes and Bell too. We have to unload the system parts from the aircraft and ship it to Culver City. There the XM-26 systems will be assembled and sent back to us. A plane is standing by to take it. We have to get the two B Models ready to ship as well. In Culver City, the system will be completed and married to the stuff down there in storage. The missiles themselves are being taken right off the production line at the plant in Tucson and will be shipped to us. There's a C-141 on standby at Davis-Monthan Air Force Base ready to fly the missiles up here. Everything is coming to us and we will consolidate it and get it over to McChord to fly out on two C-141 aircraft on the twenty-second. Any questions?"

"Sir, I take it that Hughes headquarters is aware that we're deploying to a combat zone?" Mr. Hugh McInnish Jr. asked.

"If they didn't know yesterday, I'm sure they do now. Hope your contract had an extra pay war clause in it. Ours doesn't," Feore said with a smile. "One last thing. This is a classified mission, so don't be telling everyone where we're going or when. Okay, if there are no more questions, we have a lot of work to do. Sergeant Hartsell, if you need additional manpower to get the aircraft ready, let me know."

"Sir, I think right now with Specialist Lehrschall, Evans and Taylor, we have enough, but I won't hesitate to let you know."

The next seven days were spent preparing the aircraft once the XM-26 components were removed. An Army U-21 aircraft was standing by at Grey Army Airfield, and as soon as the last component was loaded, the aircraft took off at 1800 hours for the flight to Culver City, California, and the Hughes Aircraft Factory, where the remainder of the systems were in storage. Three days later, a C-141 aircraft arrived at McChord Air Force Base. Its cargo wasn't unloaded but additional cargo was added, to include test equipment, spare parts and maintenance tools. On the evening of the twenty-first, two UH-1B aircraft were loaded aboard the second C-141 along with the components for the XM-26 system. At first light in the morning, the team rode a blue Air Force bus across the tarmac to the aircraft and loaded each aircraft, occupying the bucket seats along the sides of it. As the aircraft rose through the dense overcast, family members could only imagine when they might see their loved ones again and only prayed that they would.

28

CHARLIE HEATS UP

14 **April** 1972
   11th Battalion, 2nd ARVN Airborne Brigade
   FSB Charlie

Since their arrival, the 11th Battalion had experienced probes on the perimeter and harassing fire from the surrounding NVA positions. Things began to heat up on the morning of the twelfth. The probes prior to then were generally platoon-size and none presented a major threat to the ARVN soldiers in their prepared positions. Duffy had spent his days adjusting air strikes on known and suspected anti-aircraft positions that ringed the firebase and made it increasingly difficult for resupply aircraft to land. Twice, Duffy had been wounded by fragments from incoming mortar or small-arms fire. None of the wounds were life-threatening, and he considered them more of an annoyance than anything serious. He wasn't about to be medevacked for these cuts.

"*Incoming!*" Duffy yelled as he heard the sound of a freight train growing louder before the 130mm artillery round impacted on the firebase. This was new as the NVA hadn't employed this large-caliber weapon before. Previous incoming was from mortars, which are silent in their approach. Diving into his bunker adjacent to the command bunker, Duffy grabbed the hand mike and called Lieutenant Colonel Kama.

"We're getting hit by 130mm. I need a FAC ASAP," Duffy requested.

"Roger, Covey Five-Eight-Zero is coming on station at this time and is waiting for your call," responded Major Griswold, Colonel Kama's assistant.

"Roger, I am QSY at this time,"[1] Duffy said and switched frequency to the FAC aircraft.

"Covey Five-Eight-Zero, Dusty Cyanide, over," Duffy transmitted.

"Dusty Cyanide, Covey Five-Eight-Zero, Understand it's a bit frosty this morning, over."

"Covey, we're being hit by a large one due west of my location. Estimate on an azimuth of zero-eight-five. How copy? Over." Duffy had noted the general direction from which the round was coming before he'd entered the bunker.

"Roger, Dusty Cyanide, I have good copy and will take a look. Over."

Covey Five-Eight-Zero was at eight thousand feet and flying west of Rocket Ridge. Looking down, he was hoping to spot the gun, but he knew it would be difficult to see unless it was firing since the jungle canopy offered good concealment from aircraft. Generally, when the NVA spotted a FAC aircraft, they would stop shooting until the aircraft was out of position to observe the fire or had departed.

* * *

Twenty kilometers west of Firebase Charlie, the NVA had carved a cave out of the side of a mountain. Within that cave was a 130mm Russian-designed artillery tube. Beside the NVA gun crew stood a Russian officer with a radio. Overlooking Firebase Charlie was another Russian officer with a radio and binoculars.[2]

"Red Fire, Bird's Eye Six, fire mission," the observer transmitted.

"Bird's Eye Six, go ahead," the gun officer replied.

"Red Fire, target is bunkers on Hill 1015," the observer said, passing on the coordinates for the target.

"Roger, Bird's Eye Six, I have good copy. Wait one." Shortly, the 130mm cannon belched flame and a round soared towards Hill 1015. Bird's Eye Six observed from his overwatch position on the adjacent hill. The round impacted but did little damage.

"Red Fire, drop forty," Bird's Eye Six instructed.

"Roger, drop forty." This time the round was a direct hit on a bunker, which was destroyed.

* * *

ALL MORNING, Colonel Bao had been directing the battle from the command bunker, successfully allocating fire support and reinforcing the perimeter where needed. The western side was again taking the brunt of the ground assaults. Sitting next to a radio and studying his map, he cocked his head as he heard the sound of incoming artillery. The impact was loud and raised a cloud of dust in the TOC, both from the floor up and from the ceiling down. *Damn, that was close*, he thought as he looked at the ceiling. He didn't hear the next round but only saw the flash of the explosion for an instant.

Duffy heard both rounds and immediately knew that the second may have hit the command bunker. He had been in his bunker when it hit. Grabbing his M16 rifle, PRC-77 radio and helmet, he exited his bunker, running to the command bunker, which was now a smoldering pile of sandbags and broken timbers. Several ARVN soldiers were pawing through the mess, attempting to pull out any survivors. As Duffy reached the bunker, he heard the sound of another incoming round.

"*Incoming!*" he yelled and threw himself on the ground. In the next instant, his bunker went up in an explosion. The round was a direct hit on his bunker. *Son of a bitch, they must have a spotter on the hill*, he was thinking as he picked himself up. Grabbing his radio, he made a call.

"Covey, Dusty Cyanide, over."

"Dusty Cyanide, Covey Five-Eight-Zero, go ahead."

"Covey Five-Eight-Zero, they have a spotter on the hill to our north. We've got to take him out or the gun that's supporting him. Over."

"Dusty Cyanide, I have a flight of two with napalm inbound. I can hit that hillside with it. Over."

"Roger, do it, over," Duffy transmitted and looked at the adjacent hill. Moments later, the first of two F-4 Phantom jets streaked across the face of the hill. As it did so, two torpedo-shaped objects fell from the wings. As they hit the tops of the trees, the entire hillside burst into orange-and-black flames. The second aircraft was right behind the first but lower on the hillside as he dropped his deadly ordnance. *Hope that fried your ass*, Duffy was thinking as Bao's broken body was removed from the bunker. Duffy approached him. The gaping chest wound told Duffy that Bao was not long for this world.

"Colonel Bao, I'll call for a medevac aircraft to get you out of here," Duffy said, attempting to ease Bao's pain. Bao grasped Duffy's hand and pulled him closer.

"Duffy, tell my wife I loved her true. Tell my children to remember me. Tell my paratroopers to never surrender. You my officers, one final salute."[3]

"Hey, sir you tell them. We'll have you on a bird shortly," Duffy said softly and with as much enthusiasm as he could muster, attempting to encourage Bao.

"You not good bullshitter, Duffy. You have no poker face." Bao began to laugh, only to cough up blood. Duffy held his hand as Bao stopped coughing and his breathing became more labored. Finally, his breathing stopped.

Bao's body was wrapped in his poncho and placed in a single grave. As the fighting along the perimeter was ongoing, no large ceremony was held.

"Major Le, you are now in command," Duffy said as he and Major Le, the battalion executive officer, walked away from the grave. "What are your orders for me?"

"I need you to take out enemy guns. Air-defense guns, mortars and artillery. Can you do?" Major Le asked.

"Can do if we have air support," Duffy responded.

"Good," Le said and turned to Major Doan, the battalion Operations officer. "See to it that Duffy has a security element covering him as he calls air support."

"Sir" was all Doan said in acknowledgment, and he had a fire team surround Duffy and move with him for the remainder of the day as he called in air strikes and directed attack helicopters against the increasing attacks along the perimeter.

29

REALIZATION SETS IN

14 APRIL 1972
11th Airborne Battalion
FSB Charlie

"MAJOR LE, I don't think we're going to be able to hold much longer," Duffy said as the sun began to set in the west. All day, the enemy had been applying pressure on the perimeter. Finally, two NVA battalions had been able to breach the southwest wire and get into the trenches, methodically moving from bunker to bunker, clearing the trench line. The paratroopers were making a gallant effort, but the numbers were overwhelming. The paratroopers for the 11th Battalion were making the NVA pay a dear price for their actions, but there were just too many enemy soldiers pouring into the trench line. Le and Duffy were occupying a foxhole in the center of the firebase as almost every bunker had been destroyed.

"I think you right. We execute our plan. I tell units to execute plan. We pull back to east side and go through wire," Le said.

"Roger. I'll call the gunships and cover the withdrawal," Duffy stated as he put his PRC-77 mic to his lips. "Panther Three-Six, Dusty Cyanide, over," he transmitted, looking at the Cobra gunship a couple of thousand feet above him.

"Dusty Cyanide, Panther Three-Six, over."

"Panther Three-Six, we're about to echo-echo out the east side. Lay your fire on the trench line on the west side. How copy? Over."

"Dusty Cyanide, understood. We're rolling in now," Captain Bill Reeder said as he pushed the nose of the AH-1G gunship into a steep dive, focused on the trench line. He could clearly see people moving, with one group heading east and being followed by another. The lower he got, the clearer it became who was friendly forces and who was NVA. Panther One-Three was right behind him. Reeder's copilot/gunner commenced to lay a stream of 7.62 minigun fire into the trailing group along with 40mm grenades. Reeder began punching off 2.75-inch folding-fin rockets with seventeen-pound warheads into the trench line as well. He had some flechette rockets on the inboard rocket pods but refrained from using those in close proximity to friendly forces. Hearing the rockets impacting, Duffy paused for a moment to evaluate the damage. Major Le was right next to him.

"Keep going, Major. I got this," Duffy said.

"We team. I cover you," Major Le said, sighting down his barrel along the trench line.

"Panther Three-Six, Dusty Cyanide, adjust fire. Drop three meters," Duffy yelled into the microphone. Panther aircraft responded to his request and brought the fire in closer.

"Ah, I hit," Major Le yelled after a piece of shrapnel from the rocket ripped into his chest.

"How bad?" Duffy asked, pulling at the major's shirt.

"I think bad. You hurt too," Le said, pointing at the wound

in Duffy's shoulder. Duffy hadn't felt the hit. This would be his fourth wound since arriving at FSB Charlie. Ripping Le's shirt open, Duffy recognized that Le had sustained a sucking chest wound. Immediate first aid was required, and Duffy knew just what to do. Grabbing a LRP food packet, he bit the plastic packet in two.[1] One half he applied to the exit hole in Le's back and the other to the entrance wound in Le's chest. He then applied a compress over both wounds. "That should hold you for a time, Major," Duffy said encouragingly.

"Duffy, I no good. You take command now," Le ordered. Duffy said nothing but nodded. Four soldiers were providing security, and Duffy now instructed them to make a field-expedient stretcher out of a hammock and carry Le, which they did.

Duffy and the two soldiers carrying Major Le proceeded to follow the lead elements passing through the wire in an orderly, disciplined fashion. Walking wounded were being assisted by their fellow soldiers. Duffy and Major Le were bringing up the rear with Major Doan leading up front with one of the company commanders. About one hundred and fifty soldiers were all that was left of the original four hundred and seventy men of the 11th Airborne Battalion.

As they moved, they could hear the NVA attempting to follow them down the mountain. Duffy continued to talk to Panther Three-Six and Covey Nine-Nine. Four hundred meters from the perimeter, Duffy paused and made a call while the remainder of the force paused to catch their breaths.

"Covey Nine-Nine. We no longer own the hilltop. Moving northeast at this time down the mountain. Target request, over."

"Dusty Cyanide, send it, over."

"Covey Nine-Nine, request BUFF strike Charlie. They own it and we're four hundred meters northeast of there. Estimate two battalions of NVA, over." A few minutes later, Duffy had his answer.

"Dusty Cyanide, Covey Nine-Nine, Arc Light is diverted and will be over Charlie in twenty minutes. Will advise of prerelease, over." Duffy and his group of one hundred and fifty soldiers continued down the mountain, moving away from Charlie as quickly as they could considering the number of wounded they had with them.

"Dusty Cyanide, Covey Nine-Nine, over."

"Covey Nine-Nine, Dusty Cyanide, go ahead."

"Dusty Cyanide, one minute to drop, over."

"Roger, understood, we're clear." Duffy immediately began notifying everyone to get down, open their mouths and hold on to their helmets. Even though they were six hundred meters from Charlie, the shock wave would still be considerable.

"Dusty Cyanide, drop, drop, drop," Duffy heard over his radio, and he knew from experience that in ninety seconds the world of what had been Charlie would disappear. He was not disappointed when the first bomb exploded on target.[2] The plan for the evacuation was for Duffy and the force to link up about ten kilometers from Charlie with 113 Company. All night, Duffy, Le and Doan kept the paratroopers moving. Occasional gunfights broke out with NVA forces patrolling in the area. In each gunfight, more casualties were accumulated.

"Incoming!" someone yelled as the first of the 105mm rounds slammed into the group.

Crap, that's friendly fire, Duffy was thinking as he got on the radio to contact Lieutenant Colonel Kama.

"Check fire, check fire!" Duffy yelled on the radio to Kama. "Who the hell is shooting this shit?" he asked once the incoming fire had stopped. Injured soldiers were being treated. Three were dead and seven more were wounded.

"For God's sake, do not approve any more fires until you check with me," Duffy directed and read off the coordinates of his party's location. That was when he was informed that 113

Company was not going to be able to conduct the linkup. The enemy was too numerous between their forces.

Duffy and his party continued to move in the pitch-black jungle. Throughout the night, the vegetation grabbed them, the insects ate them and the NVA sniped at them. Duffy was physically exhausted and assisted by a young paratrooper at times, especially in cross streams as he was experiencing temporary flash blindness.

The ambush at first light was a complete surprise and they had walked right into it. The first indication was the PKM machine gun opening up on the right flank of the trail they were traveling on, followed by the explosion from a claymore mine. When caught in an ambush, the only thing to do is get out of the kill zone quickly and that was what the young paratroopers did, but some panicked and ran in the wrong direction, never to be seen again. Wounded in hammocks were dropped in the kill zone.

Duffy managed to get out of the kill zone and surrounded himself with thirty-five soldiers in a small clearing. Major Doan and Major Le were with him. "Let's get some security out and I'll see if you can get choppers to pull us out now," Duffy said as Major Doan began to organize a security perimeter around the small clearing that they had stumbled into. As they established the perimeter approximately one kilometer from the ambush site, they could hear the NVA calling their names, which they had learned from an ARVN prisoner they'd captured.

"Duffy, you surrender or you die" was heard in the distance. Surrender had not crossed Duffy's mind. Instead he pulled out his emergency radio that transmitted on the Guard frequency for all aircraft to hear.

"Any aircraft, this is Dusty Cyanide requesting assistance, over."

Almost immediately he heard, "Dusty Cyanide, Covey Triple Nickel. What is your location?"

After a few minutes, Duffy looked down at Major Le with a smile for the first time in many days.

"We have four aircraft coming to get us. Keep everyone quiet and lay low," he directed and commenced to move around their small perimeter, encouraging the soldiers.

30

DALLAS NIHSEN

15 APRIL 1972
H Troop, 7/17th Cav
En Route to Kontum

MAJOR JAMES M. GIBBS, commander of H Troop, 7/17th Cav, was leading a flight of four UH-1H aircraft to Kontum when he got a radio call.

"Any aircraft in the vicinity of Kontum, Covey Five-Five-Five, over." Gibbs knew Covey was the call sign of the FACs that worked the area.

"Covey Five-Five-Five, Embalmer Six, over."

"Embalmer Six, Covey Five-Five-Five. Troops in contact and need immediate extraction. One Uniform Sierra and thirty-seven ARVN paratroopers. Can you assist?"

"Covey Five-Five-Five, I have a flight of four slicks and two Cobras. Let me see if I can be released from our current mission and assist. I'm taking the slicks into Kontum POL to refuel, but I can send the Cobras immediately. What's the friendly location and call sign? Over."

Covey Five-Five-Five passed the coordinates for Duffy's location and his call sign. The two Cobra gunships immediately broke off from the four UH-1H aircraft and proceeded to Duffy's location. In Gibbs's cockpit, work began to request a change of mission to assist.

"Dennis, you handle getting the flight into Kontum POL and I'm going to see if we can get a mission change," Major Gibbs instructed his copilot, Warrant Officer Dennis Watson. Mr. Watson was probably the most experienced right-seat pilot in the unit. The only reason he wasn't an aircraft commander was the fact that in his short time in-country this was his third unit of assignment. Every time he was sent to a unit, it was ordered to return to the States and he didn't have enough time in-country to qualify to rotate back with the unit. While Mr. Watson maneuvered the flight of four into POL, Major Gibbs contacted the aviation battalion operations and explained the situation. A mission change followed shortly.

"Covey Five-Five-Five, Embalmer Six, over."

"Embalmer Six, Covey Five-Five-Five, over."

"Covey Five-Five-Five, Embalmer Six is a flight of four inbound to Dusty Cyanide's location, over."

"Roger, Embalmer Six. Break, Dusty Cyanide, did you copy Embalmer? Over."

"Roger, Embalmer Six, Dusty Cyanide, I'm talking to Undertaker Two-Two, over."

"Roger, Dusty Cyanide, I have Undertaker Two-Two in sight. Wait one."

In the distance Major Gibbs could see his two Cobras as they rolled over and dove towards the tree line, punching off rockets as they did so. As he approached, Gibbs took the number four slot in the flight as he wanted to be able to coordinate the actions of his flight of two and four. As he assumed a high orbit to assess the ground situation, he monitored the communications.

"Cobra, Cobra, they're twenty-five meters away! They're in

that wood line—go get 'em," Dusty Cyanide transmitted. Gibbs watched as Undertaker Two-Two rolled over into another dive and punched off two more rockets.

"Cobra, Cobra, they're twenty-five meters to my sierra, to my sierra," Duffy directed Undertaker.

"Roger, Dusty, we're inbound. Keep your heads down," Undertaker announced. The sound of a minigun could be heard.

"Dusty Cyanide, Embalmer Six, over."

"Embalmer Six, go ahead."

"Dusty Cyanide, I want you on that first aircraft that comes in, over."

"Embalmer Six, that's negative. If I leave, they can't communicate. I'll be on the last aircraft. I have four wounded to get out on the first aircraft," Duffy transmitted in a calm voice. Gibbs realized that Duffy was correct. Only he could speak to the aircraft, and his remaining until the last ensured that the aircraft would continue to extract his soldiers.

As Duffy directed the Cobra gunships, the first of the Embalmer flight entered the one-ship landing zone. In an orderly but expedited fashion, several Vietnamese paratroopers dashed from around the perimeter to the waiting aircraft with two of the wounded. Chalk One was on the ground for less than five seconds when dust began to swirl around the aircraft, indicating it was taking off.

"Chalk One is coming out!" was transmitted as the aircraft departed the ground.

"Chalk One is taking fire!" was almost immediately heard, and it was obvious as green tracers streaked after the departing aircraft. As Chalk One cleared the tree line, a stream of minigun fire ran alongside the aircraft compliments of Undertaker as he rolled in behind the UH-1H.

"Chalk Two on short final," Gibbs heard as he observed the second aircraft entering the landing zone. As with the first, the skids of the aircraft were just touching the ground when another group of paratroopers jumped into the aircraft along with two wounded soldiers in hammocks. The aircraft departed immediately.

"Chalk Two is clear" was transmitted as the aircraft departed over the tree line with what appeared to be only a few rounds fired at it. Gibbs continued to watch as Chalk Three made his approach.

"Okay, Dennis, let's get in position to get in as soon as Three-Three comes out. You have the aircraft, but I'm going to get on the controls too in case you're hit," Gibbs instructed Mr. Watson. "Dallas, you guys get ready on the guns." Watson maneuvered the aircraft into position. Specialist Dallas Nihsen was the crew chief for Major Gibbs and had flown with him almost every day. The gunner, Specialist Bird, was on his first mission, having transferred into the unit from the infantry.

"Chalk Three, short final." Chalk Three came in hot and had to make a drastic deceleration to stop his aircraft in the landing zone. As soon as he touched down, the paratroopers were aboard.

"Chalk Three coming out! Three is taking fire!" everyone heard over the radio. Mr. Watson was coming in hot and on short final when the tree line opened up with small-arms fire on his aircraft.

"Does anyone see the friendlies?" Watson asked as he cleared the tree line to land.

"No, but we're taking fire," Specialist Bird yelled as his M60 machine gun answered. On the left side of the aircraft, Specialist Nihsen was also firing. Not seeing any friendlies and taking fire, Watson had to make a snap decision.

"Chalk Four is making a go-around," Watson transmitted as he dropped the nose and increased his power, rapidly exiting the landing zone.

"Sir," Watson said, getting Major Gibbs's attention, "if I

didn't see a B-40 rocket, I'll kiss your ass!" A look of surprise crossed Major Gibbs's face at the comment as he hadn't seen the B-40 rocket, having been too busy talking to Undertaker Two-Two as Watson commenced to circle the landing zone in another attempt to land. Bird was busy attempting to get his gun back in operation as it had a double feed with rounds stuck in the barrel.

"Six, you think you can get back in there?" Undertaker Two-Two asked.

"Affirmative. I couldn't see the people that time. I don't think we had a smoke left from number three. Over," Major Gibbs responded.

"Six, they're located along the wood line."

Major Gibbs and Watson were both scanning the tree line, looking for a friendly face. Over the intercom, Gibbs asked, "Bird, Nihsen, did either of you see friendlies down there?"

"Yes, sir, I saw them," Bird answered. Over the radio, Undertaker Two-Two was asking Dusty if he was still at the same location.

"Undertaker Two-Two, we are moving whiskey...er...to the november echo, over."

"Undertaker Two-Two is rolling hot with twenty mike-mike, stand by." And Gibbs saw Undertaker roll into a steep dive. His 20mm pylon-mounted gun vibrated the entire aircraft when he opened fire. It was apparent where his rounds were hitting as trees were cut down as well as people unlucky enough to be in the open.

"Major! There are bad guys on the trail. Son of a bitch is carrying a rocket," Nihsen reported. Gibbs attempted to see the trail with the individuals but only caught a quick glimpse.

"Undertaker, we got people all along these trails our your nine o'clock. Over," Gibbs reported.

"Dusty, Undertaker Two-Two, how was that?" Gibbs and Watson only received a garbled response to the question from Dusty. Then they clearly heard, "Still got small-arms. We've moved about twenty-five meters. We're going to stop here. We got five people left, over." Gibbs immediately acted.

"Two-Two, this is Six. I'm on a supposed final. I don't really know where the people are."

"Six, stay on course. I have you and them. They're twelve o'clock, over," Two-Two reported. Watson held his heading and began to lose altitude to be right on top of the trees. To his front, Watson could see a burst of minigun fire impacting forward of his aircraft.

"Okay, watch for the friendlies," Major Gibbs said as they approached the landing zone. He peered over the instrument panel, scanning the tree line. The closer they came to the clearing, the greater the intensity of the small-arms fire grew.

"I got yellow smoke," Major Gibbs suddenly said and pointed to the eleven o'clock position off the nose.

"I see it," Watson said calmly as he negotiated a slight change in heading towards the smoke.

"Six, the friendlies are across the tree at your twelve," Undertaker Two-Four said, laying down another burst of minigun fire. "Bad guys are in the trees."

"I see them," Bird said, still attempting to unjam his M60 machine gun.

"Okay, I see them," Gibbs said, allowing Watson to continue his approach. The occasional sound of tapping on the side of the aircraft was heard, and it was all on Watson's side. "I got friendlies on my side, Two."

"Clear left, ease it down," Nihsen said as the aircraft cleared the trees and began its descent into the tight landing zone. The explosion in front of the aircraft got everyone's attention.

"Crap! We're taking incoming!" Bird yelled.

"That's a rocket!" Gibbs responded.

"Six, I have it and rolling hot," Undertaker Two-Two reported as he punched off two rockets of his own into the origin of the RPG round.

"Clear right," Bird said, still attempting to get his M60 machine gun functioning.

"Watch the blades," Major Gibbs said with a strain in his voice as the aircraft lowered into the clearing. "I'll watch the instruments." Watson was concentrating on staying clear of trees and small brush that could be catastrophic if they got a tail rotor strike.

"Okay, sir, you're clear down over here. Just kind of hold it and let them crawl in. It's going to be rough," Bird said as the aircraft came to a three-foot hover above the stump-filled clearing. Seconds seemed like minutes as Watson held his concentration on hovering the aircraft while each individual climbed aboard, causing the aircraft's center of balance to shift slightly.

"Three are in," Bird yelled, still attempting to clear the jam in his M60. Nihsen wasn't shooting as there was no contact on his side of the aircraft.

The aircraft continued to rock from the shift in balance, which Watson was overcoming. Major Duffy and three of the ARVN soldiers were attempting to climb in the aircraft. Duffy and Major Doan, the battalion operations officer, were the last to climb in when Doan yelled and began to fall back, his foot mangled and injured. Duffy reached out and grabbed his web belt and began pulling him back into the aircraft. That was when Bird noticed the bandages on Duffy.

"Sir, we have wounded on board. This major has three bandages and the ARVN major has just been hit. The major is pulling him aboard," Bird yelled over the intercom, frustrated as he couldn't get his weapon functioning. Watson's concentration was momentarily lost as the first round came through his side window and passed between his head and the aircraft bulkhead. Then a second round followed the first, but with a much heavier sound as that round slammed into and through the corner of the transmission wall.

"Hey, hey, I'm hit," Nihsen yelled as he fell forward in his seat, being held in only by his harness. The aircraft continued to rock as Duffy pulled an ARVN officer onto the aircraft.

"Go, go, go," Bird yelled, and Watson added power and climbed out of the landing zone. Duffy gave a thumbs-up to Gibbs, indicating all were aboard as he moved to the left side of the aircraft. As the aircraft cleared the trees, Major Gibbs was calling Nihsen but not getting an answer. From his seat he couldn't see behind him, but he knew from the motion of the aircraft that something wasn't right.

"I have the aircraft. Look and see how Nihsen is," Gibbs instructed Watson. Before releasing the controls, Watson glanced at the engine instruments.

"Forty pounds," Watson read off on the torque gauge as the aircraft steadily moved forward. Despite the number of hits the aircraft had sustained, the master caution panel wasn't showing any damage. Releasing the controls, Watson turned in his seat and looked down into the eyes of the wounded Vietnamese major whose head was resting on the back of the radio console. Watson continued his gaze to Nihsen's position, where Duffy had moved to as Nihsen was no longer in the aircraft but suspended from his harness, partially in the aircraft and partially hanging out. Duffy was pulling him in and began applying a bandage to his back where a bullet that had come through the side window and the corner of the transmission wall had hit him.

"Six, Two-Two, did you get the Uniform Sierra? Over."

"Two-Two, that's affirmative," Gibbs responded as he concentrated on staying low-level above the trees and exiting the area. "I have wounded on board and am heading to Kontum hospital." Switching to intercom, Gibbs asked about Nihsen's condition.

"Sir, the major says he thinks he'll be okay if we get to a hospital. The round hit him in the back and went clear through. The entry wound is patched and the major is working on the exit wound," Bird responded. Watson looked back at the major and confirmed with a nod what Bird had said. As he turned to look back at Duffy, he made eye contact with the Vietnamese major, who had removed his soft cap. With a smile and a nod, the major extended his hand holding the hat and presented it to Watson. The message was unspoken but clear: "Thank you."

A few minutes later, Gibbs heard the intercom come alive.

"Sir, Nihsen is gone" was all Bird said. Nihsen had died in Major Duffy's arms.

31

DAK PEK IS THE FIRST TO FIGHT

19 **April 1972**
Border Ranger Battalion
Dak Pek

VANN WAS BEING STRETCHED THIN. A late riser normally, he had been called and asked to come to the SRAG headquarters at 0700. Normally he would still be in bed until 1000 hours.

"Okay, why am I here?" Vann asked as a cup of coffee was placed in his hands.

"Sir, we have a situation developing at Dak Pek," Colonel Snell said. He was due to rotate back to the States in the next couple of days and was really looking forward to going. "A large NVA force hit the camp this morning and it's still under pressure. We have a FAC over the camp, but no advisors are up there, as you know."

"What unit is located there?" Vann asked, attempting to get the cobwebs out of his head.

"Sir, that's the 88th Border Ranger Battalion. Their commander is one of the best in the province," Snell added.

"I remember meeting him once. What support have we given him?"

"Earlier, we got an AC-119 Stinger aircraft to move up that way and offer assistance," Colonel Snell stated. "We haven't gotten a BDA on that action as of yet. Dak Pek is out of artillery range except for the tubes at Ben Het, which are firing in support, but it isn't much. And Dak Pek does have four-deuce mortars."[1]

"Well, keep me informed on this. The NVA have got to take out that camp if they want to move forces down Highway 14, so this trip wire will tell us their progress just like Ben Het will give us warning on Highway 512," Vann explained.

"Sir, we've also had a report from Colonel Kaplan, the 22nd Division advisor, that the 1st Battalion of the 42nd is in contact north of Dak To II. They're surrounded and the 42nd is attempting to get a relief force to them, but it almost appears to be a half-hearted attempt," Snell said.

"What the hell is Dat doing about it?" Vann asked as his frustration level increased.

"According to Kaplan, very little. Dat refuses to move forces, saying that the North Vietnamese soldiers are superior. He's hoping that airpower will save the day," Snell said, knowing that this would not satisfy Vann.

"I knew that Dat was a corrupt son of a bitch and should have had him fired long ago. Unfortunately he has close ties to the Saigon power brokers. I tried to get Dzu not to accept him as a division commander, but Dzu was afraid to buck the Saigon warriors. Now we're going to pay for that. Where is the 1st Battalion?" Vann asked, taking a very serious interest in this development and moving close to a map posted on the wall.

"Sir, they're right here, about four klicks north of Dak To II."

"We need to get that battalion out of there. If they're allowed to be taken, the rest of the regiment will toss in the towel immediately. Let's get some B-52 support for them. Is there an advisor with them?" Vann asked, already knowing what the answer would be.

"No, sir. I believe the FAC is talking to them with a Vietnamese ride-along. I'll check and see what we can do," Snell said, knowing there wouldn't be much and the Vietnamese Air Force was going to have to provide the air cover.

"Has General Wear been informed?" Vann asked, taking a sip of coffee and staring at the wall map.

"Sir, General Wear was informed, but he's having another coughing attack and we told him to get back to bed. Sir, maybe you need to talk to him about his medical condition. It doesn't appear that the medical facilities here are treating him very well," Snell said in a low voice.

"I'll speak to him. I'm going to need him when this fight starts. Change of subject, what have we heard from Delta?"

"Sir, they're still in contact. Colonel Kama said he spoke with Captain O'Brien, and as long as they have resupply, they're good at holding their position. They got a resupply yesterday and we're scheduling another for today."

"Good. If we lose Delta and Firebases 5 and 6, then we can expect an attack at Dak To II and Tan Canh. Those firebases are the only thing keeping the NVA at bay right now."

"Lieutenant Colonel Schorr notified us that the 40th abandoned their positions in Pony and Hoi An and pulled back into English. He said that they only have two of the three battalions, now having lost a battalion in the withdrawal from Pony and Hoi An. He's confident that English can hold out against anything the enemy throws at them," Snell briefed.

"English is a strong position. Duc should have no problem holding that place with two battalions and supporting artillery. Chuc should be able to put some fire under Duc and get him to hold that place," Vann offered. "What about the 41st Regiment?"

"Sir, they've been pretty quiet. They're sitting at LZ Crystal. They're sending out patrols in the daytime but hunkering down at night according to the senior advisor, Lieutenant Colonel Stovall. He has a cav team out there today conducting reconnaissance around Crystal. I believe the cav commander is flight lead on this one."

"Good. Crystal is astride Highway 1 and the closest firebase to Qui Nhon. They've always been in a quiet sector. With them and English, we can focus our attention on Rocket Ridge and Dak To II," Vann said as he finished his coffee and departed.

32

LZ ENGLISH FALLS

19 APRIL 1972
    40th Regiment
    LZ English

THE MORNING SILENCE was broken by the sound of increasing gunfire along the perimeter of LZ English. Refugees from the surrounded villages of An Do, Binh How, Dai Loc, and Ba Le began streaming down the road towards English, it was reported to Duc. They all had the same story: "Beaucoup VC." Accompanying the refugees was also an increase in the number of incoming mortar rounds impacting around the district headquarters. Schorr was not concerned about LZ English as it was a formidable position. The arrival of Major Hacker and Lieutenant Eisenhower the previous day told Schorr the situation was worse than he expected.

"Hey, guys, let's see if we can calm Duc down a bit," Schorr said, finishing his morning coffee and waiting for a pause in the incoming rounds that had been hitting along the perimeter and wire. The night had been spent attempting to calm down Duc, who had planned a withdrawal from the firebase. The three advisors took turns throughout the night sitting in the command post, attempting to advise the staff on actions to take. Overhead, the TACAIR could be heard and friendly artillery was registered around the firebase as well.

"Right behind you, sir," Josh said, retrieving his steel pot and following Schorr at a slight jog to the command post. As they entered, they could hear Duc talking in an excited and elevated voice.

"Seems English is to be evacuated," Josh said in a low tone to Schorr, who quickly turned and asked, "You speak Vietnamese?"

"Not great, sir, but enough to understand what he's ranting about." Just then, Duc spotted the two Americans. He rapidly approached Schorr.

"English evacuate. General Dzu ordered. We go Quin Ngo. We leave 1200 hours," Duc said.

"Calm down, sir. We have a plan and plenty of support. The perimeter is holding just fine," Schorr pointed out, but Duc was not listening. "Sir, we have TACAIR and artillery laid on to cover your withdrawal and I have the cav sending us helicopter gunships."

"1st Company will move first, followed by headquarters and then 2nd Company. I give order we depart at 1200 hour," Duc announced.

"Yes, sir, all the support from TACAIR, artillery and attack helicopters will be here at 1200 hours," Schorr attempted to reassure Duc. He was starting to doubt his success, however.

"Josh, I'm going to run back to the advisor bunker and make a call. How about staying here and keeping an eye on Duc?" Schorr asked.

"Sure, sir. I'll come get you if there's a problem," Josh responded and took a seat in the corner so he could observe the staff dysfunction.

Arriving back at the advisor bunker, Schorr was about to

make a call when three mortar rounds landed inside the perimeter and very close to the command bunker. Before Schorr could make his call, Josh tore into the bunker.

"Sir, you best come quick. Duc is bugging out!" Josh yelled.

At first Schorr thought he'd misunderstood Josh, but then it registered. He sprinted out the door and saw Duc heading for his M113 armored personnel carrier along with his staff. Grabbing Duc's arm, Schorr stopped him in his tracks.

"Sir, what the hell are you doing? We have a good plan. Stick to the plan," Schorr said aggressively. Initially Duc just stared back at him with a deer-in-the-headlights look. Then he jerked his arm back.

"We go now. We go now," Duc said, turning and picking up the pace to reach his vehicle, which was already running. The other staff tracks were positioning as well. Schorr could do nothing but watch as Duc and his staff drove out the gate and headed in a cloud of dust towards Quin Ngo. This exodus was not unnoticed by the soldiers manning the perimeter and engaging the enemy.

Shit, I've got to let higher know about his. Vann's fair-haired boy just deserted his command, Schorr was thinking when he arrived back in the advisor bunker.

"Sir, what can we do?" Major Hacker asked.

"Grab some ammo and get ready to exit this place."

Schorr got on the advisor command net. "Raven Six, Raven Four-Oh, over," he transmitted, reaching Colonel Kaplan.

"Raven Four-Oh, Raven Six, over."

"Raven Six, Raven Four-Oh. Friendly troops are bugging out at any time. Request guidance. If friendlies bug out before guidance arrives, will bug out with them, over."[1]

"Raven Four-Oh, roger, wait one."

Oh, like I'm going somewhere...wait one, Schorr was thinking when Lieutenant Eisenhower stuck his head through the door.

"Hey, sir, you may want to come out and see this," the lieutenant said, almost cringing as he did so.

"What is it?" Schorr asked, not wanting to leave the radios.

"They're beginning to strip their uniforms," Eisenhower said with a troubled look.

"Damnit" was all Schorr said as he moved through the doorway when another mortar round landed. Where it hit couldn't be seen as it landed behind the advisor bunker, but there was no doubt in Schorr's mind what it hit. The rising smoke and falling debris told him his jeep was gone. Looking back to the perimeter, he saw the Vietnamese soldiers stripping off their shirts and tossing down their weapons. Even the officers were stripping down and moving to the gate. It didn't take long before Schorr, Josh, Hacker and Eisenhower found themselves to be the only ones remaining along with two Kit Carson Scouts and the wounded.[2] Fortunately, the NVA were concentrating on the departing soldiers and not on the empty firebase.

Running back on the advisor bunker, Schorr was back on the radio and placed a call to Lieutenant Colonel Stovall at LZ Crystal.

"Raven Six, Raven Four-Oh. Request immediate extraction. Friendlies have bugged out. We are departing and moving south, over. How copy?"

"Raven Four-Oh, understood."

"Four-Oh out," Schorr transmitted, then disconnected the AN/PRC-77 radio from the R-292 coaxial cable and headed out the door. As he did so, he grabbed an M-79 grenade launcher and a bandolier of ammo for the weapon as well as additional ammo for his M16. Josh had picked up a discarded M16 as well and a bandolier of ammo for it along with some magazines.

* * *

Lieutenant Colonel Stovall switched frequencies on his radio.

"Ruthless Raider Six, Raven Six, over." Ruthless Raider had been working for Stovall all morning, conducting reconnaissance around LZ Crystal. He had a flight of two UH-1H aircraft and two AH-1G aircraft.

"Raven Six, Ruthless Raider, over."

"Ruthless Raider, our advisors at LZ English say the ARVNs are leaving and they're under attack. They're calling for an immediate extraction. Can you handle that? Over."

"Raven Six, affirmative, over."

"Roger, come to Crystal and pick me up and I'll go with you, over."

"Roger, Raven, I'm five minutes from your location." Stovall attempted to contact Schorr, to no avail. *Damn, I hope we can get there in time*, he was thinking as he grabbed his steel pot and weapon and departed for the helipad.

* * *

"Okay, we're out of here. We'll head south. It appears the bad guys are fixated on the guys on the road, so we're heading away from them. Let's go," Schorr said, pointing the way to a break in the wire on the south side.

The two Kit Carson Scouts immediately moved to take the lead, heading downhill away from LZ English. At the base of the hill, they started out across a rice paddy when they caught the attention of the NVA, which started a half-hearted pursuit by one platoon. Lieutenant Eisenhower was serving as rear guard and was able to force the NVA to keep their distance. Schorr would turn on cue from Eisenhower and fire a grenade in the direction of the NVA. Josh found himself adding firepower to Eisenhower as well at times.

As they reached the far side of the rice paddy, they started up an embankment.

"Damn!" Schorr yelled out and collapsed. His leg had taken a hit and gave out.

"How bad, sir?" Josh asked, kneeling down beside him.

"Not much pain. I don't see a lot of blood, so they didn't get an artery," Schorr said as Josh tore his pant leg open and began sprinkling the wound with disinfectant. As Josh saw to Schorr, Hacker and Eisenhower along with the scouts set up a perimeter and engaged the force attempting to approach.

"As long as they don't get some reinforcements, we should have enough ammo to keep them at bay until a chopper arrives," Schorr said in an attempt to keep morale high.

"Did they say how far out the chopper was, sir?" Eisenhower asked.

"Afraid not."

This wasn't the response everyone wanted to hear. After what seemed like hours but was less than one, the sounds of rotor blades could be heard and the radio squelch broke.

"Raven Four-Oh, Ruthless Raider Six, over."

"Ruthless Raider Six, Raven Four-Oh, we are one klick south of the LZ on the side of a rice paddy. We have contact between us and the LZ approximately two hundred meters from our position, over."

"Raven Four-Oh, understood. We're coming in, be ready."

Turning to the group, Schorr said, "Okay, guys, get ready to move when he touches down. When he's on short final, empty your magazines to give him some cover fire."

The sounds of the rotor blades on the UH-1H announced his arrival to the NVA, who became more interested in the helicopter than a group of five guys. As the UH-1H approached, the NVA directed their small-arms fire at it. That was a mistake, as they soon found out.

"We're taking fire," the door gunner yelled as the tapping

sounds on the side of the aircraft grew louder and more frequent. Stovall began returning fire with his M16.

Ruthless Raider Six was flown by Lieutenant Colonel Jack Anderson, who commanded the 7th Squadron of the 17th Cav. Typical of lieutenant colonel aviators, he was on his second tour and was noted for his aggressive actions. He was also noted for his innovations. Unlike the average UH-1H aircraft, which was equipped with only one M60 machine gun on each side, Anderson's aircraft was equipped with one .50-cal machine gun on each side. Although the cyclic rate of the M2 50-caliber machine gun was slightly slower, by one hundred rounds per minute, than the M60 machine gun, it had greater penetration, longer distance and a much deadlier bullet. Hit in the arm with a round from the M60 and you live to fight another day. Hit in the arm with a round from the M2 and you lose the arm if not your life.

As Ruthless Raider Six entered the pickup zone, both guns began shooting, with the nose of the aircraft facing the enemy for the most part. Both guns were firing forward. Lieutenant Colonel Stovall was emptying the clip on his M16 in support of the two .50-cal machine guns. The NVA made the mistake of leaving their cover and charging towards Schorr and party as well as the helicopter as it came to a landing. Schorr and party opened fire with everything they had when the enemy was one hundred and fifty meters from them. They were getting kills, but the NVA pressed forward until Anderson landed and his two M2s opened fire on the advancing enemy. The enemy began to slow, stagger and die as the M2 machine guns ripped through their ranks.

"Go!" Schorr yelled as the aircraft began to touch down. The Kit Carson Scouts wasted no time grabbing him under his arms and half carrying and half dragging him to the aircraft. As they approached the right side of the aircraft, the door gunner had to cease shooting so they could get aboard. Stovall reached down and grabbed Schorr as the Kit Carson Scouts dragged him aboard and everyone else started to scramble on behind him.

"Go, go, go," the door gunner transmitted over the intercom when the last person wasn't yet aboard but was standing on the skids. Anderson picked the aircraft up and executed a right pedal turn, allowing his crew chief to continue to suppress the enemy as the aircraft performed a combat takeoff.

"Where to?" Anderson asked Schorr as they climbed to altitude.

"Take us to the nearest hospital. Thanks for saving our asses. I owe you one," Schorr said as he rested his back on the transmission wall and gave a wink to Stovall. Seated beside him was Josh.

"How you feeling, sir?" Josh asked.

"It's beginning to throb a bit. First, I want to see Duc," Schorr said.

"Sir, did you expect him to run like that?" Josh asked.

"Truthfully, no, but this was the first major engagement I've seen him in. Every other time it was small engagements, platoon- and squad-size stuff. He just wasn't ready to handle something like this. He panicked, and when he did, his soldiers did as well. If the ARVNs do this every time they get into a major engagement, they're going to lose this war."

$$33$$

THE DEFENSE

20 APRIL 1972
II Corps HQ
Pleiku

GENERAL DZU HAD CALLED a meeting to discuss the defensive plan. The debacle at LZ English had shaken him up, and he wanted to review everything with everyone. Mr. Vann was present, along with General Wear and Colonel Snell. Major Steinhauer had also been asked to attend as he'd been at LZ English when it was evacuated along with Major Hacker. Each of the regimental advisors was present as well as Kaplan and Colonel Kellar from the 23rd Division. Dzu also requested that Colonel Thinh, the Kontum Province chief, along with his advisor, Colonel Bachinski, be in attendance. Two faces he did not expect to see were Major Givens, who Dzu would learn shortly was the advisor for the 6th Ranger Group, and Colonel Lich, commander of the 2nd Airborne Brigade, along with his advisor Lieutenant Colonel Kama.

Dzu started the discussion. "Gentlemen, I want to review

the plan for the defense of our sector, but first, I must ask, who are you and why are you here, Major Givens?"

Givens stood and glanced around the room. "Sir, I'm the advisor for the 6th Ranger Group, which—" He didn't get to finish before Colonel Lich stood.

"Excuse me, General, but I've been ordered to take the 2nd Airborne Brigade and return to Saigon. The 6th Ranger Group will be replacing us starting today. I thought you knew about this," Lich said almost apologetically. Dzu flashed a confused look at Vann, who simply shrugged, indicating that he was in the dark as well.

"Where is the commander of the 6th Ranger Group?" Dzu asked in a terse manner.

"Sir, Lieutenant Colonel De will bring the 34th and 35th Battalions on the twenty-fourth and we will begin a relief in place with the 2nd Airborne Brigade units at FSB Lam Son outside of Vo Dinh," Major Givens said, feeling the heat of the moment and hoping for an out.

"Where is the 6th coming from?" Dzu asked.

"Sir, we've been in the A Shau Valley, fighting west of Hue. We have to refit and regroup before we're combat-ready again," Major Givens stated.

Vann threw him a lifeline. "Major, see me after this and we can work out the details with my operations people," he said. The relief on Major Givens's face was obvious. Dzu, however, was not satisfied.

"Who should we replace the airborne units on Rocket Ridge with until the 6th arrives?" Dzu asked.

"General, I would recommend that we bring the 53rd Regiment of the 23rd up and have them replace the airborne units until the 6th arrives. It'll only be for a week or so and the 53rd sector is very quiet," Colonel Snell offered.

Dzu thought about that option for a moment before he spoke. "I will take that under advisement and decide later."

Dzu looked at Vann, who simply raised his hand as if to say, "I got it. Calm down," then shifted his gaze around the room. "Has anyone seen Colonel Duc?" he asked. Blank stares met his question. "Can someone tell me what happened at LZ English yesterday?" His voice betrayed his anger.

Josh looked around and stood. "Excuse me, sir, but I was there until we were extracted."

"And who are you?" Dzu asked.

"General, this is Major Josh Steinhauer, an observer from Washington, looking at the advisors' role in Vietnam," Vann answered. "He was at English yesterday with Colonel Schorr, who was wounded," he explained and then turned to Josh. "Major, tell the general what you saw."

"Sir, everything was planned for a departure at 1200 hours. At about 1000 hours, we started receiving some accurate incoming artillery. Colonel Duc came out of the command bunker at about 1030 hours and said to leave immediately. He got into his APC and rolled out the gate with several others, to include staff and subordinate commanders, following him. When the troops saw them leave, the soldiers tore off their uniforms, dropped their weapons and ran out the gate behind them. By 1115, only the wounded and the advisors were left in the camp. We left at about 1120 and went out the south side of the perimeter," Josh explained.

Dzu just stood for a moment and said nothing. Finally, he turned to Vann. "Let's review our plan for the defense of Kontum."

Going to the map board, Vann began, "We intend to defend at Dak To II and Tan Canh with the 42nd and 47th Regiments of the 22nd. They will hold and force the enemy to bunch up and be subjected to B-52 strikes. Colonel Dat, you have to get your forces out front on the high ground. Make contact with the enemy as soon and as far out as possible so we can bring maximum airpower on him," Vann said.

"We have been fighting this war long time. I know what I need to do," Dat said with a show of anger and indignation.

"Colonel Dat, if you don't force him to bunch up so we can hit him with B-52s, you're going to be the first division commander to lose your division, because you're going to be overrun unless you get out in front of them," Vann said.

"Oh, that not happen," Dat said, almost laughing.

Vann turned to Colonel Kaplan. "I'll send you a postcard in the POW camp."

"Not to me you won't because I won't be in one," Kaplan responded and pointed at Dat. "You can address it to him." Kaplan had already voiced his frustrations with Vann about Dat's lack of leadership and pessimistic attitude. Dat really expected the United States to return to the ground battle with troops despite Kaplan telling him it would not happen. Dat was also convinced that the North Vietnamese were superior forces. General Wear witnessed this exchange and figured it was going nowhere good, so he stepped into the conversation.

"Gentlemen, it appears that currently Rocket Ridge is holding the enemy at bay. Dak Pek has reported that they're still in control of their compound and they have a body count of over two hundred with few casualties. What should concern us at this point is this action with the 1st Battalion, 42nd north of Dak To II. There's an indication that this may be the 2nd NVA Division, which we've been looking for. We need to confirm that and have a plan to deal with it, Colonel Dat," Wear said, but Dat wasn't listening or didn't acknowledge that he understood. There was a momentary pause in the conversation that provoked Dzu to pick up the briefing.

"We need to ensure unity of command, so I have decided that General Dat will be responsible for Dak Pek, Dak Sang, Ben Het, Dak To II, Dak To and Tan Canh. Those forces in those locations report to him. The forces on Rocket Ridge will now report to the 6th Ranger Group. All forces in Kontum City will be under the command of Colonel Thinh, the province chief, and Colonel Tuong will command all forces in Pleiku. The 23rd Division will be responsible for his sector but also expand to control Highway 19 and An Khe, ensuring the road stays open. This road must be kept open or we are going to run low on supplies," Dzu directed. Vann was seen jotting down a note. "General Dat, please tell us how your forces will be positioned," Dzu asked.

Dat had regained his composure from his discussion with Vann. "I have the 47th Regiment in Dak To II with one tank company as well as the 9th Airborne Battalion. One company from this regiment is on Rocket Ridge. The 42nd Regiment is in Tan Canh along with my command post and one battalion from the 41st Regiment. The 1st, 4th and 2nd Battalions of the 42nd are in Tan Canh along with the engineer battalion and the reconnaissance company. The 3rd Battalion is located at Dien Binh on Highway 14 eight miles southeast. One of 3rd Battalion's companies is on FSB 5 and one platoon is on FSB 6. I also have positioned four tanks at Tan Canh. Then I would ask that when the relief in place is made between the airborne brigade and the Ranger group, one battalion from the Ranger group comes to Dak To II. Supporting the division is fifty tubes of artillery in a combination of 105 and 155mm howitzers."

Vann cringed when it was mentioned that the 47th would be holding Dak To II. The 47th was commanded by Colonel Tran Huu Minh, in Vann's opinion one of the most incompetent commanders in the South Vietnamese Army.

"Excuse me, Colonel Dat, but the 1st Battalion was surrounded a few days ago and the relief force hasn't reached them. I believe we have had only sixty-three of the original three hundred and sixty make it back to Tan Canh," Kaplan said. If looks could kill, Kaplan would be dead as Dat stared at him.

"Please explain, Colonel Dat," Dzu asked.

"Sir, we're in contact with the battalion commander and they're in a fighting withdrawal at this time" was Dat's answer.

Kaplan said nothing during the brief but didn't appear to be happy. When Dat announced that four tanks, M41s, were at Tan Canh, he showed obvious disgust, which Dzu noted. "Colonel Kaplan, you have something to say?"

"Sir, tanks are a mobile resource. To place them in a static position at Tan Canh is the wrong employment of these vital assets. They should be consolidated and remain mobile to take advantage of their speed and maneuver and to be employed as a counterattack force," Kaplan said. He didn't divulge that Dat and his armor commander had already had this discussion and Dat had overruled the commander.

"Where is the 14th Armor now?" Dzu asked.

"The 14th is at Ben Het to meet any force coming down Highway 512. The 19th is providing security between Pleiku and Tan Canh," Dat responded.

"How many tanks do you have that are operational?"

"Between the 14th and the 19th, we have fifty M41 tanks," Dat responded.

"In fixed positions," Kaplan pointed out. Dzu was on the spot for a decision as to what to do with his most mobile force.

"What obstacles have we emplaced?" Dzu asked Dat.

"Sir, the Highway 14 and Highway 512 bridges have been prepared with demolitions by the engineers for destruction. In addition, we have antitank killer teams at both locations and a recoilless rifle guarding the Highway 512 bridge," Dat announced with a degree of confidence.

"Colonel Dat has his plan and his resources" was all Dzu would say. Kaplan rolled his eyes and gave up the argument.

"Colonel Thinh, what forces do you have in Kontum at this time?" Dzu asked.

"Sir, at this time I have two Ranger battalions and the Regional and Popular Forces."

"We have a ground plan," Dzu announced, "but what about our logistics?"

Lieutenant Colonel Dick, the SRAG G-4 advisor, fielded the question. "Sir, as of the sixteenth, we had only a three-day of supplies in Kontum since Highway 19 was closed at the An Khe Pass. We've since been receiving resupply by the US Air Force with C-130s, and soon C-141s will be joining the flow. Some of the C-130s will bring in forty-five-hundred-gallon fuel bladders. Those aircraft bringing in cargo will depart with refugees and take them to Tan San Nhut. The C-141s can carry over three hundred passengers on their return flights. As long as we control the airfield at Kontum, we should have adequate supplies until the road can be opened," Dick concluded.

"Are the Koreans working on opening the road?" Dzu asked, looking at Snell.

"Sir, Mr. Vann has spoken with the Korean commander and they're working on the issue. However, it appears that it'll be a few more days before it's cleared and then a week to repair the road so trucks can cross," Snell explained.

Vann had been all for having the two regiments positioned far forward to bunch the enemy so the B-52s could pound the enemy back into the Stone Age. Now, having heard Dat's plan, he wasn't so sure that Dat was going to be able to pull it off. General Wear had argued for a delaying action by the regiments falling back into Kontum. Vann had originally been opposed as he felt that what would commence as an orderly withdrawal/delaying action would quickly turn into a rout, with Vietnamese soldiers running for their lives minus their equipment and certainly not standing and fighting.

"General Dzu, maybe we should consider having a delay plan and withdrawal plan back to Kontum that would be an on-call execution. Colonel Kaplan and Colonel Dat can work out the details and get back to us the day after tomorrow. Would that be acceptable, Colonel Kaplan?" Vann asked.

Damn, boss, why couldn't you have come up with this a couple of weeks ago so we could have planned and rehearsed it? Kaplan was thinking. "Yes, sir, I believe we can have a plan ready for you in two days," he announced without looking at Dat. Vann looked over at Dzu and then Wear, and both were indicating by their facial expressions that they approved.

34

GENERAL MINH'S FINAL BRIEF

20 APRIL 1972
  B-3 Front HQ
  Base Camp 609

GENERAL HOANG MINH THAO wanted to review the final plans with the commanders. Seated around the table were Colonel Kim Tuan, commander of the 320th Division; Colonel Nguyen Chon, the 2nd Division commander; Colonel Khuat Duy Tien of the 64th Independent Regiment; and all regimental commanders of the divisions as well as battalion commanders. Thao wanted everyone to understand his commander's intent. Once everyone was seated, General Thao began.

"Gentlemen, I have called you here for one last discussion before we launch our attack. We have successfully driven the ARVNs off the two southern firebases on what they call Rocket Ridge. The two northern firebases are still occupied and we must remove those people as well. Once we control that ridge, we can then complete the destruction of forces in Tan Canh and Dak To II. I believe we can do that now as the two northern firebases can control Highway 512 with artillery but not Highway 14. Their occupation will delay our ability to take out Ben Het and move down Highway 512, but that is only a minor matter. It appears that they expect our main attack to come down Highway 512 as they have positioned the 14th Armored Squadron with twelve tanks at Ben Het. This prompts a minor change in plans," Thao said, refocusing his look at Colonel Tuan. "Colonel Tuan, I want you to establish an ambush site at the bridge over the Dak Poko River on Highway 512. There is high ground there and excellent ambush sites. This force must prevent the tanks at Ben Het from reinforcing Dak To II. Understood?"

"Yes, sir, it will be done," Tuan responded and began writing some notes.

"Colonel Chon, you and your engineers have worked a miracle pushing that two-hundred-kilometer road through the jungle and not being detected. That has allowed us to move supplies, men and tanks within striking range of Dak To II. The engineers should be congratulated for even constructing bunkers almost to the wire without being detected. Thankfully the enemy does not believe in active patrolling or we would not have been able to accomplish this," Thao said before he paused and acknowledged the 7th Engineer Regiment commander with a smile and a nod.

"Colonel Curong, unfortunately your seizure of Firebase English did not force Dzu to shift forces to the east, but your closure of Highway 19 at An Khe and Highway 14 between Pleiku and Kontum has seriously disrupted the enemy's ability to resupply his forces at Tan Canh and Dak To II. My congratulations. Are you going to be able to continue to keep Highway 19 closed?"

"Sir, the Koreans along with the 44th Regiment of the 23rd Division are working together to open Highway 19. I think we can hold it for another week, however," Colonel Curong said.

"I know you will do your best, Colonel. In the next three days everything and everyone will be in position, and I believe we should commence our ground attack on the morning of the twenty-fourth. In the meantime we will continue to concentrate our artillery fires on both Tan Canh and Dak To II. When the assault commences on Tan Canh, we will shift all our fires to Dak To II. This will prevent reinforcements from Dak To II from reaching Tan Canh. My intent is to pound both locations before the ground attack commences, with priority for the artillery on the enemy's artillery positions first, then crew-served weapons and command bunkers. The biggest threat we will face is the airpower that they might bring against us. We have sufficient air-defense weapons with the 12th Air Defense Battalion in the 2nd Division sector. They must keep the enemy's attack helicopters away. We have been given the Russian air-defense missile and will employ that against his jets if possible," Thao said, pausing and looking at the faces of his subordinate commanders. All he saw was confidence around the table.

"Okay, Colonel Chon, will you discuss your ground plan with us?" Thao said, sitting down. Chon stood but remained in place.

"The 2nd Division has moved into positions on the high ground north of Tan Canh and Dak To II. We can observe the interior of both places and have identified their artillery positions as well as command bunkers. In addition, we have located their ammunition supply points and tank positions. Rather than keeping the tanks in a mobile reserve, they have positioned them as if they were fixed fighting positions. The 66th Infantry Regiment, 37th Sapper Battalion, and the 7th Tank Company for the 297th Tank Battalion will make the main attack on Tan Canh. The 1st Regiment will make a supporting attack from the opposite side of the compound. They will be supported by the 40th and 675th Artillery Regiments, who are in position at this time. Once Tan Canh has been overrun, the ground assault on Dak To

II will commence with the 1st Regiment of the division supported by the 10th Sapper Battalion. The 7th Tank Company will, upon overrunning Tan Canh, dispatch four tanks down Highway 512 to Dak To II. I anticipate that we will control both locations by 1200 hours and have eliminated the enemy totally by 1700 hours," Colonel Chon outlined.

"Very good, Colonel Chon," General Thao said. "Colonel Tuan, please tell us about your plans." As Tuan stood, Colonel Chon took his seat.

"General, the 320th will continue to apply pressure on the two northern firebases as well as continue to remove any forces between the ridge and Highway 14. The last southern firebase, I believe, will fall tomorrow as we are building a road to that location and tomorrow will move tanks up to the firebase. I believe we can have the last of the enemy removed from the ridge by the twenty-fifth and begin to move against Ben Het. We have forces moving towards Polei Kleng at this time and they have been building a road towards that objective. This will position us for the assault on Kontum," Tuan stated.

"Very good, Colonel. I anticipate that your division will be in the best condition for the assault on Kontum with the 2nd Division supporting you from the north, but will finalize our plans for this at a later date," General Thao said, standing. "I will be available to discuss any further concerns that you have. I believe that we have a solid plan, and I only see success in this first phase. Let us go forth and hand our people victory!"

35

FSB DELTA FALLS

21 April 1972
  6th Airborne Battalion
  FSB Delta

CAPTAIN O'BRIEN HAD RISEN early as he was suspicious of the sounds he had heard during the night. The LPs had reported the sounds of heavy engines all through the night as well as the sound of chainsaws.[1] Aside from that, the night had been quiet...too quiet in his mind. For the past twenty days they had been under constant probes and assaults. The wire around the firebase held numerous bodies in various stages of decomposition and the stench was becoming overwhelming. Soldiers wore bandannas around their faces to help reduce the odor, but it didn't do much good. As it would be light soon, O'Brien moved around the perimeter to make sure that everyone was ready and to give some encouragement to the soldiers. In his opinion, properly led, these were good soldiers.

The day before, a company of Rangers from the 6th Ranger Group had been inserted to reinforce the airborne soldiers that had been in the fight for a month. Looking at the two groups, it was easy to see who was airborne and who was Rangers. The Rangers had been in combat for the better part of a month as well and they looked it. Torn uniforms, sunken cheekbones for lack of food, and dark circles under their eyes that were obvious to anyone. The airborne troops had maintained their uniforms and had been well supplied with rations, so their appearance was better. Looking at their positions also indicated a higher degree of discipline as fighting positions were well maintained. The Rangers in just one day had allowed trash to accumulate in their fighting positions, and repairs to the bunkers hadn't been made. O'Brien made a mental note to talk to the Ranger company commander. As O'Brien walked along the north perimeter, he noticed some commotion.

"Dai'uy," O'Brien half whispered, gaining the company commander's attention, "what is going on?"

"This soldier is LP. He say they come. He hear heavy engine sound. He say many soldiers walking up hill," the Vietnamese captain said, pointing at a young soldier standing next to him. O'Brien could see fear written all over the soldier's face and knew he needed to do something fast to calm the fears.

Pulling out his map and laying it on the ground, he pulled the soldier down. "Show me on the map where your position was and where you heard the sounds," he directed the young man. O'Brien already knew the LP's position but wanted to steady the kid. Finally the soldier pointed on the map right where O'Brien knew the LP to be and then dragged his finger to where he thought the sound was coming from. O'Brien took out his grease pencil and placed an X at that point.

"Dai'uy, I'm going to call for fire support. Be ready, because they're going to come at you as soon as the rounds hit them," O'Brien said. The captain acknowledged O'Brien with a nod and began moving along the perimeter, instructing his soldiers.

O'Brien jogged back to the command post and told the

battalion commander the situation. He then got on the radio, calling a fire mission for artillery after he put a call into Colonel Kama and requested an air strike at first light. Shortly, the sound of artillery firing could be heard in the distance from the east, with impacting rounds following almost immediately afterwards. His intention was to start the artillery close to the perimeter and walk it out towards the location of the heavy equipment. Almost immediately after the first round impacted, automatic weapons fire started, and it was AK-47 by the sound of it. Grabbing his PRC-77 radio, O'Brien jogged back to the previous location on the perimeter. Green tracers criss-crossed the perimeter and red tracers reached out to engage muzzle flashes.

"Dai'uy, what have you got?" O'Brien asked as he dove into the trench line under fire.

"Artillery hit very close. Enemy was almost in wire when it hit. Very good that artillery begin here and not out there," the Vietnamese captain said with a smile.

Surveying the situation, O'Brien decided to call for his final protective fires. Reaching the fire direction center for the battalion, O'Brien ordered the FPF to be laid in since the enemy was on the perimeter. This was a full-blown ground attack. Before the FPF started, three barrels, partially dug into the ground and facing the enemy, erupted, throwing a fountain of flaming thickened diesel fuel over a wide area containing attacking enemy soldiers. The defenders watched the flaming bodies stopped in the wire and now dying. Soldiers quickly engaged and mercifully shot those engulfed. This caused the enemy to withdraw at that point, but the attack continued all along the perimeter, and as first light came, so did supporting artillery and mortars from the North Vietnamese observers who sat on the surrounding hills.

Throughout the day, O'Brien continued to move around the perimeter, directing artillery fire and attack helicopters when he could get them along with TACAIR fighters.

TACAIR fighters were at a premium along with B-52s that were supporting the battle raging around Quang Tri to the north. The fight in III Corps around An Loc was still undecided as the 5th Airborne Battalion had sacrificed the 1st Company the day before as they were pushed off a hill mass known as Windy Hill and were retreating to find a landing zone for extraction. TACAIR across Vietnam was in high demand.

As the day wore on, the ground attack didn't falter but continued, with several points on the perimeter being penetrated and then taken back by the defenders. Enemy artillery was out of range for friendly artillery to engage and O'Brien was hoping that the attack helicopters or the FAC could identify the enemy artillery and take it out, but no success in that effort was being realized. O'Brien had to face facts—the battalion might not be able to hold out. Ammo was running low and no resupply was able to get to them. Getting on his radio, he called Lieutenant Colonel Kama.

"Six-Five, Six-Five-Bravo," O'Brien transmitted.

"Bravo, Six-Five, go ahead" came the response from Kama.

"Six-Five, I don't think we can hold out much longer. We're low on ammo and their artillery fire is damn accurate. TACAIR is the only thing really keeping them at bay, and it'll be dark soon, which will end that support. Over," O'Brien reported.

"Bravo, when you think it's time to get out, you're authorized to do so. Your counterpart is getting the same order now," Kama informed him.

O'Brien went looking for the battalion commander almost immediately. When he found him, he approached slowly as the colonel didn't look happy.

"Sir, I've been told that evacuating is your decision. Whatever you decide, I'm with you," O'Brien said. For only a moment, the colonel looked at him.

"We go now!" the colonel said, which surprised O'Brien. "I

get report from 1st Company. Tanks on west perimeter. We go now. Go east."

O'Brien had been in the advisor bunker talking to Kama and didn't know about the tanks. With all the explosions from incoming rounds and small-arms fire, he hadn't heard the tanks approaching. Not waiting for further instructions, O'Brien grabbed his PRC-77 radio and stuffed it into his backpack. In his mind, he needed water, ammo and that radio. As he moved to the eastern perimeter, he observed the airborne soldiers around the perimeter collapse in an orderly fashion towards the escape route out the wire on the east side. He also noticed the mad scramble by the Rangers towards that same opening.

As it was now 1930 hours, Covey Triple Nickel had been replaced by Covey Five-Four-Six.

"Covey Five-Four-Six, Six-Five-Bravo, over."

"Six-Five-Bravo, Covey Five-Four-Six" was heard as Covey circled above in the fading light at eight thousand feet.

"Covey Five-Four-Six, Six-Five-Bravo is moving out the east side of the base. We have tanks at the west side perimeter, over."

"Roger, Six-Five-Bravo, I'll take care of that problem in a minute," Covey responded. Moments later a rocket slammed into the main gate of the firebase and emitted a white column of smoke. This was quickly followed by several explosions and a swath of napalm over the tanks and the enemy soldiers around them, delivered by two F-4 Phantom jets. O'Brien's last transmission from Firebase Delta was at 1930 hours, informing Kama of the situation and their direction of movement.

* * *

MR. VANN HAD BEEN RECEIVING reports from Colonel Kama on the situation on FSB Delta. However, he had another problem that had to be taken care of, one that prevented him from flying up to observe the action. Walking into General

Wear's office, Vann observed his deputy. Wear did not look good physically. The bloody handkerchief on his desk told the story.

"General, you look like shit," Vann said.

Wear looked up from what he was reading. His breathing was labored. "Hell, I'll be okay just as soon as I shake this whatever it is," Wear said.

Vann moved closer to Wear's desk. "General, you need to get to a hospital, and something more than what we have here or in Kontum," Vann said.

Wear just looked up at him. "You're going to need me in the coming days. I can't be leaving you high and dry. Not now."

Vann stood for a moment, staring at his confidant. Finally, he dropped to his knees beside Wear's desk and clasped his hands together. "George, please go away and rest. I'm going to need you later to help with Kontum."[2]

"Maybe you're right," Wear said with resignation. "I'll make the calls and try to get to the Philippines tomorrow if I can get a hop."

"Good. I'll have a plane standing by to fly you to Tan Son Nhut as soon as you're ready to leave," Vann said, standing up and walking to the door. He turned. "George, just concentrate on getting better and then getting back here."

Vann went to his office and picked up the phone. His first call was to lay on an airplane to carry Wear to Saigon. His second call was to General Weyand at MACV headquarters.

"Weyand, Vann here. Hey, I'm putting George on a plane and sending him to the hospital in the Philippines. Whatever it is that he has is really getting bad. I'm going to need a replacement and quick," Vann said.

"Well, John, I don't think I have any generals sitting around with nothing to do," Weyand replied.

"Yeah, you do. General Hill, the former deputy commander for the 101st, is sitting at Cam Rahn Bay twiddling his thumbs. I've worked with him before and want him," Vann responded.

"Let me look into this and I'll see if we can break him loose and send him your way. I'll get back to you." Hanging up the phone on Vann, Weyand dialed Brigadier General John Hill's number at Cam Rahn Bay.

General John Hill was a West Point graduate and had a distinguished combat record in Korea. He was an Army aviator and had been the assistant division commander of the 101st Airborne Division, which had only recently returned to the States. Hill had known John Paul Vann for years and the two had even worked together at one time. Hill wasn't a fan of Vann, thinking Vann was arrogant, abrasive and self-centered, but he knew if anyone could convince the Vietnamese to do anything, it was John Paul Vann.

"General Hill, General Weyand here. Look, we have a situation in II Corps and we need you to get up to Pleiku and take over as the senior military officer at SRAG II," Weyand outlined. "You'll be working for John Paul Vann, who's the director there."

"Sir, am I being asked if I want the job or being ordered to the job?" Hill asked.

"You're being ordered. Why, do you have a problem with Vann?" Weyand asked with some concern.

"Sir, if I'm being ordered, then I'll pack and get up there right away. If I'm being asked if I want to work with the guy, my answer is hell no. I know John, but I'm a soldier and I take orders. I'll get up there as soon as I can. I have a few things that I'll need to clean up here before I can head up there," Hill replied.

"Good, I'll let him know that you'll be there soon," Weyand said, hanging the phone up.

The next day, General Wear departed for Clark Air Force Base in the Philippines. He never returned to SRAG II.[3]

36

THE END BEGINS

23 April 1972
  22nd Division HQ
  Tan Canh

COLONEL KAPLAN WALKED into the division command post after his morning coffee at 0600 with Lieutenant Colonel McClain, Major Wise, Captain Dobbins and Captain Yonan in the advisor bunker. All month, the base camp had been receiving incoming artillery rounds and mortars, but this morning was starting off with what appeared to be a bit more intensity. Major Wise and Lieutenant Colonel McClain, Kaplan's deputy, accompanied him. Upon entering, Kaplan's usual routine was to read night dispatches from SRAG II. One dispatch caught his eye.

"Hey, guys, look at this," he said, calling Wise and McClain over. "This is from Captain John Kellar, the district advisor. He sent it to SRAG last night at 2330 hours. Seems he reported enemy vehicles moving west to northwest. SRAG II says they were trucks."

"God, I hope they're right. From the buildup we've seen

lately and the increased incoming artillery, I hope to God they're not tanks," McClain said. As they discussed the possibility of tanks, they were interrupted by the sounds of an aircraft approaching.

"Sounds like an OH-58. Probably Vann dropping in for a discussion with Dat. Has anyone seen Dat this morning?" Kaplan asked.

"Probably still hiding in his bunker," Wise said under his breath. "I'll go see what the helicopter is bringing us," he announced as he picked up his steel pot and headed out the door, pausing long enough for the latest incoming round to hit and explode. Then he sprinted out the door towards the approaching aircraft. Moments later he returned, trailing behind Mr. Vann.

"Good morning, gentlemen. Where is Colonel Dat?" Vann asked.

"Sir, we haven't seen him this morning. He's probably still in his bunker," Kaplan explained.

"No matter. We want you to start your plan on withdrawing from Tan Canh and Dak To II. We're planning to move the troops off FSB 5 and 6 as they're no longer tenable. Start displacing your artillery back to Binh Dinh. How are you going to displace the battalions back?" Vann asked.

"Sir, the plan is to first displace ten tubes of artillery and then begin to displace the infantry battalions, half a battalion at a time, starting with the 47th. We lost a tube and nine hundred rounds of 105 ammo yesterday when an incoming round landed right on the tube," Kaplan explained.

"Good, execute the withdrawal plan. With all the FSBs falling into the hands of the enemy, staying here is not the most prudent thing to do. We will have a new plan for you tomorrow on your next positions around Kontum. Any questions?" Vann asked.

"Is Dat getting an order to execute?" McClain asked.

"He should have it within an hour. Contact me if he doesn't get it or questions it. I'll be in the air, watching the extraction on Five and Six," Vann said as he headed back outside to join his aircraft.

"Jon, why don't you get with the Ops people and get them started on issuing an order? We want to be able to close out as soon as possible," Kaplan directed.

"Yes, sir," Major Wise said and moved over to the operations section in the division command post.

The division command post was one hundred feet long and thirty feet wide. It sat six feet above ground and about two feet below ground. It was constructed of creosote timbers and sandbag walls three feet thick. Window openings were along the sides with an entrance door at each end. A double roof protected the top from incoming artillery rounds. The interior was divided by sandbag walls with a commo section, operations section, intelligence section and advisor section. Under normal circumstances it was more than adequate, but these were not normal circumstances.

After coffee, Captain Raymond Dobbins had gone to the 42nd Regimental command post, where he served as the acting senior advisor. The 1st Battalion had been in contact and stragglers were still coming into the base camp. Dobbins was convinced that the enemy was nearby and closing in on the camp. He had moved outside and was sitting on top of the regimental bunker, looking for enemy movement along with the regimental commander. The perimeter had been cleared for five hundred meters out of any vegetation or anything that would afford cover and concealment to the enemy. He was easily scanning the open terrain despite the incoming artillery and mortar fire.

An M41 tank returned through the main gate and stopped to offload a wounded crewmember. Dobbins watched as the tank suddenly blew up. *What the hell?* he thought. *How the hell did they get so close with an RPG?* he was asking himself when he called Kaplan and reported that the tank had been destroyed by an RPG rocket.

In the division command bunker, Kaplan and McClain couldn't understand how an RPG with an effective range of two hundred and fifty to three hundred meters could have destroyed the tank. The enemy wasn't that close.

"Hey, Major Carter," McClain called out. Major Carter was the senior advisor to the 14th Armored Cavalry Regiment and just happened to be in the command bunker at the time. Carter approached. "Is it possible for an RPG to take out a tank at a range of over five hundred meters?" McClain asked.

"Possible, yes. Likely, no. It would have to be a damn fine gunner to achieve that, and I doubt if the weapon has any accuracy over three hundred meters. Motor burnout couldn't possibly carry the round past maybe three hundred and fifty— why?" Carter asked.

"We just got a report from Captain Dobbins that a tank was destroyed and the closest enemy was about five hundred meters away," Kaplan added. "Let's go have a look at this."

All three officers headed outside and moved to the location of the tank. Arriving, McClain began examining the damage.

"What is all this copper wire?" he questioned as he began rolling up about thirty feet of fine copper wire.

"Here's the tail fins, and there's some wire attached as well," Kaplan said, bending over and picking it up. "Let's get back to the TOC and examine this stuff." Before they left, Carter climbed on the tank and examined the silver-dollar-sized hole in the turret. A closer examination of the inside revealed three dead soldiers and an interior totally destroyed. Returning to the command post, they began a closer examination.

"Sir, the writing on these fins is Russian," Wise stated, looking closely at the fins.

"This copper wire must somehow control this thing, activating these four jet nozzles," Kaplan pointed out.

"Sir, I think we're looking at an AT-3 Sagger missile," Carter said. "The range on these things is about two klicks and it's guided to the target through these wires, with a gunner flying the missile to the target."

"If that's true, then this changes things in a big way. How do we defeat the damn thing?" Kaplan asked.

"We can't," Carter said. "If it can't be seen, it can't be killed. Only thing is the thing can't be effective at night as the gunner can't see the targets. I think—" Carter didn't finish as an explosion ripped through the division command post and darkness engulfed everyone.

Kaplan was regaining consciousness as the darkness and blurred vision began to disappear. Picking himself up slowly, he felt the blood oozing down the side of his face. McClain was talking to him, but he couldn't hear a word he was saying. Finally his hearing began to return.

"Sir, are you alright? Sir?" McClain repeated as he and Carter took Kaplan under the arms and assisted him in standing.

"Thanks, I think so," Kaplan said, wiping the side of his face and noticing the blood on his hands. "Where is Wise?"

McClain began looking around in the darkness and found Wise under a pile of sandbags from a collapsed wall. Wise was moaning but not moving.

"Sir, I got him, but he's hurt pretty bad, it appears," McClain said as he began pulling sandbags off Major Wise with Carter's assistance. What light there was in the destroyed command post was coming from the small side windows, the gaping hole in the side of the command post where the communications section had been and the burning creosote timbers. The acrid smoke was beginning to choke the survivors. There were twenty dead Vietnamese soldiers scattered throughout as well as a number of wounded.

"Mac, let's get Wise out of here and as many of the wounded as we can. This place is going to burn down or collapse soon. We need to get everyone out and now," Kaplan ordered. He assisted in getting Major Wise out of the burning command post. Once everyone that was alive was out, Kaplan took a head count of the wounded and called for a medevac aircraft.

Turning to Major Julius Warmath and Captain David Stewart, the division signal advisors, who had been in the advisor bunker when the AT-3 had destroyed the division command bunker, Kaplan said, "Warmath, Stewart, get comms up in the advisor bunker and notify Pleiku of our situation. We need medevac aircraft for twenty to thirty." Both officers took off at a sprint for the advisor bunker.

"Mac, while we wait for medevac, how about getting with Dobbins and setting up the division command post in the 42nd Regiment command post? I'll wait here and direct the medevac operations," Kaplan suggested.

"I'll get right on it," McClain said and then pointed his finger at Kaplan. "And you get something on that cut on your head. At least a field dressing."

Again Kaplan wiped his hand over the side of his face and it came away with fresh blood. Within an hour, the first medevac aircraft arrived and so did Mr. Vann.

Kaplan explained what had happened and his take on the AT-3 missiles. After he explained, Vann asked, "Where the hell is Dat?"

"Sir, he was uninjured and is reestablishing the division command post over in the 42nd Regiment command post. He's over there right now with Lieutenant Colonel McClain," Kaplan said.

"I noticed that all the medevac aircraft are US. The Vietnamese are supposed to be extracted by the Vietnamese medevac aircraft," Vann pointed out.

"Sir, we haven't seen a Vietnamese medevac aircraft in weeks.

I know we called for them this morning, but none have come in. If we wait on them, most of the Vietnamese wounded will die," Kaplan explained. Vann didn't seem happy with the explanation.

"Okay, let's load some of the wounded up on my aircraft and I'll get them to the hospital in Kontum...and I'll see about getting Vietnamese medevac aircraft out here," Vann added.

"Sir, can I ask how the extractions are going on Five and Six this morning?" Kaplan inquired.

"They haven't started yet. We're trying to get VNAF helicopters to conduct the extractions. Our aircraft are pretty well committed right now. I'll let you know when the extractions commence. You take care, Colonel," Vann said as he moved off to his aircraft.

37

TAN CANH HEATS UP

42nd Regiment Command Post
Tan Canh

CAPTAIN RAY DOBBINS lay on top of the regimental command bunker to observe the perimeter and call in air strikes. He had seen the one tank destroyed by the AT-3 and was looking to adjust air strikes on any enemy positions he could pinpoint. 1st Battalion, or what was left of 1st Battalion, had linked up with four tanks and was attempting to break contact and move back into the perimeter. However, they were so close to the enemy, even danger close was too close. The NVA had learned over the years to "grab the Vietnamese by their belts and hang on" to prevent air strikes or artillery from supporting them. It was a tactic that had been used since the early days of engaging the French.

"Covey Triple Nickel, Beagle Five, over."

"Beagle Five, Covey Triple Nickel, over."

"Triple Nickel, from target reference point one-oh-one, one

hundred meters north, two hundred meters west, troops under trees. Over."

"Roger, Beagle Five, from TRP one-oh-one, one hundred meters north and two hundred meters west, troops under trees, over."

"That's a good copy, Triple Nickel."

"Roger, Beagle Five, wait one." Dobbins lay on his back, looking skyward. The tiny twin-engine centerline-thrust Cessna aircraft, with the nomenclature of O-2 for the Air Force, was at eight thousand feet, and only a flash of reflected sunlight gave away his location to Dobbins. As Dobbins watched the small aircraft, it entered a steep dive and descended rapidly. At one thousand feet, a 2.75-inch rocket leapt from under the wings and streaked towards the area that Dobbins had given as the target. To watch the rocket, Dobbins had to flip onto his stomach. He smiled as the round impacted right where he wanted it.

"Covey, Triple Nickel, that's it, over."

"Roger, stand by." Dobbins raised his binoculars and concentrated on the target area. Suddenly, there was a string of explosions cutting a swath through the trees and then the sound of an F-4 Phantom jet streaking away. This was quickly followed by two objects dropping from the wings of a second F-4 jet and tumbling into the trees, resulting in a huge fireball as the napalm ignited. Watching the area, Dobbins could see people running from the trees, engulfed in flames. They didn't run for long. Dobbins didn't have time to take in the scene as more targets were presenting themselves.

"Beagle Five, Triple Nickel, over."

"Triple Nickel, Beagle Five, go ahead."

"Beagle Five, I have to break station. I'm bingo on fuel. Covey Five-Eight-Oh will be replacing me in about an hour as he's refueling now. How copy?" This was not the news Dobbins wanted to hear, but he understood.

"Triple Nickel, I understand, but could you ask him to make it fast? More targets are presenting themselves. Over."

"Roger, I'll ask. Triple Nickel out."

Suddenly Dobbins felt a bit lonely. He would have to place calls for fire through artillery channels and use the tubes that were on the base. The call had to route through Major Carter, who had replaced Major Wise as the division operations advisor, who would forward it to the Vietnamese batteries.

"Raven Three, Raven Three, Beagle Five, fire mission," Dobbins transmitted.

"Beagle Five, Raven Three, be advised, the guns have been abandoned. The gun bunnies are sitting in their bunkers and refuse to come out and man the guns as long as we're receiving incoming. Raven Five is down there now kicking butt to get them shooting. I'll let you know when they're up, over."

"Raven Three, it best be quick as Covey just broke station and it'll be an hour before we get the next Covey aircraft. Any chance we can get the locals to fly an air strike? Over."

"Beagle Five, I'll see what I can get us. They're pretty much committed in other places if you know what I mean. Over."

"Roger, Raven Three. Let me know when the artillery is up. Beagle Five out."

Dobbins continued to observe where fire was coming from so he would have targets when Covey returned or the artillery was up and ready to fire. The enemy, however, did not hesitate to engage the remaining M41 tanks with Sagger missiles. Before the sun set, the remaining M41s would be either destroyed by the missiles or abandoned by the crews for fear of the missiles.

For most of the day, Dat sat in a corner. Kaplan couldn't get him to make a decision or even speak much.

"Colonel Dat, we need to push out and find the enemy. Patrols need to move further out so we can pinpoint the enemy's locations and get the B-52s on them," Kaplan advised.

"No use. We will be overrun at 0600 in the morning," Dat

said and sat there ignoring the actions and conversations around him. Kaplan decided it was time to get him relieved. Kaplan couldn't make the call from the command post, so he went over to the advisor bunker and got on the radio.

"Rogues Gallery, Raven Six, over."

"Raven Six, Rogues Gallery, go ahead."

"Rogues Gallery, we have a situation here. Dat has given up and is resigned to the fact that this place is going to be overrun in the morning. Any chance we can replace him? Over." Vann did not return the call immediately but thought about Kaplan's request.

"Raven Six, I already considered this and spoke with Dzu. He agreed and offered the position to Colonel Tuong, who turned down the opportunity. Dzu feels that if we pull Dat out now, it may start a panic. Best we just leave him there. You're running the show, it looks like. Over." This was not what Kaplan wanted to hear.

"Roger, Rogues Gallery. I'll do what I can. Raven Six out."

Two hours later, Kaplan called the nine advisors into the advisor bunker for a meeting. The advisor bunker was set deeper in the ground than the division command bunker, so it wasn't as noticeable. It was generally used to store supplies for the advisors and served as sleeping quarters. A complete communications array back to II Corps and SRAG headquarters had been set up by Major Warmath and Captain Stewart.

"Alright, we have everyone here, so let's start. Vann and I spoke this morning and the possibility that this place is going to fall is pretty good. If that happens, on my call, everyone is to immediately assemble at the helo pad on the west side, next to the minefield. Bring only yourself and any equipment you have in your immediate possession, like your weapon, ammo and a radio if you have one. Leave everything else. Understood?" Kaplan asked.

"Sir, what about Colonel Brownlee and Captain Carden at Dak To II? Do they have an E&E plan?" McClain asked.

"They do, and Brownlee went over it with me. Once we leave they'll be pulled out right behind us."

"What's the plan for Dat and his staff?" Dobbins asked.

"Dat and his staff are on their own," Kaplan said with frustration in his voice. "We have aircraft to get us out and not our counterparts. I'm sorry, but we can't get everyone out. Say nothing to them because if they see us moving to that pad or know our plan, they'll mob the aircraft. Dat is sitting in a chair, doing nothing, and he's been that way for the past six hours. He believes they'll be overrun in the morning and feels he can do nothing about it. Okay, if no questions, let's get back in the fight and see if we can hold this place. Dobbins, how about you walk the line and see how the troops are doing since they know you the best?"

"Yes, sir," Dobbins said and headed for the door.

For the rest of the day, shelling continued, but the enemy made no effort to storm the base. However, they did change their tactics.

The massive explosion lit up the late-afternoon sky and the shock wave rolled across the compound.

"What the hell just happened?" asked Kaplan inside the 42nd Regiment command post. Initially no one could answer the question, but it quickly became obvious as additional explosions were heard.

Dobbins had been out on the perimeter and witnessed the whole thing.

"Sir," he said, entering the command post and moving to the map board. Pointing at the high ground north of the compound, he began to explain what he had seen. "On this high ground that overlooks the compound, I saw nine or ten RPGs fire at once and all directed at the ammo dump. One must have been successful as the entire ammo dump went up in one massive explosion. These secondary explosions are our own rounds cooking off from the initial explosion," Dobbins explained. "Sir, I think we lost the entire supply of ammo." Kaplan saw any hope of saving the base camp going up in smoke.

At 2100 hours, the news didn't get any better. Warmath approached Kaplan in the command post.

"Sir, we just got a report from Captain Cassidy, the senior advisor in Dak To district compound, that tanks are moving through Dak Brung hamlet up Highway 14 towards Dak To headquarters. He's requesting Spectre gunship support," Warmath said.

"Approved, and see if they can get here quick," Kaplan said, and Warmath was back on the radio with a request. An hour later, the sound of a four-engine aircraft could be heard when the radio call came in.

"Raven Six, Spectre Two-One-Oh, over."

"Spectre Two-One-Oh, Raven Six, contact Tango Bravo Three on four-five-double-oh, over," Kaplan directed.

"Roger, QSY at this time."

* * *

CAPTAIN CASSIDY SAT on the perimeter of his small compound in Dak To. His force consisted of the Popular Force, which was composed of about fifty Montagnards that were very loyal to him, but not so much to the South Vietnamese and even less to the North Vietnamese. He wasn't sure how they would react when faced with tanks, although they had been issued the M-72 LAW rockets. As he peered into the darkness, only illuminated by his watch, which read 0326 hours, his radio came to life.

"Tango Bravo Three, Spectre Two-One-Oh, over."

Cassidy grabbed up the hand mike so fast it startled the young soldier standing next to him.

"Spectre Two-One-Oh, Tango Bravo Three, over."

"Tango Bravo Three, good evening. I understand you have some targets for us this fine evening, over."

Looking skyward, Cassidy could now hear the aircraft but couldn't see it in the night sky. *Son of a bitch is a cheerful dude*, he was thinking as he keyed his mike. "Spectre Two-One-Oh, we have a report of tanks moving south on Highway 14 in the vicinity of Dak Brung..." And Cassidy read off the coordinates for the hamlet.

"Roger, Tango Bravo One. We'll mosey up that way and take a look. I'll let you know what we see. Over."

"Roger, Tango Bravo One standing by." *I hope you kill whatever you see*, Cassidy thought as he laid the hand mike back down.

SPECTRE TWO-ONE-OH CONTINUED to fly north. With the sophisticated onboard equipment, he was able to see clearly the ground that he was passing over. In addition, he had a 105mm howitzer mounted in the left-side door that was computer-controlled and extremely accurate. Other weapons on that side of the aircraft were two 20mm Gatling guns, each capable of firing four thousand rounds a minute. Within ten minutes, the aircraft was over the target area and found what he was looking for.

"Tango Bravo One, Spectre Two-One-Oh, over."

"Spectre, Tango Bravo, go ahead."

"Tango Bravo, we have eleven tanks moving south towards your location. We are engaging."

"Roger, Spectre, Tango Bravo out." The broad grin on Cassidy's face was a reassuring sign to the Montagnard soldiers standing next to him even if they didn't understand the transmission.

Spectre Two-One-Oh engaged the tanks with his 105 howitzer, firing high-explosive (HE) rounds. This type of ammunition was effective against everything except tanks. To destroy a tank, a high-explosive antitank (HEAT) round was required, and Spectre wasn't carrying any of these rounds this evening. Two hours later, Spectre reported back to Cassidy.

"Tango Bravo One, Spectre Two-One-Oh, over."

"Spectre, Tango Bravo, go ahead."

"Tango Bravo, we killed three tanks vicinity of Dak Brung and probably gave the crews in another six the scare of their lives. We're bingo on fuel and breaking station. Good luck."

"Spectre, thank you for your assistance. Safe flight home. Tango Bravo One out" was all Cassidy could say. The tanks were coming.

38

TAN CANH FALLS

24 April 1972
22nd Division HQ
Tan Canh

KAPLAN WAS ATTEMPTING to catch a few minutes of sleep. He had monitored the situation at Dak Brung but was confident the tanks couldn't reach Tan Canh. The bridge on Highway 14 had been rigged with demolitions as well as the one on Highway 512. Both bridges could be blown if the tanks approached. The order had been given earlier to destroy the bridge on Highway 14.

"Colonel, Colonel...wake up, sir," McClain said, standing next to where Kaplan lay on the floor.

"Okay, I'm awake. What time is it?" Kaplan asked, accepting a cup of coffee that McClain handed him as he sat up.

"It's 0400, but we have a problem, I think," McClain said as Kaplan started to stand.

"Oh, what's that?" Kaplan asked, fully awake.

"Seems that the bridge across Highway 14 wasn't blown. In

fact, it looks like charges were never put in place. Captain Kellar just reported that enemy tanks just rolled past his position without firing a shot and they're headed this way," McClain explained. "The artillery battery that's by the main gate reports hearing the sounds of track vehicles."

"Shit, let me get over there and see for myself," Kaplan said, grabbing his steel pot and sidearm. Running the hundred and fifty meters from the command bunker to the artillery battery, Kaplan started to hear the sounds of track vehicles approaching. Kaplan was in a foot race to see who would get to the battery first. He won.

"Dai'uy," Kaplan said, seeing the battery commander. Through his interpreter, Kaplan told the battery commander to lower his tubes and engage the tanks with HEAT rounds. Immediately, the battery commander started barking orders and the tubes were lowered. The engagement was brief. As best Kaplan could tell, the tanks stopped and retreated and one fuel truck was hit and destroyed. No tanks were hit, but a round did hit five feet in front of one tank. Kaplan congratulated the battery commander just to keep up the appearance of success. This was not the time to destroy what morale the soldiers had.

Earlier in the night, Dobbins had convinced Lieutenant Colonel Thong, the 42nd Regiment commander, to deploy anti-tank teams around the perimeter and along the road from Dak To to Tan Canh. The teams managed to destroy two tanks before they ran back to the safety of the compound. A 106mm recoilless rifle team was in position to engage but ran instead without firing a shot.

Returning to the command post, Kaplan talked with Dobbins, McClain, and Yonan about the defensive posture of the compound.

"Sir, why don't I go out by the main gate with Lieutenant Colonel Thong as that appears to be where the tanks are going to approach? Being right there, the two of us can best direct the fight against them," Dobbins offered.

"Sounds good, but don't get cut off if it turns to shit. You know the exit plan," Kaplan directed.

"Sir, I don't intend to," Dobbins said and departed.

"Sir," Yonan said, "I'll climb to the top of the water tower and direct air strikes from there. It's high enough that I'll have a good three-sixty view of the perimeter and can direct the strikes from up there."

"Good idea, but don't get cut off, understood?" Kaplan said.

"Understood, sir," Yonan said as he picked up a PRC-77 radio to talk to the FAC. Everyone departed and moved to take up positions to report to Kaplan how the battle was actually going. Kaplan didn't like directing the battle from inside a bunker and relying on the reports that the Vietnamese commanders were sending. He needed people to be able to verify what he was hearing. He didn't have long to wait.

"Raven Six, Beagle Five, over."

"Beagle Five, Raven Six, go ahead."

"Raven Six, three colored flares were just fired on the south side. We have tanks leading infantry approaching from the southern tree line in formation. Over."

Kaplan glanced at the clock on the bunker wall. It read 0510 hours. *Did Dat know they would attack at this hour?* The sounds of incoming rounds only added to his stress as these sounds were from the north.

"Raven Six, Raven Four," Captain Yonan transmitted from the top of the water tower.

"Raven Four, go ahead."

"Raven Six, tanks on the north high ground are engaging. Infantry are approaching the north perimeter. Over."

Kaplan quickly glanced at the wall map for the locations of the friendly forces. The north perimeter was held by the regimental reconnaissance company, probably the best company in the 42nd Regiment.

"Roger, Raven Four. Are they holding?" Kaplan asked.

"Affirmative, but they're not going to be able to hold if the tanks leave the high ground and attack."

Kaplan looked at the map again. There were no reserves to plug holes in the perimeter. From the sounds outside the bunker, he could tell that the tanks on the high ground were picking targets within the compound with impunity as he had no resources to use against them. As he studied the map, the entire front of the command bunker suddenly exploded. A tank round had hit the top of the bunker above the doorway and it collapsed. Kaplan moved and began pulling sandbags down and out of the way. As he did so, reality set in. *What the hell am I doing? I'm relegated to a squad leader for ten Americans. Dat is out of the fight. I can't see what's going on outside. Tanks are moving against the perimeter. I've got to get my people out of here. Better to die on your feet than to suffocate or burn to death in a bunker.*[1] Looking around, he saw those Americans in the bunker staring at him, waiting for orders.

"Everyone out. We're going now. Notify Dobbins and Yonan to get their asses to the PZ." His last act was to grab a PRC-77 radio and move out. What he had seen convinced him that there was nothing that he or the other advisors could do.

"Rogues Gallery, Raven Six, over."

Moments later he got a response. "Raven Six Rogues Gallery, over."

"Rogues Gallery, we need extraction now. Over."

"Raven Six, understand and am inbound. Move to the PZ. Flight of two Oscar Hotel Five-Eights," Vann transmitted. Surrounding Kaplan were McClain, Stewart, Warmath, Major Carter, Lieutenant Johnny Jones and Staff Sergeant Walter Ward as well as Specialist Fourth Class Frank Zollicoffer and Captain Kellar. Dobbins and Yonan weren't there yet, but Kaplan knew they had to get moving as a tank had already broken through the perimeter.

"Okay, let's move out," Kaplan said, carrying an M16 rifle that he'd found on the ground. As the small party moved, they witnessed more tanks breaking through the perimeter. ARVN soldiers were in panic mode, running in every direction. All organized resistance had collapsed. Reaching the proposed pickup point, everyone lay down in a small ditch on the side of the road. As they lay there, the sound of an approaching tank could be heard. Stress levels were already high, and now they were going higher.

"Hey, sir," Lieutenant Jones whispered, "I have a LAW. Want me to take it out?"

"Lieutenant, be my guest," Kaplan said, shaking his head at the young officer's bravado.

Jones knew the best place to hit the tank with the LAW was in the rear, where the engine was located and the armor was the lightest. Slowly, he began crawling in the ditch towards the approaching tank. As it passed him, Jones got to his knees, prepared the LAW for firing and set his sight on the engine compartment before he pressed he trigger. Nothing happened. The rocket misfired and the tank proceeded none the wiser down the road and around a building.

"Nice try, Lieutenant," Kaplan said to the dejected young man. Moments later a second tank appeared, following the path of the first. McClain also had a LAW and waited for the tank to pass their position before he attempted to engage. His LAW malfunctioned as well.

"We can't stay here. This place is like Times Square with tanks and people running around," Kaplan said, looking about. "And where the hell are Yonan and Dobbins?"

"Sir, I don't know about Dobbins, but Yonan is still on top of the water tower. There are two tanks parked at the base of the tower," Sergeant Ward said, handing a pair of binoculars to

Kaplan. Kaplan scanned the area and could see Yonan and his Vietnamese counterpart on top of the tower, trapped by the two tanks.

"Okay, we have to move. There's that old road in the middle of the minefield. What do you think if we move to it?" Kaplan asked.

"Sir, I've seen some of the ARVNs moving through the minefield safely. I think I can find that trail and get us through it," Sergeant Ward offered.

"You really think so?" Kaplan asked.

"Well, sir, I'll take the point and we'll find out. Everyone walk single file behind me and attempt to step where the man in front steps," Ward said as he stood and moved to the edge of the minefield. Everyone lined up behind him in single file and they began moving. Each step was done in anticipation of an explosion. Finally they reached the old road and again lay down as not to attract attention. As they lay there, they saw several ARVN soldiers attempting to run through the minefield only to be killed by an exploding mine.

"Raven Six, Rogues Gallery, over," Kaplan heard on his radio, and everyone's spirits rose immediately.

"Rogues Gallery, Raven Six."

"Rogues Gallery is a flight of two inbound. Over."

"Rogues Gallery, be advised we moved from intended PZ two hundred meters west, over."

"Understood you are in the minefield," Rogues Gallery responded, puzzled at the new location.

"Affirmative, but we're on the old road. It's clear, over."

"Roger."

Turning to the group, Kaplan said, "Okay, there are two OH-58s. McClain, Stewart and I will wait here while you six get on those aircraft," Kaplan said. Warmath and Jones as well as Ward started to object, but Kaplan quickly put an end to the discussion. "I don't want to hear it. You're getting on those aircraft." Several ARVN soldiers had joined the group. None were designated to get on an aircraft.

* * *

VANN WAS FLYING the first aircraft with Mr. Robert Richards, followed by Captain Dolph Todd piloting the second aircraft. Flying at treetop level, the aircraft made a beeline for Tan Canh. As they approached, Vann executed a power climb, quickly sacrificing airspeed for altitude, and began to orbit above the compound. Looking down, he could see the tanks moving around the camp and a small group of people moving through the minefield. Others were attempting to get through the minefield, only to be blown to pieces as exploding mines detonated. As Vann watched, three tanks moved to the original intended pickup point and stopped.

"Rogues Gallery, Raven Six, over."

"Go ahead, Raven Six."

"Rogues Gallery, we have moved to the old road in the middle of the minefield. Over."

"Roger, Raven Six, I have you in sight. I see three Tango Five-Fours on the helipad. Can you see them? Over."

"That's a negative as the road sits about five feet down behind a small ridge. Over."

"Roger, stand by, we're coming in," Vann said and lowered his collective, executing a rapid descent. As the two aircraft made their approach, they came in very fast. Captain Todd in the second aircraft landed hard, fearful of one or all the tanks opening fire upon them, but none did. Both aircraft landed without taking any hits from enemy fire. The six advisors quickly loaded the two aircraft. Vann was the first to pick up to depart when panicking ARVNs grabbed the skids as the aircraft lifted off. The overloaded aircraft struggled to get in the air. Vann decided to land at Dak To II as he was sure the dangling

ARVNs would fall to their deaths before he could reach Pleiku, and he still had three advisors to pick up at Tan Canh. As the advisors climbed out of the choppers, they were told to wait as the airfield and a UH-1H would be in shortly to pick them up. The ARVNs quickly disappeared when they reached the ground.

As Vann applied power and began to lift off, a burst of gunfire came at his aircraft, with several rounds hitting sensitive components. The master caution light came on as well as the master caution warning horn. The master caution panel lit up like a Christmas tree. Vann was struggling to keep the small helicopter in the air and immediately returned to Pleiku. Captain Todd got off unscathed and returned to Tan Canh to pick up Kaplan, McClain and Stewart. He then proceeded to take them to Pleiku.[2]

39

ESCAPE AND EVADE

24 April 1972
47th Regiment
Dak To II

EACH MORNING AT APPROXIMATELY 0800, Colonel Kaplan would receive a UH-1H to use as a command-and-control aircraft. This morning was no different. Once in the OH-58, Kaplan was on the radio making contact with the Gladiator aircraft.

"Gladiator Seven-One-Five, Raven Six, over."

"Good morning, Raven Six, Gladiator Seven-One-Five will be working for you today. What have we got? Over," First Lieutenant James Hunsicker transmitted.

"Seven-One-Five, Tan Canh has been overrun. Do not, repeat, do not go there. Proceed to the airfield at Dak To II. There are six advisors there for you to pick up and bring to Pleiku. How copy? Over."

"Raven Six, I have good copy and am proceeding to Dak To II. What's the situation there? Over."

"Seven-One-Five, there's contact in the vicinity of Dak To II, so be careful. Avoid departing northwest, over."

"Roger, Seven-One-Five out." Hunsicker flipped to the intercom to talk to the crew. Specialist Fifth Class Rickey Vogel was serving as the crew chief and Specialist Fourth Class Charles Lea was door gunner. Mr. Wade Ellen was the peter pilot for the day and new to Vietnam.[1]

"Okay, guys, change in plans. Tan Canh has been overrun. The advisors made it to Dak To II, so we're going there to extract them. There are six. We may take some fire around there, so be on your toes. Any questions?" Hunsicker asked.

"I'm good," Lea responded at the same time as Vogel indicated the same.

Gladiator Seven-One-Five proceeded to fly to the airfield at Dak To II and quickly spotted the six advisors on the airfield. Incoming artillery and mortars were impacting on the compound, but the airfield appeared to be ignored. When they landed, the six advisors quickly jumped in. Hunsicker turned to observe the advisors boarding and then turned to Ellen.

"Okay, you have the aircraft, and let's head for Pleiku," Hunsicker directed.

"I have the aircraft," Ellen responded, taking the controls.

"You're up, sir," Vogel said as the last advisor boarded the aircraft.

"Coming up," Ellen announced, and the aircraft came to a gentle hover and proceeded to move forward, building speed and altitude.

As the UH-1H lifted off, Ellen took a northwest heading. A half mile from the airfield, three anti-aircraft guns opened fire at the departing UH-1H, which immediately began trailing smoke.

"Taking fire!" Vogel yelled and then went silent. His gun didn't return fire. The sound of a sledgehammer hitting the aircraft could be heard as the master caution horn began to blare along with the entire master caution panel lighting up. Lea began shooting as the aircraft lurched to the left in a roll. He glanced quickly to the front. Ellen was slumped forward towards the radio console. Hunsicker was attempting to straighten the aircraft, which was losing altitude rapidly when it hit the trees. Blackness rolled over Lea.

Lieutenant Colonel Brownlee and Captain Carden could only stand and watch as the aircraft careened into the trees and a fireball erupted. Brownlee retrieved the hand mike on the PRC-77 radio that he was carrying. Lieutenant Colonel Brownlee notified Raven Six, who was still in the air. "Raven Six, Sparrow Six, over."

"Sparrow Six, Raven Six, go ahead."

"Raven Six, be advised, Gladiator aircraft with advisors has been shot down. No survivors, over."

The news hit Kaplan like a punch in the gut. His goal was to get everyone out safely, and he had failed in that mission.

WHEN MAJOR WARMATH WOKE, he just lay still for a moment, trying to comprehend what had happened. *We took off and suddenly there was a pounding noise followed by a horn and then we dropped suddenly...what is that smell?* The sound of someone moaning got his attention and he began to look around. Captain Kellar and Sergeant Ward were next to him and both appeared to be waking up as well. As Ward attempted to sit up, he let out a low moan. "My back! Oh shit."

Kellar looked over at Warmath. "Sir, are you okay?" he asked.

Warmath started to sit up again but stopped halfway and lay back down. "I think I dislocated my shoulder. What the hell happened?"

"Sir, I think we were shot down," Kellar answered, looking around. The aircraft wreckage was twenty feet away and still burning. The pilots, Hunsicker and Ellen, could be seen in the cockpit still. Jones lay beside the aircraft, partially in and partially out. As Kellar looked around, he saw movement in the brush on the far side of the burnt aircraft. Slowly he approached to find Specialist Franklin Zollicoffer, the crew chief, semiconscious. The door gunner, Specialist Charles Lea, was attempting to drag him further away from the aircraft. It was obvious that Specialist Zollicoffer had a broken leg, but the bone hadn't protruded through the skin. It was also clear he had other injuries that were more serious but less visible. Major Carter was still inside the aircraft and wasn't moving or moaning. He appeared to have died from a bullet.

After a few moments, Warmath took charge of the situation. "Okay, we're all busted up to some extent. We'll probably have company shortly and I'm not talking friendly either, so when they arrive, be submissive. No hero crap. Don't pick up a weapon. Understood?" he said, scanning everyone. "Kellar, you and the gunner don't seem to be hurt, so if you want to take off, go ahead. I'll stay with the crew chief and Ward."

"Sir, we'll stick with you guys for now. Let me see what we can salvage and use," Kellar said as he started gathering up undamaged material, which wasn't much. Some seat belts, some canvas, a two-hundred-and-fifty-foot climbing rope, a case of C rations, two flight helmets and four steel pots. As the day wore on, activity was heard around them, but no one came to check on them, which piqued Kellar's curiosity.

"Sir, I'm going to do a bit of a recon to see where we're at," Kellar said, standing up.

"I'll go with you, sir," Lea offered.

"Okay, let's go."

Kellar and Lea moved off towards the north but didn't get far. The Dak Poko River appeared. It quickly became obvious that they had crashed on a small island in the middle of the river. *No wonder no one has come looking for us*, Kellar was thinking. *There may be hope yet.*[2]

* * *

BY 1000 HOURS, Captain Dobbins and Lieutenant Colonel Thong came to the conclusion that all was lost and they could do nothing else. Thong's soldiers located at the main gate on the eastern perimeter had accounted well for themselves, but as more tanks and enemy infantry poured in on the north and south sides, both knew any further resistance was useless.

"Dai'uy, follow me," Thong said and started off at a slow jog towards his bunker. Artillery was impacting on the compound, but they reached Thong's bunker unscathed. As they ran, Dobbins looked back and noticed about twenty ARVN soldiers following them.

Reaching his bunker, Thong motioned for Dobbins to enter. Dobbins wasn't crazy about the idea of getting into a bunker with one way in and the same way out.

"Dai'uy, get in quick," Thong insisted.

My fate is in his hands now, Dobbins was thinking as he ducked into the small bunker. Thong was right behind him and immediately moved his bed aside, revealing a skillfully camou-flaged trapdoor. Opening it, Thong jumped down into a chamber and motioned for Dobbins to follow. As soon as Dobbins was down, the twenty ARVN soldiers followed. *Damn, I must have been the only one that didn't know about this place, and the ARVNs know to stick to the advisor as supposedly I'll get extracted*, Dobbins was thinking when Thong reached up and closed the door. Thong said something in Vietnamese, and the twenty ARVNs immediately became silent in the cramped confines of the small hiding place.

Throughout the day, the sound of battle could be heard above them, sometimes distantly and at others very loud. As the day wore on, the sounds became fewer and less frequent, however. By 2000 hours that evening, the sounds hadn't been heard in over two hours. Thong looked at Dobbins and motioned that it was time to take a look. Gingerly, Dobbins opened the door and heard nothing. Closing the door, Dobbins gave Thong a thumbs-up and mouthed "all clear."

Thong began speaking to the twenty Vietnamese soldiers, who listened intently to the escape plan. The soldiers would leave in groups of four and make their way to the perimeter and through the wire, escaping into the surrounding countryside. The first group of four departed into a night lit by the full moon. It seemed that all was well until a machine gun opened fire. Dobbins and Thong couldn't know if the first group had been spotted and killed or what. The decision was made to wait a couple of hours and let the moon set before attempting again.

At midnight, the entire group came out of the bunker and began moving towards the wire. Thong and Dobbins were at the tail end of the group as the ARVN soldiers were throwing caution to the wind in their haste to get through the wire. Suddenly night became day when a Spectre gunship dropped illumination flares. The enemy saw the running soldiers and opened fire. Dobbins and Thong were about to start running when the shooting started and they dropped down into a pig pen. The stench was overwhelming, but at this point Dobbins didn't care.

Lying in the pig shit, Dobbins had nothing else to do but observe the enemy. Tanks were still along the perimeter, and it was the sound of their heavy machine guns that had killed previous attempts to reach the countryside. Overhead, Dobbins heard a FAC, and suddenly all the tanks released smoke canisters to mask them from it. The smoke was thick and spread out enough to mask not only the tanks from the FAC but anyone running between the tanks to the countryside.

"Thong, we go when the tanks pop smoke. We go fast. Okay?" Dobbins said.

Thong studied the situation for a moment and smiled.

"Okay, Dai'uy," he said, then gave orders to the few ARVNs still with them.

As the FAC passed over the area a second time, the tanks popped their smoke canisters. As the smoke covered the tanks, Dobbins, Thong and the ARVNs took off at a sprint to the tree line through a break in the wire. Everyone reached the jungle. After a short break, they moved south for several kilometers before an aircraft spotted them, and the next day they were picked up.

40

———————

PREP FOR COMBAT

24 APRIL 1972
  1st Combat Aerial TOW Team
  Ton Son Nhut

EVERYONE HAD an opportunity to sleep on the long flight over from McChord Air Force Base outside Tacoma, Washington. What wasn't expected, at least not by the new arrivals, was the change in weather from cool and rainy to humid and hot. They also didn't expect the reception party that awaited their arrival. As the two C-141 aircraft taxied to the tarmac and stopped in front of a fortified hangar, the tailgate ramps were lowered. Waiting for the aircraft were a team of maintenance people, forklifts, trucks and generators. Everything needed to quickly get two UH-1B aircraft back in the air. Lieutenant Colonel Feore led the team members off the aircraft and approached a colonel standing at the head of the army of workers.

"Sir, Lieutenant Colonel Feore reporting as ordered," Feore said, rendering a proper salute as he approached the officer, who returned the salute and extended his hand.

"Colonel Todd, Deputy Commander, 1st Aviation Brigade," he responded. Turning slightly, he added, "This is Major Grayson. He and his people will take care of getting your aircraft unloaded and your people settled in. Tomorrow morning, your aircraft should be ready to mount your special systems and commence your training. Your people can get some rest and acclimate to the area for today. Any questions?"

"No, sir. We do have some very precious ammo on that other aircraft along with our special equipment," Feore pointed out.

"That special ammo will remain on that aircraft and we will have US Air Force guards around it as well. Let's you and I go over to my office and talk for a few and then I'll take you over to the BOQ," Todd offered.

"Major Grayson, Mr. Hugh McInnish is head of our civilian contact team, and SFC Hartsell is NCOIC for the enlisted members, which are a total of four," Feore explained. "Any specific questions about the aircraft, I'm sure they can answer. I don't know if you're aware, but the aircraft belong not to the Army but Hughes Aircraft Corporation. We're just borrowing them," Feore added and smiled at the expression of confusion on the major's face.

"Thank you, sir. I'll get with them immediately," Grayson said and moved off with his team to the C-141 that had shut down and exposed the two UH-1B aircraft inside.

"This way," Todd said, motioning to a jeep and driver. The drive to his office was quick and nothing of importance was said. When they arrived, Todd instructed the driver to take Feore's bag to his BOQ room and return. Stepping into the air-conditioned office was a relief for Feore at this point. Perspiration had penetrated his uniform down his back and under his arms.

"I had forgotten how hot it gets here," he said, accepting a cup of coffee from Todd, who motioned for him to sit down.

"Well, it got a lot hotter yesterday, and I ain't talking weather. How soon can your aircraft be ready?"

Right to the point, Feore thought. "Well, sir, it'll take one day to have the birds ready and another day to run systems checks, so we can be in the air, say, the evening of the twenty-fifth, tomorrow night," Feore indicated.

"Good. Then tomorrow night or the next morning, we're moving you to Long Binh. You will be under the operational control of the 1st Aviation Brigade—more specifically, under my control. When you get to Long Binh, I want you to continue with your system checks and conduct training. We're in a midintensity fight and we have a couple of pilots that have been in the thick of it standing by to give your guys some pointers on the threat and changes in tactics. The enemy has used surface-to-air shoulder-fired missiles that helicopters can't get away from. We also want to make some modifications to the pilot seats, exchanging them for some with armor protection. That'll cause some weight and balance adjustments and recalculations," Todd outlined.

"Sir, you mentioned it got a lot hotter yesterday...," Feore stated, not finishing his sentence.

"It did. What we feared would happen did. On 30 March, the NVA launched an attack across the DMZ with two divisions supported by armor, and a third division attacked out of Tchepone down Highway 9 through Khe Sanh, also with tank support. The ARVNs were slow in reporting this to us, until some US Marine lieutenant colonel raised the flag on the fourth of April and got our attention. On the fifth of April, the NVA launched another major attack with three divisions across the Cambodian border from Snoul down Highway 13, knocking off Loc Ninh and Quan Loi and beating on the doors of An Loc. And they're supported by tanks. Right now, the fight up there is T-54s against LAWs. Yesterday, they launched a third major attack coming out of the triborder area, hitting Tan Canh and Dak To, and again leading with tanks. We have nothing but LAWs to help up there. If the ARVN don't stop them and they get to Kontum, they can cut the country right in half. Your aircraft are going to go to Pleiku as soon as you're satisfied they're operational. From Pleiku, you'll support the forces in MR-II but will take your missions from me. Questions?"

"Sir, I didn't realize how desperate this mission was," Feore exclaimed, almost in shock.

"We didn't either. Initially we were going to decide who needed you the most, MR-I, defending Quang Tri, or MR-III, blocking them from coming on to Lai Khe. Now we have no choice. You've got to go to MR-II," Todd pointed out.

"What about the tanks approaching Quang Tri?"

"We have some time there. That Marine lieutenant colonel took it upon himself to blow the bridges over the rivers leading to Quang Tri, so he bought us time. Hell, if he hadn't done that, the damn NVA would be sitting in Hue by now. As for MR-III, the ARVNs are moving the 21st ARVN Division as we speak to push up Highway 13 and open the road to relieve An Loc. They have some tanks with that division. But there are no friendly tanks in MR-II and that's why we need you there. Now when you get to Pleiku, we will conduct live fire training up there. That C-141 with your ammo on board will depart here as soon as the rest of our gear is off and deliver it there for you. It'll go into a separate secure ammo facility for safekeeping. They're expecting it. I understand you have a rep from Missile Command."

"Yes, sir. Mr. McGinnis."

"Good, I'll tell Major Grayson to see to it that he's on that flight with the missiles. Someone will meet him there in Pleiku and get him settled if that's okay and you don't need him here," Todd asked.

"No, sir, that will work."

"When you're at Pleiku, your support will be provided by the 17th Aviation Group. H Troop, 17th Cav, and H Troop, 10th Cav, are operating out of Pleiku and will be conducting reconnaissance missions to find targets for you. The 361st Aerial Weapons Company, call sign Pink Panthers, will provide escort support when you're on a mission. Your call sign will be Hawk's Claw," Todd explained, pausing for a moment. "Well, you look tired. The driver is outside and will take you over to the BOQ. When you're ready, just call and the driver will be back to pick you up. A crew bus is on standby to support your people and will remain with you until we go over to Long Binh," Todd said, standing and extending his hand. "You have no idea how happy we are that you've arrived. Good luck and good hunting."

41

DAK TO II

Lieutenant Colonel Brownlee watched as the UH-1H helicopter exploded in the trees half a mile from the runway on the northwest side. Light contact had commenced the night before with ground probes and concentrated artillery, but no major ground assaults had taken place. He believed that this was about to change. In the distance, he could hear the battle at Tan Canh, but it appeared to be decreasing.

"Let's get up to the command post and see what Minh has been doing and the situation around us," Brownlee said, and Carden followed along.

"Do you think there would be any survivors?" Carden asked, taking a last look at the towering black smoke from the burning aircraft.

"I don't think anyone could live through that. Vann has been notified, so he may send a scout over to check out the crash site. Not our concern right now as we can't do anything," Brownlee said, moving towards the 47th command bunker. Along the perimeter, the sound of small-arms fire was increasing, but incoming artillery was decreasing. *Probably the start of the ground assaults around here*, Brownlee was thinking when he entered the 47th command post. It was empty!

"What the—" Brownlee said. Minh and the entire staff had deserted the command post and were gone. Calls from units on the perimeter went unanswered.

"Sir, what are we going to do?" Carden asked hesitantly.

"Captain, we're going to get the hell out of here. Nothing we can do. There's no commander or staff to advise. Let's get to our bunker, grab what we can and get the hell out of here. We're on our own now," Brownlee said, heading for the door. Reaching the advisor bunker, Brownlee put a call into Kaplan and notified him of the situation and told him their plan to escape and evade. While he was on the radio, Carden stood in the doorway. What he saw sent a chill down his spine.

"Sir, you best see this."

Two T-54 tanks had moved on to the airfield. One took up a position on the west end of the runway, ready to engage any vehicles coming from Ben Het down Highway 512. The other took up a position in the middle of the runway and turned its 100mm main gun on the compound. Systematically, it began destroying one bunker after another.

* * *

THE 14TH ARMORED Regiment was located at Ben Het. Dat had positioned the unit there days before with the intent to stop enemy armor moving against Ben Het. If Minh had conducted active patrolling, he would have known that the T-54s weren't coming from the west but from the north over a two-hundred-kilometer road that the enemy had cut through the jungle the prior month. Even close-in patrols would have discovered bunkers that the NVA had dug just outside the perimeter of Dak To II. When the 14th rolled out of Ben Het to counterattack, they had fourteen M41 tanks, which had a 76mm main gun. They were no match for T-54s with a 100mm main gun and better armor.

Moving down Highway 512, the force came to the bridge at Dak Mot over the Dak Poko River. This was a bridge that should have been rigged for demolition but had not been. The column was halfway across the bridge when the NVA sprung the ambush. Occupying the high ground overlooking the bridge, the enemy engaged the force with RPGs from above, quickly destroying nine of the twelve M41s. The surviving three turned and headed back to Ben Het.

* * *

CARDEN CONTINUED to watch the two T-54 tanks on the airfield while Brownlee began burning documents, to include the codebooks. As Carden watched, movement caught his attention. Two M41 tanks appeared from the east. Carden's spirits rose as now the two T-54s could be destroyed. At eight hundred meters, the M41 opened fire, hitting the tank in the middle of the runway. The rounds hit squarely but caused no damage. Slowly the turret on the T-54 rotated. On its first shot, one M41 exploded in flames. It took two shots to kill the second M41.

"Sir, we need to go and now," Carden said, convinced that their bunker with antennas on top would be hit shortly. Brownlee decided he could do no more and headed for the door. At this point small-arms fire was sporadic and most of the ARVN soldiers had abandoned the perimeter and were running in panic. Some were discarding their uniforms; almost all had dropped their weapons and load-bearing equipment.

"Let's head south to the river and get across," Brownlee said as he started jogging in that direction. Brownlee had been fighting a bad cold for the past couple of days. In addition, he was a big man and not used to running. Carden was keeping pace with him with little difficulty, heading for the footbridge across the Dak Poko River. As they got closer, they became more cautious. Reaching the footbridge, they discovered numerous ARVN bodies on the bridge and in the surrounding waters. All had been cut down attempting to flee south.

"We can't cross here. Let's move downriver. I know of a shallow fording site there," Carden said as he had been out on a few patrols in the area.

"Lead the way," Brownlee said, gasping for air. The duo moved seven hundred meters downstream without encountering anyone. The fording site was fifty meters across and waist-deep, but the southern bank was steep and high.

"Captain, you go ahead and cross. I'll follow you when I catch my breath," Brownlee said.

"Sir, are you sure? I don't feel right leaving you here," Carden said with concern.

"Yeah, by the time you cross and scale that bank, I'll be ready to come over, and then you can help me up the bank," Brownlee said.

"Alright, sir," Carden replied and waded into the river. As he crossed the fifty meters, he scanned the southern bank for any movement. *I'm a sitting duck if anyone is on these banks*, he was thinking as he moved quietly across the slow-flowing river. Reaching the south side, he began the climb up the steep bank, grabbing vegetation to help pull himself up. At the top, he turned and waved to Brownlee, who was sitting on the bank. It appeared that his breathing was still labored. Brownlee simply waved to him to move on.

Damnit, sir, get your ass over here, Carden thought as he waved again. Brownlee again waved for him to move on. Carden paused for a moment, then decided to move into the jungle and give Brownlee time to catch his breath. As he moved cautiously, he suddenly heard movement to his front and saw a figure rise up.

"Don't shoot, Dai'uy. It is me," Carden heard from the brush. He recognized the voice.

"Is that you, Chi?" Carden asked in a whisper.

"Yes," Sergeant Cao Ky Chi, their interpreter, said with a wide grin.

"Damn, I'm glad to see you. The colonel is back on the river-bank. We need to go back and get him moving," Carden explained.

"I go with you," Chi said and began to follow Carden. Suddenly Chi grabbed Carden and squatted down. The sound of Vietnamese voices could be heard to the north. Then a gunshot was heard.

"Chi, what's going on?" Carden asked.

"Enemy was calling to colonel. They want him to surrender and drop weapon," Chi said. "We wait." Carden did not argue but took the interpreter's advice and waited an hour before they cautiously moved back to the riverbank. Colonel Brownlee was nowhere to be seen.[1]

"We go now," Chi said. "We go south. I know friendly location for us." Carden and Chi moved south towards FSB 5 and joined a group of friendlies waiting to be extracted north of FSB 5. They were picked up the next day.

42

COMMAND DECISIONS

25 APRIL 1972
SRAG II HQ
Pleiku

THE PREVIOUS DAY had been a disaster for Vann's plan of stopping the enemy and pounding them with B-52 strikes. Today, some B-52 strikes were going to be dropped, but the question was where. Throughout the night, reports from Spectre and Stinger gunships indicated that tanks were everywhere. Spectre reported killing between thirty and fifty tanks in the Dak To II–Tan Canh area alone. Covey reported that an F-4 with the new laser-guided bombs had destroyed three 105mm howitzers that the NVA were attempting to move that morning.

Vann was just entering his office when Brigadier General John Hill was coming down the hall.

"Damn, I'm glad to see you," Vann said as Hill approached him.

"I was told to report here to be your deputy and senior military officer," Hill said, sounding less than enthusiastic, and Vann caught it.

"Look, John, I know we've had our differences, but I need you right now. Wear came down with something and I had to send him to the hospital in the Philippines. Here, step into my office and let's go over some stuff. We have a staff meeting in half an hour with Dzu to go over what happened yesterday. It was a disaster. After the staff meeting, we'll take my helicopter and I'll give you a tour of the area and then we can talk about your role as I see it and as you see it. Fair enough?" Vann asked.

"Sounds good," Hill replied and they commenced to have a quick discussion about the respective staff members and General Dzu.

General Dzu had asked for a combined II Corps–SRAG II staff meeting to see where they were and what needed to be done to salvage something. President Thieu had already directed that no ground would be given up, and yet there was nothing Dzu could do at this point to retake Tan Canh or Dak To II. Someone was going to have to take the blame for this, and he felt it was not going to be him. Major Steinhauer sat in the back at the request of Mr. Vann. Josh had spent the night in the command center monitoring the radios and was well aware of the disaster.

"Before we get started, I want to know why you allowed this to happen," Dat said, looking directly at Colonel Kaplan.

"Sir, I was not the commander of the 22nd Division. Colonel Dat was. It was his responsibility to train and lead his division. Not mine," Kaplan said as tactfully as possible.

"You advisor. You should have advised him better," Dzu said, pointing his finger. Before Kaplan could respond, Mr. Vann jumped in.

"General, Colonel Kaplan is an advisor...not a commander. If Dat didn't take his advice—and he did not—there's nothing that Colonel Kaplan could have done. We made you aware of this inaction along with Colonel Minh. The 22nd has had bad commanders even before Dat. Major General Le Ngoc Trien, the previous commander for two years before Dat, openly told his officers and soldiers that they couldn't defeat the NVA on the battlefield. That kind of leadership poisoned the soldiers. If you want to blame someone for this, blame him, but you will not blame my officers for piss-poor leadership," Vann said. All of the Americans took note that Vann backed them to the hilt. The word of his support quickly spread throughout the advisor ranks. "Now can we discuss what our losses are?"

Lieutenant Colonel Dick, SRAG G-4, took the podium. "Sir, our major components captured include twenty-three 105mm howitzers, seven 155mm howitzers, and ten M41 tanks. Over fifty artillery pieces have been destroyed long with fifteen tanks that I know of. Naturally, an unknown number of individual weapons, mortars, radios, jeeps, and 106 recoilless rifles have also been lost along with thousands of rounds of small-arms and artillery ammunition. Of the captured artillery pieces, we can expect those to be used against us in the coming fight."

Vann looked at Dzu. "General, most of your artillery officers have attended the US Artillery School at Fort Sill. One of the first things they learned is never to allow the enemy to seize the guns. Destroy them before allowing them to fall into enemy hands. For American artillery soldiers it's a mark of honor, but your officers failed to demonstrate honor when they simply ran away," Vann said, hoping the sting would be felt by Dzu. Dzu said nothing.

"Anything else, Dick?" Vann asked.

"Not really, sir. The resupply by the 374th Tactical Airlift Wing from Taiwan continues to flow. They have fifteen C-130s bringing in supplies each day. Seven bring in ammo, three bring in fuel and five bring in rice. VNAF C-123s have been hauling supplies as well and taking out refugees. I suspect we're going to be flying out a lot more of the refugees as they come down Highway 14 from Dak To," Colonel Dick said.

"Let's talk refugees. Major Givens," Vann called out, turning in his chair.

"Sir," Givens responded.

"Tell us what you've seen," Vann directed.

Givens stood up and began to speak. "Sir, I'm located at Vo Dinh at the 6th Ranger Group Headquarters. We've seen a major increase in refugees moving down Highway 14 towards Kontum. The road is being shelled by the NVA. Civilian bodies cover the road. Three buses of civilians were ambushed with RPGs and B-40 rockets, killing everyone. The NVA are making no effort to win the hearts and minds of the people but are killing anyone and everyone. ARVN soldiers are mixed in with the civilians, identified only by their uniform shirts and trousers. They have no equipment or helmets or weapons. They look like they're out for a Sunday stroll," Givens reported.

"Thank you, Major," Vann said, turning to face Dzu, who said nothing and looked away. Finally Dzu looked around the room and saw Colonel Ba, commander of the 23rd Division.

"Colonel Ba, what is the status of your division?" Dzu asked.

"Sir, my command post close Kontum last night. Now we occupy basement of old Special Forces Camp B-24, halfway between airfield and northwest perimeter. Lieutenant Colonel Kellar, my advisor, and I will make sure division is settled in and start to look at plan to defend. The 44th Regiment still in An Khe, but I expect them here soon," Ba outlined. "The 45th Regiment left Pleiku on the twenty-third, moving by convoy from Pleiku to Kontum. It was ambushed and had to return to Pleiku. We move back up the road now to clear this obstacle. The 53rd Regiment is now in defensive positions around Kontum," Ba concluded.

"Very good, Colonel Ba, we will talk again later today," Dzu responded and glanced at Vann. "So, what is the status of our forces now?" he asked, and Colonel Snell stood. This would be his last briefing as his time in Vietnam was over and he would be flying home in the coming days.

"Our disposition at this time is that Firebases 5 and 6 have been extracted for the most part. We have people moving through the jungle from both firebases. Captain Carden hooked up with one group yesterday. The 71st and 95th Border Ranger Battalions are at Ben Het. They've had light contract but nothing significant, but they report vehicles moving on the road. The 90th Border Ranger Battalion is at Dak Seang and has been in contact but holding out. The 88th Border Ranger Battalion is at Dak Pek. The 62nd Border Ranger Battalion is at Polei Kleng and has had only minor contacts through patrolling. I reminded everyone that the strength of each of these battalions is approximately one hundred and fifty people. Talking with Captain Truhan and Captain Sparks at Ben Het, it appears that three to four hundred survivors from the 47th have reached their location. We're working to ger VNAF aircraft up there to extract those people and bring them to Kontum. The 34th and 35th Battalions of the 6th Ranger Group began arriving yesterday, and they're at FSB Lam Son in the vicinity of Vo Dinh and replacing the 2nd Airborne units. They have a good blocking position across Highway 14 north of Kontum," Snell reported.

"And the status of the 22nd Division?" Dzu asked. Snell shot a look of surprise at Vann, who leaned over very close to Dzu.

"It doesn't exist any longer. You need to reconstitute it somewhere with new commanders and new people. I would recommend you do that at Ban Me Thuot." The expression on Dzu's face told Vann that Dzu hadn't even considered reconstitution yet.

"Gentlemen, thank you for this update. The staffs will prepare defensive plans for Kontum and get them to you shortly. I am available to meet with anyone today. Good day," Dzu announced, indicating the meeting was over. As everyone stood to leave, wondering what had been accomplished, Vann touched Dzu's elbow.

"We need to talk," Vann said, and Dzu nodded and led the way to his office. Upon entering, Dzu pointed to an overstuffed chair for Vann to sit in.

"We're liable to have two problems with Ba," Vann started. Dzu quickly jumped to his defense.

"Colonel Ba is a good commander. Why we have problem with him?"

"I don't doubt he's a good commander, but we have a problem. First, he's the same rank as the 6th Group commander and the district commander. The airborne brigade is leaving now, but what battalions are being left don't report to Ba but separate airborne command in Saigon. None of those guys have to take orders from him as they're of equal rank and all work for different commands who give them orders. Unity of command is going to be a problem. We need a senior officer here to pull the command together with everyone reporting to that one commander," Vann explained.

"I see your point," Dzu mumbled.

"The second problem, and I'm going to fix this quickly, is that the senior advisor, Colonel Kellar, and Ba do not get along. Kellar flies the helicopters and leaves the advice to subordinate advisors. Kellar has to go, but I need to find a replacement for him, and I'll start working on that this afternoon. While I work on that, you think about what we do for unity of command here at Kontum. Okay?" Vann asked.

"I will think about it. Maybe move my chief of staff to take the command of Kontum's defense," Dzu pondered as Vann departed.

43

PRIORITIES

25 April 1972
SRAG II HQ
Pleiku

Vann and Hill had been out all afternoon, flying in Vann's aircraft, viewing the area. Hill was somewhat familiar with the area, having been spent two previous tours in the northern part of Vietnam. As Vann flew, he pointed out the key hamlets, roads, and firebases, and Hill made notes on his map. Hill was a rated Army aviator, so Vann's normal pilot got the afternoon off. Upon returning, Vann and Hill went to Vann's office.

"Can I offer you a drink, General?" Vann asked.

"No, I'm good" was Hill's response. He wasn't a frequent drinker and never while on duty. Once seated, Vann decided it was time to outline his priorities for Hill.

"First, let me say I'm glad to have you here. The loss of Wear could not have come at a worse time, but he really needed to get to a hospital.[1] Weyand called and said he tried to come back from the Philippines but Weyand met him at the plane and put him right back on it with orders to report back to the hospital. He told him that you were already here in place," Vann informed him.

"I've known Wear for several years. We served together in Korea. Good man. Hope he'll be okay," Hill expressed.

"I suspect that a long hospital stay is in his future. Anyway, here are the things I need you to make your priorities. First, I need you to organize and coordinate fire support. They've never fought as a division, so they don't understand coordinated and prioritized fire support. The Vietnamese have almost no idea of concentrated artillery support. They don't understand the relationship of direct support and general support for artillery or priority of fires. This may have been one of the factors that caused them to lose Tan Canh and Dak To II. Massing fires is not normal for these commanders," Vann pointed out.

"Does the division have a fire direction center?" Hill asked.

"I don't think so as the batteries are generally so far apart it wasn't ever used. Each battery had their own FDC, but nothing to coordinate and prioritize fires," Vann explained.

"Okay, I'll get on that one quick. What's next?" Hill asked.

"Next, I think we need to cut the size of the DTOC. There are so many people in there that they're tripping over each other and the people that need to be in there can't get a thing done," Vann indicated.

"I was going to say something about that as I noticed that there were a lot of people in the meeting this morning that didn't need to be there. The chaplain advisor...that's a first," Hill said, chuckling slightly. "I'll get with Lieutenant Colonel Bricker and discuss it with him."

"Bill Bricker is new. He's replacing Snell and only arrived three days ago. This might be a good time to make the changes," Vann agreed. "The third thing, and this is major—airspace management and control. We have so many aircraft, from fighter bomber jets, Navy, Air Force, Marine, to prop VNAF bombers, to B-52s to Army helicopters and gunships and VNAF helicopters when they show up. Add Spectre, Spooky and Stinger aircraft at night to that mix. I'm amazed that we haven't had a midair or an air strike on friendlies," Vann lamented.

"Let me talk to the 1st Aviation Brigade, who owns all the US helicopters in-country, about getting someone to assist in that endeavor. Do you think the Air Force will cough up someone to go help with managing high-performance aircraft?" Hill asked.

"Can't hurt to ask. Do you have someone in mind for managing helicopters?" Vann inquired.

"Yeah, Colonel John Todd, the deputy commander for the 1st Aviation Brigade. He would make a good air boss. The other thing I want to do, with your permission, is move third-echelon aircraft maintenance out of Pleiku back to Cam Rahn Bay. I suspect that if Charlie makes a major push against Kontum, he may be making a second push against the facilities in Pleiku. We're going to need a sustained round-the-clock maintenance program when things start heating up," Hill stressed.

"Sounds fine to me. Nothing sacred about having maintenance at Pleiku," Vann indicated and paused. "On another subject, what's your first impression on the advisors you've met?"

Hill sat back in his chair and thought for a moment. "I thought you might be asking me that question. Kaplan seems to be a very capable advisor, and if Dat would have listened to him, they may have been able to hold out a bit longer. The mess with the 22nd can't be held against Kaplan. Have we had any word on Brownlee or Yonan?" Hill asked.

"No, nothing," Vann replied, wringing his hands and shaking his head. "What do you think of Kellar?"

"I'm not so sure about him. In the meeting, he struck me as less than enthusiastic about being an advisor, and whenever Ba said anything, he rolled his eyes. Does he get along with Ba?" Hill inquired.

"From what I've seen, not very well. Ba is a good commander, but Kellar would rather fly his helicopter than sit with Ba and give advice. I'm hearing that they don't socialize, and Kellar really doesn't give him much advice, so I've been told," Vann said.

"Do you have a replacement in mind?"

"Yeah, Colonel Rhotenberry is due to replace Kellar in September. I think I can get him over here right away from the States. Do you know him?"

"I do, and he's tougher than a woodpecker's lips. He would be a good man to have if you can get him. Any others for backup?"

"There's a Colonel John Truby who's the senior CORDS advisor for II Corps that I think I can get if we can't get Rhotenberry," Vann stated and paused for a moment.[2] "We're going to need replacements for some of our regimental advisors. Lieutenant Colonel McKenna with the 44th Regiment is doing a good job and has a good rapport with Colonel Tien. Lieutenant Colonel Schorr was wounded, so we need a replacement for the 40th Regiment, which is going to have to be reconstituted along with the 42nd and 47th. Brownlee is missing, so we need someone for the 47th Regiment. Captain Dobbins was acting senior advisor to the 42nd and did well, but we really need to get a lieutenant colonel in there. Major George Dodge is acting senior advisor with the 45th and has done good, so we can keep him in place. The 53rd hasn't had an advisor for a long time. We need someone there," Vann outlined.

"I'll talk to Colonel Pizzi about filling those slots ASAP," Hill indicated.

"What do you think of the Vietnamese commanders you've met so far?" Vann asked.

"Well," Hill said, leaning forward in his chair, "Dzu appears to do what you tell him to do, which makes life a bit easier for you, I imagine. Colonel Ba seemed okay. Colonel De, the 6th Ranger Group commander, didn't impress me, and the 2nd Airborne Brigade commander struck me as all talk and no action. Colonel Long, the province chief, seems to have a burr up his ass if you ask me. He may be a problem when things get tough. The Vietnamese staff seemed okay, but I was a bit surprised to see none of them answering Dzu's questions."

"In mixed company, Dzu usually directs his questions to the advisor staff. He doesn't want to embarrass his people," Vann replied. "Oh, there's one other thing I need you to see to."

"What's that?" Hill asked, suspicious of this request.

"Need you to ensure that the airfield at Kontum stays operational. We lose that airfield, we're in trouble with Highways 19 and 14 under the guns," Vann pointed out.

"I'll get over there and see what we can do to make that happen. Not to change the subject, but I have noticed a lot of people here at Pleiku that don't appear to have jobs. What's up with that?" Hill asked.

"Several units have rotated home recently. However, support units for those units have not. We have a lot of logistic folks here that don't have jobs or enough work to keep them busy. If any were combat arms trained, I would make advisors out of them, and several have come forward and volunteered to stay on," Vann said.

"Then I say get them out of here. If they were combat arms people, I would agree to put them in as advisors, but being logisticians, we can't, so get them out of here. Ship them to Cam Rahn Bay. That will cut down on our resupply needs as less mouths to feed. Give me the word and I'll make a call to have the units transferred out of here and move them to Cam Rahn Bay or wherever," Hill indicated.

"Do it" was all Vann said.

Hill stood. "If there's nothing else, you've given me a full plate to work on, so I best get started. I have a few phone calls to make to MACV before they all go out for their afternoon cocktails."

"And I will get on the phone about getting Rhotenberry over here or Truby out of Nha Trang if I can't," Vann said, standing and heading to his phone. Over his shoulder, he looked at Hill as he departed. "Talk later tonight after dinner."

44

TRUBY GETS INVOLVED

Colonel John Truby received the call the previous day that he was being reassigned to SRAG II in Pleiku. John Vann had flown down to Nha Trang and picked him up and briefed him as they flew back to Pleiku. Rhotenberry had a medical procedure and couldn't come over until September. Truby was very familiar with the Central Highlands and had worked well in the past with Vann. Last night Vann had flown him over from Pleiku and introduced him to Colonel Ba. Truby was impressed. Kellar was nowhere to be seen as he had already departed for another assignment.

"Good morning, Colonel Ba," Truby said, entering Ba's work area in the 23rd Division command center. The command center had been set up in the basement of a building. The first floor of the building had been covered with empty fifty-five-gallon drums standing upright. Over them was a layer of wood timbers supporting sheets of plywood and tin. On top of the plywood and tin were filled sandbags two layers high. It was believed that this would protect the basement from incoming artillery.

"Good morning, Colonel. We walk perimeter this morning?" Ba's question came across as a statement. When the two had met the previous evening, Truby had asked if Ba had walked the perimeter that the division was expected to defend. He had not, and Truby had suggested tactfully that they needed to do that so they could best determine where to put forces and identify avenues of approach and locations for reserve forces, kill zones and the forward defense positions. Ba had never done a division perimeter defense. Truby had written an exercise at the Command and General Staff College at Fort Leavenworth in the late 1950s and had a good understanding of what was involved in the planning for such an action. They had planned to be out all day. On a map, they had drawn out a tentative plan and now wanted to observe the plan on the ground. At the first stop, it was clear that the plan was going to have to be changed.

"Colonel Truby, this not good. We have unit boundary here and this looks like likely avenue of approach. Only one unit should be here covering this avenue," Ba pointed out.

"You're absolutely right, Colonel. If the enemy comes down this avenue along a boundary between two units, he would split those units and roll right in to the city. We need to adjust this boundary so only one unit is covering and responsible for this avenue," Truby agreed. Ba turned to his operations officer, who was accompanying them, and said something. The staff officer wrote some quick notes on a notepad.

"I think final protective fires should be laid along telephone line, but I let battalion and regimental commanders decide that," Ba said, pointing at a row of telephone wires two hundred meters to their front. Truby said nothing but simply nodded approval. As they continued to walk and discuss the defense, they came upon soldiers digging foxholes. The foxholes were rather shallow, being only two feet deep.

"Colonel Ba, these foxholes are too shallow. This dirt is easy to dig. The holes should be four to five feet deep to offer the most protection," Truby pointed out. "In addition, if they're that deep, the soldiers can squat down in them if a tank approaches, let the tank roll over the hole and then stand up and fire a LAW into the back of the tank, which is the most vulnerable part." Ba was staring at Truby the whole time he was talking. Everyone was staring at Truby as he talked—privates, sergeants and junior officers. Ba broke out in a smile. He slowly turned to the private that was in the process of digging and began to coach him on the proper way to dig a foxhole. After he finished, every soldier was back to digging, and amazingly, all had smiles. Truby felt that he was working with a professional soldier and a good teammate.

Walking on to the next location, Truby and Ba were discussing the upcoming battle that they knew was approaching. The discussion had turned to the pros and cons of a perimeter defense versus leaving Kontum to conduct a movement to contact.

"In Kontum, I think perimeter defense is better than movement to contact," Ba said.

"Why is that, Colonel?" Truby responded.

"Going after the enemy in the jungle and fighting on ground that he has chosen is like going into a man's house with all the lights turned off and him waiting for you with a gun. Let the enemy come to me, on ground that I have selected, across kill zones that I have chosen and against prepared positions that I have emplaced. That make me man in dark house with gun waiting," Ba said with a smile.

"I can't argue with your philosophy, Colonel," Truby answered with a bit of a chuckle.

As they were finishing their tour in the late afternoon, they stopped outside of the Popular Forces compound. Truby pointed out some problems that he'd noted with their defensive positions and Ba began to make on-the-spot corrections when Colonel Long, the province chief, came out. Initially it appeared to be a cordial conversation between the two Vietnamese colonels, but then it turned heated. As best Truby could understand, Long didn't appreciate Ba making corrections to his units' deficiencies even though Ba was responsible for the overall defense of Kontum. Long pointed out he wasn't in Ba's chain of command and didn't have to respond to Ba's orders. Truby made a mental note that he was going to have to talk to General Hill about this.

The next morning, Ba called a meeting to discuss the defensive plan for the perimeter. He asked that all commanders attend, to include the province chief, Colonel Long; the 6th Ranger Group commander, Colonel De; and the 2nd Airborne Brigade commander. Truby was one of the first to arrive, followed by Ba's staff. At the appointed time, none of the other commanders had arrived nor sent any member of their staff. *How in the hell is Ba going to be able to conduct a division perimeter defense if none of the subordinate commanders support him?* Truby was thinking when he left and headed to see General Hill.

"Sir, you have a minute?" Truby asked, entering Hill's office.

"Sure, what's up?" Hill asked, sitting back in his chair behind his desk. He motioned for Truby to take a seat.

"It seems that the province chief, the 6th Group commander and the airborne commander feel that they don't have to take orders from Ba. All three aren't in his chain of command, all three report to different headquarters and all three are of equal rank to Ba. Unity of command is lacking under this current arrangement. Unless those three get on board, Ba isn't going to be able to hold this perimeter," Truby outlined.

Hill thought for a moment. "I see your point. Let me take this up with Vann and Dzu and see what we can do to rectify the situation. Strange as it sounds, I don't think Dzu even has command authority over those three. I will get back to you," Hill said, quickly jotting down a note.

45

GOOD AND BAD NEWS

29 APRIL 1972
SRAG II HQ
Pleiku

THE STAFF WAS HAVING an afternoon update with Vann and Hill as well as General Dzu. They would review the events of the last twenty-four to forty-eight hours and lay out the events of the next twenty-four to forty-eight hours.

"Okay, let's get started. Pahl, you're up," Vann said, taking his seat. Colonel Pahl stepped up to the podium and placed a VGT on the overhead projector of a map of the area.

"Gentlemen, in the past forty-eight hours, the enemy appears to be holding his tanks at Tan Canh and Dak To II. Ben Het reports sporadic contact and enemy movement eastbound along Highway 512. There has been sporadic contact in the vicinity of Polei Kleng. On the twenty-sixth, the enemy quickly moved in an occupied Dien Binh after the airborne pulled out. From prisoner reports, we believe the 141st NVA Regiment are the ones that have moved in. There have been—" Pahl did not finish before he was interrupted by General Hill.

"What? Who authorized that withdrawal? Were they in contact?" Hill asked, looking at Colonel Bricker.

"Sir, we had no reports of them being in contact and we were notified after the fact," Bricker stated. Hill just shook his head.

"Continue, Colonel Pahl," Hill said, making a note.

"There have been probes at FSB Lam Son against the 34th and 35th Ranger Battalions as well as some artillery and mortar fire. Spectre is reporting vehicle movement along Highway 14 and Highway 512 but very little past Dak To," Pahl stated and checked his notes. "Aircraft that have been looking for Brownlee and others have reported pockets of enemy forces, and we've been plotting those locations and passing them on to operations for targeting. They're definitely in a holding pattern at this time with only reconnaissance elements moving towards Kontum. Any questions?" Pahl asked as he wrapped up his portion.

"Why do you think they're not continuing the attack?" Vann asked.

"Sir, it could be a couple of factors. First, they may be waiting on the 320th to finish clearing operations between Rocket Ridge and Highway 14. Second, they may be refitting and resupplying. A third possibility is the rigid doctrine of the North not to change plans in the middle of an operation. A fourth possibility is they may want to soften up Kontum before they launch a ground assault as they've done in Tan Canh, Dak To II, An Loc and Quang Tri, according to reports," Pahl outlined. "Any other questions?" There were none.

"Sir, I will be followed by Colonel Bricker," Pahl announced. Bricker stood and moved to the podium.

"Sir, in the past forty-eight hours we have been policing up stragglers from the 22nd Division. Three hundred and fifty were picked up at Ben Het yesterday and flown to Kontum. We're assembling them in one of the old SF camps. We're going to need to have a decision soon on where to move them to so the division can be reconstituted. Reports are that they're a bit out of control and generally tearing the place up," Bricker said, glancing at General Dzu, who didn't make eye contact.

"Colonel Kaplan and I will look into this, Mr. Vann, and get back to you," General Hill said. Vann just nodded.

"Yesterday, Colonel De, commander of the 6th Ranger Group, displaced his headquarters to FSB November—"

"Who authorized that move?" Hill interrupted Bricker with a look of concern.

"Sir, I have no idea. He used VNAF helicopters and reported the move after it was completed," Bricker stated.

Hill turned in his chair and looked at Colonel Todd, who had just arrived and was taking over as air boss for all helicopter operations. "Did you know about this move?"

"No, I didn't. I'll look into it," Todd said.

Hill looked back at Bricker. "Where are the 34th and 35th Battalions? Are they still at FSB Lam Son?"

"Yes, sir, I believe they are, but De hasn't had contact with them," Bricker said.

"Well, damnit, tell De to make contact with them. We can't afford to have two battalions sitting out in a blocking position and not have contact with them," Hill said, his level of frustration obvious to everyone. "Alright, continue."

"We've received authorization to move the third-echelon maintenance units at Pleiku to Cam Rahn Bay, and those units have been notified to prepare to depart. Delta Company, 1st of the 12th Infantry, has been attached to the 17th Aviation Battalion at Pleiku and is serving as an immediate reaction force. On a positive note, ROK headquarters has reported that as of this morning, Highway 19 is open. This was confirmed by Lieutenant Colonel McKenna, the senior advisor with the 44th Regiment, who left this morning to go on R&R."

"Well, that is some good news," Hill said with a smile.

"Yes, sir. On a sad note, Bravo Troop, 7th of the 17th Cav, began standing down yesterday. We couldn't convince MACV to keep them in-country a bit longer."

"Damn. That will hurt. I hope we don't lose any other units to the drawdown," Vann said.

Bricker continued, "We've been notified by MACV that Colonel Donald Swenholt, US Air Force, will be joining us tomorrow to coordinate air assets. He'll be bringing a control party with him as well."

"Excellent. I want his people to have all the support we can give them," Hill said.

"Sir, I would like Colonel Todd to follow me as I believe he has some good and interesting news," Bricker said as Todd stood.

"Mr. Vann, General Dzu, General Hill," Todd said formally. "Tomorrow, a unique aviation unit will arrive in Pleiku. The 1st Combat Aerial TOW Team, call sign Hawk's Claw. There are two aircraft UH-1Bs equipped with the XM-26 TOW weapon systems. Each aircraft carries three missiles on each side and engages targets ideally at three thousand meters and three thousand feet."

"What do they engage?" Dzu asked.

"Sir, ideally, they engage and destroy tanks," Todd said. Dzu shot a look at Vann and a smile broke out on his face.

"Really!" Dzu asked.

"Yes, sir. This is their first commitment in combat, having been sent over this past week from California, where they've been in testing. The aircraft are actually owned by Hughes Aircraft, who also owns the weapons, but they're being flown by Army pilots that have been doing the testing. Once they arrive, they'll be prepared and I'll keep you posted on the first mission and the results," Todd explained.

"I would very much like to see this aircraft," Dzu indicated.

"Sir, as soon as it's ready I'll invite you down to look at it," Todd offered graciously.

The remainder of the staff briefed pertinent points that needed General Hill's attention, but nothing earthshaking was noted. As the briefing began to break up, General Hill asked if Mr. Vann, General Dzu and Colonel Truby could stay behind, which they did. After the room was emptied, General Hill turned to Truby. "Tell them what you told me."

Truby looked at Vann and Dzu. "Ba has a unity of command problem, and if we don't correct it, he can't conduct a division perimeter defense of Kontum. Ba commands the 23rd Division and has only the 54th Regiment in the city under his command. The Ruff-Puffs, 6th Ranger Group, and the airborne brigade commanders don't feel that they have to take orders from him as they're not in his chain of command and are of equal rank. They're ignoring him and not working with him at all," Truby stated.

"We need a general officer to take command of the defense of Kontum," Vann said.

"That would be nice, but we don't have a general officer to use," Dzu said.

"Well, it's obvious that De and Lich are going to dance to their own tune and that's not going to work," Truby said.

"Why not bring in the rest of the 23rd Division?" Hill said. "Bring the 44th and the 45th Regiments into Kontum. Give Ba his entire division. Move the 6th Ranger Group outside to the surrounding hamlets and blocking positions along with the airborne brigade. Hell, we're liable to lose all the airborne troops at a moment's notice anyway depending on the whims of Saigon. Let's not put them someplace of importance and have them pulled unexpectedly," Hill expressed.

For a moment, everyone exchanged looks. Finally Dzu spoke up. "I will order the 44th and 45th Regiments to move immediately to join the 23rd Division here in Kontum. Colonel Ba will have his entire command." Everyone nodded in agreement. "Let us discuss where we should put the 6th Ranger Group and the airborne brigade after dinner tonight."

46

SITUATION UPDATE KONTUM

28 APRIL 1972
Senior Province Advisor
Kontum

COLONEL STEPHEN BACHINSKI was serving as the senior advisor to Colonel Long, the Kontum Province chief. One of his duties was to provide an end-of-month report to MACV on the situation in the province. Bachinski stared at his typewriter, a bit unsure of how he was going to write this month's report. Finally, he decided that it would be best to jot down his thoughts before he put them in message format.

"Refugees: There are currently eight thousand refugees in the processing center and another eight thousand being taken in by family. Most have nothing more than what can be carried. Daily flow continues down Highway 14 and Highway 19 to Kontum, as well as from surrounding hamlets.

"Civil Service: Civil service employees that are supposed to see the refugees are adequately taken care of with food, medicine, accommodations and transportation out have turned to taking care of family first and are even fleeing themselves.

"Regional and Popular Forces: Desertions in both forces have reduced the force by fifty percent. Soldiers care about family first and getting them out of the combat zone. Their capability to add to the defense is limited.

"Sanitation: Sanitation is poor, with too few facilities for washing or waste. Water from the river is contaminated with feces, urine, and bodies of both humans and animals. Wells are providing potable water but must be guarded.

"Medical services: Medical services are nonexistent. Medical supplies are gone. Medical personnel have departed for the most part, leaving patients to fend for themselves.

"Food: Food supplies have offered minimum nutrition but have supported the current population.

"Departures: With all roads closed, departures are limited to air transport. US and VNAF aircraft have been significant in extracting civilians from the airfield to Tan Son Nhut. VNAF helicopters are selling seats to depart Kontum to Pleiku.

"Atrocities: Atrocities are reported daily. Reports from hamlets and refugees indicate that priests, policemen, government officials and hamlet leaders are immediate targets. Children, to include both boys and girls, are moved into the jungle, not to be seen again. Military-age men are forced to dig trenches or fighting positions.

"Conclusion: Poor military and civilian leadership over the years has contributed to the present conditions. At the present time, it is not believed that Kontum can be retained against a concerted enemy push as there are insufficient forces to repel such an attack and there is a lack of unity of command.

"Recommendation: MACV should anticipate and plan an evacuation of all US personnel from the province."

With his bullet points, Bachinski prepared his report and forwarded it up the chain, which did not include SRAG II as it was a military organization and Bachinski was in the State Department chain. When it was incorporated into the final report that General Abrams received, it mirrored what Vann had told him in private communications. Abrams decided it was best to talk to Melvin Laird, who passed his comments on to the president in the Oval Office.

"Mr. President, General Abrams and I had a talk. The situation in MR-II is deteriorating with the collapse of the 22nd Division at Dak To II and Tan Canh. This has hurt the morale of the Vietnamese forces in general and especially those attempting to defend Kontum. Senior Vietnamese military leadership is bending and breaking in some cases and that has had a trickle-down effect on the midgrade leadership. There are exceptions, as in the case of General Truong, the MR-IV commander. In MR-I, the corps commander, General Lam, is incompetent at best, and the 3rd Division commander is bending under the pressure. President Thieu has issued an order to the corps and division commanders in Quang Tri, Hue and Kontum that they will hold in place at all costs. He has further directed that Highway 13 from Lai Khe to An Loc be opened by 2 May.

"Abrams also reported that the disposition of troops northwest of Kontum is a reinforced Border Ranger battalion at Ben Het, another battalion at Dak Pek and a third Border Ranger battalion at Dak Seang. These battalions, I should point out, are about the size of a reinforced US rifle company and not as large as a US battalion. In Kontum area, there's the 6th Ranger Group, one regiment of the 23rd Division with four infantry battalions, two airborne battalions, forty-eight tubes of artillery and eighteen tanks. He also noted some friction in the command as there's no one central commander authority for Kontum. The enemy, on the other hand, is resolved to carry this through as he has the initiative, disregard for the expenditure of men or material, and discipline obtained through fear among his soldiers and the civilian population, brought about by intimidation and brutality. Civilians are being totally ignored and are being targeted. The enemy isn't attempting to win the hearts and minds of the people. Just the opposite, they're punishing the people for not supporting them."

Nixon contemplated what Laird had just told him and did not answer immediately but turned in his chair to look out the window while he considered his response. Finally, he turned back to face Laird.

"There is no doubt that with the will, we have the ability to decimate the enemy's ability to supply his forces. It's a question of will for us to do that. I do. However, we have to overcome the bureaucrats in the Defense Department, who will join with their compadres in the State Department to find ways to erode the strong, decisive action that I want and have indicated we will take. The JCS and NCS have got to develop some ideas on actions that are strong, threatening and effective."

"Sir, we resumed the bombing campaign over North Vietnam at the beginning of last month. The situation around An Loc appears to have stabilized to some degree. The thrust in MR-I has been halted. Right now Kontum is the danger spot. I'll discuss with JCS about increasing B-52 strikes in the area as well and see if we need to move more aircraft to the region."

47

WITHDRAW FROM FSB LAM SON

1 May 1972
23rd Division HQ
Kontum

With Highway 19 being opened, Major Josh Steinhauer decided to drive over to Kontum with his driver. Josh had heard about the debacle at Tan Canh from Lieutenant Colonel McKenna before he left to go on R&R. Josh wanted to observe what was taking place at Kontum with the defeat of the 22nd Division. As they entered Kontum, it quickly became obvious what the impact was.

"Sir, I've never seen so many people all moving down Highway 19 towards the coast," Sergeant Howard said as he weaved through the traffic of humans walking down the road, on both sides.

"They're running scared. I think I've seen enough military-age men in the last hour to man a regiment, and from their haircuts and clothing I'll bet they were deserters. This isn't good," Josh said, noting that no one was carrying a weapon or any military equipment. Slowly the jeep wound its way through the city and reached the headquarters for the 23rd Division. As Josh exited the jeep, the rumbling sounds of B-52 bomb strikes could be clearly heard and the dust rising from the ridge north of the city could be easily seen.

"Damn, that's close, sir," Howard said, looking at the rising wall of destruction. "Do you think the NVA are that close?"

"I suspect they might be. Mr. Vann isn't going to be wasting B-52 strikes on the monkeys," Josh said as he walked towards the entrance to the command bunker. "Wait here and I'll see what we can see or do next." Once inside, he noticed organized chaos, which was typically found in a command bunker under siege. As he stood there looking, someone from behind him asked, "Who are you and what are you doing here?"

Turning, Josh was looking at a US Army colonel. His name tag said Truby. "Sir, I'm Major Josh Steinhauer, on special assignment from the DOD IG office. I've been sent over here—"

"Yeah, I know all about you, Major. Was wondering when you were going to get here. How does the 44th Regiment look to you? You've been there for almost the past month, right?" Truby asked.

"Yes, sir. The regiment looks pretty good. The commander is aggressive and the chain of command appeared to be competent. Lieutenant Colonel McKenna seems to have a good rapport with the commander, Colonel Tien. Major Swachek is the deputy and filling in now that McKenna is on R&R," Josh reported.

"Good, come over to the map board with me," Truby said, leading the way to a map board posted on a table with clear plastic over it. On the plastic cover were red marks indicating enemy locations. As Josh looked at it, he thought they must have gone through a box of grease pencils marking it. "Right now we have the 34th and 35th Ranger Battalions at Fire Support Base Lam Son. The commander moved his headquarters without informing anyone to Fire Support Base November, here," Truby added, pointing at the location. "We've had no contact with the commander, Colonel De, or the battalions. The advisor, Captain Givens, is attempting to find out what's going on. I'd like you to drive up there and assess the situation. The road is clear, so that shouldn't be a problem. Report back to me when you get there and let me know what's going on. Do you have a radio?" Truby asked.

"No, sir," Josh said, studying the map and marking locations on his own map.

"I'll get one for you." Truby turned and directed an American sergeant to get an FM radio and take it to Josh's vehicle. "Your call sign will be Traveler. Mine is Golden Boy. Call me on forty-five-double-oh. Any questions?"

"No, sir. You do understand that I have no authority to order anyone to do anything. I'm over here just as an observer," Josh said.

"Good, and you're going to observe. Best get going," Truby said and pointed to the door.

Outside, Howard was positioning the FM radio between the front seats when Josh arrived. "Where we off to sir?"

"Howard, we're going for a little ride. Take 19 west to the intersection of 14 and turn north. We're going to Fire Support Base Lam Son. Should take us about thirty minutes as it's only eight miles from here."

"Yes, sir. I know where it is, just off 14. Been there a couple of times over the year," Howard said as he put the vehicle in gear and rolled out the gate. On Highway 19, the traffic flow for the most part was going east towards Kontum. It consisted of people walking, bicycles, motor bikes, oxcarts, and a few cars and trucks. The trucks were initially civilian, but as they turned onto Highway 14, some of them were military and they were full of troops. The foot traffic changed as well from mostly civilians to mostly military the closer they got to Lam Son.

Arriving at Lam Son, Josh was surprised at what he saw. Four M41 tanks sat outside the perimeter, blown to pieces and still burning. Most of the infantry soldiers had departed. The artillery battery was still present and manning the guns. An American officer was in an apparent argument with a Vietnamese officer, demonstrating wild hand and arm movements and elevated voices. Josh approached.

"Excuse me, Captain, but what's going on here?" Josh asked. The captain hadn't seen him approach and was a bit startled to turn and see a strange major standing behind him. The Vietnamese officer simply walked away towards the artillery battery.

"Sorry, sir, I didn't see you. I'm Captain Givens, the advisor to the 6th Ranger Group, which was located here until about an hour ago," Givens said.

"Okay, what happened an hour ago? Where are they now?" Josh asked.

"This morning we took some incoming artillery. Nothing serious and no casualties. We've had ground probes for four days now, but again, nothing major. Four tank crews that were outside the perimeter unassed the tanks and took off this morning at 0500. The enemy quickly seized the tanks and started to drive off. I called in an air strike and stopped that from happening. Two days ago, Colonel De moved his command post to November after we had a few incoming artillery rounds. About an hour ago, and I haven't yet figured out who ordered it, the 34th and 35th Battalions packed up and left for November. There's no one here providing security for the battery, and the battery commander now intends to load his people up and move out too. This firebase is being abandoned without a real fight," Givens said with disgust dripping off each word.

"Are they taking the tubes with them?" Josh asked.

"I don't believe they are, sir," Givens said as the first truck departed with the gun crews. They weren't bringing their guns.

"Get an air strike on those artillery tubes. Do you have a ride out of here?" Josh asked, looking around for another jeep.

"No, sir. I sent my deputy out earlier to try and turn the battalions around and send them back. Mind if I get a ride with you?" Givens asked, picking up his PRC-77 radio.

"Nah, jump in and let's get that air strike," Josh directed. "Howard, let's get out of here."

A half mile down the road, Howard pulled the jeep to the side of the road as Captain Givens talked to a FAC aircraft orbiting above. The white phosphorous rocket marked the center of the artillery battery. Moments later, the first of two five-hundred-pound bombs exploded, causing secondary explosions of artillery ammunition and tossing 105 howitzers into the air like rag dolls. A second jet dropped napalm canisters, destroying almost everything else on the firebase.

The first blocking position in the plan to defend Kontum's perimeter was gone.

48

BOMBING TACTICS

1 MAY 1972
SRAG II HQ
Pleiku

COLONEL DON SWENHOLT, USAF, had arrived the day before with a small air control party. Prior to his arrival, Captain Chris Schudder had been the air ops advisor for II Corps. Captain Jack Finch was the air advisor for the 23rd Division. This was about to change. Colonel Swenholt called a "blue suiter" meeting at SRAG II Headquarters.

"Gentlemen, we have been brought here to work air operations for this operation, to include flight following, airspace management and air operations. So far this has all worked for some reason and we haven't had any friendly engagements or midairs, but things are going to get a lot more concentrated in the days to come. Captain Finch and Captain Schudder, I want you two to take over coordination and allocation of B-52 strikes as well as close-air support requests." Both captains exchanged looks and nodded that they understood. "You'll work here and not over at II Corps headquarters. You will not share any information with the Vietnamese on the number of B-52 strikes scheduled or where those strikes are going to be employed. Your maps will be covered at all times. Is that understood?" Swenholt asked.

"Yes, sir, but can I ask why?" Captain Schudder asked.

"Mr. Vann feels that we're not getting good intel from the Vietnamese. He wants to keep the B-52s in his hip pocket as the carrot to get the intel we need for the strikes to be effective," Swenholt said, pausing. "Now we're going to request a change in the bombing tactics. Right now the three B-52s in the flights follow one behind the other on their drops down the middle of the box. We're going to ask them to fly in echelon wingtip to wingtip, which will cover the width of each box and be more effective. Instead of blowing dead bodies into the Stone Age, we will only blow live bodies into the Stone Age."

"Sir, we're going to have to move the boxes further from the friendlies in that case," Captain Finch said with some concern in his voice.

"No. The boxes will still be danger close to the friendlies, and that will be three hundred meters," Swenholt said, "but only with the approval of myself or Mr. Vann. You two will not have that responsibility in case some friendlies do get hurt. You plan for danger close at five hundred meters."

"Yes, sir. When does this start?" Finch asked.

"Effective immediately. In fact, grab your map and let's see what we have planned for today and tomorrow," Swenholt directed. Finch got up to retrieve the map.

"Sir, General Dzu wants to bomb every abandoned firebase and every hamlet north and west of here. Mr. Vann said we wouldn't as we still have advisors and civilians in those areas that may be trying to get back to Kontum. He's directed us to use TAC fighters directed by the FACs in those areas and provided us with some boxes for the BUFFs. Each box is one kilometer wide and three kilometers long. Bingo Control is located here in Pleiku, so we get fairly accurate strikes. The problem we have is getting an accurate DBA after the strike. On several occasions, Mr. Vann has flown out in his chopper and waited for the strike to go in. He then flies into the strike box and conducts a visual reconnaissance to count bodies," Captain Schudder pointed out as Captain Finch returned with the map and spread it out.

As Swenholt studied the map, he asked, "What are the typical loads that we've been getting?"

"Sir, we're getting a mix of five-hundred-pound and seven-hundred-fifty-pound bombs, which is about seventy thousand pounds on each bomber. They generally come out of Utapao, but we're starting to get planes out of Guam as well," Schudder replied. After a moment, Swenholt looked up.

"Okay, I want you to get with the intel folks and have them show you the avenues of approach from this ridge—"

"That's Rocket Ridge, sir," Finch interrupted.

"Okay, from Rocket Ridge to Kontum. Also suspected locations where they'll have artillery positioned that can hit Kontum. Get with Ops and get the locations on all known and suspected friendly locations. Once you have that, I want the entire area around Kontum indicated in at least one box and possibly two. Flight routes will be parallel to friendly lines, so some boxes may run east–west and some north–south. Got it?" Swenholt asked.

"Yes, sir, we'll get right on it," Schudder replied with a broad smile.

"Once you have all that plotted, get it over to Bingo Control so they can direct the BUFFs to the correct box," Swenholt directed.

49

TOW TO THE FIGHT

2 May 1972
  1st Combat Aerial TOW Team
  Pleiku

THE MORNING STARTED AS USUAL, with strong coffee, powered eggs, undercooked bacon, sawdust bread and half-cooked pancakes on the menu. Warrant Officer Carroll Lain had graduated from flight school, and instead of heading right to Vietnam like ninety-nine percent of the graduating warrant officers, he had been sent to Hunter Liggett to fly aging Bravo-model Hueys. His initial disappointment was quickly replaced with excitement when he discovered he would be on a test program for a new weapon system, the XM-26 TOW antitank weapon system. The system had been ground-mounted for the past year and was in infantry battalions but had never been mounted on helicopters. When the call came to get to Vietnam, no one was upset as they were about to test the system out on real targets.

"Hey, sir, what have we got today?" Lain asked as he sat

down next to Captain Roy Sudeck, the team's Operations officer and aircraft commander for the C&C aircraft for the day.

"Right now we're on standby. The cav is out looking for some targets for us. Pink Panthers will be flying cover for us, and I have the C&C aircraft that will provide pickup, if we need it," Sudeck said.

"I hope we don't need it, sir," Lain commented as he sipped his coffee.

"I do too. I'm going over to Operations. See you over there. Who you flying with today?" Sudeck asked, standing up.

"I believe I'm flying with Mr. Whiters, sir," Lain said. CWO Whiters was the senior warrant officer in the team and had two previous tours in Vietnam.

Over in Flight Operations, Lieutenant Colonel Feore was looking over the weather report for the day. "Looks like we'll have some cloud cover today but should be good for flying," he said when Mr. Hugh McInnish and Mr. McGinnis walked in. Both were civilians overseeing the project. McInnish was with Hughes Aircraft and McGinnis was with Missile Command. SFC Hartsell followed them, wiping his hands on an oily rag.

"How does everything for today's mission?" Feore asked.

"Everything looks fine. Specialist Lehrschall and that new kid Specialist Wayne Evans are at the aircraft and all set to go," Hartsell commented.

"Good, now all we need is the cav to find something for us," Feore said. "Good morning, Chief," Feore greeted Mr. Whiters.

"Morning, sir, I'm going to head out to the aircraft. If Lain shows up, would someone send him out?" Whiters said.

He headed back out the door with his flight gear. As he did so, the radio came to life.

"Hawk's Claw Three, Pink Panther Three-Two, Over."

"Pink Panther Three-Two, Hawk's Claw Three India, over," the Operations clerk responded. All heads turned to the clerk, who had everyone's attention.

"Hawk's Claw Three India, Pink Panther Three, we have contact. Four, I say again, four Mike Four-One tanks." Pink Panther transmitted the location.

Before he could finish, Sudeck and Hartsell were out the door and running to the aircraft. They were quickly followed by Lieutenant Colonel Feore, who was flying the C&C aircraft with Sudeck. Lain was just approaching the Flight Operations door when it flew open with Sudeck in the lead. Lain didn't need an invitation or even question what was happening. He knew.

Lehrschall and Evans saw the pilots sprinting towards the aircraft and immediately untied the blades and donned their flight gear. McGinnis and McInnish were right on Feore's heels to get into the C&C aircraft. As the aircraft cleared the airfield at Camp Holloway, Sudeck contacted Pink Panther for an in-flight brief, which he received in detail. Whiters monitored the transmission.

Turning to Lain, who occupied the left seat, Whiters said, "Okay, we'll get to three thousand feet and at a range of three thousand meters engage the first of those four tanks."

"Roger," Lain responded.

"Okay, just don't be nervous. Fire just like you did the other day with your two practice shots. Don't rush it and stay focused on the target. You do that and you'll have a kill," Whiters said.

"Thanks, sir...no pressure, right?" Lain said, looking at the aircraft commander and smiling.

"That's right, no pressure," Whiters said, returning the smile. "Of course if you miss, I'm sure that the colonel will have you scrubbing the latrines with your toothbrush for the duration."

"Yeah, no pressure," Lain said. As they continued to fly northwest towards Kontum and the coordinates that Pink Panther had passed, both crew members held their M60 machine guns ready to engage. The air-defense threat was noted as high since a heat-seeking missile had been introduced by the

NVA. Several aircraft in the Quang Tri area had been shot down. The aircraft were equipped with an extension on the exhaust to direct the heat signature of the engine upward into the rotor blades, which dissipated the heat quickly, so the crews were told. Both gunners also held a thermite grenade that they would throw if they saw a missile launch as the grenade put out a much higher heat signature than the engine exhaust.

"Hawk's Claw Three, Pink Panther Three-Two, over."

Whiters could see the AH-1G Cobra attack helicopter that was covering an OH-6 scout helicopter working just above the trees. *Those OH-6 pilots must have some big balls*, Lain was thinking as he watched the little aircraft slowly moving over the jungle canopy.

"Pink Panther Three-Two, Hawk's Claw Six-Five, over," Whiters answered.

"Hawk's Claw, little bird will make one pass and drop smoke. Four Mike Four-One tanks are there. Over."

"Roger, Pink Panther, I have little bird in sight, over." As Whiters and Lain watched, the little bird suddenly turned sharply along a stretch of Highway 14 and tossed a white phosphorous grenade out. When it exploded, the white cloud couldn't be missed, nor could the four tanks up against the jungle tree line.

"Have you got the tanks?" Whiters asked, turning towards the tanks about four thousand meters away.

"I got them," Lain said as he placed his face into the sight unit stabilizer telescope and locked onto the first tank. Whiters steadied the aircraft at three thousand feet and closed the distance. As they passed through what Whiters thought was three thousand meters, he told Lain he was cleared to fire. The missile leaped off the rail and to the untrained eye appeared to wobble in front of the aircraft. Lain remembered his training and continued to hold the sight on the target. As he did so, the missile stabilized in the center of the sight and impacted on the tank.

"First kill," Whiters reported.

Before the day was over, the 1st Combat Aerial TOW Team would kill four tanks, one 105 howitzer and one two-and-a-half-ton truck, all US equipment abandoned at FSB Lam Son.[1]

50

———

CONFIDENCE BUILDERS

2 MAY 1972
23rd HQ
Kontum

COLONEL BA and Colonel Truby had been visiting the perimeter daily, inspecting positions and equipment and speaking with leaders, advisors and soldiers. Overall, they were pleased with what they were seeing.

"I think soldiers are doing well," Ba said. "However, whenever the soldiers ask about tanks, they appear to lose"—he paused—"how you say *su tu tin*?"

Truby looked at Josh, who was walking with them and had stayed with Truby since the fall of FSB Lam Son.

"Confidence," Josh said. Ba's head snapped around to look at Josh.

"*Ban noi tieng Viet?*" Ba asked. Truby's head rotated between Josh and Ban, now confused as to what was being said.

"*Mot chut,*" Josh replied.

"Okay, you two! What did Colonel Ba ask you?" Truby asked.

"Sir, he asked if I spoke Vietnamese and I responded that I spoke a little," Josh said. "I generally keep that fact to myself as it's let me eavesdrop on a lot of conversations over the course of this assignment."

"Good to know," Colonel Ba said with a smile.

Truby looked at Ba. "So the troops are expressing their concerns about tanks. We need to raise the confidence level and fast. They've got to believe in the LAW rockets. They've got to believe they can destroy those tanks with the LAWs, especially if they fire in volley."

"What 'volley'?" Ba asked with confusion on his face, looking at Josh.

"*Tinh co?*" Josh said.

"Volley," Ba repeated, still confused.

"Volley fire is when three or more soldiers fire their LAWs at the same tank at the same time. One LAW will kill the tank, but soldiers' confidence increases when three LAWs hit the tank at the same time," Truby explained.

"We show soldiers this technique. We get tank and set up range. Make soldiers go shoot tank with LAW in volley. We can do that," Ba said, and his aide started writing a note.

"Sir, the guys in An Loc have been using the LAW to knock out tanks down there for a month now. Maybe if we could get photos of those tanks with some of the defenders sitting on them and pass those around, that might build their confidence," Josh offered.

"Major, you just named your mission. Get some of those photos...oh, I forgot, you really don't work for me," Truby said.

"Sir, I believe that falls within the realm of my assignment. I'll make some phone calls to a contact I have there in An Loc," Josh said.

Looking back at Colonel Ba, Truby said, "I'll talk with Vann and see what else we can do to raise the confidence level. I have an idea that might be a big confidence builder and have immediate impact." He looked at the far hills.

Later that afternoon, the sound of LAW rockets impacting on the side of an abandoned tank could be heard as Vann and Truby met at the airfield. As Vann climbed out of his helicopter and the engine noise died, he heard the impacting rounds.

"What's that? Are there tanks probing the perimeter?" he asked with deep concern.

"No, sir, that's confidence building. We're going to need a lot more LAWs. Ba has all the soldiers shooting at abandoned tanks with LAWs to build their confidence. He has the 106 crews even practicing their shooting and then examining the damage to prove that they can knock out a tank. Up until now, the 106 was only shooting beehive antipersonnel rounds, not HEAT antitank rounds. That might be why they ran at Tan Canh," Truby pointed out.

"Good point. I'll talk to the folks and get us more LAWs... and 106 rounds. Anything else he's doing to raise their confidence in killing tanks?" Vann asked.

"Well, that major from the DOD IG suggested we get photos of killed tanks with smiling killers from An Loc and pass those out. Let the troops see that they can kill tanks. He said he has a point of contact at An Loc and was going to put a call in for the photos," Truby said as they walked across the tarmac.

They paused to watch a C-130 that was back taxiing down the runway with its ramp down. As he did so, five pallets of supplies rolled off the back. A large military forklift followed behind and picked up each pallet separately, moving it off and clearing the runway. Five pallets were dropped in thirty-seven seconds according to Vann's watch. By the time the C-130 reached the end of the runway and turned to depart, the runway was cleared. The C-130 never shut his engines down and never stopped on the runway for fear of enemy observers adjusting artillery or mortars on the aircraft. A few VNAF C-123 aircraft did pause long enough on the tarmac to pick up refugees that were organized into groups. Initially, the groups, once organized for the loads, would mob the aircraft, be it a C-123 or a CH-47 helicopter. Master Sergeant Lowell Stevens solved this problem with fourteen US soldiers armed with baseball bats maintaining control of the group. Word quickly spread that one should stay with the assigned group if they didn't want to play baseball—US soldier-style baseball.

"Damn, that was a fast offload," Vann said, turning to continue walking. "What were we talking about?"

"Sir, I said that DOD major—" Truby didn't get a chance to finish.

"Yeah, he's going to get photos from An Loc. I'll call General Hollingsworth and see if he can expedite that request. I'll see if I can get him to come up and give a talk to the commanders about the battle down there. That ought to raise their confidence level. They've been holding out through two major attacks so far. A lot of air support is saving their ass, along with the fact that there's no way to retreat. Highway 13 is closed, so the ARVNs are stuck in An Loc and have to fight. In a way I'm glad that Highway 19 is under fire—otherwise we might find these guys turning tail and running. President Thieu issued an order today that no Vietnamese forces will retreat from An Loc, Kontum or Quang Tri, although Quang Tri is a done deal. They're holding the south bank of the My Chanh River now," Vann said, handing a piece of paper to Truby. "Read this from Abrams."

To: All advisors and personnel
From: Commander, MACV

Subject: Airlift of ARVN commanders

Effective immediately, no ARVN commander will be airlifted out of a defensive position by US aircraft or helicopters unless such evacuation is directed personally by the RVNAF Corps Commander. Inform your counterparts.

"I'LL BE sure that all my people and the ARVNs know this. I guess he's serious," Truby said, folding the message and putting it in his pocket. "Not to change the subject, sir, but can we get some air strikes on targets that are closer to Kontum? Something that the people in the city can see and hear? A napalm strike on that ridgeline or a B-52 strike. Something to show them that there's support for them, at least from the air. Spectre at night is impressive," Truby said.

"That's something I wanted to talk to you about. I'm keeping the B-52 strike boxes close hold. Only US personnel will be allowed to see and designate the target boxes. This is about the only carrot I have to hold to get them to respond to the situation. Dzu is falling apart. He's convinced he's going to be court-martialed for Tan Canh. I think he'll find a way to get transferred if he doesn't get relieved in the coming weeks. Colonel Swenholt has formed the Air Management cell and has guys coordinating the B-52 strikes. Discuss it with him. I'll give him a heads-up that you're going to talk to him. I suspect that in the coming weeks, a B-52 strike close to the city will be more than show—it'll be a necessity."

51

WELCOME TO POLEI KLENG

5 May 1972
  62nd Border Ranger Battalion
  Polei Kleng

Polei Kleng was occupied by the 62nd Border Ranger Battalion. Originally established in 1966 as a Special Forces camp, it sat at the end of Highway 511 and twenty-two kilometers west of Kontum. Between it and Kontum was the Dak Poko River. This was Major Steinhauer's first look at the camp as the OH-6 approached. He immediately noticed a large contingent of civilians in the camp as they landed.

"Thanks for the lift," Josh said as Captain Jim Stein gently set the aircraft down on the designated pad.

"No problem. You call, we haul," Jim said with a smile. Jim was a scout pilot with the cav troop. He'd just happened to be heading out this way on a scout mission and Josh had asked for a ride. Above, two Cobra gunships orbited, watching over the little bird. They were hunting for tanks this morning as the Hawk's Claws were on standby to come shooting if they found something. As Josh jogged away from the aircraft, an American officer was standing off to the side to meet him.

"Good morning, sir, and welcome to Polei Kleng," Captain Geddes MacLaren said, extending his hand. Saluting in the combat area was discouraged, as a sniper would love to shoot an officer and they knew that the senior officer would be the last to exchange the salute.

Accepting the hand, Josh said, "Thanks, glad I was able to get out here today."

"Why don't we head over to the command bunker and meet the rest of the crew?" MacLaren said, pointing the way.

"How many of you are here?" Josh asked, knowing that there couldn't be too many Americans in the camp. Vann was attempting to find people to fill advisor positions.

"Just me and First Lieutenant Paul McKenna."

"McKenna," Josh responded with surprise. "No relation to Colonel McKenna with the 44th, is he?"

"No, sir, no relation and I get asked that all the time. The ARVNs that know Colonel McKenna are convinced he is. It scares them that he'll tell his father, so I let them think it," MacLaren said with a chuckle as he ducked into the command bunker, where one American officer with a baby face was over-looking a map with an ARVN officer. They both looked up at Josh.

"Gentlemen, this is Major Steinhauer. He's here to observe us for...what exactly are you observing, sir?" MacLaren asked.

"I'm here observing how you work with your ARVN counterparts, that's all," Josh said, extending his hand to the American. "You must be Lieutenant McKenna."

"Yes, sir," McKenna responded, accepting the handshake.

"And, sir, this is Major Buu Chuyen, the commander of the 62nd Border Ranger Battalion," MacLaren introduced.

"How do you do, sir?" Josh said, accepting the ARVN officer's less-than-firm handshake.

"Good, welcome," Chuyen said. Josh detected a lack of enthusiasm, however, in Chuyen's voice.

"Sir," McKenna said, breaking the awkward silence that seemed to come after the introduction. "We have a report from a patrol that we sent out this morning that they found what they believe to be tank tracks. We reported that and the cav is now on station, looking to see if they can find something in this area," he indicated, pointing at a location on the map.

"Yeah, it was a cav bird that brought me out here," Josh said, studying the map. "What contacts have you had?"

"We got the usual incoming mortar rounds and some light probes on the perimeter, but nothing major as yet. If they did find tank tracks, I suspect that's going to change soon," Captain MacLaren indicated. "Sir, how about a walk around the camp?"

"Sure, let's go," Josh said and followed MacLaren outside. "Let me ask, am I correct in thinking that Major Chuyen isn't happy to see me here?"

"I don't think that's it, sir. I think the reports of tanks have him spooked. He's already talked about an exit plan with the executive officer, Captain Phan Thai Binh. Binh is a good man and has more backbone than Chuyen in my opinion," MacLaren said as they walked through the camp. Josh noted several bunkers that were raised higher than he would like to see and several antennas on each of the larger bunkers scattered throughout the compound. Again he noted the large number of children and women, all Montagnards.

"They're the families of the soldiers," MacLaren said when Josh asked about them. "This battalion is Montagnards, and the families travel with the husbands. Having them here helps keep the soldiers here and fighting that much harder to protect them. The Montagnards are fearlessly loyal to their families and to each other, I think more so then you'll find with the Vietnamese ARVN."

"I had forgotten, but in the previous century in the US

Army, wives were camp followers as well, although today if you said an Army wife was a camp follower, she'd probably hit you with a rolling pin. Hell, some don't even like being called dependents now. You have to refer to them as spouses," Josh said.

"I know, my wife is one that claims she's not a dependent but a spouse. She even refers to me as her spouse instead of husband. What is this Army coming to?" MacLaren said, half laughing.

"What if the camp is hit? Is there a plan to get them out?" Josh asked.

"Yes, sir. We have a preplanned exfiltrate route on the east side through the minefield with claymores on the sides to clear the area. Everyone knows to meet on the east side but they don't know the exact lane," MacLaren said.

Walking through the compound, Josh wasn't surprised at the smiling faces and warm greetings he was getting from the elders. Typically, a group of kids were following them, hoping for a piece of candy or a cigarette. When they returned to the command post, McKenna immediately approached.

"The scout bird found the tanks. Two of them. He called out another aircraft called Hawk's Claw," McKenna said with a look of confusion. "Sir, do you know who these Hawk's Claws are? Never heard of them."

"Yeah, they're new in-country and have a weapons system capable of killing tanks at a range of three thousand meters and very accurate," Josh informed them. "Much more accurate than the old SS-11 system where you had to fly the missile to the target. This system, you put the crosshairs on the target and keep them there and within ten seconds that target is dead." McKenna and MacLaren exchanged wide grins.

"I like these guys already," MacLaren said.

* * *

"HAWK'S CLAW THREE-SEVEN, Undertaker Two-Seven, Over."

"Undertaker Two-Seven, Hawk's Claw Three-Seven, over."

"Hawk's Claw, I have two tanks for you." Undertaker read off the location. "My little bird is orbiting around the tanks and will mark when you're in position. He's taking negative fire, over."

"Roger, Undertaker, we're five minutes away," Chief Warrant Officer Lester Whiters said. Whiters was flying today with Chief Warrant Officer Dixson. Whiters was on the gun today. He allowed Lain, the most junior warrant in the unit, to get the first kill, but he was going to get one as well.

"I see the little bird. Painting the tops of the blades makes it pretty easy to spot them above the trees," Dixson said.

"As blind as you are, I'm surprised you can see the instrument panel," Whiters said, taking a jab at the second senior warrant officer in the unit.

"You know if you miss this target, I'm never going to let you live it down. One shot, one kill, remember? No excuses," Dixson said, returning the jab.

"Undertaker, Hawk's Claw, over."

"Go ahead, Hawk's Claw."

"Undertaker, have him pop smoke, over," Dixson said.

"Roger." Moments later, a cloud of red smoke drifted up from the trees. Whiters scanned the area through the sight.

"Damn, I see the smoke, but the vegetation is in the way and masking the tanks. Let's go higher and see if we can get a better angle," Whiters directed, and Dixson applied power to initiate a higher altitude.

"How's this?" Dixson asked.

"Still no good. The damn vegetation has them covered for the slant range we need. I don't think we're going to get them," Whiters said with a look of disgust as he pulled back from the sight.

"Hey, Undertaker, Hawk's Claw, over," Dixson transmitted.

"Go ahead, Hawk's Claw."

"Undertaker, we can't get the target as the vegetation is too thick for the slant range and altitude we need. I'm afraid we're not going to be able to help you today. Over."

"Understood, Hawk's Claw. We'll talk to the FAC and rectify this problem. Thanks for trying. Better luck next time. Undertaker out."

* * *

"Sir, I just got a call from the Undertaker aircraft and the Hawk's Claw couldn't hit the tanks. Something about slant range and vegetation too thick. Undertaker is calling in the FAC to take care of those tanks. Said he would report back when they're done for," McKenna said. "I just hope they take care of them quick."

52

POLEI KLENG HEATS UP

6 May 1972
62nd Border Ranger Battalion
Polei Kleng

Josh woke up to the smell of coffee. Opening his eyes, he saw an elderly Montagnard woman smiling at him and extending a cup of coffee to him. McKenna was already up and out of the bunker and MacLaren was sitting on his cot with a cup already in hand.

"Don't know her name, but ever since we arrived here she's come every morning with a cup of coffee for each of us. It's at the point that when we get a care package and it has a can of coffee, we just give it to her along with some other goodies. Truthfully I think she saves the grounds and reuses them, but, hey, we have coffee in the morning," MacLaren said, nodding appreciation to the woman, who just returned the smile and began cleaning up the bunker and coffee cups.

"It's nice to wake up to, I'll admit that," Josh said, taking a sip. "What's on the schedule for today?"

"Well, sir, you've seen the camp. I was thinking I'd see if we could get a chopper laid on and get you out of here. You may want to go over to Ben Het if you haven't been there. Not that we don't enjoy your company," MacLaren said.

"I haven't been to Ben Het, but isn't it cut off now since Dak To and Tan Canh fell?"

"They're still not in a fight. Got some light probing, but nothing serious. Might be because they have three or four M41 tanks up there on their compound. It's a pretty formidable place with two Border Ranger battalions located there. Charlie may be thinking twice before going after that place. It's an old SF camp like this one and sits on a small rise with a commanding view and clear fields of fire for five hundred to a thousand meters. Wish we were on a small rise. Could make all the difference," MacLaren explained.

"Maybe I'll fly up that way. Have to run that by General Hill, but he's given me pretty much free rein to go anywhere."

"Okay, then I'll go over to the command post and see if I can lay a bird on for you," MacLaren said as he finished his coffee and headed for the door. He never made it.

The concussion wave from the impacting artillery round outside blew MacLaren back into the bunker. Josh immediately rolled onto the floor, landing on top of the Montagnard woman, who was faster to hit the floor than he was. She wasn't smiling but fear masked her face. A second round impacted, followed by others, but all much further from the advisor bunker.

"It sounds as if they're walking rounds across the compound," MacLaren said, shaking his head to clear it. "I need to get to the command bunker. Meet me there." He started back towards the door on unsteady legs.

Josh rolled off the poor woman and motioned for her to stay. She acknowledged that she had no intentions of leaving that bunker and slid closer to the wall. Josh grabbed his boots and did a quick lace-up. The first item of his uniform he put on was his steel pot. He had slept in his pants. Grabbing his shirt, his load-bearing equipment and his weapon, he headed for the door. *I'm a freaking aviator and artilleryman, not a grunt, and this looks to be the second time in two months that I'm going to play grunt,* he thought as he moved quickly across the compound.

Reaching the command bunker, Josh found Major Chuyen, Captain Binh and the two advisors in deep conversation. Chuyen appeared to be concerned with tanks, and the advisors were telling him this was mortars and artillery fire, not tanks, but he wasn't listening. Finally, Chuyen left the command bunker as more artillery impacted.

"I'm going to check the perimeter," McKenna said after a few moments.

"I'm going to get a FAC up and see if they can spot the artillery," MacLaren said, picking up a hand mike.

"Why not let me do that as I'm an artillery guy, and you go check the perimeter too? Seeing you out there may keep these guys' confidence levels up," Josh said, reaching for the hand mike that MacLaren was holding.

"Not a bad idea, sir. Call back to SRAG and they'll send out a FAC," MacLaren said, handing Josh the handset. "I'll check back in after I make a sweep of the perimeter."

"Okay. Be careful" was Josh's final instruction as MacLaren slipped out the doorway.

An hour after Josh contacted SRAG, Covey Triple Nickel arrived on station and almost immediately the artillery fire stopped. A Covey aircraft was able to remain on station until late in the afternoon. Almost immediately after the FAC departed, the artillery bombardment started again, and it was much worse.

Everyone on the compound was in a bunker. It appeared that the best bunkers to be in were the ones located along the perimeter.

"Son of a bitch," MacLaren said, looking out the door of the advisor bunker.

"What?" McKenna asked.

"They must have an observer adjusting fire because they're systematically destroying every bunker. We best—" MacLaren didn't finish his sentence when the 122 millimeter round slammed into the top of the advisor bunker, causing the ceiling to partially collapse. All three Americans were slammed to the floor. As Josh began to clear his head, he started choking on the dust.

"Damn, we've got to get out of here," he heard MacLaren say. "Where's Paul?"

"I'm over here, sir. I'm pinned down under this beam and sandbags," Lieutenant McKenna said, attempting to crawl forward. Josh immediately began pulling sandbags off the young officer while MacLaren was attempting to lift a four-by-four timber that was across McKenna's back.

"Are you okay?" Josh asked.

"Yes, sir, I think my cot is destroyed, however," McKenna said, noticing that the cot appeared to have taken most of the impact of the timber. As soon as McKenna was free, all three moved out of the destroyed bunker and dashed to the western side of the perimeter.

"There's an open foxhole. Let's get in there," MacLaren said, jogging ahead of everyone. "I'm done with overhead cover at this point." Dropping into the hole, which was just big enough for three people, especially Americans, they watched as each bunker within the interior of the compound was systematically destroyed by artillery fire. The bunkers with an antenna on top were the first to be destroyed.

"They've got to have an observer someplace to be this accurate with their fires," Josh said, peering over the top of the foxhole.

"It'll be dark soon and then they won't be as accurate," McKenna said.

"It won't matter as they will have destroyed everything by then. We need to find Chuyen and get him ready. There will be a ground attack, I'll bet, as soon as this artillery is lifted," MacLaren said.

"I'll go look for him, sir," McKenna said, immediately pushing himself out of the foxhole and sprinting towards the western perimeter. Josh and MacLaren continued to observe the destruction. Finally Josh had had enough.

"Do you think someone from inside the compound could be adjusting this fire?" Josh asked, looking at MacLaren. MacLaren just stared at Josh for a moment.

"Sir, I never thought of that, but as there's no ground that overlooks the compound, and as accurate as this fire is, that is a possibility."

"I'm going hunting. It shouldn't be too hard to find out. Which bunkers haven't been destroyed? That should tell us if it's one of our own people," Josh said as he pulled himself over the lip of the foxhole and paused for the next round to impact before he sprinted off towards the east.

Alone in the foxhole, MacLaren could only sit and watch as one bunker after another was destroyed by incoming artillery fire. He knew that the Montagnard soldiers on the perimeter must be terrified by this pounding. They were used to the occasional mortar rounds that had hit the compound over the years, but not this sustained and systematic artillery fire. McKenna suddenly appearing and dropping into the hole unannounced scared MacLaren for an instant.

"Damn you, Paul, you scared the shit out of me! Where the hell is Chuyen?"

"Sir, Chuyen has already di di," McKenna said with an expression of disgust on his face, taking a quick look around. "Where's the major?"

"The major thinks the spotter may be in the compound and went looking to see if he could find someone. You say Chuyen has already taken off. When and where did he go?"

"About thirty minutes ago, according to Captain Binh, who has taken command. He said Chuyen took off through the evacuation gap in the western perimeter," McKenna indicated. "On the bad side, I saw some red flashing lights on the western tree line. I think we're in for a ground assault."

"Son of a bitch. Well, our assignment was to advise the battalion commander, and he's gone, so I'm calling for extraction," MacLaren said as he picked up the hand mike on the PRC-77 radio that he'd carried into the foxhole.

* * *

CAPTAIN JIM STEIN was finishing up another seven-hour day of flying, looking and snooping over the Vietnamese landscape. He and his door gunner were looking forward to a hot shower, cold beer and dinner when the radio began crackling with incoming traffic.

"Scalp Hunter Four-Five, Pink Panther Three-Two, over."

"Pink Panther Three-Two, Scalp Hunter Four-Five, go ahead."

"Scalp Hunter, we have a request to proceed to Polei Kleng and extract two advisors, Over."

"Roger, Pink Panther, I'll head that way. I'm good on fuel. Over."

"Scalp Hunter, we'll be joined by the Undertakers and provide cover for you, over."

"Roger, what's the situation there? Over."

"Polei Kleng has been receiving artillery fire all day. It appears that they're about to get hit with a ground assault. Over."

"Roger, I'll drop to treetop level. Did they say where they'll be?"

"I was told they would be on top of a bunker with broken antennas. We'll lay down fire in front of you going in and coming out, over."

"Roger, understood. I'll let you know when I drop down. I have you in sight, I believe. Flight of four guns, correct?"

"Roger, Scalp Hunter. I have you in sight. Polei Kleng is at your eleven approximately ten klicks. Over."

"Roger."

* * *

"WHERE THE HELL IS THE MAJOR?" McKenna said, peering over the top of the foxhole.

"I don't know, but he best get his ass here quick. An OH-6 is inbound to pick us up with gun cover. When he lands, we sprint to that bunker with the broken antenna or any damn place he lands and climb in. Not waiting on the major," MacLaren said.

* * *

"PINK PANTHER, Scalp Hunter dropping to low level. Approach will be west to east. Rotation beacon on, nav lights off. Over."

"Roger, Scalp Hunter, we have you. Will commence fire in five, over."

"Roger, Pink Panther."

In the front seat of the gunship sat First Lieutenant Tim Conroy. Tim had developed into an excellent gunner in the front seat of the Cobra gunship and would soon be moving up to aircraft commander in the back seat of the Cobra.

"Hey, Tim, let's lay a carpet of forty mike-mike down in front of Scalp Hunter when he makes his run. We'll use the rockets on the perimeter while he's on the ground and use rockets and the rest of the forty mike-mike when he's coming out, okay?" Captain Bill Reeder, the aircraft commander, directed.

"Got it" was all Tim said as he grabbed the handles on his sight and began selecting his weapon system from minigun to 40mm grenades.

A few minutes later, as they watched Scalp Hunter but also the approaching compound with intense small-arms fire on the western perimeter, Reeder contacted Scalp Hunter.

"Scalp Hunter, Pink Panther, we're going to commence fire, over."

"Roger, do it," Reeder heard above the sounds of an M60 machine gun being fired by the Scalp Hunter gunner.

"Open fire, Tim." And the aircraft began to shake slightly with each round fired.

Immediately Captain Stein noticed the small explosions from the impacting grenades forward of his aircraft clearing a path to the engaging compound. Clearing the wire around the perimeter, Stein started a rapid deceleration in the faded light, looking for a bunker with a broken antenna on top. Running figures were everywhere. Some just running, others running and shooting with some red and some green tracers. *Damn, the enemy is inside the wire*, he realized as he saw the green tracers from the enemy's AK-47 assault rifles. Spotting a bunker that could qualify, he plopped the aircraft down, cutting some wires holding the broken antenna. It collapsed away from the aircraft.

"Shoot anyone approaching who isn't large," Stein told his gunner.

"I got them and they're hauling ass this way," the gunner said as Stein felt two bodies fly into the aircraft along with some tapping sounds on the side of the aircraft. Both advisors were firing.

"*Go, go!*" Stein heard over his earphones and, checking his gauges out of habit, he began to apply power. The gunner's M60 and two M16 rifles continued to spray the area as the aircraft lifted off and cross the wire.

"Pink Panther, Scalp Hunter is coming out," Stein said as he crossed the wire and immediately noticed 40-millimeter rounds and rockets walking a path in front of his aircraft. Reaching the western tree line, Stein went into a power climb and headed for Mr. Vann's headquarters.

Where in the hell is that major? Captain MacLaren wondered as he looked back on the embattled compound.

53

BORDER CAMPS FEEL THE ENEMY

7 May 1972
SRAG HQ
Pleiku

"WHAT?" Vann said with an elevated voice as Captain MacLaren and Lieutenant McKenna stood in front of his desk, with General Hill standing off to the side. "Why in the hell didn't you get Steinhauer out of there? And what the hell was he doing there?" he demanded, looking at all three with his eyes emitting daggers.

"Sir, Steinhauer came to me and asked if he could go out there and do his job. Observe the interaction of advisors and their counterparts. We hadn't had any trouble out that way, so I thought that was a safe place to let him go to as opposed to Ben Het or some other place," Hill said.

Transferring his gaze to the two officers standing in front of his desk, he said, "And you two just left him there..." He left the rest of the sentence hanging in the air.

"Sir, it wasn't like that," MacLaren said. He knew this could go badly for him as the senior advisor. "If you'll let me explain—"

"Well, I'm waiting," Vann answered.

"Sir, when we were being systematically hit with artillery taking out bunkers, the major thought that there may have been a spotter in the compound directing the artillery and went to find the person. We never saw him after that. He'd been gone almost two hours when the bird landed. The compound was under a ground assault and the enemy was within the wire. The chopper landed and it was a running gun battle to get to it. It wasn't about to wait around. We feel bad about this, sir, but there was nothing we could do," MacLaren said. From his explanation and facial expressions, Vann surmised that the captain was sincere and was telling the truth.

"Okay, I understand. You'll be glad to know that Steinhauer is okay. He's with Captain Binh, who has taken charge. The compound is surrounded by anti-aircraft guns, so getting a bird in to get him out is our of the question for now. He's stepped in to advise Binh and work the artillery and Spectre. I guess in his previous life before being a pilot he was an artillery officer," Vann said, pausing for a moment. "I have to call General Brooks at MACV since the major works for him, so get out of here and let me make that call," Vann said with a smile.

* * *

MAJOR STEINHAUER FELT it safe to move as the sky to the east appeared to show some light. There had been no small-arms fire for the past four hours. As he started to stand, he noticed Captain Binh lying next to him.

"Dai'uy Binh, are you okay?" Josh asked, lightly shaking the officer. Binh didn't move initially but then opened his eyes and turned his head to Josh.

"A-OK, Major. You?" Binh asked.

"I good," Josh responded standing up fully. Binh followed.

"We go inspect perimeter. I walk two hours ago. All look good. Why you no fly out?" Binh asked as they slowly but cautiously walked through the destroyed camp. Montagnard women were already getting cooking fires started. Some were assisting the wounded one minute and corralling children the next.

"I would have, but I was on the other side of the perimeter when the chopper landed and I couldn't get to them," Josh explained.

"I glad you no go. You do good with Spectre last night. It break ground assault back," Binh said with a smile. During the night, Spectre had arrived on station as the ground assault was reaching a climax. Josh had directed the gunship with its 105mm howitzer and 25mm Vulcan cannons, making multiple orbits over the besieged camp. The results the next morning were obvious when the sun came up as the field in front of the wire was littered with dead NVA soldiers.

Walking through the camp, Josh noted that some bodies were being carefully picked up by the Montagnards. Others were being tossed in a pit and lye being poured on top with a thin layer of dirt. Binh noticed Josh taking an interest.

"We honor our dead. We toss enemy in pit" was all Binh had to say when the distinct sound of an explosion was heard in the distance, followed by the sound of a freight train approaching. No one needed to yell "Incoming" as everyone was already moving to take cover. It was going to be a long day.

* * *

CAPTAINS STEPHEN TRUHAN and Robert Sparks were sitting in the advisor command post when they got the word that Mr. Vann was inbound in his helicopter. Truhan was the advisor for the 95th Border Ranger Battalion and Sparks was the advisor for the 71st Border Ranger Battalion at Ben Het. They both left the command post and started walking down to the helipad to meet with their boss.

Ben Het was a large compound about twelve kilometers west of Dak To II. The 2nd NVA Division had bypassed the compound for the most part in its advance on Tan Canh and Dak To II. Located on a small rise, it had a commanding view of the surrounding terrain and the tree line had been pushed back approximately eight hundred meters. A well-developed berm surrounded the perimeter along with concertina wire and minefields. Within the compound were the families of the soldiers as well. When the two advisors reached the helipad, Vann's aircraft was on short final.

As Vann exited the aircraft, his pilot began the shutdown procedures. Both advisors waited for Vann to approach them. As he did so, he extended his hand. Being a civilian, even though he held an equivalent rank of major general, he didn't warrant a salute, nor was saluting in the forward areas encouraged.

"Morning, gentlemen," Vann said as the two officers shook his hand. "How goes it?"

"Sir, we've had some incoming mortars over the past week, but nothing serious," Truhan said.

"There've been some ground probes but nothing more than the typical stuff that we've seen over the course of the year," Sparks added. Vann was looking around as they spoke.

"You know, gentlemen, this is one strong position. I hope you get hit with a regiment when they come, maybe more," Vann said, to the surprise of both officers.

"Sir, you care to explain that comment?" Truhan asked with a bit of surprise.

"You have a strong position here. A well-developed compound located in an excellent position with good fields of fire. The river on the south will make it difficult for someone to bypass you. If they attack, they'll be bottled up in front of you, making them an ideal target for B-52 strikes, and that's what I'll give you," Vann said, looking up at the sign over the entrance to the camp. "That sign is most appropriate, Ben Het and Loving It. I do love Ben Het." As the three walked up to the interior, it appeared that an angry discussion was breaking out between the commander of the 71st Border Rangers and a large group.

"Excuse me, sir, while I see what this is about," Sparks said, starting to move away.

"Wait, I'll go with you," Vann said, keeping pace with Sparks. Truhan followed just out of curiosity as the 71st wasn't his responsibility. Vann's Vietnamese language skills were excellent and he quickly recognized the problem.

"Captain Sparks, it appears you have a mutiny on your hands," Vann said.

"Sir?" was Sparks's only response as his Vietnamese skills were insufficient to keep up with the discussion.

"It seems that the soldiers of the 71st want their families flown out of here or they're not going to fight," Vann explained and then turned to the 71st commander and the spokesman for the mutiny. The conversation was conducted in Vietnamese, and the more Vann talked, the calmer things appeared to become. Finally, the commander smiled, as did the spokesman for the group, and handshakes were exchanged all around before the two groups separated.

Vann turned back to Sparks and Truhan. "I got to get going. I agreed to lay on some CH-47s and fly the families out starting tomorrow. I need to get back and lay on some VNAF aircraft to do that. We'll fly them down to Pleiku as we have enough refugees in Kontum as it is. Get these people ready to go. The people, not their chickens, pigs or water buffalos. I'll have my staff get word to you in the morning when the lift will start. You guys have a good day. I'll find my way back to my aircraft," Vann said, walking off with long strides.

"Thank God he was here or this could have really been a mess," Sparks said as Vann passed under the entrance sign to Ben Het. An hour later, the first of many artillery rounds impacted on the compound. There would be no lift in the next day as the incoming artillery never ceased.

* * *

ALL DAY, rounds had been falling on Polei Kleng. Josh and Binh continued to move as much as possible to encourage the soldiers hunkered down in foxholes. Fortunately, the enemy was concentrating his fire on the already destroyed bunkers and not the perimeter. The sky was overcast, with low clouds preventing the FAC from being able to look for the firing guns. Josh recognized that this was the prelude to a ground attack that would come later in the day or maybe after dark, which was a typical tactic of the enemy. He was on the radio, talking to the II Corps artillery advisor, Lieutenant Colonel Stanislaus Fuesel.

"Sir, I need planned final protective fires around Polei Kleng. We're going to be hit with a ground assault tonight and the weather is going to preclude getting air support," Josh said.

"Major, I hate to tell you this, but you're well beyond anything we have that could support you with artillery. The range on the 105s is only eleven klicks and the 155 is only a little further. Let me talk to the air people and see if we can get some B-52 strikes in your neighborhood. They're controlled and can bomb through the clouds pretty accurately," the colonel said.

"Okay, sir, I guess I have no choice," Josh said, hanging up the radio mike and turning to Captain Binh. "We best lay the mortars in to fire our final protective fires before it gets too late."

They both departed the bunker and headed for the mortar pits, which were still intact. An hour later, two klicks to the west, it was obvious the first of several B-52 strikes was arriving as the sound of rolling thunder was heard and a rising column of dust could be seen.

That evening, the ground attack was less than the previous evening and easily repelled.

54

CHANGE IS COMING

8 May 1972
SRAG II HQ
Pleiku

General Hill had walked over from II Corps headquarters to see Vann. As he approached Vann's office, Vann spotted him and motioned him to come in. Vann was on the phone and pointed to a pot of coffee and two cups. Hill got the message and poured two cups of coffee, placing one on Vann's desk and taking one of the overstuffed chairs facing Vann's desk.

"I understand, General. Tell the president I agree with your assessment and we need to do something fast," Vann said. "Good, I will be waiting for your call. Have a good day." He hung up.

"What was that all about?" Hill asked.

"That was General Cao Van Vien, Chairman of the Joint Vietnamese Staff. He and the president have concerns about Dzu's ability to continue, and I frankly can't blame them," Vann said, reaching for his coffee.

"Dzu has been talking to me and being relieved is exactly what he wants. He thinks he's being set up for a court-martial for the fall of Kontum. He's willing to take the blame for Dak To II and Tan Canh but doesn't want Kontum landing on his head. Even faked illness to get relieved the other day," Hill said with visible frustration.

"Well, he may have succeeded. They're looking for a replacement. Seems he's been pestering Vien to relieve him. He figures since they relieved Lam up in I Corps, he would be next on the chopping block. I don't think he's in the same boat as Lam as I understand that Lam was aloof in the whole thing when Dzu was staying engaged. We just had bad intel and a crappy division commander in Dat," Vann explained.

"Who have they got in mind?" Hill asked.

"Well, that's the problem. They've offered the command to several lieutenant generals, and all have an excuse not to take the command, from being too busy in their current assignment to drop everything to hangnails. Pompous cowards!" Vann said in an elevated voice. "They're looking at offering it to major generals with a promotion. We should know something in a day or two," he said in frustration. "What you got?"

"Well, not great news for you. Polei Kleng got hit again last night, but not as bad as the first night. Air-defense guns are still encircling the place, so we can't get a chopper in there, but that major is doing a hell of a job as an advisor. He got with Lieutenant Colonel Fuesel and requested B-52 strikes around the compound. Thinks it may have reduced the force planned to hit them last night," Hill explained.

"Good, so they're still in the fight," Vann commented.

"The weather is supposed to be better today, so the FAC will get up and provide some support to them. Wish we had some artillery within range of them, but we don't. Now for some not-so-good news," Hill said.

"And...?" Vann said, setting his coffee cup down.

"Ben Het is reporting indications of track vehicles. And they believe they've been hit with 160mm mortars," Hill said.

"If they got hit with 160mm mortars, they're in for a ground assault. Hell, I don't think the 160 has been used in Vietnam ever. Let's get the intel weenies on that and order up B-52 strikes in support of Ben Het. Let the TACAIR work for Polei Kleng," Vann said.

"I already talked to Colonel Swenholt and that's what he recommended and is doing as we speak."

* * *

"COVEY TRIPLE NICKEL, TRAVELER SIX, OVER," Josh transmitted. Days earlier, Hill had given Josh the call sign of Traveler and Josh added the Six to it as he was now in charge at Polei Kleng. *If someone doesn't like me adding the Six, they can come out here and relieve me*, Josh was thinking.

"Traveler Six, morning. Covey Triple Nickel has a full package for you today with fast movers and VNAF Skyraiders. I just got an indication of an artillery piece and that'll be first this morning. If you have other targets for me, just send them. BUFF won't be with us today as they're working north of here. Over."

"Roger, any artillery you see, go for it...or tanks. Over."

"Haven't seen tanks from up here. If you have some suspected locations, let me have them and we'll see what turns up, over."

"Roger, will let you know. Traveler Six out," Josh said, ending the conversation. Looking skyward, he saw the tiny gray O-2 Skymaster enter into a steep dive and punch off one rocket that burst in the trees to the west of the compound at the base of Rocket Ridge. It was followed shortly afterwards by two F-4 Phantom jets unloading two loads of napalm across the face of the ridge. Throughout the day, Josh was thankful that the artillery wasn't pounding them as the FAC stayed on station until it was too dark to see.

55

ALL HELL COMES

9 MAY 1972
 62nd Border Range Battalion
 Polei Kleng

DURING THE NIGHT, a Spectre gunship orbited above the compound. Anytime a potential target appeared, it was quickly eliminated. At 0400, Spectre departed station. Captain Binh immediately began moving around the perimeter, making sure everyone was awake and prepared. The most dangerous time, he believed, was the time between the Spectre gunship departing and the arrival of a FAC above. This morning he would not be wrong. Josh was on the radio, seeing if a B-52 strike could be diverted to support them at first light or sooner. The answer wasn't what he wanted to hear. What he did hear was a sudden and overwhelming volume of small-arms fire along the eastern perimeter.

Sprinting to the perimeter, he quickly found Binh. "Dai'uy, what have we got?" Josh asked as he squatted down next to Binh.

"OP says full assault. He say maybe twenty tanks leading!"

Binh said, fear clearly coming through his voice.

"Binh, settle down. We talked about this, and your people are trained on how to use the LAW rockets. You have your tank killer teams out and they'll take care of the tanks. The FAC will be on station pretty soon and bring in plenty of air support," Josh said when he heard a loud and strange-sounding explosion on the eastern perimeter. "What the hell was that?" he asked rhetorically. Then it dawned on him.

"Binh, did you blow the exfiltration route?" Josh asked in surprise.

"We go. Get families out," Binh said as Josh noticed that most of the women and children were congregated towards the eastern perimeter. *Damn, they knew hours ago that they were getting out of here*, Josh thought. "Lieutenant Kchong lead them out. Wait for all to withdraw and go Kontum," Binh said as two LAW rockets were heard, followed by an explosion and a cheer.

Looking over the berm, Josh saw that a T-54 tank was on fire, but others were slowly moving past it with infantry following. The defenders were holding their own and not running. A second T-54 went up in smoke and the tanks slowed, waiting for infantry to catch up. But the infantry was in no hurry to join the tanks or clear the area ahead of the tanks due to the intense small-arms fire and mortars from the Rangers.

Binh kept looking over his shoulder to the eastern perimeter as the families were moving through the wire. Josh was wondering when the mad dash by the soldiers would occur as he'd experienced at LZ English the month before. He didn't see anyone moving but all continuing to engage the enemy. Another T-54 blew up—a victim of the tank killer teams. All the tanks had stopped now and so did the infantry. They were all frozen when two more tanks exploded.

"Binh, your tank killers are eating them up," Josh said with enthusiasm. "We can hold this place."

"Families go, we go after them," Binh said. Josh realized that the pressure of the three days of artillery bombardment had taken its toll on their nerves.

"Look, Binh," Josh said, peering over the berm as the stalled attack. "Look, the tanks are retreating!" he yelled. "We can stay!"

"We go now," Binh said and began issuing orders to the subordinate commanders to pull back. Josh was disappointed that they weren't staying but understood. He was impressed, though, at the orderly withdrawal as the perimeter collapsed towards the exfiltration route. As the soldiers moved through the wire, Binh took up a position inside the wire and off to the side to cover the withdrawal. As the last soldier moved through the wire, Binh pulled out a clacker and connected it to two wires and pumped it. All around the perimeter, claymore mines ignited, effectively neutralizing any enemy forces that stood outside the wire. Binh was the last one through.

The movement west was slow due to the families. Lieutenant Kchong was in the lead with a small contingent to clear the way and lead the families to the Dak Poko River. If they could make the river and cross it, they would be safe. Unfortunately, the NVA knew that and wanted to stop them. A running gunfight ensued.

When Josh and Binh reached the river, Binh established a perimeter on the western bank while the women and children crossed. In some places they had to swim, but in most places they could wade. The Rangers on the perimeter were in a close-in fight due to the vegetation. At one point Rangers were seen in hand-to-hand combat. Mortar rounds began hitting the eastern bank and the river full of women and children. Josh could do nothing to assist but continue to engage. Finally Binh gave the final order for everyone to cross. Those on the eastern bank laid down a base of fire to cover those coming across. When Josh reached the far bank, he took a head count. There was a trail of bodies from the compound to the river as only ninety-seven people total had reached the far shore.[1]

56

66TH NVA REGIMENT COMES CALLING

9 MAY 1972
   Ben Het Compound
   Ben Het

ALL NIGHT, reports of track vehicles had reached the advisor command post from the Ops and LPs positioned outside the wire. As the reports came in, Truhan and Sparks plotted the locations on their maps and reported the results to SRAG headquarters. What was surprising them was that the tanks weren't coming from the west as anticipated but the north and east, from Dak To II.

"I think Vann might get his wish, but they're not going to be stacked up on the west side for a B-52 strike," Sparks said.

"Let's just be thankful that they haven't been pounding us all night with artillery. They're launching the FAC first light and will get some helicopters out here as well," Truhan said, hoping to relieve his fears and Sparks's.

"It's always nice to have company," Sparks said. His tone was joking, but he was dead serious. Suddenly intense small-arms fire broke out on the perimeter. The TA-1 field telephone rang.

"Yeah?" Truhan said. Sparks listened to the one-sided conversation as the mortar pits came to life and those within them started lobbing mortar rounds out to the perimeter.

Hanging the phone up, Truhan looked at Sparks. "That damn dumbshit led them through the minefield."

"What...the freaking dog led who through the minefield?" Sparks asked.

"Dumbshit must have been coming back from his nightly romp into the jungle and the NVA were watching him. According to the guys on the perimeter, the NVA were following Dumbshit through the minefield when they spotted them. We have a full-blown assault on the perimeter. Let's get Spectre on the horn," Truhan said. Picking up the hand mike, he made the call.

"Any Spectre aircraft, Rocket Eight-Eight Bambino, over."

"Rocket Eight-Eight Bambino, Spectre Oh-Two, over," he heard a moment later.

"Spectre Oh-Two, we're under attack at Ben Het and need your assistance, over."

"Bambino, we're about ten minutes away. Will be coming your way, over." Truhan and Sparks exchanged looks that expressed relief. The relief was short-lived.

"Dai'uy, Dai'uy, tanks come," a young Vietnamese soldier said. Ty was an interpreter for the two captains and ran back and forth between the battalion commanders and the advisor bunker often.

"Where, Ty?" Truhan asked.

"Come main road," Ty said, pointing towards the gate.

"Spectre Oh-Two, Bambino, we have tanks approaching, over," Sparks transmitted.

"Roger, I have one in sight at this time, appears to be approaching, over."

"Roger, take him out, over." Both advisors departed the advisor bunker to witness this tank. Truhan grabbed a radio so he could communicate with the aircraft orbiting above. Reaching the perimeter berm, the advisors could see the intensity of the small-arms fire as well as the lumbering tank two hundred meters down the road leading a couple of other tanks. Moments later, the tank exploded from a burst from the aircraft above. Another tank drove around this tank, took the lead and accelerated towards the main gate.

"Spectre Oh-Two, nice shooting, but we have another pressing towards the main gate. Over," Sparks transmitted.

"Roger" was all Spectre said. Moments later, a shower of sparks covered the tank as 40mm rounds exploded all over it. Smoke appeared out of the engine compartment, but the tank continued to roll forward. As it rolled through the main gate, the antitank mine on the side of the road took off one track as the tank came to a stop. It didn't move.

"Spectre, you killed that one. We have heavy contact on the eastern perimeter, over."

"Roger, we'll move over there." Both Truhan and Sparks began to head out when movement at the gate caught their attention.

"Wait one," Sparks said and pointed. A Montagnard Ranger was crawling in the ditch beside the road. When he was about fifty yards in front of the tank, he slowly rose into a kneeling position and placed a LAW on his shoulder. The round slammed into the turret of the tank, blowing the top hatch open. Sparks slapped Truhan on the back.

"Damn textbook engagement," he said and gave a thumbs-up to the young soldier, who was looking around with a wide grin. Both advisors continued to move along the perimeter to the north, working their way to the eastern side. As they reached the northern perimeter, the undeniable sound of a track vehicle alerted them. Looking over the berm, they spotted the cause of the noise. Twenty-five feet away, a PT-76 amphibious tank was stuck. The tracks were wrapped in concertina wire, and as the driver attempted to move forward, the tank just dug deeper into the mud. It was going nowhere.

"I'll take care of this," Truhan said, grabbing a LAW and moving towards a bunker to the side of the tank. Arming the LAW rocket, he rose up, centered the tank in the sight and squeezed the trigger. Nothing! *Son of a bitch, it's a dud. What the hell was the malfunction procedure again?* he was thinking when the turret on the tank began to rotate in his direction. *Shit, they've spotted me.* He scrambled to crawl into a bunker under a spray of machine-gun fire from the tank. When the shooting stopped, Truhan peeked through an opening in the sandbags. To his surprise, the crew was climbing out of the tank. The engine was still running. Before they could leap off the tank, Montagnard Rangers cut them down with small-arms fire. Truhan and Sparks continued to work their way around the perimeter and were pleased at the fight the Montagnards of both battalions were putting up.

"Rocket Eight-Eight Bambino, Hawk's Claw Oh-Three, over." Both advisors turned to each other with curious looks that said *Who is this?*

"Hawk's Claw Oh-Three, Rocket Eight-Eight Bambino, over."

"Rocket Eight-Eight Bambino, Hawk's Claw Oh-Three is inbound to your location. I have the capability to kill tanks, over."

"Hawk's Claw Oh-Three, we have negative tanks at this time in our vicinity, over."

"Bambino, I have one sighted at your main gate! Engaging now." Before Truhan could explain that the tank at the main gate had already been killed three times, something caught his eye as it slammed into the dead tank, which immediately began emitting black smoke.

"Bambino, we got a kill on that one. He won't bother you again, over."

"Hawk's Claw Oh-Three, be advised that tank was killed three times already. It was dead, over."

"Roger, Hawk's Claw will chalk that one up. Hawk's Claw breaking station as there are no more targets. Hawk's Claw out."

Truhan and Sparks looked at each other in disbelief. "Effective weapon against a dead target. Wonder how it does against a real live tank," Sparks said, and both began laughing. They didn't laugh for long.

Reaching the northern area, they realized that about one-third of the perimeter was now occupied by the NVA. Spectre had broken the back of the assault, but not before a portion of the perimeter was overrun. The Montagnard Rangers were holding the attackers at bay, and the fight was coming to a standstill. As long as the NVA didn't get reinforcements, Truhan and Sparks thought they could hold.

57

HELICOPTER SUPPORT

9 May 1972
361st AWC
Kontum

SITTING in the refuel point at Kontum, Pink Panther Three-Two was flight leader for a flight of two. Captain Bill Reeder was aircraft commander and Lieutenant Tim Conroy was his front-seat gunner. Tim, being the gunner, was outside the aircraft, refueling the aircraft, which they had just rearmed.

"Pink Panther Three-Two, Pink Panther Three, over" came over the unit VHF frequency.

"Panther Three, Panther Three-Two, over."

"Panther Three-Two, can you take another mission? A resupply bird is taking a load of LAWs to Ben Het and needs escort. Over."

"Roger, we're available," Reeder said, wishing he wasn't available. It had already been a long morning. Armed with all the information for the hookup with the resupply aircraft, Reeder briefed his wingman and Tim, and the two aircraft departed for the linkup in flight. It didn't take long for the Cobra gunships to catch the UH-1H, a much slower aircraft.

"Rocket Eight-Eight Bambino, Pink Panther Three-Two, over."

"Pink Panther Three-Two, Bambino, over."

"Bambino, we're inbound escorting a resupply to you. Where do you want it and what is your enemy situation? Over."

"Pink Panther, drop it on the helipad next to the airfield. We have people standing by to unload. Be advised, avoid the eastern perimeter. Anti-air fire has been light today, over."

"Roger, we're five minutes out," Reeder reported, watching the UH-1H drop to low-level altitude heading towards the airfield. As the aircraft approached, small-arms fire began, intensifying as the UH-1H pressed forward to deliver its load. To protect the aircraft, Reeder entered a steep dive as Conroy opened fire with both his nose-mounted minigun and the 40mm grenade launcher. The enemy ceased firing at the UH-1H and turned its attention on Panther Three-Two, not with small arms but with .51-cal anti-aircraft guns that had been silent up until now.

* * *

TRUHAN AND SPARKS watched as the UH-1H attempted to avoid the small-arms fire that was reaching into the sky for them. Suddenly a loud gunfire sound not heard all morning caught their attention as the baseball-size tracer rounds of a .51-cal anti-aircraft weapon opened fire on the descending Cobra gunship. In horror, they watched as smoke streamed out of the engine area on the Cobra.

"Pink Panther is going down, Pink Panther is going down" was heard over the radio as the Cobra crashed two hundred meters south of the runway. Truhan grabbed a pair of binoculars and trained them on the downed aircraft.

"Whatcha see?" Sparks asked, watching things unfold with his naked eye.

"The front-seat canopy just popped open. That guy is getting out, or I should say falling out. He looks unstable...wait... he's moving to the back to help the rear pilot, who's hanging out of the cockpit. Looks like his leg is hung up on something. He's moving but can't get out. The fire is increasing...the front-seat guy is moving to the other side of the aircraft...I can't see him now. Shit, the fire is going to roast that backseat guy who's hanging upside down. Here, take the glasses," Truhan described. Handing the binoculars to Sparks, he picked up his M16 rifle and raised it to his shoulder.

"What are you doing?" Sparks asked with a look of concern as Truhan took aim at the pilot dangling out of the aircraft.

"I'm not going to let that guy burn to death," Truhan said as his finger slowly took the slack out of the trigger. The flames were climbing up the side of the aircraft towards the pilot when a gust of wind blew a pillar of smoke over the scene. Truhan lowered his weapon, anticipating that the smoke would clear quickly and then he would shoot. When the smoke did clear, the pilot was nowhere to be seen as the aircraft had exploded.

* * *

BILL REEDER WAS SUSPENDED over the side of the aircraft with his foot caught on something. As he hung there, unable to get free, he continued to kick with his legs. The heat from the fire was increasing. Tim attempted to pull him out but was unsuccessful.

"Let me get a fire extinguisher," Tim yelled and went to the other side of the aircraft to retrieve it. Reeder continued to struggle when a gust of wind blew smoke around him. Suddenly he was free and dropping headlong to the ground, hitting head-first. A searing pain shot through his spine.

Oh God, let me get away from this fire,[1] Reeder was thinking as he crawled through the low brush. Suddenly the aircraft exploded, with the remaining ammunition beginning to cook off. This incentivized him to crawl even further despite his pain. Overhead, he could see his wingman engaging the enemy that he suspected were around him and moving to the crash site. *Where the hell is Tim?* He wondered. As he lay in the taller grass about one hundred meters from the burning aircraft, he heard the sound of an approaching UH-1H. He attempted to raise himself up and stand, but the pain was too intense and all he could do was sit, which didn't get him above the vegetation. *Crazy fool Huey pilot is looking for us. He's going to get his ass shot down too,* Reeder thought as small-arms fire from AK-47s was heard all around him. They were engaging the Huey, which quickly departed the area.

* * *

"Scalp Hunter Four-Five, Undertaker One-Three, over." Jim Stein had been flying most of the daylight hours. He and his observer were butt sore and tired when the call came in from the flight leader that had been covering them throughout the day.

"Undertaker One-Three, Scalp Hunter Four-Five, go ahead."

"Scalp Hunter, we have an aircraft down vicinity of Ben Het. We've been asked if you can get them, over."

Without hesitation, Jim responded, "Roger, Undertaker One-Three, let's head that way." He turned in the direction of Ben Het, glancing at his fuel gauge. *We should have enough to get there and back,* he thought.

"Scalp Hunter, we got a report from the FAC that he has two mirror flashes in two locations about one hundred meters apart next to the down aircraft, over. Also, two Pink Panthers will be joining us up there."

"Roger, I'll start over the bird and orbit out from there. Always like more company in the air, over."

"We'll cover you and be looking. Sun is setting, so we may not have enough to see a mirror flash," Undertaker One-Three responded.

Approaching Ben Het, Jim's observer was the first to spot the smoldering remains of an aircraft.

"Sir, I see the aircraft, or what's left of it. It's about two hundred meters south of the airfield," he said, pointing towards it. Jim was already at treetop level and flying as fast as the little bird would safely fly.

Approaching the downed aircraft, Jim commenced an orbit, looking for a friendly face. An occasional tapping sound could be heard on the side of the aircraft, and Jim's eyes glanced at the instruments and master caution panel each time.

"Undertaker, it's getting too dark to see. I'm going to turn on my landing light to see if I can spot someone. Cover me," Jim announced and flipped on his landing light. It was a beacon for the green tracers. Undertaker and Pink Panther set up an immediate racetrack of four Cobra gunships engaging the enemy while Captain Stein maneuvered over the trees.

"Sir, I see someone! He's at your three o'clock in that bomb crater," Jim's observer yelled. Jim quickly turned the aircraft and placed the landing light on the downed crewmember. The man was on his knees, head bowed almost as if in prayer.

"Alright, I can land there. You get out and help him in," Jim ordered, maneuvering the small aircraft to the lip of the crater. His observer was out of the aircraft as soon as the skids touched the ground. He helped get the pilot to his feet and half carried, half walked him to the back seat of the aircraft.

"Go, go!" yelled the observer as he climbed aboard. Jim

pulled in as much power as he dared and departed as quickly as the little bird would carry him.

"Undertaker One-Three, we've got one and are heading to the hospital in Kontum," Jim reported as he began to climb for altitude. "It's getting too dark to continue to look for the other. I'm sorry."

Before he gained much altitude, the observer sitting in the front seat next to him announced, "Sir, this guy is about to fall out."

"Okay, let me put us down and you get in the back with him," Jim said, looking for an immediate place to land and informing Undertaker. He quickly found a place, and the observer switched seats and grabbed Tim, holding him for the flight to Kontum.

"How bad is he?" Jim asked his observer. "Can he make it to the 67th Evac in Pleiku?"

"I think so, sir."

"Good, that's where we're headed, then," Jim said, switching his intercom switch to communicate on the unit VHF frequency.

"Undertaker One-Three, Scalp Hunter, over." There was no answer. Jim repeated the call, and again no answer. *Damn, we must have taken a hit in the radio black boxes*, Jim thought. But when he looked down at his radios, they were all turned off. *What the...?* flashed through his mind as he turned the radio back on.

"Undertaker One-Three, Scalp Hunter, over."

"Where did you go, Scalp Hunter? I have you covered but haven't heard from you, over."

"We had a technical problem that's resolved now. We're heading to the 67th Evac Hospital in Pleiku, over."

"Roger. It's too dark to look for the other guy. Maybe tomorrow early we can come back, over."

* * *

BILL REEDER LAY in the tall vegetation, listening to the small OH-6 scout helicopter cruise over the vegetation, looking for them. He attempted to get their attention, but in the fading light and with his back, he was unable to. *God, I hope they find Tim*, he thought as he lay there listening. His morale increased as he heard the little bird land and then take off again.[2]

* * *

CAPTAIN JIM STEIN was pushing the little bird as hard as he dared to get Tim to the hospital.

"Hey, sir, do you know this guy?" the observer asked.

"I don't know. What's his name tag say?"

"Conroy, sir."

"Oh, hell, he was the front-seat gunner that covered us that night at Polei Kleng," Jim said and attempted to milk another knot of airspeed out of the aircraft.

"Pleiku Tower, Scalp Hunter Four-Five is fifteen minutes out, declaring an emergency to 67th Evac, over."

"Roger, Scalp Hunter, you are cleared to 67th Evac pad. We'll notify them and have them standing by, over."

"Thank you, Pleiku Tower," Jim said. Suddenly, a bright yellow light appeared on the master caution panel.

"What is that, sir?" the observer in the back said, noticing it as well.

"It's the twenty-minute fuel warning light. We should be okay," Jim said, attempting to reassure his observer. He never slowed his approach as he made a hard deceleration landing on the pad and was immediately met by medical personnel, who took Tim out of the aircraft. Jim shut the aircraft down immediately and followed the gurney inside. He wanted to know Tim's condition so he could report it back to the Pink Panthers.

The inside of the emergency room was confusion to the untrained eye and just business as usual to those that worked there. It took Jim a few minutes to find someone who knew something of Tim's condition. They went and found a doctor who was treating Tim.

"How is he doing, Doc?" Jim asked.

"Captain, I hate to tell you this, but that man has been dead for hours," the doctor said.

"Oh, bullshit. We were talking to him twenty minutes ago," Jim said in an elevated voice.

"Captain, that's not possible. The man's body temperature is so low he had to be dead for a couple of hours. I'm sorry, but there's nothing we can do," the doctor said and turned to take care of others. Jim couldn't believe what he'd just heard and slowly walked out, leaving a hole in one of the walls as he did so.

* * *

THROUGHOUT THE EARLY EVENING, the Montagnard Rangers continued to work at clearing the NVA out of the bunkers on the perimeter. Spectre had isolated those enemy forces in the perimeter bunkers from the main body, which had retreated. Truhan and Sparks could hear one of the enemy soldiers moaning from what they believed were wounds sustained in the fight. As they observed one of the bunkers, the young man was pushed out of the bunker by the others and allowed to make his way to the Montagnards. First aid was administered almost immediately in the hope that others would decide to surrender as well. This humanitarian act would pay big dividends an hour later.

"Dai'uy," Ty said, coming into the advisor bunker.

"Yeah, Ty?" Sparks responded.

"Prisoner says big attack planned for at 0500 in the morning. Says big force will attack," Ty said.

"Did he indicate where this force is located?" Truhan asked, pulling out a map and spreading it on the table.

"He say they right here," Ty indicated, pointing at the map.

"Shit, that's a klick out in the jungle right there," Sparks said, turning to look at the location, which could be seen through the doorway.

Picking up the hand mike to the radio, Truhan made the call. "Rogues Gallery, Rocket Eight-Eight Bambino, over."

A few moments later, they heard, "Bambino, this is Rogues Gallery, over."

"Rogues Gallery, request a BUFF mission, immediate. We have the location of a large force that's planning on hitting us at 0500. Over."

As expected, there was a delay before he got a response as the transmission had to be relayed through a U-8 signals aircraft that was orbiting between Pleiku and Ben Het. Through this aircraft was about the only way they could transmit over the distance. Finally, Rogues Gallery's voice was heard.

"Bambino, how bad do you want this air strike? Over." Truhan and Sparks exchanged looks of amazement and confusion. Finally, Truhan keyed the mike.

"Rogues Gallery, how bad do you want to retain this compound? Over," Truhan asked.

At 0230 the following morning, they learned how badly Mr. Vann wanted to retain the compound. The B-52 strike was laid in one thousand meters from the perimeter. No ground attacks occurred that day.

58

CHANGE FOR THE BETTER

10 MAY 1972
    II Corps HQ
    Pleiku

GENERAL HILL HAD BEEN SUMMONED to Dzu's office. This didn't happen often and struck Hill as a bit unusual, especially at such an early hour. Entering the headquarters, Hill immediately got the impression that something was amiss as people wouldn't make eye contact and were speaking in hushed voices. Reaching the outer office, Hill was ushered right into Dzu's office without the usual ceremony.

"Ah, good morning, General Hill," Dzu said cheerfully. "Please be seated," he offered, pointing to one of the overstuffed chairs that adorned every high-ranking Vietnamese officer's office. "May I offer you some tea or coffee?" Dzu asked, and before Hill could answer a tray appeared with both liquids and three cups along with pastries.

Okay, what the hell is going on? Hill was thinking when another Vietnamese officer walked in. He wore the rank of a major general. *Oh Jesus, are they replacing Colonel Ba as division commander?* Flashed through Hill's mind as he stood up.

"General Hill, allow me to introduce you to Major General Nguyen Van Toan. General Toan, General Hill, your advisor," Dzu said as General Toan extended his hand. Physically, Toan was a big man for a Vietnamese. Vann had warned Hill the night before that Dzu was going to be replaced shorty, but Hill hadn't realized it would be this quickly, nor by a major general when the position called for a lieutenant general. Dzu had been relieved.

"How do you do, sir?" Hill said, accepting the extended hand.

"Well, thank you, General Hill. We work well together. Kill many enemy very soon," Toan said, maintaining eye contact with Hill and holding the handshake a bit longer than was natural.

"Gentlemen, let us sit and have some drink while we talk," Dzu said, breaking the handshake and staring contest. Everyone moved to an overstuffed chair surrounding the coffee table. An aide poured coffee or tea, presented each with a cup and then departed.

Major General Toan had been the I Corps armor commander. Trained at Fort Knox, Kentucky, he understood tank warfare and armor tactics. In I Corps, Lieutenant General Lam, the I Corps commander, had not paid attention to the advice Toan had given him on the employment of armor there, and the results had been disastrous. Lam had been relieved and Toan was attempting to rebuild his reputation. Over the course of his career, Toan had been in and out with the powers in Saigon. Accepting this assignment, he hoped, would put him back in their good graces.

"General Hill," Dzu said, getting Hill's attention. "This morning I executed my last official act."

"And that is, sir?" Hill responded, bracing himself for the announcement.

"This morning I ordered the 23rd Division to move the 44th Regiment from An Khe to Kontum. They will begin flying from An Khe to here this afternoon and tomorrow begin arriving in Kontum," Dzu said, very pleased with himself. Turning his attention to General Toan, he said, "This will allow Colonel Ba to have his entire command here in Kontum."

"That's good and should make things much easier for Colonel Ba to control. I look forward to meeting him," Toan said.

"Colonel Truby is the senior advisor to Colonel Ba and they work well together," Hill interjected.

"I'm sure they do," Toan said and paused for a moment, checking his watch. "General Hill, I'm scheduled to meet Mr. Vann. Would you care to accompany me to meet him?" he asked as he stood, leaving his unfinished cup of tea. Hill quickly rose, accepting the invitation, which he felt was more of a command.

"Be happy to take you to him, sir," Hill replied and turned to Dzu. "And to you, sir, my best wishes whatever your future holds."

"Thank you, General Hill," Dzu responded but did not extend his hand, nor did Hill.

* * *

Lieutenant Colonel McKenna had been on R&R in Singapore for the past ten days. The night before, he had arrived at Pleiku and signed back in from leave. This morning he hadn't been able to sleep, which was typical of people coming back into Vietnam after so many days away from the small-arms fire, incoming mortars and the threat of death around them. Before the sun rose, he walked out of the flight terminal, where he'd spent the night, to get some air, bumping into a Vietnamese officer standing with his back to McKenna.

"Oh, excuse me. I didn't notice—Captain Diem! What are

you doing here?" McKenna asked in surprise as the officer turned around. "Why are you not in An Khe?"

"You gone long time," Diem said, shaking McKenna's hand. Diem was a company commander in the 44th Regiment. "We go Kontum," Diem said, pointing across the runway at hundreds of soldiers waiting to board VNAF transport aircraft or CH-47s. "You go Kontum. Okay?"

"Okay, Diem, I go Kontum too," McKenna said without a smile.

"Come, I take you to Major Swachek. He have jeep and Hao over there."

59

HELICOPTER VS. TANK

12 May 1972
B/7/17th Scalp Hunters
Kontum

THE PREVIOUS DAY, the airfield had been subjected to incoming artillery throughout most of the day. Reprieves came while the FAC was on station, but the onslaught would resume as soon as the FAC left the area. In the early-morning hours, the 7th Air Force declared Kontum too dangerous for their aircraft and ceased all daylight operations. Planes were landing in the dark without engine shutdown and with minimal time on the ground. FACs were flying out of Pleiku.

"Morning, gentlemen," the Operations officer said, addressing the four crews that stood in front of the Flight Ops counter. "Kontum is getting shelled by 130mm artillery, which commenced yesterday morning. Those guns have a maximum range of thirty kilometers, so they're well outside the range of any artillery Kontum has that they could throw at them. Your mission today is to be looking for those guns as well as any tanks you might see out there. Start your recon in the Vo Dinh area. Any questions?" There were no questions as the mission brief had been the same almost every day for the past three weeks.

"Okay, if no questions, here are your mission sheets, and good hunting."

Each aircraft commander took the mission sheet and departed with their copilots. First Lieutenant Craig Smith was flying an OH-6 this morning, so he had no copilot. His observer gunner, Sergeant Robbie Robinson, was already at the aircraft getting his ammo loaded along with hand grenades, white phosphorous grenades, and smoke grenades as well as a few thousand rounds of 7.62mm machine-gun ammo for his M60 machine gun that he carried.[1]

"Morning, Robbie. How does everything look?" Craig asked. Although Robbie wasn't a crew chief, he had learned to inspect the aircraft and in the case of an emergency, Craig had taught him how to land the aircraft. It wouldn't be a pretty landing, but any landing you can walk away from is a good landing.

"She looks good, sir. What we got today?" Robbie asked with his usual level of enthusiasm. Nice thing about flying with him, he always had a positive attitude, Craig thought.

"We are going to be scouting around Vo Dinh and working our way along Highway 14. The brass is concerned about tanks coming down that road and some artillery that's shooting at Kontum from out that way," Craig said, putting on his chicken plate chest protector. "Let's mount up and do this," he added as he watched the two Cobras crank their engines.

They flew out towards Vo Dinh, intercepting Highway 14 about three kilometers south of Vo Dinh.

"Undertaker Two-Eight, Triple Nickel, over," Craig transmitted to the Cobra lead aircraft.

"Triple Nickel, go ahead."

"I'm going to slow up and start working along the road."

"Roger, I have you in sight and am tracking." The Cobras

were at altitude but had been warned about a new anti-aircraft missile that the NVA had recently acquired. It had been used in the III Corps area, everyone was told, but hadn't been seen in the II Corps area of operations. Low to the treetops, Craig had to worry about small-arms fire and not heat-seeking missiles. Slowly, Craig's OH-6 scout helicopter worked in an S pattern, moving along the sides of the road and only crossing the road to check out the tree line. Never did he fly down the road. That was a sure way to get shot up. After an hour, something caught his eye.

"Hey, Robbie."

"Yes, sir?"

"Did you see that pile of bamboo up ahead when we crossed the road on that last pass. Did that seem odd to you?" Craig asked over the intercom system.

"I saw it. I've seen piles of logs on the side of the roads but never a pile of bamboo. Do you want to check it out?" Robbie asked.

"Yeah, we'll take a closer look when we get up there," Craig answered and toggled his intercom switch to talk to Undertaker.

"Undertaker, Triple Nickel, over," Craig transmitted.

"Go ahead, Triple Nickel."

"Undertaker, I have a pile of what appears to be bamboo off to the side of the road up ahead. I'm going to take a closer look. Over."

"Roger, Triple Nickel, I have you covered."

The closer Lieutenant Smith approached the pile, the more concerned he became. "Robbie, watch this pile closely. Something doesn't seem right," he said, positioning the pile on Robbie's side of the aircraft as he had the only weapon that could return fire effectively. As the OH-6 approached the bamboo pile, his neck began to tingle. *Something isn't right here,* he was thinking.

"Robbie, hit that pile with a burst," Craig ordered, and Robbie opened fire with his M60 machine run.

"Hey, sir, bamboo doesn't cause ricochets and we have ricochets!" Robbie yelled. "I think there may be a tank under that pile."

"I think you're right," Craig agreed and contacted Undertaker. "Undertaker, we think we have a tank under this bamboo pile. Have you got any HEAT rockets?" Craig asked.

"Negative. Let's get the FAC on this," Undertaker directed.

Craig already had the FAC tuned in on his FM frequency and depressed his transmit switch. "Covey Two-Nine-Eight, Triple Nickel, over."

"Triple Nickel, Covey Two-Nine-Eight, over."

"Covey, I have a possible tank location. Are you prepared to copy? Over."

"Roger, send it over."

Craig sent the coordinates.

"Triple Nickel, I have a good copy and am on station. Can you pop smoke on the target? Over."

"Covey, Triple Nickel, will do now, over." Switching back to intercom, he said, "Robbie, get a smoke ready. I'm going to make another run at it for Covey."

Craig turned towards the bamboo pile and passed over the top at maximum airspeed as Robbie dropped a smoke grenade that tumbled into the tree line on the side of the road. Pulling away from the rising smoke, Craig reported smoke out and waited.

A few minutes later, he heard, "Triple Nickel, Covey Two-Nine-Eight, did you pop smoke yet? Over."

"Covey, that's affirmative. It's gone now. I'll make another pass and drop. Wait one," Craig said, shaking his head. "Okay, Robbie, another pass."

"I'm ready. I'll make this one a yellow. He should be able to see it. Goofy grape may have been too difficult to see from up there," Robbie said, excusing Covey for not seeing the smoke. Craig turned again and approached the tank from a different angle, swiftly passing over it and Robbie engaging with his M60 machine gun.

As they pulled away, he transmitted, "Covey, smoke out, over."

"Roger. Over."

Waiting for Covey to confirm the smoke, Craig asked Robbie if he thought he was doing any good shooting at a tank with the M60 machine gun.

"Well, sir, I'm not hurting the tank, but I am letting the enemy inside it know they ain't fooling anyone. Maybe they'll panic and attempt to drive off."

Craig just chuckled to himself.

"Ah, Triple Nickel, Covey here. I'm not seeing any smoke, over."

Well, damn, if you would come down from ten thousand feet, you would see it, damnit, Craig was thinking when he keyed the mike.

"Roger, Covey, I'll make another pass. I have you in sight right above me and we're along the highway, over."

"Roger, Triple Nickel" was all Covey replied.

On the third pass, Craig received the same response from Covey. Covey couldn't see the smoke grenades. Craig was reaching a frustration level that he hadn't experienced before. *Is this guy blind?* He was thinking.

"Alright, Covey, I'm going to make one more pass and this time I'm dropping a Willie Pete.[2] You should be able to see that damn thing," Craig said. "Okay, Robbie, this time drop a Willie Pete right on top of the pile. I'm going to slow down so you have a clean drop." Craig lined up and came towards the bamboo pile, executing a rapid deceleration.

Suddenly the pile moved as the tank raised his main gun and fired at the OH-6. Craig had hovered so close that when the tank fired, the concussion wave of the shot severely damaged the rotors, knocking one off. They went into a wild gyration with Craig doing everything humanly possible to control the aircraft, which now had only three rotor blades instead of four. The round missed the helicopter completely. Robbie stopped shooting, hanging on for dear life as the aircraft spun and wobbled.

"I can't hold it, we're going in!" Craig said over the intercom.

"Triple Nickel, Undertaker, get the hell out of there" was the last thing Craig heard before the aircraft crashed in low brush fifty meters from the road. Once the dust settled, both on the ground and in Craig's head, he began shutting down the aircraft, which was still running despite the fact that it had no rotor blades now.

Fuel off, battery off, he remembered. "Robbie, get the hell out of here," he yelled, receiving no answer. Robbie was already out of the aircraft with his M60 machine gun and was grabbing up several grenades. As Craig exited the aircraft, he looked up to see Undertaker punching off some rockets in the vicinity of the tank.

"Covey, this is Undertaker. Triple Nickel just marked the tank's location with his crashed helicopter and a Willie Pete. Do you see them now? Over." Undertaker was pissed and Covey got the message loud and clear.

"Roger, Undertaker, I have the target and have a flight of four coming in, over."

"Roger, Covey. Just keep them on the tank's side of the road and not the side where Triple Nickel crashed. We have movement around Triple Nickel and I believe it's the crew," Undertaker directed. As Undertaker worked with Covey, the C&C aircraft began making an approach to pick up Craig and Robbie. Running to the approaching UH-1H, Robbie began to limp, then stopped.

"Hey, sir, I think I've been shot," Robbie said, dragging his hand across his ass. "Damnit, I have been shot...in the butt," he said as he examined the blood on his hand.

"Well, if you can walk, let's move before you get shot in the other cheek, magnet ass," Craig said with a smile and assisted Robbie into the awaiting UH-1H.

As Craig and Robbie were picked up, Covey commenced to put air strikes into the area. After eight flights of F-4s had decimated the area with bombs and napalm, the tank was finally revealed. Hawk's Claw had come out earlier but due to the vegetation couldn't locate the tank. After the last bombing run was made, the tank was exposed and Hawk's Claw made the kill. What amazed everyone was the fact that eight air strikes couldn't kill this point target.

60

HOSPITAL MOVE

12 MAY 1972
Kontum Hospital
Kontum

DR. PAT SMITH had run the hospital in Kontum for thirteen years. She was from Seattle, Washington. Trained as a registered nurse, she had come to Vietnam to work for two years in a leper colony with the Montagnard people. She'd fallen in love with her work and the people. During Tet of 1968, the original hospital had been overrun and destroyed by the Viet Cong. She'd been spared as the patients and staff had covered her with their bodies while the Viet Cong moved through the building, looking for her. Since then, the hospital had had to be moved, and for the past five years, it had been located in an abandoned French Catholic school. It had eighty-eight beds inside but now was supplemented with Army tents on the grounds outside. The hospital had eleven foreign nationals serving in various capacities and thirty Montagnard assistants.

Over the past weeks, her patient load had increased significantly and now included not only Montagnards but also ARVN soldiers. Medical supplies were running low despite the efforts to bring supplies in by air. Frequently Colonel Bachinski, the senior advisor to the province chief, would come by to see that she was getting her share of the supplies coming in as well as food. Everything was on rations since the roads were open only intermittently.

"Dr. Smith, I have spoken with Mr. Vann. This shelling is going to continue and only get worse. He's anticipating that we're going to have a major ground attack in the coming days, and truthfully, we're not sure we can hold. We think you should consider taking your children and staff and flying down to Pleiku and maybe work out of that hospital. If this place does fall, they're going to need you there. We've evacuated about fifteen thousand refugees so far to Pleiku and are trying to get more out as long as the airfield stays open. I can get a helicopter in here to move you out very quickly," Colonel Bachinski offered.

Initially Dr. Smith just stared at him. He could tell by looking at her that the woman in her late forties was tired. Slightly overweight, with short-cropped hair, she must have been attractive in her younger days, he thought. Time and this environment had taken a toll on the woman. Finally, she asked, "What about my patients? What will become of them?"

"We'll start getting them out on the military aircraft at the airfield. If you're not here, those coming in with wounds won't come here but to the airfield, where we can prioritize them and get them on planes to Pleiku."

As Colonel Bachinski waited for an answer, Dr. Smith looked around and the many memories flooded back to her. The terrifying night during Tet; the night they'd heard noises outside the door to the hospital and called American soldiers, thinking it was the VC attempting to get in, only to discover after a few rifle shots that the intruder was a tiger prowling the grounds; the little boy shot in the stomach by other children playing with a gun; the three girls shot by the VC when they were playing in the river.

Finally, she looked back at Bachinski. "You know, back in 1965, South Vietnam turned down an offer for a fifty-nine-thousand-strong Montagnard army trained by US Special Forces and armed with US equipment. They would have cleaned out the VC in the Central Highlands in three weeks." Her eyes welled up as she talked.

"I know this will be hard for you, but I really think you should get ready to get out of here," Bachinski said.

Resigned to that fact, she looked down at her hands. "I'll have to get the kids ready and collect their stuff, and I need to talk to the staff and hand off some ongoing actions. I can be ready in three hours, maybe."

"I'll lay on a helicopter to be here in three hours to pick up you and the kids. If you have any staff that wants out as well, let me know so I can get a couple of choppers to come in and get them," Bachinski said, pausing for a moment. "I know this is going to be hard for you, but it's best for you and your children," he said, standing and heading for the door. "I'll be back to help you load out."[1]

61

ARRIVE KONTUM

13 May 1972
  Kontum Airfield
  Kontum

THE MORNING FLIGHT from Pleiku to Kontum on the C-141 was uneventful, if you considered sitting on the floor with no seat belts, your rucksack on your legs and the pilot putting the aircraft into a forty-five-degree dive over the airfield to avoid anti-aircraft fire from the surrounding hills to be uneventful. Aside from that, not a bad flight. McKenna's jeep was loaded along with Major Swachek and Sergeant Hao, so all three had comfortable seats for the ride. Their rucksacks and personal gear occupied the back seat with Hao. Rolling off the ramp with the aircraft engines still running, McKenna was met by Major Wade Lovings, the division artillery advisor, as he drove over to the terminal building at 0400 hours.

"Good flight, Colonel?" Lovings asked.

"Not first class back to the land of the Big PX, but okay for now."

"How was R&R? Ready to get back into it?"

"R&R was great. Singapore is one hell of a place. What have we got here, besides a shitshow from what the papers in Singapore area are saying?" McKenna asked.

"Well, sir, first off, I'm replacing Major Swachek," Lovings said.

"Really, I'm going home?" Swachek asked with a look of surprise.

"I guess you are. You got a drop," Lovings said, and Swachek responded with a fist pump. "Sir, I've been told to take you over to the 23rd Division headquarters to meet with Colonel Truby as soon as you arrived. Swachek can catch a helicopter back to Pleiku to outprocess. They tried to catch you before you got on the flight but weren't fast enough," Lovings said.

"Sir, it was good serving with you," Swachek said as he pulled his rucksack out of the back for the jeep. "Hao, you take good care of the colonel, okay?"

"I do dat," Hao said with a smile.

"*Incoming!*" someone yelled, and everyone threw themselves on the ground. The round impacted off the side of the tarmac, causing no damage. The C-141 immediately began moving to the runway with refugees sprinting to get on board as the rear ramp was being raised. Lovings jumped up and climbed into McKenna's jeep.

"Get us the hell out of here," McKenna screamed as he jumped in and a second freight train could be heard coming. Hao didn't have to be told twice, putting the jeep in gear and spinning tires to get off the tarmac. The second round landed where the C-141 had been parked and now was closing in on the end of the runway. He didn't bother to ask for takeoff clearance but was at full throttle when he turned onto the active runway and took off in less distance than the aircraft was designed to do.

Arriving at the 23rd Division headquarters, Lovings and McKenna went in right away. The sound of more incoming rounds hadn't escaped their attention, nor had the chaos in the headquarters. McKenna and Lovings headed straight to see Colonel Truby, whom they met as he was coming out of his office.

"Colonel McKenna, welcome back. How was R&R?" Truby asked, stopping in the doorway.

"Good, sir," McKenna responded.

"Come in and let's go over something," Truby said, motioning towards his office. Once inside, he walked over to a wall map.

"The arrival of the 44th puts the entire 23rd Division in Kontum. The 53rd will be on the northeast side, here to here, and defends the airfield," Truby said, pointing out the left and right limits of the 53rd's assigned sector. "The Ruff-Puffs have this sector on the south side along the Dak Bla River. This is the least likely avenue of approach and it's the easiest to defend. The 45th has the northwest sector from the left flank of the 53rd to here." Pausing, Truby pointed out the sector boundaries.

"Okay, sir, where's the 44th going?" McKenna asked with a sinking feeling.

"You, sir, have from the left flank of the 45th across Highway 14, and what we see as the main avenue of approach into Kontum. We feel his main attack is coming right at you. Stop him," Truby said, looking McKenna right in the eyes. There was no smile.

"Yes, sir, I'll get with the colonel and we'll get it done. Anything else?" McKenna asked, hoping Truby would say it was a joke, but he really didn't expect that.

At that moment, Major Josh Steinhauer knocked on the door to Truby's office. "Sir, you asked to see me?" he asked.

"Yes, come in. I believe you know Lieutenant Colonel McKenna," Truby said.

"Yes, sir," Josh said, accepting the handshake McKenna offered. "Good to see you again, Colonel."

"How you doing, Josh?"

"Good, sir."

"Major Steinhauer, I'd like you to accompany Colonel McKenna and the 44th as they conduct a relief in place with the 2nd Ranger Group. Can you do that?" Truby asked, mindful that Josh didn't work for him.

"Sir, I would be glad to accompany Colonel McKenna and help in any way that I can. It all falls within my assignment," Josh said.

"That's it. Good luck," Truby said. Josh and McKenna hadn't walked two feet when a distant sound could be heard, like a locomotive train approaching. When it impacted, it sounded as if it had landed in the vicinity of the airfield.

"McKenna, come with me," Truby said, hurrying towards the doorway and down the hall.

"Lieutenant Colonel Fuesel, what are you doing here?" Truby asked, noticing Colonel Pahl, the SRAG G-2, and Colonel Tho, the corps artillery officer, when he entered the hallway.

"Sir, we were just having a meeting with the division artillery commander when the shelling started," Fuesel said.

"Truby, this is 130mm artillery hitting the airfield right now, the same as yesterday. We've never had the big guns firing into Kontum before," Pahl said. "Some of the guys did a crater analysis and figure they're shooting at max range."

"We need to get the air people working on this one and fast," Truby said, looking at Pahl. "Let's you and I get over to the Air Control Center and talk to Swenholt and Bricker about what we can do and what needs to be done." He paused and turned to Fuesel. "You stay here and work out an artillery support plan. They have forty-four 105s and four 155s. Figure out how they're going to support the forward units and figure it out fast. We can expect a ground attack any day now." He wasn't far off the mark.

62

RELIEF IN PLACE

13 MAY 1972
  44th Regiment
  Kontum

THE 44TH REGIMENT began replacing the 2nd Ranger Group at FSB November as soon as the first elements arrived on 11 May. Lieutenant Colonel McKenna, Major Lovings and Major Steinhauer headed up Highway 14 and observed the remainder of the unit moving up. It appeared that FSB November was going to be the forward edge of the battlefield for the 44th Regiment. Arriving, they met Colonel Tien.

"Colonel McKenna, glad you come. We have fight coming," Tien said with a broad smile and a warm handshake. "You rest well Singapore?"

"Yes, sir, I rest well Singapore," McKenna responded and pointed at Lovings and Steinhauer. "Sir, this is Major Wade Lovings.[1] He replaced Swachek, whose time in Vietnam is over. And this is Major Steinhauer, who's an observer from Washington."

"You spy?" Tien asked, looking at Steinhauer.

"No, sir. I'm simply observing how the Vietnamese forces are doing and working with the advisors," Josh said.

"Yes, you spy," Tien said with apparent seriousness. "Come, I show you place to stay." Tien led the way to a well-constructed bunker. From all indications it had been built by US engineers, with plenty of overhead cover and pine log construction.

"This will work well for us, Colonel Tien. Let me stow my gear and then we can walk the perimeter with you and look over the defensive plan, okay?" McKenna asked.

"Yes, I be in command bunker over there," Tien said, pointing and walking off. After the advisors stowed their gear and set their cots up, they moved off to the command bunker. Constructed like their bunker, it was in full operation and appeared it could withstand a direct hit. Upon entering, Tien waved them over to a table with a map on one side and a schematic of the defensive position.

"Colonel, we conducted a relief in place with Rangers. They gone now. We have no time to make new positions, so we take over old positions. Soldiers are now improving those positions," Tien said and began to point at the map and schematic. "This command post is here, west of Highway 14. 3rd Battalion minus one company is here, Outpost Nectar." McKenna could see that it was two kilometers north of FSB November along Highway 14. "They provide early warning and initial contact. 1st and 2nd Battalion, reinforced with one company from 3rd Battalion, is on perimeter," Tien finished.

"Sir, where is the 4th Battalion?" Lovings asked.

"4th Battalion is back guarding division TOC," Tien responded with an unhappy look. "They should be here, not guarding princes at division headquarters."

"Sir, I'll talk to Colonel Truby about getting them back. Okay?" McKenna offered.

"Okay," Tien said emotionlessly.

"Sir, can I see your fire support plan?" asked Major Lovings.

"Sir, Major Lovings had four tours with the 101st Airborne Division as an artillery officer before he joined me. He still has some connections up there with Colonel Hung," McKenna pointed out, which put a smile on Tien's face. Tien turned and called over his fire support officer, who took Lovings aside and handed him the fire support overlay.

"We go walk perimeter," Tien said, motioning for McKenna and Steinhauer to follow him. As they walked to the first position, Tien looked at Steinhauer.

"What you do, Major? You infantry soldier?" Tien asked.

"Sir, I'm an artillery officer and aviator. Now my job is to observe and report," Josh answered.

"Is here first time on ground with Vietnamese soldiers?" Tien asked.

"No, sir. I was at LZ English when it fell and with Colonel McKenna at An Khe Pass. I was also at Polei Kleng when it was overrun," Josh outlined.

"Ah, you that American. I heard about you and what you do at Polei Kleng. You okay," Tien said with a smile now.

The only thing Josh could say to that was "Thank you, sir," while flashing a look at McKenna, who gave him a wink.

"*Incoming!*" McKenna yelled as the first large-caliber artillery round impacted behind them. Everyone was down on the ground or in a foxhole. The trio inspected the perimeter, pointing out where improvements could be made as the incoming artillery continued sporadically. When they were satisfied, they returned to the command post. Major Lovings was present but didn't look happy.

"What's the matter?" McKenna asked.

"Follow me, sir, I would rather show you," Lovings said, leading the way out of the command post. He pointed. Where the advisor bunker had been located, a large hole was now present, with debris indicating that some Americans may have lived there at one time. "It took a direct hit from what I expect was a 130mm round."

"Oh crap, glad we weren't in there," Josh said, wondering why he had volunteered to come out here.

"The ARVNs are digging us a new position on the other side of the command post with some overhead cover. It should be done in a couple of hours," Lovings said.

"Okay, let's not cry over spilt milk. How does the fire support plan look?" McKenna asked, glancing at the previous advisor bunker.

"Their fire support plan looks good, but truthfully I'm not crazy about the 3rd Battalion being out there on Nectar. They should be back here to hold the line," Lovings said.

"I agree, and I doubt if they will be for long. I'll talk to Tien about bringing most of them back now and leaving a few for early warning. You two get some sleep as I think it's going to be a long night," McKenna said as he walked away to find Tien.

63

—————

US INFANTRY ARRIVES

13 MAY 1972
  23rd Division HQ
  Kontum

DURING THE EARLY-MORNING HOURS, six M-151 Jeeps rolled into Kontum and stopped at the 23rd Division headquarters. The four soldiers in each vehicle immediately did what tired soldiers do—they lay on the ground and went to sleep. After sunrise, the senior NCO woke and walked into the headquarters building. He didn't speak Vietnamese and waited until he spotted a US officer.

"Excuse me, Colonel. I was told to report to the senior US advisor here," he said.

"Well, you found him, Sergeant...Thacker. What can I do for you?" Colonel Truby asked.

"Sir, I have three TOW teams outside and was told that you would tell me where you wanted them," Thacker said.

"Come into my office," Truby said, looking around to see if anyone was observing this conversation before leading the way.

Once inside, he asked, "You want some coffee? You look like you could use some." Truby poured a cup for himself and one for Thacker.

"Thank you, sir," Thacker replied as he accepted the dark liquid.

"Okay, I was told you were coming but was also told that we're to keep you with the advisors and not let the ARVN handle the weapons, or let them fall into enemy hands. You guys are from the 82nd Airborne, correct?"

"Yes, sir. We left Bragg, stopping at Bien Hoa for four days of training, and then they sent us up here. There are twenty-three teams scattered all over the country. You get three with two vehicles each," Thacker explained.

"We have some aerial TOWs operating in the area out of Pleiku, but some of their ammo is here at the airfield. Can you use the same missile?" Truby asked.

"I'm not sure, sir, but we brought extra ammo. I'll check with our missile tech rep and see what he says."

"Okay, we're expecting a full-blown attack in the next forty-eight hours, probably twenty-four, and there will be plenty of targets for you, that I'm sure of. The main attack, we feel, will be coming down Highway 14, so I'm sending you out to the 44th Regiment. Lieutenant Colonel McKenna is the advisor there, and I'll let him know you are coming. He just left here about an hour ago. Anything you need, you coordinate with him. Any questions?" Truby asked.

"No, sir," Thacker said, recognizing that this conversation was concluded. "I'll get my boys rolling."

"Wait, I want one team to stay here at the headquarters. Have the NCOIC report to me and I'll take care of him and his people. Take two teams out to McKenna."

"Yes, sir. We'll get rolling in fifteen," Thacker said and headed out the door. Truby thought he would treat himself to a few minutes of sleep in his office, but it was not to be.

"Colonel Truby," Ba said, sticking his head in the door.

"Yes, sir. What can I do?" Truby said, standing.

"We have increased radio traffic from enemy. He talk much. US signal intercept say he say he attack tomorrow morning at 0400 hours," Ba said.

"That makes sense as Charlie likes to attack at night or early morning, but normally he precedes his attacks with heavy artillery barrages for a couple of days. I wonder why that hasn't happened," Truby said, thinking out loud. "Have you pushed out patrols to locate his forces?"

"I have, and they have not had contacts as of yet today. We see."

* * *

"COLONEL, I was told to report to you," Sergeant Thacker said, approaching McKenna. McKenna had seen the M-151s approaching but had no clue what was mounted on the vehicles or who the squad of US soldiers were.

"Okay, who told you and what are those things on the jeeps and who are they?" McKenna asked, slowly approaching the jeeps.

"Colonel Truby said to come and report, and those, sir, are the infantry soldiers' answer for killing tanks at three thousand meters in ten seconds," Thacker said with pride. "We're from the 82nd Airborne Division and were sent over here five days ago to kill tanks. That, sir, is the ground-mounted, tube-launched, optically tracked, wire-guided BGM-71 missile system, TOW for short. Colonel Truby said I wouldn't be disappointed working with you and you would provide me some tanks to kill," he added, oozing with confidence. "The infantry squad is from Delta Company, 1st of the 12th Infantry, 1st Cav Division, and is my security detail."

"I've read about the system but have never seen one,"

McKenna said, walking around the jeep. "What do you need from me?"

"Sir, I need a clear field of fire over as long of an area as possible on the likely avenue of approach. Some cover would be nice as well," Thacker added.

"Follow me, Sergeant," McKenna said, leading the sergeant down the small hill that November sat on. At the base of the hill, McKenna stopped and pointed down Highway 14. "How's this? I don't want you on the hilltop because when he attacks, he's going to shell the crap out of it. This pine tree grove will offer some concealment. If they close on you and it gets too hot, you can pull out and easily get behind the hilltop. What do you say?" McKenna asked.

Sergeant Thacker took a moment to answer, looking at the pine grove they were standing in and examining the open country in front of his position. "Sir, I think this will work just fine. Good concealment, good exit route, good observation and level ground to our front, with no folds for him to hide in," Thacker said, turning to face McKenna with a broad smile. "I'll get the team and move them down here."

"Good, I'll get another squad of infantry and marry you up with them while you get the team." And the two began walking back up the hill. Reaching the top, McKenna explained to Tien what the TOW could do and Tien immediately assigned a squad of soldiers to provide security to the TOW team, which moved downhill into position. As they were moving off, Steinhauer approached McKenna.

"Hey, sir, would it be okay with you if I took the jeep and went forward to Nectar? I want to see how they're putting in up there and what they do when they spot the first tanks," Josh asked. "Might give us an indication of what the others are going to do."

"Great minds think alike. I was going to ask if you would do that. I want to keep Lovings here to work with the fire support as he was the advisor for the division artillery. Take Hao with you...wait, you speak Vietnamese and don't need him, do you?"

"No, sir, and I know how to drive a jeep too," Josh said with a smile.

"Get out of here and keep me posted," McKenna said with a smile. *Glad that major is around. He's been in so many tight spots with me and always has stepped up*, he was thinking as he made his way back to the command post bunker. Major Lovings was just getting off the radio.

"Hey, sir, I just went over the final protective fire plan with division. I think we're wired in pretty good, as long as they don't hit all three regiments at once. The other regiments are asking for the same thing as us. We all have two batteries of 105 in direct support. The 155s are being held in general support. Colonel Hung said he would remain in the division fire support cell if we needed him. Our two batteries have our plan. We should be good—shit, *incoming!*" Lovings yelled as he dropped to the floor.

The round impacted in the middle of the fire support base and was quickly followed by a second and others. The barrage had started. McKenna, lying on the floor next to Lovings, glanced at his watch. It indicated it was 1750 hours. It was going to be a long night.

Josh had heard the first round pass over his head as he drove north on Highway 14. *Damn, I'm glad I'm not on that hill now*, he was thinking when an ARVN soldier stepped out of the brush and waved him down.

"Where you go? You no go dat way," the soldier said and motioned for Josh to get off the road. Off in the woods, he led Josh and finally stopped. "Here."

Josh got the message but decided to hold off speaking Vietnamese unless he had to. He wanted to eavesdrop on what the Vietnamese were talking about. As he exited his jeep, a Vietnamese lieutenant approached him.

"You..."—the lieutenant paused, trying to think of the right words—"*phat dien*, Major, but welcome."

"You're right, Lieutenant, I am crazy for being here. Take me to the commander, please," Josh said with a laugh, and the two proceeded to the battalion commander's position. Josh could see quickly that it was a well-prepared position with cover and concealment.

"Mind if I just wait here with you, Colonel?" Josh asked as they arrived at the colonel's position.

"You here see if we run. We no run. We withdraw orderly once I give order," the colonel said with some pride. "You stay. You see." Josh didn't have long to wait. A TA-1 field phone began to buzz shortly afterwards. Josh looked at his watch out of force of habit. It read 1915 hours.

"Major," the colonel softly said. "Tanks come."

* * *

"COLONEL TRUBY, report of tanks from Nectar," Ba said with a look of concern.

"Are they still manning Nectar?" Truby asked.

"They still there. No engagement yet," Ba said. "We get air support."

It was a statement, but also an ask from Ba.

"I'll call Vann and lay on support. We need it here early, before daylight if possible," Truby said, reaching for the phone. Voice communications were still possible thanks to an Army U-8 and U-21 fixed-wing aircraft on station almost twenty-four hours a day providing radio relay between Pleiku and Kontum. This aircraft supplemented the single-sideband radio that was the primary communications source.

"Mr. Vann, Colonel Truby here. Things are starting to heat up. We have artillery hitting our forward positions, and tanks have been spotted on Highway 14. I suspect we're going to be in a fight in the morning. Can we get TACAIR over here at 0400?" Truby asked.

"This isn't typical for the enemy. In the past they've surrounded their objective and pounded it with sustained artillery for forty-eight hours at least before launching a ground attack," Vann said, questioning the request.

"They have in the past, but in the past they haven't been subject to the intense bombing that we've been hitting them with. Those B-52 strikes that we've been conducting for the past three weeks must have reduced their force to some extent. He may not have the artillery or the manpower to drag this out much longer, or the supplies. He's fighting on three fronts—here, Quang Tri and An Loc. His supplies must be running low and we've been bombing the crap out of the Ho Chi Minh Trail and his base camps over the border," Truby outlined. "I think he's going to hit us in the morning, especially since we've seen an uptick in his communications traffic."

There was a long pause before Vann spoke. "Okay, I guess it won't hurt to get the flyboys out of bed a bit early. I'll send in the request to have them on station at 0430. How is that? BMNT is about that time," Vann offered.

"That will do. I will keep you posted."

* * *

"WHAT THE—" Josh mumbled, looking down Highway 14. In the darkness, vehicle lights could be seen moving in the trees forward of Nectar's position.

"Colonel, what do you make of this?" Josh asked the ARVN officer who was watching through his binoculars.

"They are pulling to attack position, but why with headlights?" the colonel wondered. "I report. What time now?"

Josh looked at his watch, which was a luminescent-dial watch, Army-issue. "It's 2230."

64

HERE THEY COME

14 MAY 1972
  44th Regiment
  FSB November

"MCKENNA, TRUBY HERE," McKenna heard over the landline.

"Yes, sir," McKenna responded. *I don't need to sleep tonight.*

"McKenna, we just got a radio intercept report. The artillery commander for the 320th NVA Division just notified his batteries to commence firing at 0400 to support the attack," Truby said. McKenna took a quick glance at his watch. It was just past midnight.

"Good to know, sir. We'll be ready. Anything else?"

"I've spoken to Vann about getting air support up early. There has to be some light for them to see, so I expect we may have some support by 0530. Spectre should be over your area or will be shortly. Nothing else. Good luck."

Placing the receiver for the TA-312 field phone back in the

cradle, McKenna went to find Colonel Tien. Tien was in the command bunker and had just received the same news. Quickly, the word was passed to the subordinate units.

Major Steinhauer got the information and passed it to the colonel before he received it from the Vietnamese chain of command.

"Hope they know not to come before then," the colonel said, half joking. "Come, we walk perimeter. Talk to soldiers." Moving out slowly the two walked towards the forward positions. At each fighting position, they spoke softly to the soldiers, giving encouragement. Josh was impressed by what he saw. The confidence the soldiers showed had not been present when he was at LZ English, but he had seen it at Polei Kleng. They were at ease with the commander, asked good questions and were eager to show that they knew what was expected of them. When they finished visiting each unit, they walked back to their position to the sound of some sporadic gunfire. An ARVN officer approached and said something that Josh understood but still played ignorant.

Turning to Josh, the colonel said, "They probe right flank."

"Sir, let me see if I can get Spectre up here." And Josh got on the radio.

An hour later, he heard, "Traveler, Spectre Two-One, over."

"Spectre Two-One, Traveler. We have sporadic contact on our right flank along Highway 14. We also have seen lights fifteen hundred meters north of our position, over."

"Traveler, Roger. Are all your people in positions and not moving about? Over."

"That is affirmative, Spectre, over." Josh heard the droning of the aircraft's four turbine engines above but couldn't see the aircraft in the dark, moonless night. It sounded as if the aircraft might be in an orbit.

"Traveler, Spectre Two-One, over."

"Go ahead, Spectre." Although he couldn't see the aircraft, force of habit had Josh peering up into the night sky.

"Traveler, you have company slowly approaching your right flank. You also have a large concentration of people and what appears to be vehicles, tanks, about fifteen hundred meters north of your position. I can take care of people, but we don't have the tank capability tonight. Am I cleared to engage?"

"Spectre, can you confirm my location? Over," Josh said, hoping that Spectre was looking at the right group of people and not his people.

"Roger, Traveler. Do you have a red-lens flashlight? Over."

"Roger, Spectre."

"Flash your red lens three times. Over," Spectre instructed. Josh removed his flashlight and made sure the red lens was on it. *Flash a white light at him and he's liable to think we're shooting at him,* Josh was thinking while he made sure the lens was attached properly.

"Traveler, I have your red lens and it confirms your position. Am I cleared to engage? Over."

"Spectre, you are cleared." No sooner had the words been transmitted than a molten red stream appeared from out of the darkness, heading to the ground. As Josh watched, he was amazed that although the stream appeared to be continuous, only every fifth round was a tracer round. Initially, the ground on the right flank was swept, and then the area fifteen hundred meters to the north was engaged. Because of a small dip along the jungle tree line, Josh couldn't see the rounds impacting, but he was sure it was effective, especially when he saw ricochets rebounding into the air.

SERGEANT THACKER HAD his two teams of two vehicles each well positioned in the pine grove. Private First Class Angel Figueroa was the gunner on the jeep next to Thacker's position.

"Sergeant Thacker, wake up," Angel said softly. He didn't like waking up the sergeant, but then most people don't like disturbing a sleeping bear.

"I'm awake, and this better be good, Private," Thacker said without moving or opening his eyes as he lay wrapped in his poncho liner.

"Sergeant, I think I see a tank on Highway 14," Angel said.

"You think or you do...which is it?" Thacker said with his eyes open now.

After a short pause, Angel said, "I do, Sergeant."

Now Thacker was up and moving to the jeep. "Let me see," he said, getting behind the sight and pressing his eye to it. "Oh shit, it is a tank," he announced as he stepped back and pointed for Angel to get on the gun.

Angel looked surprised and hesitated just for a moment. "Really?" he asked.

"You're the gunner, now get on the weapon and kill that mother," Thacker ordered.

Immediately Angel scrambled into the firing position and took aim. Just before he fired, he looked to check the backblast area as he'd been trained to do. This was his first time shooting at a real target that would shoot back. Aiming carefully, he depressed the trigger. With a loud ignition and a flash, the missile leaped out of the launch tube. At first it appeared to wobble as it raced out, but the further it got, the more settled it became and centered on the sight, just before it hit a tree.

"What the hell?" Sergeant Thacker said, watching through his binoculars.

"The tank is moving and it moved behind that tree. Nothing I could have done," Angel exclaimed as his teammate loaded another missile.

"Engage again," Thacker ordered and Angel complied. This time no tree stepped in front of the missile. Approximately eight seconds after launch, the turret of the tank was blown into the air.

"Nice shooting, Specialist Angel Figueroa. You just got promoted," Thacker said with a smile. "Reload—I suspect we're going to see more."

* * *

JOSH SAW the explosion to his front right side and knew it wasn't a Spectre kill. He wasn't looking towards Highway 14 when the missile flew into the tank, so he didn't know what had happened, but it was a dead tank and that was all that mattered.

* * *

"OKAY, it's 0400. Where are they?" Truby asked in frustration as he was waking up. "This damn waiting is nerve-racking."

Ba was standing over him with a cup of coffee. "You sleep good. Intercept say that attack not until 0430 now. Here," he said, handing Truby the coffee.

"Thanks," Truby said, standing up and looking around.

"It start soon," Ba said, and Truby picked up his steel pot and placed it on his head. Everyone waited for the artillery to start falling, and they waited and waited—nothing.

"What the hell? It's 0440. He's late," Truby said out loud to no one and everyone. "Have we had any reports of ground probes?"

"Just the usual, but nothing significant," Ba said, equally confused. As they stood looking at the map, the division intelligence office came in and spoke to Ba. Truby watched the exchange but, not being very proficient in the language, couldn't keep up. Finally Ba smiled and issued an order before he turned to Truby.

"He believes attack is not late. We early. NVA use Hanoi time. One hour later than our time. He think artillery start at 0530 now. I think he right," Ba said. "I notified all units to be prepared. Also, TOW team and Major Steinhauer report one tank killed. Good job," Ba said with a thumbs-up and a smile. The intelligence officer was correct and at exactly 0530, the artillery barrage commenced.

BATTLE OF KONTUM

13-14 May 1972

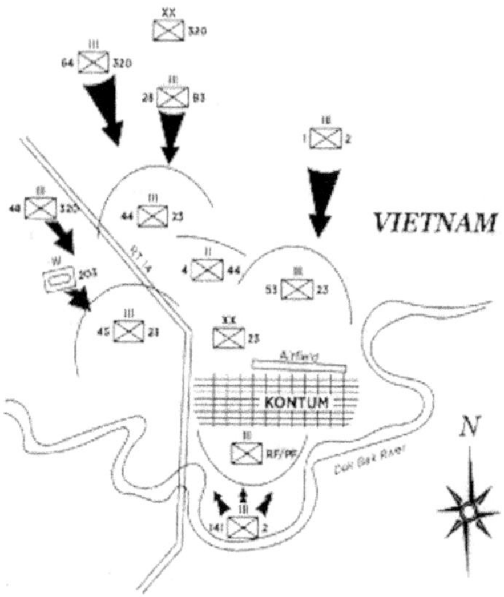

65

——————

FIRST ASSAULT

No place was being spared from the artillery barrage that the 320th NVA Division was laying on. Each of the forward regiments was reporting incoming artillery and ground probes. About the only unit that wasn't being hit with artillery was the Ruff-Puffs on the south side, but they did have probes along their front lines. As the fighting intensified, reports of the enemy strength filtered into the division command post.

"Well, he started the artillery right on time. I will bet at 0600 we'll see a full-blown ground assault," Truby said, looking at the map and the enemy movement being posted on it.

"What time TACAIR come?" Ba asked.

"They should be on station at 0600 as well. The FAC is up right now. As soon as we have some daylight that the fighters can see, they should be all over them. Spectre last night probably took them down a notch or two," Truby boasted.

* * *

"RAVEN FOUR-FOUR, Traveler, we are pulling out, over," Josh announced over the FM frequency.

"Traveler, Roger," McKenna responded. *I hope this is orderly or it could start a panic*, he was thinking as Tien approached him.

"3rd Battalion is pulling back. All good. I put in reserve position when they get here," Tien said. "Commander reports all good and orderly."

"That's good to hear but I never doubted it," McKenna lied. Tien believed him. Thirty minutes later, Josh ran into the command bunker.

"They're right on our heels and leading with ten tanks," Josh said.

McKenna immediately turned to Lovings as the sounds of small arms intensified.

"Lovings, we need artillery FPFs now. We've got to separate the infantry from the armor," McKenna directed.

"I'm on it, sir," Lovings said and turned to his Vietnamese counterpart. Moments later, artillery could be heard passing overhead from south to north, but not a lot. Reports filtered into the command post from the frontline battalions that the enemy was progressing. The artillery was insufficient, as it appeared that only two batteries were engaging.

"Lovings, ask Division to give us everything they got or we're going to be overrun. It appears we have two regiments coming at us and one is a tank regiment, we think," McKenna said. Again Lovings and his counterpart went into a huddle and were on the radio to division artillery.

Moments later, Lovings said, "Sir, I spoke to Colonel Hung. It appears that 53rd and 45th Regiments are being hit but not as bad as us. He's giving us everything for a brief period," Lovings said.

"What is everything?" McKenna asked as he was also attempting to talk to Covey Triple Nickel.

"Sir, we have priority of fire on forty-four 105s and five 155s, and they're about to shoot the FPF. Might tell Covey to stay high and not over us," Lovings said.

Almost immediately, the rolling thunder of artillery rounds from the south passed over their heads. The impact was terrifying as the entire front only five hundred meters in front of the troops erupted, and then it began walking through the enemy towards the frontline troops, stopping only two hundred meters in front of the ARVNs. Suddenly the NVA tanks found themselves alone as the infantry retreated or were killed. Any vehicles on Highway 14 were killed by the TOW teams. Any not on Highway 14 were being engaged and killed by ARVN soldiers with their M-72 LAWs if the tanks got within range.

Over in front of the 45th Regiment, the situation was similar. Rather than the artillery massing on the attacking enemy, Covey was directing air strikes with devastating results as VNAF A1-E Skyraiders, A-37 jets and F-4 Phantoms strafed and bombed the attacking elements of the 64th and 28th Regiments. Major Dodge had been on the radio as soon as Covey was switched over to the 45th Regiment. From his position, Dodge could see the first attack faltering when the napalm had swept over the attackers.

"Covey Triple Nickel, Raven Four-Five, over."

"Raven Four-Five, Triple Nickel, go ahead."

"Covey, that strike broke their back. Can you find deeper targets that may be the second wave? Over."

"Raven Four-Five, I'll move back a bit and see what we have further north. I want to keep the aircraft east of the Red Ball as there's too much artillery going in over there for me to bring them in close."

"Roger, Triple Nickel, understood. Raven Four-Five out,"

Dodge concluded, placing the hand mike back down. He felt pretty good that they had repulsed this first attack.

From inside the division command post, Truby could only listen to the action. All the division assets had been allocated and there was nothing left. At this point it was the battalion and regimental commanders' fight, and Truby felt like he had nothing to contribute. Suddenly, one transmission got his hopes up.

"Raven Six, Hawk's Claw Three, over."

Grabbing the hand mike, Truby quickly responded to the call. "Hawk's Claw Three, Raven Six, over."

"Raven Six, Hawk's Claw Three is a flight of two with escort. Understand you have targets for me, over."

"Hawk's Claw Three, contact Raven Four-Four." And Truby handed the Hawk's Claw aircraft off to McKenna and the 44th Regiment as they were the only ones reporting tanks. That fact was of concern to Truby as well. *Where are the tanks?* he was thinking. *Should be a lot more.*

* * *

"RAVEN FOUR-FOUR, HAWK'S CLAW, OVER."

McKenna hadn't worked with Hawk's Claw and had only read about them and their capabilities. This would be his first opportunity to see them in action. The sun was breaking over the eastern horizon, and it was easy to spot enemy tanks before the regiment's positions. Most had stopped when the artillery had decimated the supporting infantry as they weren't about to attempt to charge into the regiment's positions without supporting infantry.

"Hawk's Claw, Raven Four-Four, over."

"Raven Four-Four, we're a flight of two with escort. Understand you have targets for us. Over."

"Affirmative, Hawk's Claw." McKenna read off the coordinates of the tanks. "We'll cut off the artillery so you can work the area, over."

"Roger, we're over your location at this time and ready to engage. Cease fire on the artillery, over."

McKenna didn't have to tell Lovings to do so as he'd monitored the conversation and immediately issued a cease fire to the division artillery. From his position, McKenna could observe the area in front of the regiment's positions. Almost as soon as the artillery ceased, enemy soldiers began to stand and move forward, as did tanks, thus exposing themselves to the Hawk's Claws.

"Hawk's Claw Three-One, Scalp Hunter Two-Oh, over."

"Scalp Hunter, Three-One, over."

"Three-One, I have two tanks attempting to cross this riverbed. One is on the bank and the other is halfway across. Over," Scalp Hunter reported as he zipped along at treetop level. "Dropping smoke...now." Hawk's Claw began scanning the terrain ahead until he found the plume of yellow smoke rising from the riverbank. His eyes fixed on the object in the middle of the stream. From where he was, it appeared to be a large rock, until he observed it through his sight.

"Well, hello," Chief Warrant Officer Danny Rowe whispered to himself. "I got him. Just put me in position," he said to his pilot, Chief Warrant Officer Edmond Smith.

"You got it," Smith said as he began to lower the collective and lose altitude.

"Pink Panther Four-Oh, we have target sighted and are moving into position."

"Roger, we're with you," Pink Panther flight leader said. At altitude, Captain Redick and Lieutenant Colonel Feore were in the command-and-control ship, watching the action.

"Okay, we're at three thousand and I estimate twenty-seven hundred meters," Smith said. "Evans, Lehrschall, are you two ready?"

"Ready as ever," Evans responded, exchanging a look of anticipation with Lehrschall. Both heads snapped front again when the missile suddenly leaped from the tube. Mr. Rowe held steady on the target despite some turbulence and watched as the missile closed on the tank in the river. The top hatch was open, and seconds after the missile impacted, a plume of flame shot out the open hatch, throwing what appeared to be the body of the tank commander out of the hatch that he was standing in.

"Second target, engaging," Rowe said as he moved his sight onto the tank on the riverbank. As soon as it was locked on the target and before he could launch the missile, he noticed the crew was already climbing out of the tank. He launched the second missile. Score another kill for Hawk's Claw.

By 0800, the attack against the regiments was pretty much over, or so everyone thought.

66

ATTACK CONTINUES

14 May 1972
23rd ARVN HQ
Kontum

JOHN VANN STRODE into the 23rd Headquarters, accompanied by another US Army officer. His name tag said Rhotenberry. Colonel Rhotenberry was originally supposed to be the 23rd Division senior advisor, but he had been undergoing a medical procedure when Colonel Kellar was relieved. Rhotenberry was originally scheduled to arrive in September, but it was requested that he come right away. The procedure had to be done, so he arrived as soon as he could and Truby was told when he took the assignment that it would only be temporary.

Colonel R. M. Rhotenberry was now entering his fifth tour in Vietnam and as an advisor. He had a distinguished combat record in Korea and was exactly the man that Vann wanted for this assignment.[1]

"Colonel Ba, Colonel Truby, allow me to introduce Colonel Rhotenberry," Vann said, approaching Ba and Truby.

"Hot damn, my replacement," Truby said. Ba simply acknowledged the introduction with a nod as Rhotenberry extended his hand, which Ba accepted.

"Colonel Ba, I've heard much about you and your leadership. I look forward to serving with you," Rhotenberry said.

"Together we will defeat this enemy," Ba replied.

"Now, gentlemen, I would like you, Colonel Truby, to stay on a bit longer and help with the transition while Colonel Rhotenberry has time to observe and come to some conclusions, say maybe for another five days. Would that be acceptable?" Vann asked.

"Yes, sir, fine by me," Truby answered. "How do you feel about it?" he asked Rhotenberry.

"Mr. Vann and I already talked about it and I'm good if you and Colonel Ba are," Rhotenberry replied, glancing at Ba.

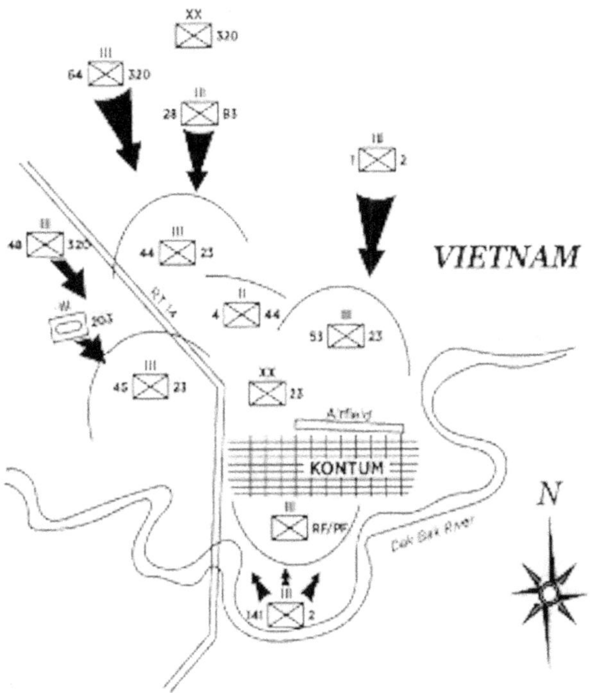

"I think satisfactory," Ba said with caution. He had just gotten comfortable working with Truby and now would be switching advisors again. First Kellar, then Truby, now him. *Does this revolving door ever cease?* Ba was thinking.

"Good, it's settled, then," Vann said, turning to Ba. "Colonel Ba, how about a rundown of this morning's attack?"

Ba moved over to the map and the sketch of the defensive perimeter. "Attack come at 0530 with artillery shelling. Ground attack come at 0600. Main attack against 44th Regiment. This attack led with tanks. No tanks against the 45th and the 53rd Regiments. I think the 44th fight with the 48th Infantry Regiment and the 203rd Tank Regiment. Same time, the 45th Regiment fight 64th Regiment of the 320th Division and the 28th Regiment of the B-3 Front, independent regiment. The 53rd Regiment fight 1st Regiment, 2nd Division. In the south, the Regional Popular forces fight probed by the 141st Regiment of the 2nd Division. The attacks stopped before they penetrate by TACAIR, artillery and those helicopters with the antitank missiles. Now we prepare for the next attack," Ba concluded.

"When do you expect that to occur?" Rhotenberry asked.

"I think tonight. I think main attack come at 45th Regiment or 53rd Regiment. The 44th Regiment hurt them too much today," Ba indicated with a smile.

"Where do you consider your weakest point in the defense?" Rhotenberry asked Ba.

"I have concern for the south. Regional Popular forces many times go home at night see families. We have to keep on them to stay in position. In the north I have concern area between 45th and 53rd Regiments. The weak link in defense is boundary between two units. That is the point that I worry about. We have 4th Battalion from the 44th Regiment in reserve. I moving them to position behind this boundary in case I need to reinforce," Ba explained. His explanation seemed to appease Rhotenberry.

Throughout the day, the 23rd units continued to improve their positions in anticipation of another attack. Covey continued to operate over the battlefield, looking for targets, especially the 130mm artillery pieces that were shelling Kontum and the units. Away from Kontum and the populated areas, the

B-52s continued to unload on suspected NVA locations, but caution had to be exercised due to the number of refugees on the move and the absent ARVN soldiers that were attempting to E&E back to friendly lines. Consideration was also being given to the fact that several American advisors were still missing. As night came, pucker factors increased.

The intensity of small-arms fire, RPGs and mortars all along the forward defenses erupted at 2000 hours. McKenna, Lovings and Steinhauer immediately went forward to see if they could assist in any way. Returning to the command post, they updated Tien on what they had seen.

"Colonel Tien, I believe you have three battalions closing in on you. They got very close before they were discovered. We have some hand-to-hand fighting in the forward positions. We also have some forces behind us, engaging the 3rd Battalion. I recommend that we request a Spectre gunship," McKenna said.

"Do it" was all Tien said, redirecting his attention to his operations officer, who was rendering a report from one of the battalions.

"Can we get more artillery?" Tien asked.

"Sir, I will ask, but I doubt it. It's all been committed to the 45th or the 53rd Regiments."

* * *

Truby and Rhotenberry were in the division command post when Truby got a call from Major Dodge, deputy senior advisor to the 45th Regiment.

"Sir, they've broken through. One infantry battalion has penetrated between us and the 53rd. Not sure how long we're going to be able to hold if they start pushing follow-on forces through. We've committed our reserve already," Dodge explained.

Ba was getting the same information from the 45th Regiment commander, and the Operations officer was talking to the 53rd Regiment Operations officer. The stories were all the same. The only reserve was the 4th Battalion of the 44th Regiment, which was in a defensive posture around the division headquarters. After Ba stopped talking to the 45th Regiment commander, he stood looking at the map and the defense sketch. Truby joined him.

"I just spoke to Major Dodge with the 45th and Major Perry with the 53rd. Their stories match. The boundary has been penetrated. We have two B-52 strikes laid on and they'll be coming in the next two hours. I recommend we put them in where the enemy is concentrating his forces to exploit this breakthrough, right here," Truby said, pointing to the center of a box. Ba studied it for a moment.

"Request that" was Ba's response. At this point he had run out of options and ideas.

Truby called SRAG headquarters and spoke to General Hill. "Sir, we have a breakthrough on the perimeter between the 45th and 53rd Regiments. We want to divert those incoming B-52s to a new target." And he read off the center of mass for the bomb strike.

"Truby, I have to get this approved at MACV. Let me get back to you," Hill said, knowing that time was of the essence. Thirty minutes later he had his answer.

"Truby, Hill here. MACV disapproved your request. Said it was too close to your forces and the hamlet."

"Sir, that hamlet is gone, and if we don't get it we will be too," Truby said, not trying to mask his frustration. "Let me get back to you, sir." And he hung up.

"We need to move the troops back before they'll approve the strike," Truby said. "Colonel, do you think those two regiments can withdraw one klick in an orderly fashion without panicking?" Truby asked.

"They will," Ba said without hesitation.

"Why not mass our artillery in front of the two regiments at the point of penetration as the troops pull back?" Rhotenberry offered. "The mass artillery will hold the enemy in place while the troops pull back and keep them from rushing in behind our troops."

Ba and Truby looked at each other and both nodded.

"Get me Colonel Hung," Ba ordered, wanting to speak to the division artillery officer.

Thirty minutes later, the plan was ready to be executed. While Hung put the artillery support plan in order, Truby was back on the line with Hill. When he explained that the troops were going to pull back one klick to provide the safety zone required in thirty minutes under an artillery barrage and the B-52s could lay down a carpet of bombs in one hour, Hill passed the plan to MACV, who approved it very quickly.

BATTLE OF KONTUM
14-15 May 1972

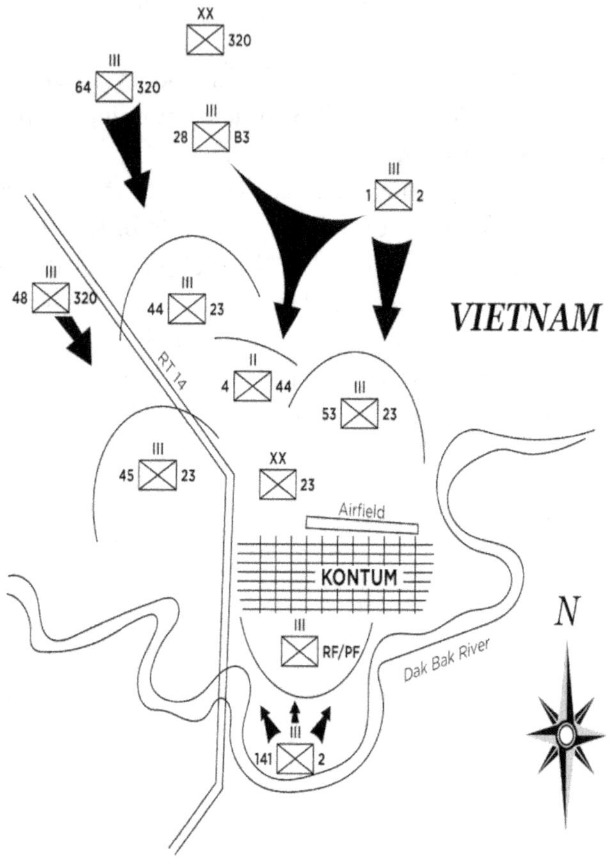

MAJOR DODGE REMAINED in the 45th Regiment command post as the units along the penetration pulled back. The units around the 45th Regiment CP were completely engaged until the rain of friendly artillery began in front of their position and extended into the rear of the penetrating forces. Reports were then received of units pulling back from the penetration to take up new positions closer to Kontum. *I hope to hell this works* flashed through Dodge's mind. If it didn't, he was sure he would be running for his life.

Once the first seven-hundred-and-fifty-pound bomb exploded, the sound of exploding bombs didn't cease for a full minute as three B-52s unloaded into the designated box. The safety zone had been ignored as one bomb detonated about three hundred meters in front of a friendly position instead of the minimum eight hundred meters. When the last bomb exploded, a deadly silence fell over the battlefield. The silence was broken a few minutes later as ARVN soldiers stood, some bleeding from their ears and noses, most shaking the ringing noise from their heads. There was no sound coming from the front or the enemy.

67

RESUME THE DEFENSE

15 May 1972
23 Division HQ
Kontum

At first light, members of the 53rd and 45th Regiments began to move back to their previous frontline positions. As they cautiously moved forward, they found no surviving NVA except one soldier. God must have been watching over that young man. The NVA attack was broken and the perimeter was restored, for the day. Ba, Truby and Rhotenberry were meeting at the division command post after a few hours of sleep.

"We must realign our defense," Ba said. "I make mistakes with way I position regiments."

Before he could speak, Truby interrupted him. "Now, Colonel Ba, you did—"

"No, I commander, I responsible. Now I must change plan. We stretched too thin on north and we have no reserve. I think we move 45th Regiment to 44th Regiment's position but closer to the city and pull 53rd Regiment back closer to the airfield," Ba announced.

"Well, what about the 44th Regiment?" Truby asked.

"The 44th Regiment had hard fight for two days. I pull him back to reserve regiment on northwest side of city. He can occupy old hospital compound for his CP," Ba indicated.

"Let me ask, Colonel Ba," Rhotenberry said, "what sector is your weakest at this point?"

"South sector. I not comfortable with just the Regional Forces there. They not disciplined as ARVN forces. We must watch southern sector closely for sappers. Also I worry about spies in the refugees. We need to get refugees out of here," Ba stated.

"I'll call Vann and see if we can get more air support to move them out," Rhotenberry said, standing and heading for the single-sideband radio. A few minutes later, he returned.

"What did Vann say?" Ba asked.

"He didn't. He's on his way here." After thirty minutes, Vann walked into the 23rd DTOC.

"Morning, gentlemen, let's talk refugees," he said, pulling up a chair and motioning for Rhotenberry and Ba to do the same. As they began to pull up chairs, Truby walked in.

"Morning, sir," Truby said, a bit surprised to see Vann there.

"Morning. Pack your stuff, I'm taking you back to Pleiku and putting you on a flight to Nha Trang. MACV called and want you back there now that he's here," Vann said, indicating Rhotenberry. Truby couldn't believe what he was hearing, but he had no objections, excusing himself to pack his gear.

"Now where were we...oh yes, refugees. We've extracted about twenty thousand so far from here. How many more do you estimate are still here?" Vann asked.

"We have people coming in all the time. Mostly Montagnards now that the enemy is pushing towards us. I would say thirty thousand are still here," Rhotenberry said, looking at Ba, who acknowledged with a nod.

"Okay, let's get the women and children to the airfield and make them the priority to get out of here. Hand the men captured weapons and put them on the defense with the Ruff-Puffs or use them as laborers. We need to keep that runway clear of debris and potholes, so use them to sweep the runway and fill in the holes," Vann directed.

"We can do," Ba said, standing and leaving the room. Rhotenberry and Vann could hear Ba issuing orders to his staff.

"We got lucky over the past couple of days, but this isn't over," Vann pointed out. "He's using some of the same tactics that we saw used in I Corps and III Corps. I think he's attempting to save his artillery and use his tanks to move up here. I also believe that our B-52s, close-air and the ground actions have taken a toll on the 320th Division. You had, what, three thousand enemy in the attacks so far. The 2nd Division hasn't been committed against this place and he has probably ten thousand troops. He'll hit here tonight or in the next couple of days. Be ready for him. I would recommend that you get Ba to push out patrols and find the enemy's front lines so we can adjust our B-52 boxes."

"Ba has already issued orders to make that happen. General Hill was in here yesterday and ripped into him about patrols and a few other things. You know, sir, that doesn't help. I've known Ba for many years and worked together down in the Delta. Ripping his ass does not get things done. I know how to work with the man. It's bad enough fighting the NVA, we don't need to be fighting with Hill," Rhotenberry concluded.

"I'll talk to General Hill and see if I can get him to back off a bit," Vann said with a snicker. "Maybe I should back off on him too."

Ba returned moments later. He wore a smile. "Combat

patrol make contact. We not probe them for change. Also, air cav find enemy northeast, northwest and southeast of city."

"Good, we'll plot those locations for B-52 strikes. I'm sure they've passed that info to your G-3 air coordinator," Vann said, standing as Colonel Ba walked back in. "Colonel Ba, you do good. Keep it up," he said, attempting to take the sting out of General Hill's tongue-lashing from the day before. Ba's face lit up and he nodded in appreciation.

Throughout the day, units moved to new locations and prepared their defensive positions. The 53rd Regiment shifted to the west slightly but withdrew closer to the airfield on the edge of the northernmost buildings, which offered some overhead cover and concealed positions. The 45th slipped due west and pulled back as well but remained outside the town. The 44th Regiment slipped south to the hospital area and took up positions blocking Highway 511 from Polei Kleng to the west and Highway 14 behind the 45th Regiment. This would allow the 44th to quickly move to reinforce the Ruff-Puffs if the need arose. Not as intense as the previous days, the moves were conducted under enemy artillery fire.

Diving into the command bunker of the 44th Regiment, Major Lovings looked at Colonel McKenna. "Sir, I suspect it's going to be a long night again tonight."

"Afraid you might be right. Wonder how Steinhauer is doing back at division?" McKenna questioned as he attempted to open a C ration can. Steinhauer had returned to Division earlier in the day while the regiments were moving.

"Sir, he's probably sitting very comfortably right about now," Lovings said as another round slammed in the 44th Regiment, close to the command post, causing dust to drop from the ceiling and rise from the floor.

"I wouldn't be so sure about that," McKenna said, taking a bite of his ham and lima beans. Suddenly a new sound was heard and the impacting explosion shook the command post.

"Holy shit, what was that!" Lovings asked as he cautiously picked himself up off the floor. "That didn't sound like incoming artillery to me."

"That wasn't. That was a tank round," McKenna responded, totally forgetting his dinner, which was on the dirt floor of the CP. He moved over to one of the windows facing towards Highway 511 and became a bit pale. Four T-54 tanks were sitting on the edge of the tree line, about eight hundred meters away.

"Lovings, get Spectre over here quick," McKenna ordered.

Map created by Infidium LLC for Matt Jackson Books.

68

BELIEVE BUT VERIFY

16 May 1972
23rd Division HQ
Kontum

"Morning, Colonel Ba," Rhotenberry said, walking into the DTOC after four hours of sleep. Almost immediately, an ARVN soldier handed him a cup of coffee. "Thank you," Rhotenberry said. He wasn't sure if the young man spoke English or not, but he was sure he would understand the sentiment.

"Morning, Colonel," Ba responded. "I think we have busy day today. 3rd Battalion moving to kill enemy penetration leftovers. 53rd moving into graveyard here on northwest to kill this group," he said, stabbing at the map with his finger.

"That's good. We should watch this action by the 53rd closely. We can't use artillery in the graveyard, so this could be a long day's fight," Rhotenberry said.

"Morning, sir," Josh said, walking into the DTOC. Josh had moved back to the DTOC during the night and found a bunker close by to crawl into and catch a couple of hours of sleep. Turned out he was more tired than he'd thought and had slept for six hours. Rhotenberry was surprised to see him as they hadn't been introduced.

"And who might you be, Major?" Rhotenberry asked, eyeing the dirty major.

"Sir, I'm Major Steinhauer and I'm—"

"So you're the IG guy I've been told about," Rhotenberry interrupted. "Mr. Vann told me all about you. I'd like to sit down and pick your brain later. Are you seeing all that you need to see?"

"Yes, sir, more than I need to see to be truthful."

"Well, how about sticking close to here today? I may be able to give you the opportunity to see a lot more before this day is over," Rhotenberry said with a smile. "There's some coffee in that pot. You look like you could use some. Help yourself," he said, gesturing to the pot.

"Thank you, sir, I'll take you up on that," Josh replied, moving towards the pot of really dark-looking coffee.

Josh stayed in the DTOC, monitoring the actions being conducted by the battalions against the penetrations that had occurred previously. At 1300 hours, Rhotenberry called him over to the map board.

"You look bored, Major. Want to get out and fly a bit?" Rhotenberry asked.

"Yes, sir. What do you need?" Josh replied.

"We have a report from the 53rd that they've cleaned out the graveyard and are pulling back. Truthfully, I don't believe it. How about you get over to the airfield? Take my jeep, and there's a UH-1 waiting to take you up and check out what's going on in the graveyard. Let me know if it has in fact been cleared," Rhotenberry asked.

"Yes, sir. I'll head out right now," Josh said, marking on his map the location of the cemetery, which was on the northwestern side of the city. Josh had been pleasantly bored sitting in the DTOC, and the chance to get out and get into the air suited him just fine as he welcomed the cooler air at altitude. The Gladiator aircraft was waiting for him when he arrived, engine turning over after just refueling. After a quick brief on what he wanted to see, Josh jumped in and that aircraft lifted off the runway.

The flight was short, less than five minutes to reach the area on Josh's map. From two thousand feet, Josh was able to observe what was happening on the ground.

"Thunder Six, Traveler Six-One, over," Josh transmitted. Radio call signs were changing frequently to confuse the enemy that Rhotenberry was sure were listening to transmissions. Josh's Traveler call sign was about the only call sign besides Mr. Vann's that didn't change. Rhotenberry had no control over aviation assets, so theirs didn't change either.

"Traveler Six-One, Thunder Six, over," Rhotenberry responded.

"Thunder Six, I'm at two thousand over the target and it appears that there are still a lot of bad guys down there and not much movement by the friendlies, over."

"Traveler Six-One, are you sure? Over."

"Thunder Six, the green tracers that I'm seeing and the ones that came up to greet us tell me I'm sure, over."

"Roger, Traveler Six-One, return to base. Out." Josh could tell from the tone that somebody was not happy.

Rhotenberry put down the hand mike and went looking for Colonel Ba, who had stepped out of the DTOC. Finding him standing next to a piss tube, Rhotenberry waited until Ba zipped his pants back up before he approached.

"Colonel Ba, I just spoke with an advisor that I had fly over the actions of the 53rd. The cemetery is not secured and is still in the hands of the enemy. Who told you it was secured?" Rhotenberry could see that Ba was immediately taken aback if not embarrassed.

"I get report from 53rd. They say all secure. Come, we call," Ba said, shaking his head and leading them to the DTOC. Arriving, Ba was immediately on the radio, talking to the 53rd commander. The conversation appeared to be a one-way conversation, with Ba hotly conducting most of it.

"He say they must have put more troops in after they secured. He send back out to secure," Ba said with a look of concern. "This may be bigger than we think."

"If they're reinforcing that action, then we've got to get that cut off," Rhotenberry pointed out as Josh walked into the DTOC. Before Josh could say anything, Rhotenberry turned to address him.

"Major, did you see any sign of the enemy reinforcing their people in the cemetery? Any at all?" Rhotenberry asked.

"No, sir. In fact, it appeared that the 53rd folks had them pretty much bottled up on three sides and the river on the fourth side," Josh replied. Ba listened but said nothing for a moment.

"Okay, we wait and see" was his only comment.

Throughout the day, VNAF C-123 aircraft were landing and rapidly offloading supplies and taking refugees out. At times, flights were delayed in landing as artillery rounds were striking the airfield when the FAC and TACAIR weren't prowling the sky. It was thought that the NVA artillery was operating from caves on the southern end of Rocket Ridge. The gun would roll out of a cave, fire and then be quickly brought back into the cave to be reloaded and wait for another opportunity to fire. Unlike US doctrine, where an artillery battery is all collocated, making it easy to resupply and coordinate fires, the NVA dispersed their guns in multiple locations, making it difficult for the FAC and air cav to locate. Although the guns were firing on the same point, each fired separately, thus not being able to mass their fires as US artillery did and ARVN artillery did not at Tan Canh or Dak To II. It was becoming obvious, however, that NVA forward observers were directing and adjusting the fires as they were more accurate than in the past.

"Major Steinhauer, need you to take another look over the cemetery. We're being told it's secure now. Chopper is inbound to pick you up," Rhotenberry said as the distant sound of rotor blades beating the air could be heard.

"Got it, sir," Josh said, grabbing his gear and heading out the door just as the chopper was setting down. The crew didn't want to be on the ground any longer than necessary as they knew they would be a target shortly for the artillery observers.

"Where to, Major?" the aircraft commander asked as Josh adjusted his headset.

"The cemetery to the northwest, and keep us at two thousand. It could be hot," Josh added as the aircraft lifted off. No sooner than it was gone than an artillery round slammed in close to where it had been sitting. As the aircraft approached the cemetery, Josh could see that not much had changed since his last visit.

"Thunder Six, Traveler, over."

"Traveler, Thunder Six, go ahead, over."

"Thunder Six, Traveler over the objective, no apparent change in conditions, over," Josh reported.

"Son of a—roger, Traveler, return to base, over." Josh could tell that Rhotenberry was pissed. Twice now the 53rd had reported the cemetery secured and twice now it was not. When Josh arrived back at the DTOC, silence prevailed. None of the Vietnamese staff were talking, or they were talking in hushed whispers. Tension hung in the air.

Captain Finch, the B-52 coordinator, was quietly sitting in his area. He glanced up and made eye contact with Josh, who walked over. "What did I miss?" Josh asked.

"Sir, you missed an explosion. When you told Rhotenberry

that the cemetery wasn't secured, he went ballistic. Ripped into Ba, who in turn ripped into the 53rd Regimental commander. Ba told him that an advisor—he didn't name you—had been up twice and confirmed that the cemetery wasn't secured. Ba told the regimental commander to get his ass there and supervise what's going on," Captain Finch outlined. "Rhotenberry then got on the radio and ripped Major Perry a new asshole for not being out there as it's the only show in the 53rd's sector. I think he's going to relieve Perry or bring in a lieutenant colonel to be the senior advisor to the 53rd. He was on the phone with Mr. Vann afterwards and I heard him talking."

"Damn, I didn't mean to get Perry's ass in a sling," Josh said, feeling a bit bad for his fellow officer.

"Hey, sir, he was in a bad situation to start with. He's a major attempting to advise a colonel with more combat experience. Not a good way to do business," Captain Finch said.

"Suppose you're right" was all that Josh said before he stepped out to grab something to eat. Even a C ration meal at this point would be good as he hadn't eaten in the past twenty-four hours. *Damn, besides something to eat, I would love to get a shower and some clean clothes*, he thought as he walked to his makeshift bunker.

Throughout the day, artillery rounds hit the city and the airfield. Major Lovings with the 44th had been timing the rounds hitting their position at FSB November. It was about one round every minute. He conducted a crater analysis and determined that they were coming from the southern end of Rocket Ridge, as he'd suspected. More disturbing, however, was the occasional mortar round that indicated it was coming from the high ground due north of the FSB November. This high ground was only three klicks north of November. Lovings determined that these were 160mm mortar rounds, some of the largest in the Russian inventory and now appearing for the first time in Vietnam.

As Josh finished the last of his C ration meal, beans and franks, a young Vietnamese staff officer exited the DTOC and looked around. Josh just sensed he was looking for him. As soon as the young man made eye contact, he trotted over. "American colonel want you, now," the Vietnamese officer announced.

"Okay, tell him I'll be right there," Josh answered, and the Vietnamese was off at a run. *Wonder what it is this time*, he was thinking as he strolled back to the DTOC.

"Major, I want you to go have another look. We're being told it's secure this time. Get as low as you can and confirm what they're telling us. Truthfully, I don't believe them," Rhotenberry said. "Chopper is inbound."

"Yes, sir," Josh said, turning and heading out the door. The chopper arrived shortly, and for the third time, Josh went out to the cemetery.

"Thunder Six, Traveler, over."

"Traveler, Thunder Six, go ahead."

"Thunder Six, we passed over the objective at five hundred feet. I lost count of the number of hits we took. This place is *not* secured. Returning to base. Over."

"Roger, Traveler, Thunder out."

Josh switched to the internal intercom system. "Hey, Chief, take us home."

"Roger, sir, is it okay if we go to POL first? I'm really low, and then I'll drop you off at the DTOC," the aircraft commander asked.

"Sure, that'll work," Josh replied, and the pilot headed for the airfield. C-123s from the South Vietnamese Air Force were delivering supplies and had been all day. The UH-1H made its approach to the airfield and went directly into POL to refuel. As soon as it was topped off with fuel, the crew was aboard and the aircraft began to hover out. The next thing Josh realized, he was on the ground as the blackness began to dissipate.

"Sir, are you okay?" a distant voice said. Josh rolled over

slowly and could see a figure squatting over him. Behind the figure was a burning helicopter.

"I think so. What happened?" Josh asked, attempting to stand up.

"Sir, we have to get to a bunker fast," the crew chief said as he half dragged and half carried Josh, who was unsteady on his feet. As they entered the nearest bunker, the next incoming artillery round impacted. A UH-1H that was parked suddenly went up in a fireball.

"What happened? Where are the others?" Josh asked, beginning to come out of his daze.

"Sir, we took an artillery round or mortar. It hit right in front of the front right side. Probably killed Lieutenant Holloman and Mr. Davis right away, and we hit and must have punctured the fuel cell on the right side, causing the fire. Specialist Pierce never had a chance when that blew. You were thrown out and I think I broke a rib on the gun mount. We were lucky."

"I'd say. Thanks. What time is it?" Josh asked.

"Sir, it's 1515 hours," the crew chief answered. "Why is that important, can I ask?"

"It'll go in my report. My watch is busted and I haven't been able to get another," Josh said, pausing. "Let's get out of here and get back to the DTOC. See if we can get you a ride out of here." Josh and Specialist Donovan began making their way back to the DTOC. Although it was only five blocks from the airfield, they had to take cover as they moved depending on how close the incoming artillery was to their position. From the sound, they could tell if it was going to impact close or far away. Most of the time, it was close. Through it, the VNAF C-123 aircraft continued to land and offload their valuable cargo. *Damn, I wish the VNAF helicopters would operate like these guys,* Josh was thinking when suddenly there was a tremendous explosion on the airfield, followed by a series of monumental secondary explosions.

"Crap, I'll bet they hit a C-123 full of ammunition," Josh said, looking back at the airfield.

"Sir, I suspect I'm going to be spending the night here. They'll close the airfield, I bet," Specialist Donovan said.

"Specialist, I'm afraid you might be right" was all Josh could say.

69

CLOSE THE AIRFIELD, AGAIN

17 May 1972
Kontum Airfield
Kontum

THE AIRFIELD REMAINED CLOSED all night while the ammo in the destroyed VNAF C-123 continued to explode. After it stopped, firefighter crews moved in with water hoses and attempted to get the fire out. Once it was, bulldozers moved in and began pushing the debris off the tarmac into a field adjacent to the runway. By 0630 the airfield was operational again and aircraft were landing with supplies.

The enemy continued to shell the city and the airfield throughout the day. Two Cobra gunships landed and had begun to rearm when an artillery round landed close and damaged both aircraft. The wounded pilots were just thankful that it didn't hit the rockets, 40-millimeter ammo and 7.62 minigun ammo they were loading. Despite the shelling, US C-130 aircraft continued to drop in with supplies.

"Kontum Approach, Greyhound Two-One, over."

"Greyhound Two-One, Kontum Approach, over."

"Kontum Approach, Greyhound Two-One is five miles west for landing."

"Roger, Greyhound Two-One, you are cleared for straight in runway 090. Winds are light and variable. Be advised we have occasional incoming artillery, over."

"Roger, Kontum Approach, I don't intend to be there long. Over," the pilot said, almost laughing.

As Greyhound Two-One approached, he went into a steep dive to the west end of the runway, intending to use as little of the runway as possible for his roll. He wanted to get down fast, unload faster and be gone even faster. The runway at Kontum was only thirty-two hundred feet long, and that was the minimum length for an empty C-130. When Greyhound Two-One touched down, he touched down on the numbers at the west end, a perfect landing using the minimum amount of runway for his landing roll. Taxiing back to the end of the runway, he lowered his ramp and his loadmaster began shoving pallets of ammo out when the first artillery shell impacted behind the aircraft. Immediately the pilot came to full throttle and began a rapid taxi to the end of the runway.

Reaching the end, the C-130 spun around and started back down the runway with the tail ramp still down and dragging on the ground like an anchor. Reaching the other end of the runway, the pilot pulled back on the yoke, but the lowered tail ramp prevented the aircraft from obtaining a proper takeoff attitude. The belly of the aircraft clipped the roof of a house before the wing hit a chimney. The impact tore the wing partially off and the aircraft began a violent turn and cartwheeled across a field.

Ambulance crews and firefighters raced across the field to the crash site. Two figures staggered out of the burning wreckage. What concerned everyone more, however, was the growing fire across the field towards the POL point with twenty-five thousand gallons of JP-4 jet fuel and three thousand rounds of 105mm ammunition that had been delivered that day. It became evident that the fire could not be contained and everyone exited the area as quickly as possible. The airfield would be closed another night.

70

ANOTHER LONG DAY

18 May 1972
   44th Regiment
   FSB November

THE PREVIOUS NIGHT, the ground probes had commenced right on time at 2000 hours. All night the frontline positions had been under attack from both incoming artillery and the ground probes. Each probe succeeded in getting a bit closer to the perimeter.

"McKenna," Colonel Tien called out. McKenna was physically exhausted and had been dozing in the corner of the CP. Snapping his head up, he looked around.

"Colonel," he responded, knowing who had called him but not knowing where he was.

"McKenna, front has been penetrated!" Tien said in an elevated voice.

McKenna was up on his feet immediately. "Notify everyone to get under cover. I'll call VT on our position," McKenna said, and he and Lovings began to make the appropriate calls, Lovings to the artillery FDC and McKenna to Rhotenberry. Tien was on the ARVN net, telling everyone to get under overhead cover. It wasn't long before the VT fuze artillery began to arrive and shower the area with hot shrapnel. VT, or variable time fuze artillery, explodes above the ground at a preset height. The shrapnel is devastating to anyone above ground, but not so deadly to those under cover with overhead protection. As the last round exploded, McKenna checked his watch. It was 0515 hours. *God, it's going to be a long day*, McKenna thought.

Vann arrived a couple of hours later and met with Rhotenberry in private. "Truth is I'm worried about being able to hold this place. I don't want to be wondering about advisors and staff if this place goes to hell in a handbasket. The 44th appears to be holding its own. The 45th is doing okay and the 53rd I have my doubts about. Their artillery is being twiddled down. We have, what, about half the artillery we started with?" Vann outlined.

"That's about right, sir," Rhotenberry responded.

"Here's what I want. I want an E&E plan. Have each advisor pick a location that they will E&E to outside the city. They're to tell that location only to you and me. No one else. I don't want an advisor to be captured and forced to tell the location for the extraction of others. When the word comes to get out, each advisor will go to their selected location. One hour after the order to E&E, a UH-1 will commence a clockwise rotation around the city, picking people up. What do you think?" Vann asked.

"Sounds like a good plan to me. What did you have in mind for the code word to execute?" Rhotenberry asked.

"Hell, do I have to think up everything? You pick a code word."

"Nunc Imus," Rhotenberry said.

"What the hell does that mean?" Vann asked with a curious look on his face.

"Sir, that's the motto of Team 33. It's Latin for 'We Go

Now.' If Charlie is listening, he won't figure it out," Rhotenberry said with a smile.

"Okay. One more thing. I want no more than seven people in here at night. The UH-1H can carry seven US people, and at night is the most likely time for this place to fall. The rest will fly back to Pleiku at dusk and come back at sunrise," Vann said.

"You're really serious about this place being overrun, aren't you?" Rhotenberry said, realizing that Vann was very serious.

"Yes, I am, and I'm not taking chances like at Tan Canh and Dak To II. Who are the seven? I think you should be one of them," Vann said, looking at Rhotenberry.

"Most definitely, I'll be here on the night shift. I'll keep Bricker, Burch, Fleisher, Jones, Hall and Finch with me," Rhotenberry read off.

"You know that there's a two-thousand-dollar bounty on Jones and Finch, don't you? The NVA know those two are responsible for the B-52 strikes," Vann said.

"I had heard that. Another reason to be sure they get out."

As Vann was preparing to leave, the usual pattern of artillery fire and mortars commenced. Most of the fire was directed at the airfield and military targets. A few rounds hit the city center and caused civilian casualties. Surprisingly, Vann saw that the people went about their business almost as usual. Shops were open, vendors were selling vegetables and soda. Food didn't appear to be in short supply at this point. For the most part the civilian population was not in panic mode.

"Do you think you'll get hit again tonight?" Vann asked as he approached his aircraft and rotated his hand above his head, indicating that his pilot should start the aircraft.

"Sir, I'll bet I can set my watch by it. It'll start at 2000 hours," Rhotenberry responded. He was not mistaken.

At the appointed time, the first probes began against the 44th's positions on the left flank of the line. Throughout the night, the line battalions reported probes and small-arms fire that showed that the enemy was looking for a weak point in the line. The intensity picked up at 0200 hours, with captured US 105 and 155 howitzers impacting in the vicinity of the 44th Regiment command post.

"Battalions report first human wave," Tien announced to the command post. McKenna and Lovings decided to move out to observe the action as the intense artillery had now shifted to behind the 44th's positions. From the top of the command bunker, the entire area was bathed in light from the aerial flares being dropped by the Spectre gunship that was orbiting at three thousand feet. These one-million-candlepower flares would remain lit for five minutes and cover a city block in light.

McKenna and Lovings could easily see the action before the front lines. The first wave of the NVA was approaching the wire under intense small-arms fire when the entire perimeter touched off their claymore mines. The entire first wave of NVA soldiers were decimated. Those that survived were quickly dispatched by small-arms fire. NVA tactics were Napoleonic in that there was no fire and maneuver to their assaults. It was a matter of walking shoulder to shoulder towards the enemy as was done in the American Revolution and Civil War. As McKenna watched, he asked himself how the hell they got soldiers to fight like that.

No sooner had the first wave been destroyed than the second wave approached. Some had no weapons but picked up weapons found on the ground. As McKenna and Lovings watched, there were no more claymore mines to impede this advance. Some soldiers were carrying ladders to throw over the concertina wire so they could get over and through this obstacle. The wire had been set at the distance that a soldier could throw a hand grenade. Unfortunately, both enemy and friendly soldiers could throw about the same distance, so a vigorous exchange of hand grenades was seen. The ARVNs were only a bit better throwing from their trench line while standing versus the NVA soldier standing in the open or lying down and attempting to throw.

Spectre was the deciding factor as he commenced engaging the follow-on reinforcements for the second wave. Some frontline positions were seized, but the bulk of the regiment was intact. At 0500 hours a preplanned B-52 strike went in parallel to the regiment's front and one thousand meters out, silencing any further activity on this Ho Chi Minh's birthday.

71

———

AIR ASSAULT

19 MAY 1972
23rd Recon Company
Kontum

"GENTLEMEN, this morning we have stopped the attack on the 44th, and now it is time to take advantage of this situation," Colonel Ba briefed the commander of the 23rd Recon Company, Major Kai, and Colonel Pham, the 53rd Regiment commander. "At 1100 hours, Major Kai, you will conduct an air insertion here," Ba said, pointing at a location on the map. As he continued to talk, Kai wrote down the coordinates. "We suspect that there is an artillery position at this ridgeline somewhere and probably hiding in a cave. Find it and destroy it." Ba turned to Colonel Pham. "I want you to push out and set up a blocking position with one battalion in case the enemy attempts to move from the recon company and attack over this open area." Pham was also writing. "We put in a B-52 strike last night in this area north of the airfield. Send one battalion into the area and see if they can obtain a BDA for us. While you are doing this, the 44th

Regiment will be doing the same in their sectors. It is time for us to push out and find the enemy concentrations. Any questions?" Ba asked, and there were none.

When Major Kai arrived to brief his soldiers, he was surprised at their enthusiasm to conduct the operation. He realized that being tied to the city and the constant nightly artillery fire was beginning to fray their nerves, and his too. Just the lack of sleep from the incoming artillery was enough even if one wasn't close to the impacting round. Even while sleeping, your senses were always attuned to the sound of an incoming artillery round. The soldiers' morale increased, Major Kai noticed, when Major Steinhauer approached and introduced himself.

"Major Kai, may I join you on this mission?" Josh asked. Rhotenberry had asked Josh to go as he was a bit untrusting after the previous day's false reports on the action in the cemetery. The recon soldiers knew that if things got bad, helicopters would come to get this American out and probably them too. Their morale rose higher when helicopters from the Gladiators arrived. Even the ARVN soldier had no faith in the VNAF helicopter support.

"Please. Stay me," Major Kai said. Despite Major Kai's limited English, Josh understood that Major Kai wanted Josh to stay close to him. Josh didn't want to divulge that he spoke Vietnamese and was finding this ruse to be very effective in learning what people didn't want him to know.

When the aircraft landed, they were quickly loaded and departed. Josh sat on the floor between the pilots in the lead aircraft and had an opportunity to observe the artillery prep on the landing zone. Typical of many missions he had flown on a previous tour as a pilot, the artillery prep was four minutes in duration, followed by the Cobra escort firing from H minus two to H-hour, when the aircraft touched down and the troops quickly exited. As the aircraft departed, Josh noticed everything became very quiet. No shooting and no jungle sounds from the local wildlife. Major Kai got his bearings after a moment and motioned for his head element to move out to the eastern tree line. All commands were with hand and arm signals. The further the company moved, the more impressed Josh became. They were extremely quiet, with no equipment rattling, no empty canteens to make noise, no talking or joking. Josh noticed footsteps were carefully placed and bushes were quietly pushed aside. They hadn't gone far when the point man raised his hand. Immediately everyone went to their knees and faced outward, except Major Kai, who moved up beside the soldier. Josh was right behind him.

The soldier, an older gentleman who looked like this was the only life he had ever known, slowly raised his hand and pointed. No words were exchanged. Josh followed his hand and could only see vegetation initially. However, the longer he looked, the more the shape of an opening appeared in the side of the hill before them. Outside the opening, some of the vegetation was burnt as if by a muzzle blast. Kai nodded and turned. Josh thought he was going to move back until Josh saw the three platoon leaders right behind him. He hadn't heard them move up. Kai again used hand and arm signals to give orders. The three acknowledged and moved ever so silently back to their soldiers. Kai took a seat and motioned for Josh to do the same.

Josh watched as one platoon of about fifteen soldiers moved silently up to opposite sides of the cave. The third platoon took up a position across the rear of the company, facing the way they had come, providing rear security. When Kai felt that everyone was ready, he gave another hand signal and the first of the forward platoons rolled into the cave. Almost immediately the sounds of exploding grenades and automatic weapons fire could be heard, but it was mostly the sound of M16s and not AK-47s. Kai tapped Josh on the shoulder and motioned him to follow.

Kai and Josh approached the entrance to the cave. Immediately Josh noticed wheel marks in the soil. As they moved further into the cave, which was now lit by electric lightbulbs suspended from the ceiling, the sound of a power generator could be heard. Empty ammo boxes lined the walls. Fifty feet into the cave, an 85mm D-44 Chinese howitzer was positioned. Josh hadn't seen one up close, so he took some time to examine the weapon. The ten dead enemy soldiers explained how the weapon was moved in and out of the cave. The maximum range was fifteen klicks, but as they were shooting only half that distance, they didn't need to elevate the muzzle a great deal, so the gun could be fired from inside the cave with just the muzzle exposed.

While Josh was surveying the gun, Major Kai's soldiers were gathering up maps and documents as well as preparing charges on the gun and ammunition that was still present. Everything was being done efficiently and quietly. Words were not being exchanged. Each soldier knew what he was supposed to do in the absence of orders and did it.

"Major, we go," Kai said, breaking Josh's train of thought. As the platoon cleared the mouth of the cave, it fell in step behind the other two platoons. Kai and Josh moved quickly forward to position between the first and second platoons in the movement. They didn't take the same route back to a pickup zone, and in fact they even went to a different pickup zone. Moments later, a deep rumble could be heard as flame and smoke exited the mouth of the cave when the artillery piece blew up. Josh was back at the DTOC in time for dinner—C ration turkey loaf.

Before Josh could enjoy his dinner, he reported to Rhotenberry.

"So how did they do?" Rhotenberry asked.

"Sir, if the rest of this army operated like that one company, this war would have been over years ago," Josh said.

"That good?" Rhotenberry said with some surprise. "Wish the others today would have done as well."

"Didn't the other battalions get done okay?" Josh asked.

"Not really. The one battalion from the 45th did get twenty-four bodies in a BDA of the last night strike, but the other battalions that were pushed out didn't go far. They're reluctant to patrol much further than a couple of klicks. We'll get hit again tonight, I'm sure," Rhotenberry concluded.

72

COMMIT THE DAMN TANKS

20 May 1972
53rd Regiment
Kontum

RHOTENBERRY WAS right and the previous night started like all the other nights, with the artillery commencing in earnest at 2000 hours. The 53rd Regiment, located on the right flank of the perimeter, was hit the hardest on its left flank. Three waves of attackers came at the defenders beginning at 0345 hours. Again the boundary between the 53rd and the 45th was penetrated at first light.

Throughout the day, the enemy forces slowly infiltrated into the penetration, pushing it closer to the frontline troops, who were falling back slowly. From the DTOC, the sound of small-arms fire, heavy machine guns and air strikes could be heard. In the early-afternoon hours the level of noise quieted down.

"Colonel Pham reports that the penetration has been stopped and his line has been restored," Ba said, walking up to Rhotenberry.

"Really," a surprised Rhotenberry responded. "And this is the same regimental commander that told us the cemetery was secured, which is still not secured. I don't believe him." Turning, he looked around the DTOC and addressed the first American he saw. "Captain Finch."

"Sir," Finch said, looking up from the map he was hovering over.

"Take the C&C aircraft and fly up to this area between the 45th and the 53rd. Tell me if it appears that the penetration has been stopped and cleared out," Rhotenberry directed.

"Yes, sir." And out the door Finch went after he grabbed his helmet. Thirty minutes later, he was back in the DTOC.

"Why didn't you call me?" Rhotenberry asked, surprised to see Finch back so soon.

"Well, sir, it seems that the people in that area of the penetration didn't like us being there and shot the shit out of the aircraft. It was clear to me that the enemy is still in that penetration and the 53rd front lines have been pushed back," Finch said. As he talked, he noticed that Rhotenberry's face was turning red.

"Show me where it is on the map," Rhotenberry said and walked over to a wall map, handing Finch a red grease pencil.

"Sir, it appears the penetration is right here," Finch said, marking a spot at the 910780 grid mark.

"You're sure?" Rhotenberry asked.

"Yes, sir, I am" was Finch's answer. Rhotenberry said nothing but went looking for Ba. Finding him, Rhotenberry took Ba aside for a one-on-one conversation.

"Colonel, two things. The first is we have a serious penetration between the 45th and the 53rd that has not been cleared despite what Pham says. That penetration is still there and if we don't clear it out before nightfall, they will reinforce it and we will have a major problem in the morning. We need to commit the reserve with tanks and clean it out," Rhotenberry pointed out.

"Pham say it not there," Ba objected.

"I just sent Captain Finch up to see for me and his aircraft was shot to shit. Did Pham go see if the penetration was gone? I'll bet not. We need to send the reserve with the tanks," Rhotenberry stressed. Ba just stood and looked at the map board.

"I call Pham and talk to him," Ba said after a moment and left. Rhotenberry could do nothing at this point but wait for a decision from Ba. Help arrived shortly.

General Toan was not one for leaving the II Corps headquarters and observing firsthand the action. Vann had finally pried him out of the headquarters and was flying around the region with him. He took advantage of this trip to drop into Kontum unexpectedly to see Ba and Rhotenberry.

"Mr. Vann, good afternoon," Rhotenberry said as Vann came through the door.

"Colonel, I'd like you to meet General Toan," Vann said as Toan followed him in. The entire DTOC came to attention immediately. Toan stood in the doorway for a moment and surveyed the room. *Guy must think he's MacArthur*, Rhotenberry was thinking, watching the little general in all his glory. Finally Toan put everyone at ease and they returned to their duties as he approached Ba and exchanged a few pleasantries.

"Colonel, what's the situation currently?" Vann asked.

Oh, this could not be more opportune, Rhotenberry was thinking. "Well, sir, currently we have a situation that Colonel Ba and I are discussing. We have a penetration between the 53rd and 45th Regiment right here. We've stopped its forward progress, but we haven't ejected them from there. We were discussing committing the reserve with tanks."

"General Toan, what do you think about sending in the tanks?" Vann asked, putting Toan on the spot. Toan turned to Ba and said something. Ba was now on the spot. Toan had just tossed the ball into Ba's court, covering his ass if something went wrong. If Ba didn't commit the tanks and all failed, it would be his fault. On the flip side, if he did commit the tanks and all failed, it would still be his fault. Toan was obviously a politician.

"I think we commit reserve with tanks. I give order," Ba said, glancing at Rhotenberry as he departed to issue the orders. The reserve battalion, 4th of the 44th, was committed with ten M41 tanks and stopped the penetration but could not eliminate it.

73

SHIFT UNITS

21 May 1972
44th Regiment
FSB November

No rest for the weary, McKenna thought as the nightly shelling commenced, continuing into the wee hours. His and Lovings's sleep now consisted of catnaps with a longer sleep lasting two hours sometime in the twenty-four-hour period.

"Colonel, wake up," a voice said. McKenna did not want to wake up. "Colonel, wake up" was repeated none too gently this time, and he did. Hovering over him was Lovings.

"What is it?" McKenna said, attempting to regain consciousness.

"The 3rd and 4th Battalions have been hit with mortars. We have, I believe, a sapper battalion between us and the 45th, reinforced with an infantry battalion," Lovings said. "We're getting indications that Highway 14 has been cut behind us and three kilometers north of the city as they got behind the 3rd Battalion.

I'm also hearing on the advisor net Perry is saying that there's a penetration between the 45th and the 53rd."

"Shit," McKenna said, sitting up. "They're coming hard this morning. Are we getting arty support?" he asked as he stood up and rubbed the sleep from his eyes.

"Just our direct support battery right now. They're hitting the in front of the 4th Battalion, which is on the shoulder of the penetration. I have Spooky coming on station in thirty minutes."

"Good. Position him over the 4th Battalion and hit the penetration. Where is Tien?" McKenna asked, looking around.

"He's in the CP, monitoring the fight," Lovings responded.

"Okay, let's get over there and see what we can do." McKenna and Lovings waited for a pause in the incoming mortars and sprinted to the CP. Tension hung in the air; McKenna could feel it as he approached Colonel Tien.

"Colonel Tien, how goes it?" McKenna asked, attempting to put a good face on the situation.

"The 3rd Battalion say road to Kontum is cut. We no go back to Kontum today." The 44th Regiment was supposed to move back to a reserve position with the 45th Regiment taking its place on FSB November. This move had been discussed for the past four days to give 44th Regiment a needed rest as the bulk of the action had been against them since they sat astride Highway 14. Tien was looking forward to the move for his regiment and himself. While Tien was monitoring the battle on the radio, Lovings tapped McKenna on the shoulder.

"Do you hear what I hear?" Lovings asked. Now McKenna did and looked out one of the openings in the side of the CP bunker. Less than one hundred meters away was a T-54 tank with its turret rotating. When it stopped, it was pointing right at McKenna.

"*Get down!*" McKenna screamed just before the 100mm tank round slammed into the side of the CP. The thick sandbag walls offered some protection and the round didn't penetrate but did some damage. Getting up, McKenna looked around. No one was hurt, but Tien was shook up. He was screaming on the radio too fast for McKenna to understand.

"Hao, what's he saying?" McKenna asked his interpreter.

Hao listened for a moment, then turned to McKenna. "He say we go now." Everyone in the CP began gathering their weapons and helmets. Tien was the first to head for the doorway and suddenly stopped with the door open. A young Vietnamese officer was standing in the doorway. Everyone breathed a sigh of relief when they recognized it was a South Vietnamese officer. The enemy had been beaten back away from the CP. Two tanks had been destroyed by soldiers with the M-72 LAW rockets.

Almost immediately, Ba was on the radio issuing orders to Tien. Ba wanted that road open and as quickly as possible. Tien realized that until it was, he was not getting off FSB November, so he had an immediate interest in getting the road secured. The 3rd Battalion was ordered to move south along the road and clear out the enemy. At the same time, the 1st Battalion of the regiment, which had already started the move to the new location in Kontum, was turned around and sent north up the road along with a battalion from the 45th Regiment. After an hour, the road was opened, but the penetration that had occurred between the 45th and the 53rd was still in place, as well as the penetration between the 44th and 45th.

In the DTOC, Captain Finch and Major Jones, USAF, were busy plotting and coordinating B-52 strikes and TACAIR. Jones was on the radios mounted in the back of his jeep in a running conversation with the FACs and Spectre gunships. Throughout the day, the sounds of thunder created by multiple flights of B-52 bombers unloading within half a mile of Kontum could be heard and in most cases seen. Black smoke rose from the distant hills as TACAIR jets laid down carpets of napalm on suspected positions, especially artillery and anti-aircraft positions.

The action caused a pause in the enemy's ability to advance. It therefore gave time to open the airfield back up. Through the late afternoon and into the night, C-130 aircraft resumed resupplying the defenders. Twelve C-130 aircraft came in after dark, replacing the lost POL with two ten-thousand-gallon bladders as well as ammunition, food and medical supplies. These were the first fixed-wing aircraft to come in since the loss of the previous C-130.

For the next two days, the 44th Regiment moved back into a reserve position on the northwest side of the city and the 45th took responsibility for FSBs November and Nectar.

74

REALIGN THE FORCE

22 MAY 1972
  23rd Division HQ
  Kontum

COLONEL BA and Rhotenberry had discussed realigning the force for the past four days. The 44th Regiment had been hit the hardest over that time as the NVA attempted to move down Highway 14. The decision was made to have the 44th Regiment and the 45th Regiment exchange places. In addition, one battalion of the 44th Regiment would be pulled to provide security around the DTOC and one battalion would be sent to the southern side of the city to reinforce the RF/PF forces. Ba issued to the order for the move to take place, which should be accomplished in one day, so it was thought.

"McKenna, we have order to move," Tien said as he read the order that division headquarters had sent. Instead of a full five-paragraph order, it was more of a fragmentary order, brief with just minimal instructions. Tien handed the order to Sergeant

Hao, who read it and then translated for McKenna. "We go" was all Hao said.

McKenna did see the coordinates for the new location and looked at the map. *This isn't so bad. We're moving into buildings and will be just north of the DTOC. The airfield is to our southeast and the 53rd CP is due east of us. Don't like that we're losing two battalions, but one will be located at the DTOC if we need it. Will need to keep an eye on our flanks as we're thin along the perimeter,* McKenna thought as he studied their new location on the north-northwest side of the city. "Colonel Tien, why don't I take Major Lovings with me and we'll do a quick recon of the area we're moving to? When I get back, I'll give you an idea of what we can expect," McKenna offered. Tien agreed as he began to issue orders. Tien decided he would leave the coordination for the relief in place between the units up to the advisors to work out.

Lovings and McKenna took Sergeant Hao and departed in their jeep. The drive took them down Highway 14 to the city and then a left turn and headed a klick into their new sector. As they moved into the area, McKenna noted that few of the buildings were damaged, most being single-story. Pulling up in front of one building, they were met by Major George Dodge, the acting senior advisor to the 45th Regiment.

"Morning, sir, welcome to the 45th," Dodge said in a chipper voice.

"Yes, it is, George. Happens every day about this time too," McKenna said with a smile. "How you doing?"

"Good. Let's go into the CP and I can brief you there," Major Dodge indicated, leading the way. The CP location was in an underground reinforced concrete bunker. At one time, this area was a French hospital and then an American hospital once the French had left Indochina and US conventional forces had arrived beginning in 1965. The bunker was constructed by US

Army engineers for the folks serving in the American hospital. It had running water and electric lights and power.

The ARVN soldiers working in the CP took little notice of McKenna and Lovings as Dodge walked them over to a defensive sketch of the area.

"I made a copy of our defensive line for you in case you want to use those positions. I recommend you do not as we've been here dug in for too long and I suspect that Charlie has a good idea of where our positions are located," Dodge said, handing McKenna an acetate overlay. On the overlay, friendly positions were marked in blue. Two arrows marked in red indicated where the penetrations had taken place, one on each side of the 45th Regiment's locations. Some red squares were also present, and Dodge pointed to them. "These are where we have enemy units located at this time but haven't been able to dig the little bastards out. One location was in a streambed between the 44th and the 45th Regiments."

"We'll keep an eye on this one. I bet they'll attempt to reinforce him in the coming days," McKenna observed. Lovings was with Sergeant Hao, talking to the fire support officer and exchanging fire support plans. "Did you get what you needed?" McKenna asked.

"Yes, sir. I gave him our fire support plan and I have his. It's based on their current positions, which we may change, but I do have his target reference points, which we don't need to change but may add to if it becomes necessary. Division has the target reference points, so they'll be able to provide coverage fairly rapidly if necessary as we move in."

"Good, let's get back to Tien and bring him up to speed," McKenna said, turning to Dodge. "Good luck out there."

"You too, sir," Dodge responded as McKenna and crew departed.

* * *

"Sir, our latest intel indicates that the enemy is running low on supplies, especially fuel. It was noted in the ground attack against the 44th the other day that one tank that approached and fired on the 44th CP was in fact out of gas. Examination of other tanks destroyed indicated that they were all low on fuel," Colonel Pahl said, looking at Vann and General Hill. "Our B-52 campaign has been tearing up his ability to resupply in those items that are expended easily, such as fuel, food, medical supplies and ammunition, especially artillery ammo," Pahl went on. "We've captured several POWs and some chu hois that have confirmed that there are shortages, to include replacements. Currently in the 48th Regiment, B-52 strikes have reduced the size of rifle companies to about ten men per company." Several people in the room showed surprised expressions. "One POW even gave us the location of the 48th Regiment command post, and we have an Arc Light scheduled for later today to hit that location."

"I want to know when that goes in and where. We want the air cav to be there when it goes in and give us an immediate BDA. I will also be up in my aircraft and want to do the same," Vann said.

"Yes, sir," Pahl answered, looking at Lieutenant Colonel Goff, the deputy G-3. "Lastly, sir, is the weather. We're approaching the monsoon season up here. We can expect low clouds, overcast skies and rain showers. This will impede the enemy's ability to resupply his forces and also impede our ability to use TACAIR." Vann looked around the room. "Where is Captain Schudder?"

"Here, sir," Captain Chris Schudder, US Air Force, responded and stood up.

"Captain Schudder, is this going to curtail our B-52 strikes?"

"No, sir. Our B-52 strikes are ground-controlled from Pleiku and overcast skies will have no effect on the 52s' ability to carry out the strikes. TACAIR might be affected to some extent—we do have the new laser-guided bombs that track a laser beam to the target, so that's not affected by overcast skies, but it will require a laser designator on the target," Captain Schudder explained.

"Alright, see me after this meeting and let's talk on how we get more laser designators," Vann said, turning back to face the front. "Laser warfare, what a strange and modern world we live in," he said with a chuckle.

75

ARVN OFFENSE

24 MAY 1972
   23rd Division Area of Operations
   Kontum

THE PREVIOUS DAY had been relatively quiet as both sides licked their wounds. The relief in place was moving along well and unobstructed. The enemy had thrown only a few rounds at the airfield and city, allowing C-130 aircraft to bring in supplies that were badly needed and extract refugees and wounded. Ba had decided the night before that it was now time to go on the offensive.

"Today we send one battalion of 44th Regiment four klicks north up Highway 14. He move south towards city, clearing along Highway 14. A second battalion we send one klick east of battalion on Highway 14 and he moves south too. We move a third battalion to a blocking position here," Ba said, stabbing the map. "At same time, I want 53rd Regiment to move forward to this location"—again he stabbed the map—"to clear out this sector and establish defensive line along here." He paused and turned to Rhotenberry. "What think you and get American helicopters?"

"Sir, I think it's a sound plan. I'll see if I can get American helicopters to support. Let's keep an eye on the 53rd, however, and make sure he moves," Rhotenberry said.

In the morning, all was set to happen. Rhotenberry had approached Josh in the early-morning hours and asked that he accompany the battalion moving into the blocking position since McKenna was flying in with one battalion and Lovings with the other. Josh couldn't say no.

"Sergeant Howard, let's roll," Josh said, getting into his jeep.

"Yes, sir," Howard responded and released the clutch, lurching the jeep forward.

"Alive, Sergeant," Josh said, quickly placing his hand on the windshield as he was pitched in his seat.

"Sorry, sir" was all Howard said as he took off towards the blocking position on Highway 14.

As they drove, Josh noticed that the flow of refugees had decreased and only Montagnards were on the road moving south. Everything they owned that was important to them was in baskets balanced on their heads. Everyone was walking, even the oldest of adults and the youngest of children that could walk. The side of the road was littered with broken vehicles, from buses to bicycles and everything in between. Some civilian bodies littered the roadside as well as ARVN soldiers from being caught on the road during some of the recent shelling. It was obvious that the NVA didn't care who was the target or present on the target when they began to fire. The other thing Josh noticed was military vehicles and troops moving north from the 45th. He arrived at the blocking position at 1040 hours and watched as the first airmobile lift flew past and began the insertions.

"How long before they get here?" asked Sergeant Howard.

"Depends on how much enemy contact they have. If they

don't get a lot, maybe three hours. We just wait and see." They didn't have long to wait before the first sounds of distant gunfire could be heard, but it was sporadic and not intense. In Josh's mind, that was good as a big firefight would result in the units being out of the perimeter even though they were supposed to be the reserve.

Before the operation kicked off, McKenna had spoken with Lovings and Steinhauer about the new location of the 44th. "Supposedly, Ba sees the 44th as the reserve, but in fact he's put us right on the line in the middle and weakened us by pulling two battalions out. He should have taken a battalion from the 53rd in my opinion instead of two battalions from us. If the enemy figures out that we only have two battalions on the line, he'll hit us the hardest or find a boundary between us and one of the others and make his main attack along that boundary," McKenna outlined. "On top of that, Rhotenberry has pulled the TOW team back to the DTOC—mobile reserve, he said. You don't keep artillery in reserve, and we shouldn't be putting our best tank destroyer in reserve too."

"Well, what are you going to do, sir?" Lovings asked.

"For right now, I'm going on this airmobile operation, but I'll talk to Rhotenberry when I get back."

The sound of distant thunder could be heard, but Josh knew it wasn't thunder but the sound of one-thousand-pound bombs falling from thirty thousand feet on NVA positions. In his mind's eye, Josh could see the plumes of dirt, trees and bodies being tossed in the air as the earth erupted. He knew that bodies were being ripped apart and, in many cases, disintegrated altogether by these instruments of war. Somehow, he felt no remorse for the actions taken against the North Vietnamese. He was sure that the enemy felt no remorse for the effect their artillery had on him or the people around him. The crack of an AK-47 close by snapped him out of his thoughtful trance and back to reality. Fleeing NVA soldiers were beginning to bump into the blocking battalion and firefights were breaking out. For the next four hours, small firefights continued to be heard when ARVN soldiers finally linked up.

"Major Steinhauer," McKenna called out, approaching Josh's vehicle. Josh looked up and at first didn't see McKenna as everyone initially looked the same in OD Green jungle fatigues, flak jackets and steel pots. Then Josh spotted the tallest person, and that was McKenna.

"How about a ride there, Major?" McKenna asked as Lovings joined the group.

"So now I understand why I'm here. I'm your cabbie service," Josh joked. Sergeant Howard just stared ahead, not sure if this was officer humor or about to get serious.

"Give us a ride and I'll give you a beer," Lovings offered.

"Two beers, one for me and one for Sergeant Howard. After all, he's driving," Josh negotiated. Howard liked the sound of this conversation now.

"Okay, two beers. You're a lucky man, Sergeant Howard," Lovings said.

"I was born lucky, sir" was Howard's only response. As the foursome drove back to the 44th Regiment CP, they discussed the operation.

"All went well. Choppers were right on time and put us down right where we were supposed to land. LZ was cold, which didn't hurt anyone's feelings, and we moved out in a pretty orderly fashion. Had sporadic contacts but nothing organized. Did see some dead NVA along the way, but saw a lot of blood trails where they dragged the dead and wounded away," McKenna offered.

"That's about the way it went for us as well," Lovings added as they pulled up in front of the 44th Regiment CP. Instead of walking into the CP, McKenna and Lovings started walking to an abandoned building next to it. Once inside, Josh saw that they had made a rather comfortable arrangement with separate bedrooms, their cots set up to include mosquito netting over the cots and individual ice chests with ice.

"The ice factory over by the airfield is still functioning. Help yourselves," McKenna offered, and Sergeant Howard didn't need a second invitation.

"So, Josh, what have you been up to?" Lovings asked.

"Pretty much just observing the interaction of the advisors and their counterparts and seeing how well Vietnamization is working. I went out on a patrol with the division recon company and it was excellent. I told Rhotenberry that if the rest of this army was that good, this war would have been over years ago."

"Yeah, Major Kai is pretty good and he's been in that position going on three years now. Before that, he was a platoon leader in the recon company. Did he tell you he attended the Ranger School at Fort Benning? They offered to keep him on as an instructor. He turned them down," McKenna offered.

"Colonel," a Vietnamese-accented voice called out from down the hall.

"In here," McKenna answered. Moments later one of the staff officers from the 44th Regiment stuck his head through the doorway.

"Colonel Tien, he say you move. You live in CP today. We back one hour move you. Thieu ta' Lovings too. Okay?" the young ARVN soldier said in his broken English.[1] McKenna and Lovings exchanged looks of displeasure but McKenna said okay.

"Well, Howard and I will leave you to your move, sir," Josh said as Howard gulped the last of his beer and headed for the door. "Thank you, sir. It was mighty good," he added, heading out.

Howard drove Josh back to the DTOC, where Rhotenberry was talking to Ba. Seeing Josh, he motioned him to come over. "How did it go?" he asked.

"Went well, sir. Colonel McKenna and Major Lovings said they had sporadic contacts and saw lots of blood trails and bodies. How did it go with the 53rd Regiment, may I ask?" Josh said.

"It went well. They pushed out and had about the same experience. They're in their new positions and digging in. Should be ready by dark for whatever comes their way... hopefully."

76

THE FINAL DAYS BEGIN

25 May 1972
53rd Regiment
Kontum

THE TRANQUILITY of the twenty-fourth was shattered at 2200 hours and the artillery was still pounding positions with artillery throughout the night. The shelling was especially heavy in the 53rd Regiment sector along their left flank, which was now shared with the 44th Regiment. At 0300 the shelling hadn't stopped and all attention was now focused on this area. Surely this was where the attack would be coming, thought Rhotenberry as he monitored reports. It appeared that the target of interest for the NVA artillery was the artillery initially located in the 53rd sector. At daybreak, Lieutenant Colonel Norbert Gannon, the new senior advisor for the 53rd Regiment, contacted Rhotenberry.[1]

"Sir, Gannon here. It appears he's focusing his artillery on our tubes. We've lost one tube already. I recommend that we move them as soon as possible to a new location because at this rate we won't have any before long."

"Okay, displace the artillery. I'll clear it with Colonel Hung. Let me know when it's done," Rhotenberry agreed.

Gannon hung up the phone and immediately went to Colonel Pham. "Sir, we need to move the artillery or you're not going to have any at this rate."

"Okay, you move. I wait here," Colonel Pham said, sitting in the corner of the bunker with his helmet and flak jacket on. He was the only person in the CP so dressed. Not a sterling example of what the commander should look like, Gannon thought as he put on his flak jacket and helmet and headed for the door. Moving on foot and dodging incoming artillery, Gannon reached the artillery batteries' position. The gun crews were all in their bunkers. Vietnamese artillery crews had a countrywide habit of abandoning their guns when receiving incoming artillery, only to return when the shelling was over.

Finding the battery commander, Gannon explained as best he could in his limited Vietnamese and the battery commander's pidgin English that the guns needed to move. Together they examined a map and decided on a new location. The challenge now would be to get the gun crews back on the guns and hook them up to trucks to be hauled to the new location. It went easier than Gannon had expected. The incoming rounds had stopped and it appeared were engaging a different location. The mention of displacing motivated the gun crews to leave their bunkers, quickly move the vehicles in, connect the tubes and move out to the new location. Gannon accompanied the battery commander and was feeling pretty good about the displacement. Quickly the tubes were placed into operation and ready to receive fire missions. Gannon notified Rhotenberry when everything was ready. This transmission was immediately followed by incoming rounds that destroyed two tubes almost immediately. The gun crews found new bunkers to crawl into and did not come out. By 1500 that day, every artillery tube in the 23rd Division had been destroyed. There was now no doubt in anyone's mind that the final push to take Kontum was coming.

While the artillery positions were under intense artillery fire, no one noticed a sapper battalion slip through the RF/PF lines at 0200 hours. Knowing that the RF/PF had a habit of going home in the evenings, the NVA took advantage of this situation. Some were dressed in ARVN uniforms that they had taken at Tan Canh and some were dressed as civilians.

"Colonel Bachinski here," Lieutenant Colonel Bachinski said in a tone that did not bode well. "We have forces crossing the Dak Bla River. It appears to be a regiment-size force reinforced with two sapper battalions. The Ruff-Puffs here are putting up a fight along with the 2nd Battalion of the 44th, but I don't think we can hold them."

"If you have to fall back, try to hold them at the Montagnard Hospital, the Catholic compound," Rhotenberry suggested.

"Roger" was all Bachinski said before the line went dead.

In the north, the enemy pushed four regiments against the three of the division along with a battalion of tanks. Colonel Rhotenberry sat in the DTOC and monitored the action through the advisor net, comparing it to what he was hearing on the 23rd command net. With each report, he would plot on his map where the report was coming from and who had sent it. Before long, he had a clear picture. The 64th NVA Regiment was attacking from the northwest on the west side of Highway 14 with the 52nd Regiment attacking down the east side of Highway 14. The 45th was embattled with these two regiments and was positioned on higher ground at FSB November. The 44th Regiment, with just two battalions, was facing the 1st Regiment of the 2nd Division and a tank battalion attacking from the north. Rhotenberry thought this would be the main attack against the 1st and 3rd Battalions. The 53rd Regiment reported the 66th NVA Regiment with one tank battalion was attacking their positions from the northeast.

This is all coming apart, Rhotenberry was thinking when he called Vann in Pleiku.

"Rhotenberry, what's up?" Vann asked.

"Oh, sir, I was just sitting here with nothing to do, so I thought I'd call," Rhotenberry said. "Actually, we're getting hit across the north and now in the south. It appears that we have five regiments supported by tanks and sappers. I think this is it. When you come in the morning, I recommend you bring everything you can get."[2]

As Rhotenberry consulted with Ba, he got a call from Captain Hall, who was at the airfield.

"Sir, we're pinned down!" Hall reported. In the background, Rhotenberry could hear small-arms fire. Glancing at the clock, he saw it was 0430 hours. "They hit us on the south side of the airfield. It appears to be a company or more in strength. The final positions along the south side are holding for now."

"Who is manning those bunkers?" Rhotenberry asked, confused as to what forces could be there to defend the airfield.

"Sir, we have some cooks, bakers and candlestick makers from the 53rd and 44th Regiments as well as some from the 42nd Regiment that have been here at the airfield, waiting to get out and sent to where the 22nd Division is being reconstituted. They're fighting pretty good right now," Hall announced.

"Hall, hold that airfield. We cannot lose it. Those people are trying to link up with those attacking from the north, and if they do, they divide our force. You have got to hold," Rhotenberry said.

* * *

FIVE OF THE defenders were US Air Force personnel. The combat control team consisted of two men and the aerial port team was a five-man team. Playing infantry soldier was not part of their job description.

"Kontum Approach Control, Boxcar Four-Five inbound for landing, over" was heard on the radio. Boxcar Four-Five was a C-130 coming in with supplies.

Staff Sergeant Malady grabbed the receiver. "Boxcar Four-Five, our house is closed! Don't land."

Captain Felix Courrington could hear the sounds of a fight going on over the talk on the radio. "Kontum Approach Control, be on the west end of the runway in ten. We are coming in, over," Felix announced and turned to his crew to brief them on his intentions. Felix had all lights turned off, even the lights in the cockpit. Instrument lights were kept on but with red lights turned down very low. He applied full flaps and slowed the aircraft to just above stall speed for its weight configuration. He never turned on the landing light but could clearly see the white numbers on the end of the runway as the wheels touched down. Immediately his copilot reversed the props while Felix stood on the brakes. In less than half of the runway, the C-130 was turned around and back-taxiing down the runway. While the aircraft back-taxied, Rick Ivars, the loadmaster, lowered the rear ramp and assisted the seven Air Force members aboard as Felix rotated the aircraft and applied full power for a short-field takeoff. Back at Tan Son Nhut, the aircraft was examined and found to have no battle damage despite all the ground fire. However, without these two Air Force elements, future C-130 cargo runs were suspended.

* * *

THE FIGHTING around the airfield didn't let up as the enemy was determined to capture this vital link to the outside. Captain Hall was back on the radio.

"Colonel, we have a problem. There are two .50-caliber

machine guns on top of the water tower north of the airfield. They're eating our lunch," he reported.

"Roger. I'll take care of them," Rhotenberry said, redialing the TA-312 field phone. "Gannon, Rhotenberry here. There are two .50-caliber machine guns on top of the damn water tower overlooking the north end of the runway. Can you take them out and quick?" he asked.

"Sir, I may just have the thing," Gannon replied and hung up without waiting for Rhotenberry's comments. Gannon was still with the artillery unit and could see the top of the water tower easily. Grabbing the battery commander, he walked him outside their tiny bunker.

"Dai'uy. You see the water tower?" Gannon asked while pointing at it. The captain nodded that he did.

"Shoot it. Now!" Gannon said as forcefully as possible. The look on the captain's face showed confusion, but he wasn't about to argue with the regimental advisor. Grabbing a gun crew and kicking them out of their bunker, he issued orders to them. Gannon watched as the crew enthusiastically went about their actions. Artillery gun crews seldom got to witness their rounds hitting a target, especially one only two hundred meters away. This was going to be different. When all was ready, the gunner pulled the lanyard and the gun fired. Almost instantly, the top of the water tower exploded in flying concrete. The gun crew was giving each other high fives and laughing as they scurried back to their bunker.

While the artillery battery was dealing with the water tower, McKenna was getting reports of .50-caliber anti-aircraft guns popping up one hundred meters east of his regimental perimeter.

"Covey Five-Two-Nine, Snapper One-Four, over," McKenna called.

"Snapper One-Four, go ahead."

"Covey Five-Two-Nine, I have a cluster of anti-aircraft .50-

calibers due east of my location at seven-seven-five-nine-oh-five. How copy? Over."

"Snapper One-Four, I have good copy and will take care of that problem. I have a flight of two Fox Fours in bound at this time. Are we cleared for Charlie Bravo Uniform? Over."

"Negative, Covey Five-Two-Nine. Too close to friendlies. Over."

"Roger, I have a couple of others en route that I'll use on this target in one-five minutes. Until then, Covey Five-Two-Nine out." Fifteen minutes later, Covey Five-Two-Nine was back on McKenna's radio frequency. "Snapper One-Four, Covey Five-Two-Nine, over."

"Covey, Snapper, go ahead."

"Roger, I have a package to deliver for you. Are you ready to accept? Over."

"Roger, Covey, you may deliver, over." McKenna looked skyward and could see the small O-2 airplane orbiting above him. Suddenly the little plane went into a steep dive and a single rocket streaked from under one wing. It was immediately passed by green tracers from four different locations surrounding where the rocket hit and released a plume of white smoke. Once the rocket was released, the little plane clawed its way back to altitude and commenced to orbit again. Moments later the plume of white smoke was replaced with a wall of black smoke and intense flames as two F-105 jets streaked across the position and released four canisters of napalm. The enemy guns were not heard from again.

Lieutenant Colonel Gannon returned to the 53rd Regiment CP after the artillery took out the water tower. Pham had remained in the corner, still dressed in his combat gear. *I'm surprised he isn't sucking his thumb*, Gannon was thinking when he received a call from a VNAF FAC.

"Snapper One-Three, Eagle Two-One, over."

"Go ahead, Eagle Two-One," Gannon responded.

"Snapper One-Three, I break station now. You have five Tangos coming towards you now. They are seven-nine-one-nine-four-oh, how copy?"

"Eagle Two-One, I have good copy and thank you." Dropping the hand mike and grabbing the TA-314, Gannon cranked up Rhotenberry.

"Colonel, I have five tanks approaching from the northwest. Are those antitank helicopters up here this morning?" Gannon asked.

"They're just coming on station. I'm sending them your way. Call sign is Hawk's Claw," Rhotenberry said.

Moments later: "Snapper One-Three, Hawk's Claw, over."

"Hawk's Claw, Snapper One-Three here. I have five tanks at seven-nine-one-nine-four-oh. How copy?"

"Snapper, we have good copy and will head out that way. Hawk's Claw out."

Gannon breathed a sigh of relief for the time being.

In the DTOC, reports continued to flow in of enemy gains and defeats. The Ruff-Puff had ambushed a force as it crossed the river and killed every one of the enemy. A UH-1H C&C aircraft was shot down on the southern edge of the city with multiple injuries. An OH-6 was shot down north of the 44th Regiment and everyone was sure there were no survivors as the aircraft blew up in flight. By 1300 the situation was looking grim as General Hill and Colonel Rhotenberry discussed the situation along with Colonel Ba.

"General, we have five regiments hitting us at once. They're supported by tanks and three sapper battalions, of which at least two have infiltrated the city. Most of our artillery has been destroyed. There's a firefight along the southern perimeter of the airfield, which is closed as of this morning to incoming resupply aircraft. There's pressure on all fronts and they're attempting to punch through between the 53rd and 45th regiments and drive into the 44th Regiment. If they break through on the north, they can link up with this force from the south and cut us in two," Rhotenberry briefed. Ba remained silent.

"So what do you need?" Hill asked.

"Sir, we need priority of all fires in Vietnam," Rhotenberry said.

"So you want me to declare Broken Arrow?" Hill asked.

"Yes, sir, if that's what it takes to get every flying machine in-country and if you want to keep this place," Rhotenberry replied.

"It's not a case of whether I want to keep this place. It's a case of we must keep this place," Hill said, standing. He walked over to the single-sideband radio and picked up the mike. "Get me Mr. Vann." Moments later, Vann answered the call. Hill said only two words, two times: "Broken Arrow, Broken Arrow."

"Broken Arrow" was the code word understood by every air asset in Vietnam that a unit was in danger of being overrun and to come to their aid. It took priority over every other mission in-country. Within an hour, the sky above Kontum was stacked with aircraft with ordnance to deliver. Covey had to bring in two more aircraft and as in the III Corps air, one aircraft was designated King FAC to handle all the traffic and hand off the fighters and bombers to the FAC aircraft working directly for the advisors on the ground. There was a constant sound of thunder from B-52 bombers and explosions closer to the city from fighter jets. Plumes of black smoke surrounded the city from the napalm being delivered on the attackers. Soon the attackers melted away as night began to fall.

In the early-afternoon lull, Major Lovings left the safety of the CP to conduct a crater analysis. As an artillery officer, he was familiar with the sounds made by different artillery pieces. Throughout the morning bombardment, he clearly heard the difference between the 85mm guns, the 122mm guns and the 130mm guns, the largest of the communist forces. More disturbing was the one sound that he was sure he was hearing. His analysis proved him correct.

"So what did you determine?" McKenna asked when Lovings ducked back into the CP.

"Just as I expected, sir," Lovings said, removing his helmet. "We're getting pounded by our own 155mm tubes. These were probably captured at Dak To II or Tan Canh and now they're using them on us."

In the DTOC, the supply situation was beginning to impact on the defenders.

"Sir," Lieutenant Colonel Dick, SRAG G-4, said, gaining Vann's attention. "We figure that the 23rd must be low on ammo, food and medical supplies since we can't get any fixed-wing into there. They called and have asked for us to get it to them somehow."

"What do you recommend? Don't tell me you're bringing me a problem without a recommendation," Vann said, almost joking.

"No, sir. I recommend that we have the CH-47s begin carrying sling loads of supplies to the soccer field and from there have VNAF helicopters fly supplies to the units. We also have been talking to the Air Force and can begin parachute drops with supplies. The Air Force said they can get it in pretty accurately as they had a lot of practice down in III Corps at An Loc," Colonel Dick outlined.

"Make it happen. I'll notify the aviation folks to get with you and start the CH-47s up. They can take out wounded after they drop the sling loads," Vann said. "Also, I'm ordering all nonessential US personnel out of Kontum and on those CH-47s. I want them all out by 1700." It was going to be a long night, Vann was convinced.

77

FIGHT CONTINUES

26 May 1972
Northern Perimeter
Kontum

Just after 0100 hours, the shelling intensified along the northern perimeter and especially on the 53rd Regiment.

"Rhotenberry, Gannon here. We're getting the crap pounded out of us. Can we get Spectre up to find these guns?" Gannon asked.

"Let me get him and move him over your way. He's been staying out of there due to the artillery barrage. I'll get back to you," Rhotenberry said as he reached for Captain Finch. "Get Spectre over the 53rd. I think they're going to get hit pretty soon."

"Yes, sir," Finch replied and moved off to make the calls. Fifteen minutes later, Gannon was on the phone.

"We have a major ground attack with tanks!" he reported. "I need Spectre now!"

"How big of a force do you estimate?" Rhotenberry asked,

glancing at Ba, who was on the radio with Colonel Pham. Pham was screaming so loud that Ba was holding the receiver away from his ear.

"I'd say we have a reinforced regiment with tanks. Appears to be ten tanks as best I can tell. The infantry has reached the wire. Do we have any artillery left?"

"We just had four tubes brought in earlier this evening. I'll get them into action to support you. Give me five minutes," Rhotenberry said and went looking for the division artillery officer, Colonel Hung. Five minutes later, the sounds of 155 artillery could be heard, outgoing instead of incoming.

Rhotenberry picked up the phone and made the call to Vann. "Here's the situation. The 53rd has a full-blown attack right now with ten tanks. The 44th has pressure as well with a regiment supported by twenty tanks. At first light I need those TOW helicopters. Can we get them?" Rhotenberry asked.

"I'll have them airborne and over you at first light along with the Cobras," Vann said.

Colonel Ba sat in the DTOC and monitored the battle unfolding along the northern perimeter. Recognizing that a penetration had been made between the 53rd Regiment and the 45th Regiment with the nose up against the 44th Regiment, Ba made the decision that it was time for a counterattack. He and Rhotenberry discussed the plan.

"I lead counterattack," Ba said, much to Rhotenberry's surprise.

"Sir?" was all Rhotenberry could come up with.

"I lead counterattack. I take 44th battalion here at DTOC and tanks from cav. We counterattack on flank of penetration from behind 53rd Regiment. I issue order," Ba said, picking up his helmet and flak jacket. "Please, you stay. I call you for help maybe," he added with a smile.

"Okay, sir, Just keep me informed," Rhotenberry said, but

he was thinking, *He's going to get himself killed or wounded so he won't be responsible when this all falls apart.*

Ba left the DTOC and joined the battalion from the 44th Regiment. He initially gave them a pep talk and then moved out alongside the battalion commander. Troops were amazed that the commanding officer of the 23rd Division would go into the attack with them. This was leadership that they'd never seen before. It made a difference in the fighting spirit of the soldiers. They stopped the penetration and managed to relieve some of the pressure on the 44th. Unfortunately, they couldn't eject the NVA from the ground they had gained. Ba decided that some things had to change.

78

FIGHT INTENSIFIES

27 MAY 1972
  44th Regiment
  French Hospital Complex

ALL NIGHT, McKenna had been monitoring the advisor radio net. From the sounds of things, the 45th Regiment was surrounded. Lieutenant Colonel Grant, the new senior advisor, was pleading with Rhotenberry to put a B-52 strike around their position and especially between them and the 44th Regiment. Two days prior the NVA had managed to slip a battalion between them, and that battalion was still entrenched, making a withdrawal almost impossible.

"Grant, Rhotenberry here. You'll get your strikes. Vann approved them. The first will be where you asked for it and it goes in at 0230 hours. The second will be north of you at 0245 hours. Now between you and me, how close is this going to be to friendly forces?" Rhotenberry asked. "You know the Air Force likes a one-thousand-meter safety zone."

"Sir, the Air Force isn't down here and I've cleared this with the regimental commander," Grant responded.

"I understand all that. How close?" Rhotenberry asked again.

"Six to seven hundred meters," Grant said.

"Oh shit! You best hope no friendlies get hit or it's going to be your ass. Understood?"

"Sir, if it doesn't go in, it won't matter as my ass will be dead," Grant responded. At 0230 hours, the first bomb exploded and the sound of thunder just outside the city continued for the next fifteen minutes as six B-52 bombers dropped their loads.

"Grant, how was that?" Rhotenberry called him as the second strike began falling.

"Sir, I think that may have done the trick," he replied.

"Well, I got a little something extra for you. Spectre is coming on station and I'm putting him over you. He should contact you shortly."

In the predawn hours, one regiment from the 320th Division and the 66th Regiment supported by tanks moved southeast parallel to Highway 14 on the east side. Another regiment that was forward of the 53rd Regiment pushed southwest following the previous day's penetration between the 45th and 53rd Regiments. The objective for the two attacks was the 44th Regiment CP.

McKenna and Lovings were in the command bunker when reports suddenly came in that the enemy was in the wire and had tanks. The sounds of AK-47 rifles could be heard, which they considered not good as the CP was behind the frontline troops.

"Do you hear that?" Lovings asked. McKenna cocked his head and began to sort through the sounds he was hearing.

"Oh shit," McKenna said when his mind identified the sound of a tank moving and moving close by. Lovings ran to the stairs and looked outside. Not fifty yards away, a T-54 tank sat traversing its turret, looking for a target. As the turret came to fix on the entrance, Lovings dove for the floor and yelled, "Get down!"

An explosion was heard, but not at the door. Picking himself up off the floor, he climbed the stairs again. Flames were roaring out of the top hatch on the tank. An ARVN soldier raised his head from a foxhole and gave Lovings a thumbs-up with one hand, holding an expended LAW in the other. A second tank saw the first go up in flames and attempted to turn around and back out. He met the same fate as the first when two LAW rockets slammed into its side and turret. Lovings moved back into the CP to explain what he had seen.

The scene in the CP was chaos. Colonel Tien was screaming into the radio to a subordinate commander. McKenna and Sergeant Hao were standing close by, with Hao making the briefest of translations. When the 3rd Battalion commander entered the regimental CP, Lovings knew that the battalion had probably broken and run. Tien took one look and announced that they were leaving and headed for the door with his staff.

"What are we going to do, Colonel?" Lovings asked.

"Grab the radio and your weapon. We're out of here and will make our way to the DTOC. Tien is running and there's nothing more for us to do if he's not going to stay and fight," McKenna said. As McKenna headed for the door, his radio came to life.

"Snapper One-Four, Big Dog Five, over," General Hill transmitted. McKenna was confused at first as to who this was as he had never spoken with General Hill over the radio.

"Big Dog Five, Snapper One-Four, over."

"Snapper One-Four, sitrep, over."

"Big Dog Five, one subordinate has collapsed and my counterpart is bugging out, over."

"Snapper One-Four, stay put. The cavalry has arrived. Big Dog out."

McKenna and Lovings exchanged looks as Tien reached the top of the stairs. He paused and then dove back into the bunker, knocking over most of his staff. The sound of 2.75-inch rockets impacting around the bunker could be clearly heard as well as the sound of miniguns. Helicopter rotor blades were beating the air into submission as the Cobra gunships pulled out of their dives and the blades made the familiar *whap, whap* sound.

Monitoring the advisor net, McKenna could understand that the 53rd Regiment was in dire straits as well. After a couple of passes by the Cobras, Tien grabbed McKenna.

"No shoot from Cobra. Too close. Shoot my men. No shoot," Tien yelled.

"Big Dog, Snapper One-Four, over."

"Go ahead, Snapper."

"Big Dog, my counterpart says to stop shooting. You're hitting his people, over."

"Snapper, tell your counterpart if we stop, he'll be overrun in three minutes, over," Big Dog transmitted. The Cobras continued to engage in front of Tien's soldiers.

* * *

"Hawk's Claw, Big Dog Five, over."

"Big Dog Five, Hawk's Claw Two-Six, over," Chief Warrant Officer Edmond Smith transmitted. His copilot gunner for the day was Chief Warrant Officer Danny Rowe.

"Hawk's Claw Two-Six, what is your location? Over."

"Big Dog Five, we're approaching Kontum from the east, approximately five minutes out, over."

"Roger, Hawk's Claw, proceed to the north side of the city. You'll find an ample supply of targets. Priority is tanks, over."

Both pilots looked at each other, acknowledging what they heard with smiles creasing their faces.

"Roger, Big Dog Five, proceeding to the north," Smith said

and switched his frequency to talk to the two AH-1G Cobra gunships escorting him.

"Pink Panther Three-Five, Hawk Claw's Two-Six, over."

"Hawk's Claw Two-Six, I monitored. Right behind you, over."

"Roger, feel free to get some licks in if the opportunity presents itself, over."

"Well, Hawk's Claw, that is mighty kind and considerate of you to allow us to have some fun as well. We appreciate that, over," Pink Panther responded.

"Assholes," Smith said to Rowe, who was snickering at the conversation. Approaching the city, Hawk's Claw turned northward and immediately spotted the tanks.

"Tallyho," Smith transmitted as Rowe looked into the sight. The altitude and distance was almost perfect, and the open uncluttered terrain in front of the 44th Regiment offered no cover or concealment for the tanks. Moments later the first missile was launched and nine seconds after that the first tank exploded. Rowe immediately slaved the sight to the next tank and fired. In less than twenty-five seconds, two tanks were destroyed. The other tankers certainly noticed, and not only did they stop but all started to retreat. Hawk's Claw did not stop but pressed the attack, engaging tanks as they attempted to move back to the tree line. With the tanks gone, the NVA infantry was on their own and subject to the anger of the Pink Panthers. Employing both flechette rockets and 2.75-inch rockets with seventeen-pound warheads, they shredded the infantry.

"Hawk's Claw Five-Six, Two-Six, Over."

"Two-Six, Five-Six, over."

"Five-Six, I'm about expended. What's your location?" Smith asked.

"Two-Six, I'm about five minutes out, over," Chief Warrant Officer Doug Hixson transmitted. Chief Warrant Officer Lester

Whiters, the oldest warrant officer in the unit, was on the weapon system this day.

"Roger, contact Snapper One-Three. He has targets for you, over."

"Roger, QSY at this time," Hixson replied and switched frequencies.

"Snapper One-Three, Hawk's Claw Five-Six, over."

"Hawk's Claw, Snapper One-Three, I have ten targets for you on my perimeter along the ninety east–west grid line, over."

"Roger, Snapper, we have them in sight and will be taking care of that problem in a minute," Hixson stated. He then informed his Pink Panther escort that they were cleared to engage infantry in the vicinity of the tanks. As the TOW missiles were launched, Pink Panther moved in with rockets and mini-guns to strike the infantry. Hawk's Claw aircraft would make three round trips today, refueling and rearming each time at Kontum. Between their strikes, King FAC handed off aircraft to Covey FACs over the 44th and 53rd Regiments.

The tanks supporting the ground attack against the 53rd were turned back, but not the infantry. Typical of NVA tactics, human waves approached the wire as soon as the Cobra gunships departed. Mortars began to support the infantry attack. Gannon was thinking, *Our luck has got to change.* God must have heard him. A mortar round landed in the ammo dump and specifically where the CS gas was stored. Suddenly the battlefield was blanketed in CS gas. Most ARVN soldiers carried a gas mask; most NVA soldiers did not. The ARVNs quickly donned their masks and resumed firing. The NVA soldiers stopped shooting and were attempting to do anything that would stop the burning sensation in their eyes and the mucus from flowing out their noses. The NVA attack faltered, then stalled, then ceased.

By 1000 hours, events had quieted down considerably for the 44th Regiment.

"I heard that there's a shower point over at the DTOC. Want to go get a shower?" McKenna asked Lovings.

"Gee, I don't know, sir. I'm just getting used to smell of us and the grit in my hair. And if we get showers, we'll probably have to put on clean uniforms and maybe clean underwear, although I don't think I have any."

"You telling me, Major, that you have not changed your underwear weekly?" McKenna asked, a bit surprised.

"Weekly? Hell, sir, I'd be lucky if I could change my underwear monthly," Lovings responded as they started digging through their duffle bags for a clean uniform.

"I change my underwear weekly, I'll have you know, Major. The first week I wear a clean pair. On Sunday night I put that pair on backwards, the following Sunday I turn the pair inside out and the fourth week I put them on inside out and backwards," McKenna said with a straight face.

"Oh shit, sir. So what do you do for the following month?" Lovings said, beginning to laugh.

"I trade that pair with Colonel Rhotenberry and each of us has a new pair for another month," McKenna said with as much seriousness as possible.

"Sir, I think I'll just go commando," Lovings said as he closed his duffle bag. Sergeant Hao drove them back to the DTOC, and Captain Finch pointed the way to an adjacent building that had a functional shower. The water wasn't heated but it was clean. Wearing clean fatigues and clean socks, the two walked back towards the DTOC when the first mortar round hit. The blast knocked both officers down.

"Oh hell," Lovings said, standing after a moment, covered in dirt and dust. "A lot of good that shower did," he said as he suddenly realized that McKenna wasn't standing but moaning. Neither had worn their flak jackets. McKenna had a large piece of shrapnel sticking out of his rear shoulder.

"Medic!" Lovings yelled as Hao came running over. "Hao,

get to the DTOC and get a stretcher. Notify them we need a medevac aircraft." Hao took off at a dead run towards the DTOC. McKenna was placed on a stretcher and carried to an aid station, awaiting a medevac chopper. When it arrived, Lovings helped carry him to the aircraft. Leaning over McKenna as he was placed in the aircraft, Lovings asked, "Hey, sir, if there's any clean underwear in your duffle bag, can I have them?" McKenna just started laughing through the pain and nodded in the affirmative.

During the day, General Toan and Mr. Vann arrived for a briefing in the 23rd DTOC. Colonel Ba had made the decision that the perimeter had to be tightened and had consulted with Rhotenberry, who agreed.

"General Toan, I intend to shrink the perimeter. We've lost too many soldiers to hold this large of a perimeter. As spread out as we are, the enemy has many routes to infiltrate. I want to pull the 45th off FSB November and bring them to the northwest side of the city. The 44th will remain in place and be on the right flank of the 45th and the left flank of the 53rd. The 53rd, I'm going to pull back to the north side of the airfield. The Ruff-Puffs in the south will pull back to the edge of the city. I'll keep one battalion of the 44th in reserve," Ba briefed.

"No," Toan said almost immediately. "We cannot give up any ground. You must maintain your current positions and you should attack to regain lost ground." Everyone was dumbfounded by Toan's order.

"But, sir," Ba started to say when Toan cut him off.

"I don't want to hear about retreating. It will be bad for morale. We must attack."

Rhotenberry had heard enough. Toan hadn't visited Kontum in a week and now he was giving stupid orders without listening to reason. Rhotenberry pushed past Ba to the map that had a piece of acetate with unit markings on it.

"General, I don't think you understand the tactical situation here," Rhotenberry said in a condescending voice that surprised Vann. Picking up a red grease pencil, he began to draw arrows on the map each time he spoke of the enemy. "Do you realize that we have a penetration between the 45th and the 44th, our reserve here?" he said, marking a red arrow between the two units. "And another penetration here between the 45th and 53rd that is pointed right at the 44th," he said, drawing another red arrow. "And this penetration on the east side of the 53rd, heading towards the airfield. How about this one in the south crossing the river? You have too much ground to cover and not enough troops. You either shrink this perimeter or call the president and tell him you cannot hold Kontum. Take your choice," Rhotenberry said, tossing the red pencil down.

The silence in the DTOC was deafening. Toan just stared daggers at Rhotenberry, but as Rhotenberry didn't work for him, there was little he could say. Finally he turned to Ba. "Do it your way, but you are responsible."

"Spoken like a true politician," someone in the back of the DTOC said softly with an American accent. The orders were issued and the 45th and 53rd Regiments began to move to new locations. The 53rd moved into a built-up area just north of the airfield, which tied their left flank in with the right flank of the 44th. The 45th moved back into the built-up area where Highway 14 entered the city and tied their right flank into the 44th Regiment and their left flank into Highway 512 and the river. The Ruff-Puffs and the one battalion from the 44th pulled into the edge of the city and tied the flanks into the river. New fire support plans were developed and forwarded to the DTOC for close-air coordination and whatever artillery support they could get from the few artillery pieces that had been flown in from Pleiku. By midnight, everyone was in their new positions and just had to wait. It was a short wait.

BATTLE OF KONTUM
1972

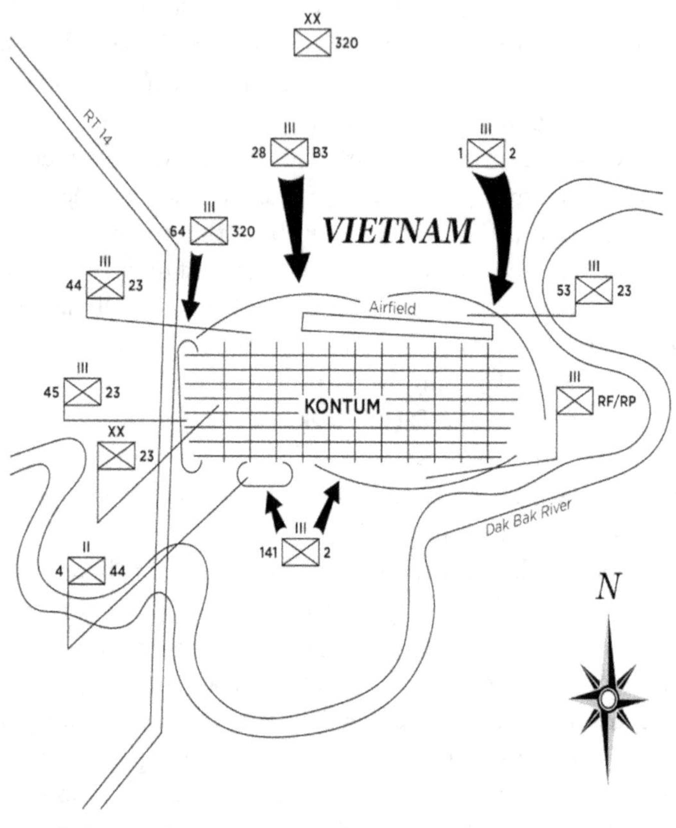

79

REINFORCEMENTS

28 May 1972
Counterattack
French Hospital

THE EVENING WEATHER TURNED NASTY, and in the early-morning hours, a light drizzle settled over the battlefield. The ARVN soldiers were thankful that they had pulled back the previous evening into the built-up area and now had positions that were dry for the most part, with overhead cover and concrete block walls for protection. They reinforced those walls with more sandbags filled with dirt. During the late hours of the previous night, NVA forces had managed to move to within forty meters of the French hospital that had been taken over by the 44th. Too close for close-air support, even from attack helicopters. Tien had to do something.

"Major Lovings," Tien said, calling him over.

"Sir," Lovings responded in his new role as senior advisor to the 44th Regiment.

"I think we need to do something about this force so close to our position. This not good."

"Sir, with this weather we're probably not going to get much in the way of close-air support after the sun comes up. There's only a little bit of artillery to support the entire division, and the chances of more coming in by CH-47 in this weather are slim," Lovings pointed out. "Sir, we could mount a counterattack, which they wouldn't expect, I bet."

"A counterattack would be risk," Tien said, studying the map and enemy positions.

"Sir, we have these intel reports that indicate that his strength is way down. POW reports are saying that most of their companies are now just ten to twenty men because the B-52 strikes have been so effective. They're low on ammo, low on food and probably as tired as we are or maybe even more so. After yesterday's fight, they may be hoping we do nothing while they run resupply and rest. If we can mount a counterattack, we might be able to push them back at the most and at the least prevent their resupply and hurt their morale. It's worth a shot," Lovings offered. Tien stared at the map for another minute.

"I will ask Colonel Ba if we can have some tanks to support a counterattack," Tien said. "I go DTOC and ask." He picked up his helmet and departed with the regimental Operations officer in tow. An hour later he was back.

"Here plan. One battalion will stay in position but shift to fill in for the battalion that we will take. We have eight tanks supporting us and they will be here in two hours. That should be time to shift soldiers. We attack on right side with support fire from frontline and tanks. Ba say tanks cannot go forward but only support by fire. I think good plan with limited objective to just clear out in front. Okay?" Tien asked.

"Sir, that sounds fine. I would say hold the tanks off until we're ready to move forward and have the tanks move up on the left flank and engage. If the enemy hears the tanks, they may expect the main attack to come from that direction and shift to consolidate on that side, weakening the side in front of our assault," Lovings offered. "We can have the battalion mortars support the attacking force once they begin to move out."

The Operations officer was listening to the conversation and nodded his approval. Two hours later the order had been issued. The shift was completed and the assaulting battalion was in position. When the tanks moved up, they did so quickly and commenced to open fire. Five minutes after they did, Lovings and Tien could see the enemy shifting forces to confront the tanks, and Tien gave the order to attack. Lovings moved up to the assaulting battalion and crossed the wire with them. The enemy was so surprised that they quickly began to pull back as they were hit hard in the flank by the assault force. By 0800 hours, the enemy had been pushed back and several POWs were taken.

The POWs, to Lovings's surprise, were teenagers. All were scrawny and appeared to be suffering from malnutrition and malaria. One of them had a command of the English language, and Lovings quickly struck up a conversation.

"What is your name?" Lovings asked.

"I call Nguyen," the young man responded.

"Nguyen, you want something to eat?"

The young man immediately nodded. "Yes, please."

Lovings dug a box of C rations out of his cargo pocket and handed it to the young man along with a P-38 can opener, which the young man appeared to know how to use. Lovings sat back and watched him devour the ham and lima beans along with the cheese and crackers and the fruit cake that came in this box. When he was done, Lovings handed him a canteen of water, which was emptied in no time.

"Officers hold all food. We no fight, we no eat," Nguyen said without being questioned. "We have no ammo, no medical, no food."

"How many men in your unit?" Lovings asked.

"We come with one hundred fifty. Now we have only thirty. Many hurt in bombing and artillery. What happen me now?" Nguyen asked.

"We'll put you in a helicopter and fly you to Pleiku. Your days in the war are over," Lovings said. Nguyen's only response was a broad smile.

While Lovings was interrogating Nguyen, Captain Finch and Major Steinhauer decided to get some air outside the DTOC bunker. When Finch had a moment of free time, he would either grab some quick sleep or go out for some fresh air. Steinhauer just wanted to pick Finch's brain about working with the ARVN staff since he had spent most of his time observing the frontline interaction of advisors and soldiers.

"So let me ask, Captain," Josh started off as he offered Finch a cigarette, "how is it working with the ARVN staff?"

"They're okay, sir," Finch said, digging in his pocket for a lighter. "They know what they need to do, just reluctant to do it and make a mistake. They lack initiative in getting things done in the absence of orders."

Overlooking the DTOC was the last standing concrete water tower in the city. The sound of the A1-E Skyraider fighter making a low pass over the tower on a bombing run to the north captured the attention of both officers, causing them to look up. As they did so, a stream of green tracers rose from the top of the water tower, and the unmistakable sound of a 12.5mm machine gun overwhelmed all other sounds.

"Damn, they're on the water tower," Finch said as a stream of black smoke exited the engine of the wounded aircraft. Josh turned and went back into the CP post to alert them to the situation. He thought Finch was behind him. Finch had other ideas.

Looking around, Finch spotted a squad of ARVN soldiers and sprinted over to them. He quickly conversed with the squad leader and together they led the squad towards the water tower. What they didn't see was a second machine-gun position at the base of the tower, until the PKM machine gun opened fire on the squad. Finch and the squad leader dove behind a pile of rubble for protection. Catching his breath, Finch looked around to assess the situation. Only three other soldiers were with him. The others lay on the ground, wounded or killed.

The previous day, Finch had found himself in a watery, muddy ditch in a similar situation, pinned down by enemy fire. *Damn, this is becoming a habit,* he thought when an M41 tank moved around the corner of a building and began firing at the tower. It was ineffective as the water tower was made of a combination of reinforced concrete and steel. The three soldiers with him continued to pop up and fire at the machine-gun position on the ground, which was well protected with concrete rubble as well.

Damn it, I need a radio so I can call for artillery, he was thinking. *Got to get to that tank and use their radio.* With that thought in mind, he began to crawl to the tank. He felt if he stood and ran, he would get shot in the back, so while his crawl took longer than he wanted, it was all he could do. A few tubes of artillery had been flown in the day before, replacing the tubes that had been destroyed since the start of the siege. Finally, he crawled behind the tank and removed the phone on the back of it to talk to the crew. They, in turn, finally were able to connect Finch to the division fire direction center.

"Fire mission," Finch said to the fire direction chief, who he knew well and spoke enough English.

"Where?" the sergeant asked. Finch didn't have a map and it took a few minutes to get the idea across that he was talking about the top of the water tower. Finally, in frustration, Finch said, "It's the only damn water tower still standing."

"Oh. I know now," the sergeant replied. "I shoot." The first round came out of the tube, which Finch couldn't see but he heard the round pass overhead and over the water tower and it kept on going.

Son of a bitch. They have the wrong charge and are hitting our own lines north of the airfield, Finch thought immediately. "Cease fire, cease fire," he screamed on the radio. They did.

"Use charge one. Understand? Charge one, high angle," Finch told the FDC. *This would work a lot better if I had mortars*, he was thinking when he heard over the radio, "Shot out," followed by the retort of the gun. He waited. Much to his delight, the top of the water tower exploded.

"Fire for effect," Finch ordered, and three more rounds landed on the now-collapsing water tower. The three soldiers that had originally accompanied him rushed the rubble and eliminated the PKM machine-gun position.

Back in the DTOC, Rhotenberry and Ba were discussing the overall situation. The soldiers of the 23rd were tired from so many days of sleepless nights and heavy engagements. Casualties were leaving gaps in the units that needed to be filled or else the perimeter, already reduced, would not be able to hold. They needed to talk to Vann and General Toan.

"Mr. Vann, Rhotenberry here. I have Colonel Ba with me and have you on speaker."

"I have General Toan and General Hill here with me and also have you on speaker. What did you need to talk to us about?"

"Sir, we're in need of reinforcements. Our casualties are beginning to affect our frontline strength," Rhotenberry said. Toan immediately launched into a discussion with Ba in rapid Vietnamese that no one could keep up with. From the tone, it was obvious that Toan was not happy about being asked for reinforcements. Finally, Vann got him settled down and brought the conversation back to English so all could participate.

"I'm not sure where we can find reinforcements for you," General Hill said, glancing at Vann and Toan. "The 40th is down in Dalat, or what's left of it, going through retraining and refitting. The 41st is the only unit left on the coast and they're holding at Crystal. The 42nd is only a fragment of itself and we have them only as stragglers now being shipped to fill out the 40th," he explained. There was silence from the group, which was finally broken by Vann.

"We do have one battalion of the 47th here at Pleiku that's been pulling security here. What about that one battalion?" Vann asked.

"Sir, at this point anything would do," Rhotenberry stated. General Toan went into an immediate tirade in rapid Vietnamese. It became clear that he was upset about losing the security that the battalion offered around the II Corps headquarters there at Pleiku.

"General Toan," Vann said in a calm, quiet voice, "if Kontum falls, do you really think one infantry battalion here at Pleiku is going to save your ass? I don't think so. Give them the battalion and hope this will save Kontum." No one said anything, surprised that Vann would have put it so delicately.

"We should transfer the third battalion of the 47th regiment immediately to Colonel Ba and the 23rd Division," they finally heard on the speaker. Rhotenberry and Ba looked at each other with expressions of gratitude. In Vietnamese, Ba thanked General Toan for his assistance. General Hill said he would arrange to have the battalion flown in by helicopter in the next three hours. Rhotenberry and Ba felt some hope for the first time in days.

"By the way," General Hill said, "how are the airdrops going?" The night before, C-130s had begun resupplying the defenders with parachute drops as the airfield was closed.[1]

"Sir, it went well last night. I understand sixty-four bundles were dropped today and we recovered around fifty of them. Some may have gone into the river. The area to the southwest along the river makes for a good drop zone," Rhotenberry said. Things were beginning to look up in the 23rd Division's world, at least for the moment.

80

A LULL

29 MAY 1972
  320th NVA Division
  Polei Kleng

LIEUTENANT GENERAL HOANG MINH THAO, Colonel Kim Tuan and Colonel Nguyen Chon as well as Colonel Khuat Duy Tien, commander of the 64th Regiment, had come together at the command of Lieutenant General Thao. Colonel Tuan's 320th Division and Colonel Chon's 2nd Division had been carrying the bulk of the fight against Kontum along with the 64th. Thao was concerned that they had not demonstrated the same success at Kontum that they had at Dak To II and Tan Canh. Thao was feeling some heat from Hanoi as the fight in his sector was the only one left that had a chance of success, since the battle in I Corps to take the imperial capital of Hue had stalled south of Quang Tri. The attempt to seize An Loc had also stalled and was being beaten back towards the Cambodian border. Hanoi wanted an assessment as to whether Kontum could be taken now.

"Gentlemen, you have done well these past weeks, but the hope of success of this entire campaign is now resting on you," Thao said as he looked at the faces of his subordinate commanders. They were faces of tired men that showed many sleepless days and nights, but such was the nature of war for leaders. "Please, what is the strength of your units at this time? Are you not getting sufficient reinforcements in a timely manner?"

Colonel Tuan was the first to speak. "Sir, the strength of my division is now one-quarter of what it was when we started the campaign and maybe even less. The ARVN soldier has proven at Kontum to have more resilience than what we found at Dak To and Tan Canh," Tuan said.

"I disagree," Chon was quick to say. "The soldiers are the same for the most part...maybe a bit better trained and disciplined, but I attribute what we are finding to better leadership in the 23rd Division than what we saw in the 22nd Division. Dat was a terrible commander and Dzu was not much better. This Colonel Ba is a fighter. He had a good reputation when he was in the Delta years ago. He is not a political puppet like so many of their officers, and that, I think, is why he has not been promoted higher. I think we have underestimated him."

"Have we underestimated him, or does he have better advisors than what Dat had?" Thao asked.

"I think the quality of the advisors is the same, at least now. The previous advisor for the 23rd only wanted to fly the helicopter and did little to advise General Canh. We would be better served if that advisor had stayed. The advisor they have now, I understand, is on his fifth tour as an advisor and understands the ARVN and us very well. We would do well to place more bounties on the advisors and remove more of the advisors. We do have a bounty on a Captain Finch and a Major Jones as they are responsible for the close-air and B-52 bomber support."

"I have seen the effect of the bombing campaign. How bad has it hurt you?" Thao asked.

"Sir, it is destroying us. Almost everywhere we go, we are in one of their strike boxes, I am told. They have boxes planned everywhere and even overlapping. The bombers come from Guam or Thailand and before they arrive, their mission and target can be changed in three hours and in some cases even less time. When they approach, they are so high we do not see them and only know we are in danger when the first bomb explodes, and then it is too late. They come over three planes abreast and wipe out an area three thousand meters by one thousand meters, and they ignore their own safety margin of one thousand meters from their own forces. We attempt to get as close as possible, but sometimes it is not enough," Colonel Tuan explained.

"Do we know where these boxes are?" Thao asked, looking around at each commander.

"No," Colonel Tuan answered. "This Captain Finch keeps the map with the boxes covered up and does not share it with his ARVN counterparts. Requests for a bombing are channeled through only the advisors, and they control everything to do with the B-52s. Mr. Vann has the final authority for the strikes and approves each one."

"What about Mr. Vann?" Thao asked. Looks were exchanged amongst the three commanders.

"If he can be eliminated, it could only be a good thing," Colonel Chon answered, and the others nodded in agreement. Thao did not respond but only acknowledged with a nod that he understood.

"Let me ask again about your troop strength and replacements," Thao said. "Colonel Tuan, you said your strength is maybe a quarter of what you started with. Can you be more specific?" Thao asked.

"Sir, my rifle companies were at about one hundred and twenty men when the campaign started. After we took Polei Kleng, we were down to eighty men per company. Since then, with a combination of the assaults, the B-52 bombings, the close-air support, the helicopter gunships and the Spectre aircraft, my companies are at about twenty men per company. We have less than half the tanks we started with. This new helicopter with the antitank missile is very effective. If our tankers see one, they stop and get out of the tank and run. They are terrified of the thing and most of the time they cannot see it because it is too far away to be seen in a tank that is closed up," Tuan explained.

"And you, Colonel Tien. Is it the same for your regiment?" Thao asked.

"Yes, sir, it is the same. His Spectre gunship can see well at night and is devastating on any night attack. During the day, the attack helicopters are the same. However, he does not appear to have much in artillery support, which is a good thing for us," Tien said.

"No, we have deliberately targeted his airfield and his artillery positions. I was hoping that if we cut off his resupply and his artillery support, it would bring him to his knees. Unfortunately, he is getting resupplied by helicopters from Pleiku and airdrops by his C-130 aircraft," Thao explained.

"Sir, what if we opened Highway 14 so his soldiers could flee? They have run away in the past. This opening may be just what we need," Colonel Tien offered.

"I thought of that, but I am fearful that this will only open a resupply route to bring in more supplies and tanks. I would rather keep them pinned up," Thao said and paused for a moment. "What is your opinion of the replacements you are receiving?"

"Sir, have you seen the replacements we're getting, when we get replacements?" Colonel Chon asked. "Sir, they are untrained teenagers. Most are scared out of their minds, having come down from up north with little training. All have undergone bombings, air attacks and artillery shellings. Most are sick with malaria or dysentery. All are underfed. They come with little ammunition and receive almost none as our supply lines cannot keep up. Our trucks are targeted almost as much as our tanks. Unlike years ago, when we could use bicycles to move supplies, we must have trucks to resupply as bicycles cannot provide what we are using today." The others remained silent, but it was obvious to Thao that they were in agreement.

"Gentlemen, we must take Kontum and quickly," Thao said. "I understand your situation. We need a good push. One good push across the airfield will link us up with the sapper battalions on the southside of the airfield. A linkup will cut their forces in half and allow us to flood into the city and then push outward east and west. Let your men rest today and do what resupply you can. Tomorrow morning I want a full assault on the north between the 44th Regiment and the 53rd, which appears to be the weakest of their regiments. Even the Ruff-Puffs in the south are putting up a stiff defense since the sapper battalion was able to slip past them. I will call for a full artillery and mortar barrage on the 53rd in the morning commencing at 0100 hours. We are low on artillery ammunition, so most of the supporting fire will be mortars. Any questions?" Everyone shook their heads and stood. The meeting was over and they knew what had to be done.

81

BY THE HAND OF GOD

53rd Regiment
Right Flank

ON THE TWENTY-SEVENTH, the 53rd Regiment pulled back and established new defensive positions on the north and northeast side of the city. The buildings offered good cover and concealment. However, most now were rubble. Lieutenant Colonel Gannon moved through the area before the regiment arrived in the withdrawal and showed Colonel Pham where the best defensible terrain was.

"Colonel, take a look at the map. Here's the built-up area we're expected to pull back into. Notice the contour lines. This entire area is on the five hundred-sixty contour line with everything to our front on the five-hundred-forty contour line. They're going to have to attack uphill to get to us and we'll have great observation of their approach. In addition, we have this swamp area and pond to your front on the north side. Sir, I don't think we could be in a better defensive position and we're closely tied in with the 44th on our left flank," Gannon pointed out. As Pham studied the map, it was as if a lightbulb had gone off in his head.

Smiling, he turned to Gannon. "I think you are right." Pointing at the map, he said, "We put one battalion along the north as he has easiest defense terrain. One battalion on east side and one battalion in reserve in center. What do with other battalion?"

"Let me recommend two battalions on the north, one on the east and one in reserve. The north is easiest to defend, but I suspect the most likely approach to our sector. If he comes another way, we can also move one of the two to reinforce the reserve," Gannon explained.

"We do that. I give order."

And on the night of the twenty-seventh, the 53rd Regiment was situated in their new positions. The attack on the twenty-eighth was against the 44th Regiment for the most part, and only the far left battalion was in contact. Gannon and Pham breathed easy. All day on the twenty-ninth, things had been fairly quiet. Patrols were sent out, units were resupplied, soldiers got an opportunity to get some rest. Gannon remembered the last time there was a lull in the battle and how things had gone the next night. He and Pham were ready for it.

"Incoming!" Gannon yelled with the first mortar round exploded followed by a steady stream of others impacting along the line on the 53rd Regiment and the 44th Regiment. The concentration was especially intense on the right flank of the northern battalions, but all the battalions were receiving some incoming rounds. Gannon glanced at his watch as he lay on the ground. It read 0100 hours. Finally reaching the command post, Gannon got on the TA-312 landline to Rhotenberry in the DTOC.

"It looks like they're coming against my northeast flank as that's where the heaviest concentration of mortar fire is. How many damn mortars have these guys got anyway? I haven't heard one artillery round yet. Just mortars, but big mothers," Gannon said.

"Finch did a crater analysis on some that hit here. He said he thinks they're 160mm mortars."

"Shit, that is a big mother—a lot bigger than the 4.2-inch mortar we have. What's the range on that thing?" he asked.

"It has a range of five klicks and it's two inches bigger in the bore than our 4.2-inch mortar," Rhotenberry replied. "We're also getting some 120mm mortar rounds on us, which is like our 4.2-inch mortar with a seven-klick range."

"I'll keep you posted if and when the ground attack starts, and I'm sure it will," Gannon said.

"I do have a Spectre ship coming up in about an hour," Rhotenberry responded. "Talk later."

Gannon placed the TA-312 in the cradle and continued to monitor the command net as well as the advisor net to keep up with the action. He knew a ground attack was coming, but where and when was the question. The sooner he knew that, the sooner he could advise Pham on what to do. Hopefully Spectre would be on station when it started.

Small-arms fire was the first indication that the ground attack was on. Gannon listened as the reports came in and Sergeant Chou, his assigned interpreter, translated. Not full translations but snippets and the essence of the calls. "Second Battalion report ground attack here," Chou said and pointed at the map. The location was the boundary between the second battalion on the right flank of the two northern battalions and the third battalion, which had the east side of the defense. "He say strong attack," Chou added. Mortar rounds were still falling in that area, and Gannon was perplexed. Why would they not have shifted their mortar fires so their forces could advance and to isolate the penetration from reinforcements? Something didn't seem right. As Gannon worked out the situation in his mind, Pham issued an order to move the reserve battalion up behind the boundary between the third and second battalions.

No need to move the reserve yet. We haven't had a penetration or even the possibility of one there yet, he was thinking as he moved over to talk to Pham about the order. Before he could get to Pham, Chou held up the TA-312. "Colonel Rhotenberry call you," he said.

"Sir, Gannon here."

"What's your situation now? The 44th has contact and I've put Spectre over him as he only has two battalions. What's your situation?" Rhotenberry repeated.

"We have contact on the northeast corner at seven-nine-oh-nine-oh-oh. They haven't breached the wire or made a penetration. Pham just moved the reserve up behind the boundary of our battalion and the 44th Battalion. Why I'm not sure and was just going to talk to him about it," Gannon explained.

"Okay, keep me posted. We'll get the Cobras up early to be on station at first light. And Jones says we should be able to get close-air support in today as the weather's going to be okay for the FACs to work. We requested a second Spectre but don't know if we will get it," Rhotenberry outlined.

"That's good news for a change. I'll keep you posted," Gannon said and hung the phone up. Pham had left the CP, so Gannon decided to lie down and get some sleep.

"Josh," Rhotenberry called out.

"Over here, sir," Josh responded and stood up from the comfortable position he had in the corner of the DTOC. Rhotenberry waved him over.

"Josh, I'm a bit concerned about the airfield. How about you take a radio and head over there and give me an update? I suspect we may see a push from the south, and I have no advisors over there."

"Sure, sir, I'll head right over."

"And take a couple of ARVNs from the security detail with

you. Don't want you out there by yourself," Rhotenberry added as he got the attention of the sergeant in charge of security. Shortly, the three left the DTOC and made their way through the rubbled streets east towards the airfield. The sounds of small-arms fire could be heard as well as incoming mortar rounds striking the northeast perimeter. To the north, Josh could see the streams of red tracers descending from the sky. *Glad I'm not under that mess right now*, he was thinking when the sound of gunfire more to the east increased suddenly. He picked up his pace, moving to the north side of the runway and jogging east. Reaching an empty fighting position, he peered into the darkness, watching the firefight to his front.

"Snapper Six, Traveler, over," Josh transmitted, attempting to contact Rhotenberry. Before Rhotenberry responded, Josh heard Snapper One-Three on the radio.

"Snapper Six, Snapper Six, Snapper One-Three, We have a breach on the east side. They're heading to the airfield. I say again, we've been breached on the east side. They're heading for the airfield, over."

"Roger, Snapper One-Three, can you contain? Over."

"Negative, our reserve is north of them. We're moving the reserve, but they'll get to the airfield. Over," Gannon transmitted.

Oh, hell, they're headed straight for me and it's just the three of us, Josh was thinking as he peered over the top of the foxhole. In the light of the full moon, Josh could see a large group of soldiers firing green tracers and racing towards the airfield. Mortar rounds from the 160mm guns began to land ahead of the approaching enemy. *There's just no way to stop this*, he was thinking when a tremendous explosion occurred next to the onrushing enemy. The concussion pushed Josh and the ARVNs back in their foxhole. When he stood back up, most of the enemy was dead or severely wounded, but they weren't attacking. What appeared to be secondary explosions were occurring in the middle of the enemy. *What the hell?* was all Josh could think for the moment. *Did a jet drop a bomb?* he asked himself, looking skyward as mortar rounds continued to fall.

"Snapper Six, Traveler, over."

"Go ahead, Traveler."

"Six, there's been an explosion at the airfield. Enemy assault appears to have been stopped. Did we just have an air strike? Over."

"Traveler, we heard it here and no air strike was in the area. We're talking to Rogues Gallery to see if he knows anything about it. Over."

"Snapper Six, Snapper One-Three, over."

"Go ahead, One-Three."

"Six, the reserve reports a massive explosion on the north side of the airfield in the vicinity of the ammo dump that was hit a couple of days ago. They're indicating that the attack has been broken and are restoring the perimeter, over."[1]

"Roger, One-Three, I have a second Spectre coming on station and he will be contacting you. Also have Shadow coming on station in one-five and will hand him off to you as well. Over."

Josh remained on the airfield until daylight, watching the reserve from the 53rd Regiment find and kill any survivors of the blast. He attempted to stop ARVNs from shooting those trying to surrender, but his efforts were fruitless.

Although the enemy had not breached the perimeter to seize the airfield, hard close-in fighting was being conducted. The enemy that had managed to reach the cover of buildings days earlier were well entrenched, and the fighting got down to close-in and hand-to-hand in some cases. Major Lovings was concerned because across the street from the front line of the 44th, a battalion of NVA soldiers were in a row of one-story buildings opposing his elements.

"Snapper One-Four, Sage Street, over," the air boss transmitted.

"Sage Street, Snapper One-Four, over."

"One-Four, I have a flight of gunships with full loads and only one-five minutes of fuel. Can you use them? Over."

Lovings quickly sent the coordinates of where to employ the aircraft and then found a good seat to watch. Looking back to the east, he saw the four AH-1G gunships at about fifteen hundred feet in a trail formation. The first aircraft pushed his nose over and began his dive. Almost immediately, rockets began to leave the aircraft in a ripple effect. The aircraft had four rocket pods of nineteen rockets each. Each rocket was the equivalent of a 105mm artillery round. As each aircraft dropped below one thousand feet, the nose turrets began spitting minigun rounds and 40mm grenades to cover their break. All four aircraft expended all their ordnance before they departed.

"Colonel Rhotenberry, Vann here."

"Yes, sir," Rhotenberry answered, wondering why Vann was calling at noon. He would usually fly in at about this time. Instead he was on the single-sideband radio, their most reliable communications with SRAG in Pleiku.

"Colonel, be prepared to meet me at the soccer field at 1430 hours. Have Ba there as well, and security. Toan is coming and a VIP. A chopper with the press will be arriving there at 1415 hours. Understood?" Vann asked.

"Ah, yes, sir, but we still have contact in the city and around the perimeter," Rhotenberry attempted to explain.

"I understand that, but have that soccer field secured," Vann ordered and hung up.

"Great, we have a fight still ongoing and now I have to babysit as well. Wonder who the VIP is," Rhotenberry was mumbling when Ba approached him.

"I get call. Vann come with Toan and VIP. Who VIP?" Ba asked.

"I have no idea. Can we move the battalion securing the DTOC to move a force to the soccer field?"

"I do now," Ba said and walked off.

Promptly at 1415 hours, a CH-47 helicopter landed at the soccer field to unload not supplies but journalists and reporters. Lieutenant Colonel McCoy, the G-1 advisor from SRAG, and Major Smith from the SRAG Information Office were herding them like cats to one side of the field. When Rhotenberry and Ba arrived a few minutes later, they kept their distance as both had a mistrust for the press, which was typical of most military officers at the time. The sounds of approaching helicopters captured their attention. To the south, three UH-1H aircraft were seen along with four Cobra gunships flying escort. As they passed over the city in a wide orbit, the three UH-1H aircraft broke off and executed steep approaches into the soccer field, landing at precisely 1430 hours. The doors to all the aircraft were open. The first and last aircraft had what appeared to be Hoc Boa ARVN soldiers. These were the bodyguards for the president. From the center aircraft, Mr. Vann exited first, followed by General Toan. They both stood next to the aircraft, waiting for the gentleman in civilian clothes. When President Thieu stepped out, everyone came to attention. The only sound heard aside from small-arms fire on the outskirts of the city was the clicking of cameras. General Toan led President Thieu straight to Colonel Ba. In a brief ceremony, Ba was promoted to brigadier general. The party remained for an hour as President Thieu walked around and conversed with the ARVN soldiers of the 23rd Division. The level of morale noticeably increased as he did so. He displayed a keen interest in the soldiers, their welfare and their jobs even as sniper fire cracked overhead. As he moved back to his aircraft, a couple of mortar rounds landed about three hundred meters away. It was noted that he didn't flinch but calmly continued to walk towards his aircraft.

Returning to the DTOC, General Ba was congratulated by

his staff and then quickly returned to work. Rhotenberry began looking over the reports from the regiments.

"General Ba," Rhotenberry said, approaching the newest general in the South Vietnamese Army. "Have you seen these reports?"

"No. Is something wrong?" Ba asked, thinking that he was about to become the shortest-serving general in the South Vietnamese Army.

"Sir, they're all indicating that the enemy is pulling back, retreating," Rhotenberry said in amazement. "Here's one from the air cav that says they're seeing large groups of soldiers withdrawing to the west and northwest. Here's another from a FAC that indicates trucks moving men west and northwest. The reports from the regiments are indicting the enemy is withdrawing as well."

"Could this be deception?" Ba asked. That was when both noticed the level of outside noise. There was none. The incoming mortars had stopped and only an occasional shot was heard and no machine-gun fire.

"General, I think it's over," Rhotenberry said, extending his hand. Ba accepted.

82

THE FINAL FLIGHT

THE HEAVY FIGHTING for Kontum had been over for four days. There were still scattered engagements around hills above the town, but the major threat had been stopped. John Paul Vann was feeling very confident that his reputation was intact and the Central Highlands would remain in the hands of the Saigon government. The defenders of Kontum, under the command of Colonel Ba, now General Ba, had stood their ground and turned the NVA offensive.

"Joe," Vann said, addressing his chief of staff and walking into his office, accompanied by two other officers, "let me introduce you to Colonel (Promotable) Kingston, General Hill's replacement."

Colonel Pizzi had already begun to stand when Vann walked, and he maneuvered around his desk extending his hand to Kingston. "How do you do? Call me Joe," Pizzi said.

"Likewise, and it's Bob, at least until I pin on the stars," Colonel Kingston said with a noticeable smile, almost a laugh. As the group maneuvered to take seats, Master Sergeant Ed Black, Vann's Filipino American administrative assistant, walked in with a tray of ice, Cokes and ginger ale and started to close the door as he departed when Colonel Pahl walked in. It was close to quitting time, and they were sure that the mixed drinks would be starting shortly. Pizzi did the honors, fixing Vann his usual ginger ale with ice.

"You're not having a drink, Mr. Vann?" Kingston asked.

"No, I'll have a glass of wine at dinner, but I'm flying up to Kontum later after the dinner, need a clear head. I know the rule is no smoking within twenty-four hours of flying and no drinking within fifty feet of the aircraft," Vann said, making a joke of the Army policy of no smoking within fifty feet of the aircraft and no drinking twenty-four hours before a flight, which was generally disregarded.

"Do you think Saigon is going to implement any changes to win over the people after this mess?" Kingston asked.

"No," Vann said quickly. "Saigon won't change its ways but consider this victory and the victory down in An Loc as a testament to their policies. Now that things have stabilized for the most part in An Loc and we're stabilized, MACV will be able to turn ninety percent of the B-52 strikes to the I Corps area and the Battle for Quang Tri, which will ensure success up there in the coming months," he added before taking a sip of his ginger ale. "The corruption in the government and the military will continue, the land grabs with the Strategic Hamlet Resettlement will continue by the upper class, and the peasants will still be sucking the hind tits. Oh, everyone is better off than they were when I came here ten years ago. People have TV now, mopeds, cosmetics and Coca-Cola, but the corruption will continue, and the rumblings of a social revolution will continue."

"What should have been done to change the circumstances?" Kingston asked. Hill and Pizzi had heard it all before and remained quiet after glancing at each other. *Here comes the history lesson*, Joe was thinking.

"From the start, we should have taken over from the French. Put American administrators in at every level of government from the presidency to the hamlet chief. Definitely at the police levels and at every level of military command. From those positions we could have rooted out the corruption that has infected every level in this country. South Vietnam has suffered at the way we did things, suggesting rather than insisting. This has been a social revolution, which we have failed to see directly but have captured by default. The enemy saw it and attempted to exploit it. South Vietnam has suffered at our hands with indiscriminate bombing, free-fire zones and wanton destruction of hamlets by soldiers. But they have also benefited and are way ahead of where they were, with a literacy rate of eighty percent versus the fifteen percent ten years ago. Today, rice production is the highest it's ever been, and modern irrigation methods have been adopted. The forced movement into the cities has created a consumer class, purchasing TVs, radios, motorcycles, and anything else the West makes. No, the country is much better off since we arrived but has a ways to go still," Vann said, taking another drink of his soda.

"What's the next move, now that we've beaten the communists back?" Kingston asked.

"We've beaten them back but not defeated them. The old strategy of Westmoreland that we could attrite the enemy was a failure, which Tet of '68 proved. All this exercise has done is given us a better position at the Paris Peace Talks and given the South time to rebuild their military. To rebuild, they need to clean up the leadership. Weed out the corrupt officers and the weak officers, mostly in the brigade level and above. The only good regimental commander we had here was Ba. The others were worthless, as is Dzu. In addition, they need some backbone instilled in them. Their soldiers will fight if properly led, supplied and put in a position where they can't run, but with the leadership at the higher levels... who knows?" Vann said with some resignation. "Okay, enough of my preaching, let's head to the mess hall for your farewell dinner, General," Vann said after a moment, finishing his drink, and the others mimicked him and stood.

* * *

COLONEL RHOTENBERRY HAD SPENT the day with General Ba, looking over the positions still held by the ARVN forces in Kontum. Along the way Major Steinhauer had joined them, as had Colonel Kaplan, the 22nd Division advisor. When they returned to the command post, General Ba invited the others to join him at dinner. Ba couldn't help but still be in a good mood, having driven the NVA off and been promoted by President Thieu two days before when he had flown in. Despite the conditions, Ba still managed to have a tolerable dinner served.

"I sorry Mr. Vann not here tonight. What time he back here?" Ba asked.

Looking at his watch, Rhotenberry responded, "He should have been back already. Let me call the airfield and see where he is." Rhotenberry excused himself and moved over to a telephone.

"Switchboard, get me Flight Operations," he said slowly so the Vietnamese operator manning the switchboard could understand him.

Moments later, he heard, "Flight Ops here."

"Flight Ops, Colonel Rhotenberry here."

"Oh, yes, sir. What can I do for you?" the American answered.

"Hey, where's Mr. Vann? Did he file a flight plan from Pleiku to here?"

"No, sir, we have no flight plan and haven't heard from him.

Let me call GCA and see if they've been talking to him. Weather between there and here is a bit skoshi tonight. I'll call you back in a minute, sir."

"Good." Rhotenberry hung up and walked back to the dining area that everyone was sitting at. A young officer was hurriedly talking to Ba. Finally, Ba said something, and the soldier rushed off.

"Something wrong, General?" Rhotenberry asked, taking his seat again.

"Unit in vicinity of Ro Uay say they hear helicopter and then hear explosion. I tell send ground patrol to check," Ba explained. Everyone exchanges looks when an American sergeant interrupted.

"Colonel Rhotenberry, there's a call in Ops for you. It's from the Flight Operations office," he stated.

Rhotenberry got up and moved to the door, talking over his shoulder. "That's probably about Vann, and he's probably delayed looking for what the soldiers heard." Reaching the desk with the phones, he picked up the receiver. "Rhotenberry here."

"Sir, this is Flight Ops desk. I spoke with GCA. They were not in contact with Mr. Vann but were tracking his aircraft on radar, until it disappeared," the voice said.

"What do you mean it disappeared?"

"Sir, they said it was over Highway 14 and heading this way when suddenly it dropped off their scope. That's all they could tell me," the American sergeant said.

"Have we got any aircraft here right now?" Rhotenberry asked with a slightly elevated voice.

"Yes, sir. I have two Cobra gunships on strip alert," Captain Donovan said.

"Bounce them and have them to proceed to the vicinity of where GCA lost that aircraft, now!"

"Yes, sir, I'll get them in the air right away and coordinate with GCA," Captain Donovan said. "Anything else, sir?"

"Yes, you have comms with Pleiku?"

"No, sir, but the Cobras will when they launch," Captain Donovan said.

"Have them contact the cav when they're airborne. I want a search team up reconning the area in the vicinity of the last reported position of Vann's aircraft," Rhotenberry directed.

"Yes, sir. Will do."

"Good, that's it for now. Call me if you hear anything," Rhotenberry responded with some concern in his voice as he ended the call. He stood for a few minutes, thinking, then returned to the table.

* * *

"PINK PANTHER THREE, Pink Panther Two-One, over," Chief Warrant Officer McDaniel transmitted as his aircraft climbed to altitude, high enough to get a call to Flight Operations in Pleiku. His wingman, Pink Panther One-Niner, was talking to Ground Control Approach at Kontum and was the lead aircraft.

"Panther Two-One, Panther Three India, over," McDaniel heard over his radio.

"Panther Three India, we're off Kontum and have been directed to proceed to the last known location of Rogues Gallery somewhere between here and your location. Panther One-Niner is talking to GCA, who has the location. Was told to launch a SEAR mission. How copy? Over," McDaniel transmitted. He could just imagine what this transmission would start.

Pink Panther Three India was Sergeant Shellback. His application for flight school was in the process of being sent with the hope that when he left Vietnam it would be to attend the Warrant Officer Candidate Program. Dropping the radio receiver on the table, he immediately grabbed the telephone and called Lieutenant Colonel Anderson. From Anderson's initial response, Shellback knew he had woken the commander of the 7th of the 17th Cav up.

"Sir, Sergeant Shellback here."

"This better be good, Shellback. I just fell off. What's up?" Anderson asked.

"Sir, Panther Two-One is in the air off Kontum. He was directed by the headquarters there to get airborne and proceed to a possible crash site of Rogues Gallery. He was further directed to get a SEAR aircraft up and work with him," Shellback explained. He couldn't see Anderson's reaction but could hear the commotion as Anderson pulled himself into a sitting position and began reaching for his pants.

"Did they give you a location?" Anderson asked, holding the phone between his shoulder and chin and attempting to get his pants on.

"Sir, he said it was between Pleiku and Kontum, and Panther One-Niner is talking to GCA for a possible location," Shellback responded.

"Alright, I'll be over shortly. Get all the information you can and get me the Nighthawk aircraft. Have them return to base, refuel and rearm and meet me in Ops. Get my crew up and have my aircraft ready. I'll take this one. Get a fire team of Blues as well and have them move to my bird. Got that?" Anderson asked as he continued to get dressed.

"Yes, sir, I got it," Shellback said as the line went dead. He began making the other calls. Ten minutes later, Colonel Anderson came through the door, followed by Chief Warrant Officer Williams, who was Anderson's copilot on most occasions.

"Shellback, what's the status?" Anderson asked, grabbing a cup of coffee from the Flight Operations pot, which was hours old.

"Sir, Nighthawk is in POL as we speak. Blues Platoon leader has a fire team with him and they're assembled at the bird along with your crew. Panther Two-One hasn't gotten back to me with any location from what he transmitted earlier," Shellback offered.

"Okay. We're going to launch and head to Kontum. I will talk to Panther Two-One when I'm airborne. How is the weather?" Anderson questioned.

"Clear here and at Kontum with some low clouds and rain between here and there around the Pao Mountain," Shellback outlined.

"Sir, we'll probably have to fly Chu Pao Pass and I'll bet dollars to doughnuts that Vann did too," Mr. Williams said.

"Probably right, Chief. Let's get going." Turning back to Shellback, Anderson said, "Notify Battalion that we're launching and why."

"Yes, sir, and good luck, sir," Shellback said as Anderson and Williams cleared the doorway.

* * *

"PINK PANTHER TWO-ONE, Pink Panther Six, over."

"Pink Panther Six, Pink Panther Two-One, over."

"Two-One, what is your location? Over."

"Six, we're just off Ro Uay," Two-One transmitted, giving the coordinates they had received from GCA. "Be advised, we have a crash site identified. One aircraft down and burning, over."

Anderson and Williams exchanged looks. "Roger, Two-One, we're en route to your location. Be there in one-five mikes, over."

* * *

GENERAL BA HAD BEEN HANDED a note, which he read slowly. Rhotenberry and the others could see his lips moving as he read the note for a second time. Slowly he looked up. "Gentlemen, note say Mr. Vann aircraft found. It crash. He dead. I sorry."

The Americans looked at each other in shock at the news. Rhotenberry began shaking his head almost in disbelief. "I can't believe it. The man did so much for Vietnam and this war effort to go in this manner. I can't believe it."

Quietly, Josh could be heard. "May he soar with the Angels on the Wings of Eagles; May he watch over those he loved and those who loved him; May he rest in peace until we all gather for the final formation on Fiddlers Green."

EPILOGUE

On 31 May, all resistance in Kontum ended and Mr. John Paul Vann declared the Battle for Kontum over. The fight in Kontum Province was over for the most part. The 320th NVA Division or what was left of it withdrew back across the border into Laos. The 2nd NVA Division, also badly decimated, withdrew back into the mountains north of Ben Het along the Laotian-Vietnamese border. Estimates put the NVA losses at twenty to forty thousand killed along with one hundred tanks and a tremendous amount of equipment and supplies destroyed in their attempt to seize Kontum and drive to the coast. No one would deny that American airpower was pivotal in the battle, but most agree that with proper leadership, the ARVN soldier held his ground.

The fighting in II Corps did continue. The 41st Regiment of the 22nd Division held out at LZ Crystal on the coast. The 3rd NVA Division initiated a siege of LZ Crystal on 1 June. The siege was broken on 6 June. The 22nd Division, under the command of Colonel Phan Dinh Niem, moved the reconstituted 42nd and 47th Regiments from Pleiku to Qui Nhon and started back north up Highway 1 to retake LZ English with almost no fight at all. The 3rd had melted back to its earlier sanctuaries in the mountains. It would be mid-June before Highway 19 from the coast would be open and supplies could begin arriving by convoys.

In a reassessment, Lieutenant General Hoang Minh Thao blamed the failure to take Kontum on the lack of aggressive action by his subordinate commanders. The three-week pause between the capture of Dak To II–Tan Canh campaign and the initial assault on Kontum allowed the ARVNs too much time to prepare. The failure to take the fire support bases on Rocket Ridge was also blamed for the failure. He felt that no blame could be attributed to him.

Mr. John Paul Vann was buried at Arlington National Cemetery with full military honors. Many that had opposed him in life honored him in death.

As in the other actions in the Easter Offensive of 1972, it became obvious that properly led ARVN soldiers were equal to their North Vietnamese counterparts. It was also painfully obvious that the leadership of the South Vietnamese Army, especially at the brigade command level and above, was greatly lacking. The corruption, nepotism and greed displayed by the upper echelons of the officer corps were rampant. Three years later, utilizing almost the same ground tactical plan, the North Vietnamese Army would roll over the defenders as the leadership was absent, as were US airpower and advisors. The success of the Easter Offensive of 1972 only awarded the South Vietnamese Army one thing, time, which they failed to use.

* * *

THANK you for reading Battle for Kontum, 1972, the sixth book in the Undaunted Valor Series. I hope you enjoyed this as much as I enjoyed writing it and will consider recommending this book to others with a few words in the form of a review.

There are more books to come. So be sure to follow me, Matt Jackson, on Amazon for updates.

KEEP READING for a sample of what's next to come . . .

WHAT'S NEXT?

THE FORGOTTEN WAR

BOOK ONE

PUSAN PERIMETER

THE FORGOTTEN WAR
BOOK ONE
PUSAN
PERIMETER
MATT JACKSON

1

—————

TF SMITH

30 JUNE 1950
  1st Battalion, 21st Infantry Regiment
  Camp Wood
  Kyushu, Japan

THE NIGHT WAS clear and still, a bit warm for this early in the year in Japan. The hot months were August through September, and then the household fans would be working overtime. The Quonset hut quarters had no air conditioning. People went to the movie theater to sit in air-conditioned comfort. For now, open screen windows would do both in quarters and in the barracks, which were less than full. Most of the soldiers lived on the economy in town.

Soldiers with less than three years' service and a rank below sergeant made less than $147 a month.[1] That didn't go far in the States in the early 1950s, but in occupied Japan, young soldiers found they could afford to live off base. Normally they had small one-room apartments with a young lady that would take care of all their needs. All the soldier was required to do was provide a roof over their heads and food. Laundry, boot shining and housekeeping were provided, along with other services. Besides the number of soldiers living on the economy, the barracks were partially empty because the unit, like all units in 1950, was so undermanned. The battalion was supposed to have three rifle companies, and it did, on paper. In truth, it had enough soldiers to man two reinforced rifle companies. The 1st Battalion had the mission of closing with and destroying the enemy. To accomplish that, it was organized with a headquarters company, three rifle companies and a heavy weapons company. The rifle companies were supposed to have six officers and one hundred and ninety-seven soldiers. The heavy weapons company was organized with five officers and one hundred fifty-five enlisted men while headquarters company had eleven officers and one hundred sixty-six enlisted soldiers for a battalion total strength of nine hundred and forty-five men. The current battalion strength was under six hundred men.

Corporal William "Bill" Dowd had just arrived that day in Japan from his infantry training and a two-week leave at home in Queens, New York. Reporting to the battalion headquarters on a Sunday afternoon, he noticed everything was quiet with few people around. Upon entering, he was immediately confronted by a staff sergeant wearing an armband that had the letters SDNCOIC.

"Whatcha need, Corporal?" Staff Sergeant Wilson asked from behind the desk he was seated at.

"Reporting for duty, Staff Sergeant," Dowd said, handing him a brown manila envelope with his military files.

"Corporal, welcome to the 1st Battalion, 21st Infantry Regiment," Staff Sergeant Wilson said, taking the envelope and tossing it in a box marked "IN." Wilson had served in the Army for almost ten years and had seen action in World War II in the

Pacific. He was considered a "lifer" by the young men in the unit but was respected for his military experience and bearing. He wasn't married. The scars on his face indicated he may have gotten too close to an exploding grenade. "Give me a minute and when the runner gets back, he'll take you to the barracks. It's 1700, so drop your stuff, get some chow and in the morning come back and they'll have you assigned to a platoon. For tonight you're restricted to the base. Any questions?"

"Why am I restricted to the base? Did I do something wrong?" Dowd asked, almost terrified that he had screwed up.

"One, you don't know Japan. Out there on your first night with no escort, the gals will have you broke in the morning and you'll probably find yourself sleeping it off in the street. Once you get a platoon, then you can go into town like everyone else. Two, there's a rumor that we may get called out for a police action in Korea, and if you're out and about, we have no way of contacting you. Hell, we'll have enough of a problem contacting all the guys that live in town and none have a telephone. And third, you're restricted because I said you were and that's the end of discussion," Wilson said firmly. "Anxious to see the sights, are you?"

"That and I played semipro baseball and played against a team from Japan one year. Wanted to see if they have a team here that I could play on," Dowd said.

"Wait one, you played semipro baseball back in the States?" Wilson asked, sitting up and taking interest in the young soldier.

"Yeah, it was a farm team for the Yankees. I played for one year as a pitcher. Then my draft number came up and now here I am," Dowd informed the staff sergeant.

"What's your MOS?" Wilson asked.

"Infantry, Staff Sergeant."

"You're probably going to be assigned to Headquarters Company. Captain Adams is our pitcher and a hell of a pitcher too. We have a ball team and if you're good enough, you'll be assigned to that platoon. They travel around Japan playing exhibition games with the Japanese and against other divisions. How does that sound?"

"Sounds fine by me. Do we have a lot of infantry training between games?" Dowd asked.

"Boy, we're an occupation force. The war was over five years ago and nuclear bombs pretty much make war obsolete. Nothing is out there that's going to get us back into infantry mode. You play ball, enjoy Japan, and in two years, you'll be back in the States and well trained to play pro ball. Now, get out of my office. See you in the morning," Wilson said, dismissing Dowd.

* * *

LIEUTENANT COLONEL CHARLES B. "BRAD" Smith commanded the 1st Battalion, 21st Infantry Regiment, 24th Infantry Division. A 1940 graduate of West Point, Brad had spent his entire career serving in the Pacific Theater in World War II and had only been out of theater to attend service schools. Life at Camp Wood on Kyushu, Japan, was relaxing for everyone. Occupation duty was considered cushy as there was little space for infantry training. All afternoon, he and his wife had listened to the reports on the radio about an incursion across the 38th parallel in Korea. Reports on the local Armed Forces Network Japan radio were sketchy at best. At 2100 hours, the phone in his quarters rang and his wife answered.

"Brad, it's for you. It's Colonel Stephens," she said with the knowing look an experienced Army wife gives when she understands the situation without even being told. Rising up off his sofa, he reached for the phone.

"This cannot be good," he whispered to his wife as he

accepted the receiver. "Good evening, sir," he said as cheerfully as possible.

"Brad, Stephens here. Get to my headquarters ASAP. Call your company commanders and master sergeant and have them meet you at your headquarters in an hour," Colonel Stephens, the commander for the 21st Infantry Regiment, 24th Infantry Division, ordered.

"Yes, sir, I'll be there in ten minutes," Brad answered, only to hear the phone hang up. Placing the receiver in the cradle, he turned to his wife. "Best get my laundry done tonight. I'll be packing it in the morning. I have to go" was all he said before he picked up his car keys and headed out the door.

Within ten minutes, he pulled up in front of the 21st Regiment headquarters building. Immediately he noticed the parking lot was full and all the lights were on. In fact, the lights were on in all the barracks as well as his headquarters building. He could see people moving around past the windows. Walking through the front door, he collided with a young officer heading out the door.

"Oh, damn. Sorry, sir," First Lieutenant Arthur Clark apologized. Brad knew Lieutenant Clark.

"It's okay there, Lieutenant. What brings General Dean's aide to our humble domain?" Brad asked.

"Oh, sir, General Dean wanted me to get some final instructions to Colonel Stephens before he departs," Clark said.

"Colonel Stephens going someplace?" Brad asked, fishing for information.

"Sir, we're all going someplace," Clark said, pausing for a moment, realizing he may have said too much. "Sir, I have to go. Have a good evening, sir." Before Brad could ask any follow-up questions, the young lieutenant was out the door.

Turning, Brad spotted Colonel Stephens heading for the regiment conference room and pointing for Brad to get in there.

When he entered, he saw that he was the last person as the other three battalion commanders along with the company commanders for the medical company, tank company, mortar company, headquarters company and service company were already standing behind their respective chairs, and numerous staff officers were positioned along the walls.

"Sit down, gentlemen," Stephens said as he came through the door and closed it. Once everyone was seated, he began. "I've received a warning order from Division. We're to be prepared to deploy from here to Pusan with further deployment to the interior of Korea to engage and repel the invasion by the North Korean Army into South Korea and drive them back to the 38th parallel. We'll fly from here to Pusan. Our heavy equipment will follow on ships and join us there. The S-3 will provide you with deployment times and the S-4 will get with your staffs on the deployment for heavy equipment and vehicles. Right now I want you to alert your people and have them pack their gear."

"Excuse me, sir, but when are we looking at deploying?" the 2nd Battalion commander asked.

"The first planes leave in forty-eight hours, and I suspect the first battalion will close on Pusan on the evening of the second," Stephens said to some very sober faces.

"Sir, what's the order of deployment?" Brad asked.

"It'll be 1st Battalion, followed by 2nd and then 3rd. Brad, you have the least amount of time, so I would get on it right away. Gentlemen, that's all I have for you. As we get more information and deployment orders, I'll get them to you. You're dismissed, except you, Brad. I need to talk to you."

Everyone stood and filed out of the room. They all knew it was going to be a long night. Once the room cleared, Stephens motioned for Brad to sit down.

"Brad, when you arrive in Pusan, there's no telling what you're going to find. I understand the refugees are flooding the place. When you get there, I'm hoping someone's going to meet you. MacArthur has sent Brigadier General John H. Church, head of General Headquarters Advance Command and Liaison Group, located at Taejon. He'll give you your orders when he sees you. Until such time as the division gets there, he's your boss. Understood?"

"Yes, sir."

"Now, you'll draw ammo for your people here. One hundred rounds per man should be sufficient. Not sure what ammo is there waiting for you, but Church will give you what you need for the mortars and the bazookas," Stephens explained. "What do you need from me?"

"Sir, I'm short people. Charlie Company is manned at ninety percent, but Bravo Company is an entire platoon short," Brad explained.

"I'll alert Lima Company to provide you a platoon. The best platoon leader over there is Second Lieutenant Carl Bernard and he has a pretty good platoon," Stephens said, pausing momentarily. "Be sure that you pack your Class A uniforms for the parade in Seoul."

Brad wasn't sure he'd heard correctly. "Sir, parade in Seoul?" he asked with a question mark all over his face.

"Look, Brad, these North Koreans aren't much but a ragtag bunch. They run up against you, they're going to turn tail and run for the hills. They probably didn't think we would come over to save the South Koreans, but we are. I'll bet we may not even get the full regiment over there before you're kicking ass and taking names all the way back to the 38th parallel." Stephens stood, extending his hand. "Make us proud, Brad, and good hunting," he said and left the room.

Brad walked back to his headquarters building, leaving his car at the regiment headquarters as he wanted time to think about what he was going to tell the company commanders. When he entered the building, a soldier at the door sounded off with a loud "Attention!" and everyone froze in place.

Brad quickly responded with "As you were," and people got back to work. To say that chaos was afoot would have been an understatement. He stopped by his office and was met by the senior master sergeant, Gent. Master Sergeant Gent was old school. "If the Army wanted you to have a wife, they would have issued you one" was commonly heard when someone complained about not seeing their wife often enough, which didn't happen in Japan very much. He had joined the Army in the early 1930s and served through the lean years of the Depression and the 1940s. On December 7, 1941, he was serving at Schofield Barracks, Hawaii, as the Japanese attacked and had spent the rest of the war in the 25th Division, slugging it out across the Pacific. He liked duty in occupied Japan.

"So, sir, are we really heading for Korea?" Gent asked, not convinced the rumor mill was accurate.

"Afraid so, Master Sergeant. We fly out in forty-eight hours," Brad said, grabbing a notepad off his desk. "Let's get into the conference room and brief the commanders. Are the unit first sergeants in there too?"

"Yes, sir, and I'll have a meeting with them when you're done with the company commanders. It's going to be a long night," Gent said. "I have people out right now rounding up those who live off post. Be interesting to see who shows up. If they don't, then they can just move back into the barracks when we get back, if we get back."

"What makes you say that? This should be a pretty easy operation according to Colonel Stephens," Brad asked as he walked past Gent.

"Sir, I served in China in the mid-1930s. These communist guys are tough, hard-core people. They can go on almost no food in the worst of weather conditions and move as silently as a snake. They won't be easy to take," Gent said.

"Sergeant, we're going to be kicking the North Koreans out, not the Chinese. The North Koreans are a bunch of peasants that got some ancient equipment from the Russians. When they see us, they'll think twice and head back north. I don't think we have too much to worry about. Let's think positive and brief the commanders and get people moving."

"Yes, sir," Master Sergeant Gent stated half-heartedly.

* * *

1 JULY 1950

THE DEPLOYMENT HAD NOT GONE AS SMOOTHLY or as quickly as everyone had wished for. The soldiers boarded trucks at 0300 hours for the eighty-mile trip to the nearest airfield. The downpour made for a cold, wet ride to the airfield. Upon arriving, Brad was approached by Major General Dean, the division commander.

"Colonel Smith, when you get to Pusan, head for Taejon. We want to stop the North Koreans as far away from Pusan as we can. Block the main road as far north as possible. Contact General Church. If you can't locate him, go to Taejon and beyond if you can. Sorry I can't give you more information. That's all I've got. Good luck to you and God bless you and your men."

Brad was aboard the first C-54 aircraft, which took off at 0800 hours. He had been awake for the past twenty-four hours, making sure everything and everyone was ready for the deployment. Upon their arrival at the K-1 Airfield in Pusan, they couldn't land due to the bad weather and had to return to Japan. Finally, accompanied by five other C-54 cargo planes, he arrived with part of his battalion. The remainder of those flying in would arrive during the night or the next day.

"Colonel, welcome to Korea. Are we damn glad to see you," Lieutenant Clark said as Brad stepped off the plane with his first load of soldiers.

"Lieutenant, what are you doing here? Is General Dean here yet?" Brad asked.

"No, sir, he's coming in tomorrow or the next day but told me to get over here and get things moving. I'm to take you to see Brigadier General Church at his headquarters in Taejon. When the last of your people arrive, they'll board a train that will take them to Taejon to meet you. I have a party here that will take care of them," Lieutenant Clark said, motioning them to a jeep that was standing by for them.

The drive to Taejon was uneventful but tedious, dodging the oxcarts, bikes, overloaded buses and refugees, all moving south towards Pusan. The ride took longer than Brad felt it should have. As they drove through Taejon, he became more concerned with the flood of refugees he was seeing than with the North Korean forces pushing the refugees south. Arriving at the headquarters building, he was quickly ushered in to see Brigadier General John H. Church, head of General Headquarters Advance Command and Liaison Group (short title: GHQ ADCOM). General Church was an elderly gentleman and probably past his prime, Brad was thinking when introduced to him. Originally Church's headquarters were located at Suwon, much further north, but as the North Koreans had moved south, he had displaced the headquarters to Taejon.

"Lieutenant Colonel Smith, we're damn glad to see you've arrived. I got word that your airflow is going smoothly and a train is standing by to haul your people up here. Sit down," Church said, pointing at a straight-backed chair. "Want some coffee?"

"Yes, sir, that would be great," Brad replied. The lack of sleep in the past twenty-four hours was beginning to catch up with him. Without being told, General Church's aide departed to retrieve the coffee.

"Let me give you a quick rundown of what's happened. North Korean forces crossed the 38th parallel on the twenty-fifth in force. They swept through Seoul and crossed the Han River on three fronts from what I've been told thus far. Intel is pretty sketchy at this point. The Republic of Korea forces initially held out and then panic set in. The result has been that they've been folding all along the front," General Church said. Standing, he moved to a map that was hanging on the wall and picked up a wooden pointer. "The main attack by the NKPA is coming down this road from Yongson to Osan. Osan is sixty-two miles north of here. If they get through Osan, they have a clear road to here, Taejon, and on to Pusan. We cannot let that happen," Church said, pausing for a moment to see if what he had just said had registered with Brad. "I really think that once you arrive, that will raise the spirits of the ROK soldiers and they'll get this panic settled. All we need is someone who won't run at the first sight of a tank."

"I understand, sir."

"Good. What I want you to do is move your unit north to Ansong by train," General Church said, tapping the location of Ansong on the map with the pointer. "Trucks will be waiting there to take you north to Osan. You're to select defensible terrain to control the road north of Osan and prevent any force you encounter from progressing to Osan," Church said, pointing at the map as he spoke. Realizing Brad didn't have a map, Church directed his aide to get him one. When he opened it, he realized everything on it was written in Japanese. Before he could say anything, Church had read his mind.

"Colonel, we don't have any good US topographic maps. Seems no one ever thought we would be fighting in this place and so there was no need for them. We're using maps left over from the Japanese occupation," Church explained.

"This should work, sir. My units will be close together, so we can make do with these. I am concerned, however, about being able to communicate information with supporting artillery," Brad said.

"No need to worry about that. The 52nd Field Artillery Battalion has arrived with one battery of artillery, 105-millimeter howitzers. Battalion commander is Lieutenant Colonel Perry and he'll meet you in P'yongt'aek. Do you know him?" Church asked.

"I know the name as his unit is also at Camp Wood, but we haven't trained together. Not much space there for training.

Certainly no live-fire exercises above company level," Brad offered.

"Do you have any questions for me?" Church asked.

"No, sir, I understand my mission. I'll need transportation for the troops. I'll have four hundred and six total when they arrive—" Brad didn't get a chance to finish.

"Four hundred and six...that's all you have?" Church said, a bit surprised.

"Yes, sir. We're short one rifle company, as are all the units. I've put together two reinforced rifle companies. We have 75-millimeter recoilless rifles and 2.36-inch bazookas as well as our light machine guns," Brad explained.

"Well, that's going to have to do. I'll arrange for transportation to get your people up to Osan by truck. Good luck," Church said, extending his hand. Brad stood, accepted the handshake and departed, intent on conducting a recon of the terrain north of Osan before his soldiers arrived. As he departed General Church's office, he was thinking, *I've just been handed a shit sandwich.*

Brad climbed into the front seat next to his driver. Major Hopkins, the battalion operations officer, jumped into the back seat.

"Okay, Dowd, we're going to P'yongt'aek. You know where that is?" Brad asked.

"Sir, I have no earthly idea," Corporal Dowd said, looking at the colonel, who had a map spread out on his lap.

"Okay, get us out of this compound and head north on that road we were on earlier," Brad instructed, chuckling. As Dowd maneuvered the jeep back onto the road heading north, it was clear the situation with refugees was no different. They were streaming past them, all going south. Brad did begin to notice ROK troops with no weapons or equipment traveling south in no orderly fashion as well.

Rolling into P'yongt'aek, Brad spotted a US Army jeep and

directed Dowd to pull over next to it. "Are you my artillery support?" Brad asked as another lieutenant colonel stepped out of the parked jeep.

"Ah, the king of battle is here to save the day. Miller Perry, 52nd Field Artillery Battalion, at your service," the man said, extending his hand.

"Just remember, the queen of battle tells the king where to put his balls," Brad joked in reply. "Brad Smith, 1st Battalion, 29th Infantry. Glad to meet you. What have you got to support me with?"

"Well, I have six 105 howitzers with vehicles and we're ready to move out when you give the word," Perry stated. "Troop strength is one hundred and eight."

"What's your ammo situation?" Brad asked.

"I have twelve hundred rounds of HE."

"What about antitank rounds?"

"That's a problem. I only have six rounds of HEAT."

"Damn" was all Brad could say. "Well, it's going to have to do. I'm heading up to Osan to conduct a recon before the troops get there. They're on a train heading for Ansong and will take trucks from there to Osan. Why don't you accompany me and we'll look the ground over together?" Brad offered.

"Sounds good," Perry said, returning to his jeep.

Passing through the town of Osan, Brad decided that it didn't offer much in the way of good defensive positions. The surrounding hills dominated the town, and the structures were mostly wood and would be subject to easy destruction. Slowly, the convoy of four jeeps rolled north, stopping occasionally to study the terrain. Three miles north of Osan, Brad had Dowd pull over to the side of the road. Perry pulled in behind him and approached.

"I think this may be a good location," Brad said, looking to his right and left. The road cut between two hills that had a commanding view of the road for about three miles. The hills offered good vegetation for cover and concealment of his position. Brad and his operations officer, Major Hopkins, began to walk the hill on the left side of the road first with Perry.

"Sir, I think we could put a platoon up here nicely with good fields of fire, a commanding view of the road, and elevated above the road where it cuts between this hill and the hill to the right. A position here and one on that hill on the right will have mutual support for each other," Hopkins pointed out.

"I think you're right. Let's look at the hill on the right." Brad started off in that direction. Reaching the adjacent hill, the three officers stood in silence for a moment, surveying the terrain.

"You know from here and that hill on the left, my FOs will have a clear field of vision to observe any force coming down from the north either on the road or following the railroad tracks over there on the right," Perry observed.

"I like this as the companies will have mutual support. The unit on the left can place a platoon on the left hill across the road. The company on the right overlooking the railroad line can curl back for flank security on the right side," Hopkins pointed out.

After a few moments of thought, Brad made his decision. "Okay, it's settled. We'll set up a blocking position on these two hills. Hopkins, I want Bravo Company on the left and Charlie on the right. Have Bravo place a platoon on that hill to the left of the road and the remainder on this hill on the right side of the road. Position Charlie to the right of Bravo and have it curl back to protect the flank on the right side. Once the vehicles have dropped off the troops, they can park along the road behind these positions. Mortars will be behind Bravo and Charlie Companies. Our CP will be behind Bravo. The aid station should also be behind Bravo and centrally located. Tell the XO to hold the field trains back in Osan. Any questions?"

"No, sir, sounds good to me," Hopkins said.

"Now what about positioning the artillery?" Brad asked, turning to Perry.

"I saw a place that I think will work just fine about two thousand meters back on the left side of the road. I'll place five tubes there and one tube with the HEAT rounds one thousand meters behind your unit on the left side of the road. That way if a tank gets through your kill zone, my guys will engage it at one thousand meters and that should be enough," Perry said.

"Okay, then, it's settled. Let's get back to Ansong and bring the troops forward," Brad said, moving back towards the awaiting jeeps.

Brad had to wait for the train to finally arrive with his soldiers on the morning of the fourth of July. The train platform at the station was packed with cheering refugees as the train pulled into the station. The soldiers on board were overwhelmed with the display of enthusiasm for their arrival, not realizing that the refugees were cheering for the train to take them out of Ansong, not the arriving Americans. The streets were lined with buses and trucks to take the soldiers north towards Suwon. When the drivers discovered they were supposed to drive north, they refused to move. Finally, soldiers capable of driving the buses and trucks were found and the vehicles were commandeered by the soldiers. The convoy departed for the long drive to Osan and passed through P'yongt'aek just after midnight. The crowds of refugees flowing south on the roads made for slow progress going north. At 0300 hours on the morning of 5 July, they arrived at the intended location to establish the blocking position. The soldiers dismounted and moved to their respective locations. The buses and trucks were parked along the side of the road to the south of the units. Colonel Perry moved his guns into the designated area and then parked his trucks in buildings off the road. Throughout the rest of the night and into the early-morning hours, soldiers work on digging foxholes and preparing their fighting positions in a steady drizzle of rain. Colonel Perry's soldiers offloaded ammunition, test-fired their machine guns and registered the howitzers. The proficiency of the gunners was so good it only took three rounds to register the base howitzer.

After the artillery had registered, Perry came up to Brad's CP. "Hey, Brad, the guns are registered and the FSO is working up a target list for us. Commo is crap with the radios because they're soaked, so I have my guy laying wire to your CP and to each of the FO positions with the line companies by field phones. Now for some good news," Perry said.

"I thought that was good news, but I'll always take more," Brad said, eager to hear this next piece.

"I have some eager beavers want to volunteer to man four .50-caliber machine guns and four bazooka teams if you want them. I told them I would check with you first. What do you say?" Perry asked.

"Hell yeah. Send them up and I'll put them with Bravo Company to reinforce his platoons along the road and a couple of the .50-cals with Charlie Company to reinforce him," Brad said.

"Good, I'll tell them to get their asses up here and report to your CP."

The night was quiet, but the rain that had pelted the soldiers the day before was still present, though not as intense as it had been. The sky was still overcast with low cloud cover. As Brad sipped a strong cup of coffee that Dowd had made, he looked skyward and knew there would be no close-air support on this day. His attention then turned to the young soldiers he was commanding. They were a new breed of soldier. Many were draftees who really didn't grasp why they had been drafted when the World War had ended five years before. In turn, the Army had attempted to appease them, making Army life as much like home as it could. To do that, physical training standards had been lowered and off-duty time had been increased, resulting in less training time. A dissatisfied soldier's complaint to a

Congressman would become a monumental headache for a commander. The overall result was a lack of discipline and a definite lack of a warrior spirit. Brad was thankful to the handful of noncommissioned officers he had that were experienced World War II servicemen.

Finishing his coffee, Brad decided to walk the line and talk to the soldiers. He wanted a sense of their level of anxiety. He thought he would start with a few of the soldiers that he had interacted with before in one way or another. He spotted a soldier with a Browning Automatic Rifle, or BAR, and recognized the young man.

"Fosness, how you doing?" Brad asked.

"Morning, sir," Fosness responded with water dripping off his helmet. "Sir, when are the reinforcements going to arrive?" he asked.

His question caught Brad by surprise. "Who told you we had reinforcements coming?" he inquired.

"Sir, that's the scuttlebutt," Fosness replied.

"Well, let's not worry about that. They'll get here when they get here."

Brad moved to the next foxhole, where PFC Vincent Vastano was digging.

"Vastano, how you doing this morning?" Vastano was noted throughout Bravo Company and the battalion for his sense of humor. It was immediately noted by Brad that this sense of humor was probably still in Japan.

"I'm okay, sir," Vincent responded with the look of a wet cat.

As Brad continued to move along, he sensed that morale was as low as he had ever seen it in the battalion. Ninety-six hours of no sleep, cold C rations for chow, rain soaking through their summer-weight uniforms, and the fear of the unknown were beginning to take their toll. Brad was about to cross the road when he checked his watch—0700 hours. He then looked north up the road just as he would before crossing a busy boulevard. The long column of tanks driving south towards his positions appeared out of the morning mist two thousand meters north of his position.

Before he could say anything, Sergeant Loren Chambers yelled to his platoon leader, Second Lieutenant Phillip Day. "Hey, sir, look over there."

"What the hell is that?" Day responded, not sure what he was seeing.

"Sir, those are T-34 Russian tanks and they're headed straight for us."

At this point, everyone was aware of what was coming and started preparing themselves. Brad ran back to his command post and cranked on the field telephone to Perry.

"Perry, we have tanks approaching from the north. I count four at this time but few infantry," Brad reported.

"Brad, I don't have commo with my FOs. The damn things are soaked in this rain. We'll have to keep this landline open so I can talk to them for adjustments."

"Roger, I'll stay off and coordinate your fires through them," Brad said and hung up. Shortly afterwards, the first sounds of outgoing artillery could be heard. Looking through his field glasses, Brad could see that the artillery fire was on target but having little effect. Even direct hits with the HE shells weren't stopping the tanks, only causing them to button up. As the first tank came within seven hundred meters of Bravo Company's positions, one of the 75-millimeter recoilless guns opened fire. Perfect hit, but little damage to the tank as it continued to move forward and in doing so began to engage Bravo Company positions.

Perry had moved to be with the forward 105 howitzer with the HEAT rounds. As the first tank passed between the two forward positions of Bravo Company, Perry told the gun crew to engage. The shot was perfect and severely damaged the tank, which did manage to pull off the road. As a second tank appeared, the gun crew fired again and destroyed that tank, but it didn't block the road. That was when the casing on the fired round jammed in the chamber, putting the gun out of action until the crew could extract the casing. Perry watched as the third tank rolled between Bravo Company's positions and the infantry opened fire with the 2.36-inch bazookas. The round bounced off the tank, causing no damage. The third and fourth tanks continued to roll past Perry's positions and into Osan three miles behind.

Brad watched in total frustration that his antitank weapons, holdovers from World War II, had no effect on the T-34 tanks. After the last tank had passed, Brad called for casualty reports and was pleased that there were relatively few serious casualties. About thirty minutes later, four more tanks were spotted approaching from the north.

"Okay, enough of this bullshit," Second Lieutenant Carl Bernard mumbled and grabbed one of the bazookas.

"What the hell are you going to do, sir?" PFC Lopez asked.

"I'm going to kill a tank, that's what I'm going to do. Wanna help?" Bernard replied.

"Yes, sir," Lopez answered less than enthusiastically.

The two crawled out to a ditch on the west side of the road. Soon, they were joined by Second Lieutenant Jansen Cox and his gunner, who had a bag of bazooka rockets. Above Lieutenant Cox on the hill, they spotted Second Lieutenant Ollie Connor setting up on the hill, overlooking the road cut. As the first tanks rolled near, they allowed the first two tanks to go through. The third tank was hit multiple times in the rear by the three lieutenants. The tank just kept on rolling. When the fourth tank rolled through, again the lieutenants opened fire. Some of the rounds hit, resulting in no damage. Some of the rounds exploded prematurely, spraying the gunners with shrapnel, as the ammo was old. Lieutenant Bernard's face was cut and burned from a round that exploded as soon as it left the launcher.

When the first tank in this group reached Colonel Perry's 105 howitzer position, it opened fire with an HE round at two hundred meters. The tank stopped and a white flag appeared out the top hatch.

"Boys, we just captured a tank. Let's go," Perry said, jumping up and running towards the tank. The driver's hatch opened and one North Korean began climbing out as another started climbing out of the top hatch. Before those two could dismount from the tank, a third soldier rose from the top hatch and immediately opened fire with a burp gun, hitting Perry in the leg. Perry's soldiers took no prisoners in this incident. Perry received first aid for the wound, but as no bones were broken nor arteries hit, he remained in the fight.

For the next hour, things appeared to be quiet for the 1st Battalion. The only bad news was delivered by the battalion executive officer, Major Floyd Martin, who told Brad that the tanks had pretty much destroyed all the buses and trucks that were parked along the road. If they pulled out, it would be on foot. Finally, the main body of the enemy came into view.

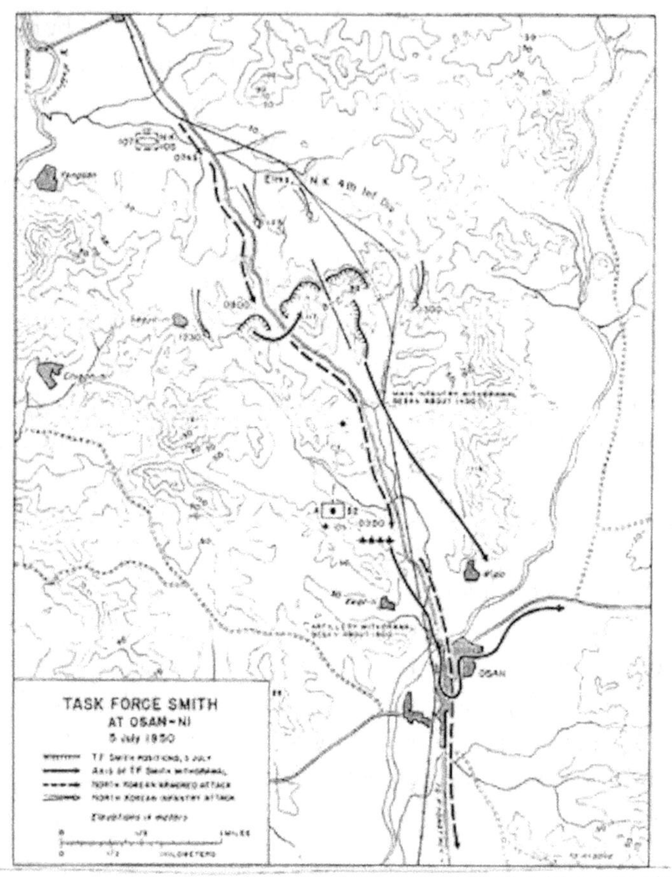

Roy E. Appleton, United States Army in the Korean War, South to the Naktong, North to the Yalu, (June–November 1950), Center of Military History United States Army, Washington DC 1992.

2

"Sir, we have company," PFC William Thornton said to his platoon leader, Second Lieutenant Cox. Grabbing his field glasses, Cox focused on where Thornton was pointing. There were thirty tanks approaching down the road, followed by infantry four abreast as far up the road as Cox could see. "Oh, shit" was all Cox said as he grabbed the field telephone and called the battalion command post. As the tanks approached, Bravo

Company used every recoilless round and bazooka rocket they had, to no avail. The tanks remained in single file and just rolled down the road towards Osan despite numerous hits on each tank. As the last tank passed the positions, the North Korean infantry began to leave the road and deploy into combat formations.

Lieutenant Colonel Perry's soldiers grabbed up two bazookas and headed for the road ditch. Perry grabbed a third launcher and rockets and headed out to join them. Moving across a rice paddy, the third tank spotted Perry and opened fire with its machine gun. Slowly the turret turned in Perry's direction. The 85mm cannon fired, knocking over a telephone pole. One of Perry's 105 howitzers zeroed in on the tank and knocked the track off. Two Koreans jumped out of the tank and went into a culvert under the road. Perry's troops killed them both. Unfortunately this tank had gotten a bit close to Perry's guns, and several gun crew members had departed in an unauthorized and hasty fashion. Officers had to start unloading ammo and feeding the guns. Embarrassed and ashamed, the soldiers returned to manning the guns.

Brad Smith sat in a position between Bravo and Charlie Companies and watched the North Koreans deploy. He quickly surmised that they were not going to attempt a frontal attack against his prepared positions but attempt to flank his positions and get behind them to cut off any possible escape. As he watched them, he began to realize that he was facing an infantry force of about four thousand soldiers against his four-hundred-man force. The odds were not in his favor at this point. Initially he saw the enemy approaching to the east of the road on two avenues, one towards Bravo Company and one towards Charlie Company. These were small forces, and small-arms fire from the defending infantry soldiers commenced as soon as the enemy was one thousand meters away. Mortar rounds, artillery and borrowed .50-cal machine guns from the artillery swept the massed formation. The effectiveness of the firing, however, demonstrated that not enough time had been spent on the rifle ranges in Japan.

Second Lieutenant John Dooley was in charge of the battalion's 4.2-inch mortars. Each round weighed about forty pounds. The gun crews were firing as fast as they could but were quickly tiring from lifting the rounds head high to drop them down the tube. As Dooley looked around, he realized that they would probably be out of ammo before the soldiers were too tired to lift another round.

PFC Thornton suddenly found himself in the role of squad leader at the advanced age of twenty. He was an excellent marksman and was carefully placing his shots at the approaching enemy infantry, but there were just too many of them and not enough ammo. Three North Koreans burst over the crest of the hill in front of him and opened fire with burp guns that surprisingly enough only hit his M-1 rifle, rendering it inoperative. Knowing he was about to die, he closed his eyes and waited. The roar of small arms was all around him, so he didn't recognize the sound of a US Thompson submachine gun firing over his head, killing the three enemy soldiers.

Captain Ross, Bravo Company commander, approached Brad in a low crouch, having run across the company frontage to Brad's position. "Sir, the commo is down. Bernard reports that they're attempting to flank his position and is requesting to pull back and join us on this side of the road. I know he wouldn't request that if he thought he could hold out. Do I have your permission to pull him in, sir?" Ross asked.

It took Brad all of thirty seconds to make a decision. "Pull him in now. Put him behind your forward platoons and we'll use him as battalion reserve," Brad directed.

Lieutenant Bernard didn't need to be told twice to move his platoon. As the order was given, the left side began pulling back to the west across the road until the entire platoon was across the road and in position as the battalion reserve. Unfortunately, a few soldiers didn't make it into the reserve position as they had decided that it was best to leave while they could and headed to Osan.

At 1300 hours, Charlie Company reported an enemy column to the west, moving to envelop them, besides the small force that had been engaging them to their front. Due to the mountainous terrain, this second column hadn't been seen until it began to cross the railroad tracks to the west. Brad and Hopkins started assessing their situation with the enemy now closing in on three sides. Something had to be done and done quickly, with more casualties falling to enemy fire, ammo running out and a lack of support.

"It's 1430 hours. Send a runner to notify Bravo and Charlie to pull back to Osan. Bounding overwatch with Charlie pulling out first, followed by the medics, battalion CP and Bravo last. Tell mortars to destroy the tubes as well as the recoilless rifles. They can't carry those weapons. We'll regroup at Osan," he said to Hopkins. "Dowd, you're with me. We're walking out of here. Hopkins, you fall back with Charlie and I'll fall back with Bravo. Let me know when you're in position to cover Charlie," Brad said with a look of disgust. He and Dowd left their position and moved behind Bravo Company.

The runners sent by Major Hopkins didn't relay the message to the company commanders as ordered but ran along the front-line positions, shouting, "Retreat, retreat to Osan." Before any of the chain of command could organize an orderly withdrawal, soldiers were out of their positions and running to the rear under heavy machine-gun fire from the flanks. Lieutenant Bernard attempted to contact his company commander on the field telephone, but there was no answer. He sent a runner to find that the company was gone.

Gathering his platoon around him, he issued his order. "We're heading south to Osan. Take only your weapons and any ammo you have. Destroy the bazookas and leave everything else. We move out in two minutes."

"Sir, what about our wounded?" one of the soldiers asked.

"We take as many as we can. Walking wounded certainly. Litter we take too. We do not leave anyone behind," Bernard said, but he knew in his heart that the litter patients would probably not make it. As they moved out, machine-gun fire at close range killed many of the litter patients and those carrying them.

PFC Thornton was wounded in the arm before the order to fall back was given. As he came out of his foxhole, he was nearly run over by two other soldiers fleeing in the same direction, causing him to fall. Lying on the ground, he saw the first of the enemy cresting the hill over the position next to his. The enemy didn't hesitate to shoot the soldier there attempting to surrender. Wounded soldiers were treated in a similar manner. The entire withdrawal disintegrated into a panicked stampede. All command and control was lost.

Brad made his way with remnants of Bravo Company down the ridge parallel to the railroad tracks. When he decided he was west of Colonel Perry's location, he turned east and went looking for Perry, whom he found.

"They've pushed us off the hills. There are just too many. I estimate a force of maybe four thousand. We can't do any more here," Brad said. The artillery soldiers had seen Brad come into their area and knew it was time to get out of there. The artillerymen removed breechblocks and sights from the tubes and set out on foot to recover their vehicles, which were on the outskirts of Osan. Perry and Brad got in Perry's jeep along with Perry's driver and Dowd and started out through Osan, only to run into three T-34 tanks parked in the middle of the street with the crews smoking and joking next to them. A fast U-turn was executed and the dirt road that led to Ansong was taken. Along the way, soldiers from the 1st Battalion were picked up by the artillerymen, thus saving about one hundred infantry soldiers.

Over the course of the next couple of days, more soldiers appeared to have reached friendly lines. All told, two hundred and fifty soldiers reached friendly lines. Lieutenant Bernard and twelve men from his platoon reached Ch'onan two days later. Of the five forward observer officers from the artillery and the machine guns, bazooka groups that had volunteered to fight beside the infantry, none survived. Colonel Perry lost an additional five officers and twenty-six enlisted men. US forces had encountered the enemy for the first time and had met defeat. It would not be the last time.

Follow Matt Jackson for updates!

ACKNOWLEDGMENTS

Writing any historical account that attempts to put accuracy into the story requires research. Unfortunately, there are only a few around who lived through these days. Those few that I was able to contact, I thank you for your time and input, Mr. Wayne Evans, Sr., Mr. Dennis Watson, and LTC (Ret.) Mark Truhan.

I would be remiss not to thank my editor, Ms. Eliza Dee of Clio Editing, for putting up with me, and Infidium.net for my maps. As always, give Momir Borocki an idea and within an hour he presents you with a great cover. My newest member of the team and one who has freed my time to pursue my research is Mrs. Margaret Daily of Rukia Publishing US, for formatting and so much more.

The one other person that deserves a major thanks is my wife of fifty-three years, who has put up with my constant time on the computer.

GLOSSARY

AC. Aircraft commander; also alternating electrical current.

ADA. Air defense artillery.

ANGLICO. Air Naval Gunfire Liaison Company. Usually deployed two to three man teams with a ground force commander to coordinate naval gunfire and close-air support.

ARA. Aerial Rocket Artillery, commonly referred to by the call sign, Blue Max.

ARVN. Army of the Republic of Vietnam. Soldiers of South Vietnam were referred to as ARVNs.

BC. Battalion commander.

BOQ. Bachelor Officers Quarters.

C rations. Canned food that could be eaten cold or hot, used by the military from World War II until the late 1970s or early 1980s.

CWO. Chief warrant officer.

C&C. Command-and-control aircraft.

DC. Direct electrical current.

det cord. White cord approximately 1/4-inch around that is highly explosive and used to quickly cut trees or blow up other objects.

FSB. Fire Support Base. Generally an circular constructed support area in the middle of the jungles approximately the size of a football field in circumference with a dirt berm five feet high. The berm would have fighting positions located at intervals. Located in the center would generally be artillery and mortars positions. In front of the berm approximately fifty feet or more from the berm would be three rows of bard wire, claymore mines, trip flares and other early warning implements.

GCA. Ground control approach, a technique used for landing aircraft, with a ground controller watching an approaching aircraft on radar and giving the pilots information as to runway alignment and altitude.

klick. Measurement of distance used by the military, consisting of 1,000 meters (one kilometer).

LZ. Landing zone, the designated location for the insertion of troops. Once an established firebase is present, it is named with the prefix LZ FSB

MP. Military police.

medevac. Medical evacuation.

NCO. Noncommissioned officer, those enlisted personnel in the military with a rank between E5 and E9; commonly referred to as sergeants in the Army, Marine Corps and Air Force and chief in the Navy and Coast Guard.

NDP. Night defensive position, usually established by company-sized or smaller units for their stationary position after dark.

NVA. North Vietnamese Army.

PX. Post exchange, the military version of Walmart.

PZ. Pickup zone, a location to pick up passengers or supplies.

RLO. Real live officer, a term applied to commissioned officers, versus warrant officers, who are appointed officers.

SF. Special Forces.

S-2. The title for the officer responsible for the overall planning, coordination, collecting and analysis of intelligence information.

S-3. The title for the officer responsible for the overall planning, coordination and execution of actions by an organization.

S-3 Air. The title for the officer responsible for coordination with aviation elements to support the actions of an organization.

thermite grenade. A grenade that is designed to destroy objects through heat rather than explode; burns at approximately 4,000 degrees.

TOC. Tactical operations center.

WO. Warrant officer, junior to CWO.

XO. Second-in-command of a unit.

REFERENCES

Andradé, Dale. *Trial by Fire: The 1972 Easter Offensive, America's Last Vietnam Battle*. New York: Hippocrene Books, 1995.

Audio Taped Interviews, *Battle of Kontum* website, https://thebattleofkontum.com/audio/index.html#11.

Bio, Brownlee, Robert W. Jr., n.d. https://www.pownetwork.org/bios/b/b175.htm.

Bio, Carter, George W., n.d. https://www.pownetwork.org/bios/c/c367.htm.

Bio, Ellen, Wade L., n.d. https://www.pownetwork.org/bios/e/e358.htm.

Bio, Hunsicker, James E., n.d. https://www.pownetwork.org/bios/h/h422.htm.

Bio, Jones, Johnny Mack, n.d. https://www.pownetwork.org/bios/j/j376.htm.

Bio, Wong, Edward Puck Kow Jr, n.d. https://www.pownetwork.org/bios/w/w110.htm.

Bio, Yonan, Kenneth J., n.d. https://www.pownetwork.org/bios/y/y007.htm.

Bio, Zollicoffer, Franklin, n.d. https://www.pownetwork.org/bios/z/z354.htm.

Burns, John C. "XM-26 TOW: Birth of the Helicopter as a Tank Buster." Master's thesis, US Marine Corps Command & Staff College, 1994. https://www.vhpa.org/stories/UH-1BTOW.pdf

Cash, John A., John Albright, and Allan W. Sandstrum.

References

Seven Firefights in Vietnam. Washington, D.C.: Office of the Chief of Military History, United States Army, 1985.

Clarridge, Christine. "Dr. Smith Provided Care, Compassion to Vietnam." *Seattle Times*, January 1, 2005. https://www.seattletimes.com/seattlenews/dr-smith-provided-care-compassion-to-vietnam/.

Collins, James Lawton. *The Development and Training of the South Vietnamese Army: 1950–1972*. Washington, D.C.: Department of the Army, 1975.

Cosmas, Graham A. *MACV: The Joint Command in the Years of Withdrawal, 1968–1973*. Washington, D.C.: Center of Military History, United States Army, 2007.

Duong, Van Nguyen. *The Tragedy of the Vietnam War: A South Vietnamese Officer's Analysis*. Jefferson, NC: McFarland, 2008.

Duffy, John J. *The Battle for "Charlie."* Self-pub., CreateSpace, 2014.

"George Wear Obituary," *Washington Post*, November 19, 2018, https://www.legacy.com/us/obituaries/washingtonpost/name/george-wear-obituary?id=1754193

"Hoàng Minh Thảo," Wikipedia, October 22, 2023, translated by Google Translate, https://vi.wikipedia.org/wiki/Hoàng_Minh_Thảo.

"John D. Lavelle." Wikipedia, September 24, 2023. https://en.wikipedia.org/wiki/John_D._Lavelle.

LeGro, William E. *Vietnam from Cease-Fire to Capitulation*. Honolulu, HI: University Press of the Pacific, 2006.

McKenna, Thomas P. *Kontum: The Battle to Save South Vietnam*. Lexington: University Press of Kentucky, 2011.

Military History Branch, Office of the Secretary, Joint Staff, MACV. *Command History, United States Military Assistance Command, Vietnam, 1972–1973*, Vol. I. Defense Technical Information Center, Washington, D.C., 1973. https://apps.dtic.mil/sti/pdfs/ADA955103.pdf.

Sheehan, Neil. *A Bright Shining Lie: John Paul Vann and America in Vietnam*. New York: Vintage Books, 1989.

Sorley, Lewis. "Courage and Blood: South Vietnam's Repulse of the 1972 Easter Invasion." *US Army War College Quarterly: Parameters* 29, no. 2 (1999). https://doi.org/10.55540/0031-1723.1933.

Webb, Willard J. and Walter S. Poole. History of the Joint Chiefs of Staff: The Joint Chiefs of Staff and the War in Vietnam, 1971–1973. Washington, D.C., Office of the Chairman of the Joint Chiefs of Staff, 2007. https://apps.dtic.mil/sti/pdfs/ADA473119.pdf.

The author enlisted in the US Army in 1968 and served on active duty until 1993, when he retired as a colonel. In the course of his career, he commanded two infantry companies, one being an airborne company in Alaska, and commanded an air assault infantry battalion during Operation Desert Shield/Storm. When not with troop assignments, he was generally found teaching tactics at the United States Army Infantry Center or the United States Army Command and General Staff College, with a follow-on assignment as an exchange tactics instructor at the German Army Tactics Center. His last assignment was Director, Readiness and Mobilization, J-5, Forces Command, and Special Advisor, Vice President of the United States. His badges include the Combat Infantrymans Badge, Expert Infantrymans Badge, Master Aviator Wings, Senior Parachutist Wings and Air Assault Badge. His awards include the Silver Star, Legion of Merit, Distinguished Flying Cross, Bronze Star with oak Leafs and Air Medal with "V". Upon retiring from the US Army, he went into private business. He and his wife have been married for the past fifty-two years and have two sons, both Army officers.

Author Matt Jackson

amazon.com/stores/Matt-Jackson/author/B09HP4L2WY

bookbub.com/authors/matt-jackson-e002f7c1-7f90-4681-9d93-1dd281a27c68

youtube.com/@mattjackson654

ALSO BY MATT JACKSON

OTHER BOOKS BY THE AUTHOR ARE AVAILABLE ON AMAZON IN MULTIPLE FORMATS INCLUDING PAPERBACK, HARDBACK AND E-BOOK:

<u>Undaunted Valor Series</u>: Follow a young man from the time he joins the military in 1968 after two worthless years in college and watch his progression from a private to an accomplished combat instructor pilot over the course of two years. All events are true, and most of the characters are people he flew with.

Undaunted Valor: An Assault Helicopter Unit in Vietnam 1969–1970

Undaunted Valor: Medal of Honor

Undaunted Valor: Lam Son 1971

Battle of Quang Tri, 1972

Battle for An Loc, 1972

<u>Crisis in the Desert Series (coauthored with James Rosone)</u>: How much different would Desert Shield and Storm have been if Saddam had carried his attack through Saudi Arabia and into the UAE? This series examines the difficulties and challenges that would have faced the allied forces if Saddam had carried the attack as well as received assistance from the crumbling Soviet Union at the time.

Project 19

Desert Shield

Desert Storm

<u>The Cost of Valor:</u> A screenplay based on *Undaunted Valor: Lam Son 1971* and currently being offered to studios. Please visit *Undaunted Valor* on Facebook for updates on the status of this effort.

Visit Matt Jackson's website: www.MattJacksonBooks.com

Contact: info@mattjacksonbooks.com

COPYRIGHT

Copyright © 2024 Battle for Kontum, 1972 by Matt Jackson

All rights reserved under International and Pan-American Copyright Convention

No part of this text may be reproduced, transmitted, downloaded, decompiled, reverse engineered or stored in or introduced into any information storage and retrieval system in any form or by any means, whether electronic or mechanical, now known or hereafter invented without the express written permission of Matt Jackson LLC.

This book is a work of historical fiction. The characters, incidents and dialogue are drawn from public sources and personal interviews as well as some fictional characters. Conversations between characters may be fiction unless duly noted.

Kindle ISBN: 978-1-960249-12-8
Print paperback ISBN: 978-1-960249-13-5
Print hardback ISBN: 978-1-960249-14-2

Printed in Ruskin, Florida, United States of America
Library of Congress Control Number: 2023919641

www.MattJacksonBooks.com
Contact: info@mattjacksonbooks.com

Interior format by Rukia Publishing US
www.rukiapublishingus.com

Cover Design by Momir Borocki

ENDNOTES

Prelude

1. Lewis Sorley, "Courage and Blood: South Vietnam's Repulse of the 1972 Easter Invasion," *US Army War College Quarterly: Parameters* 29, no. 2 (1999).

1. Another Cut

1. The term *fragging* refers to the deliberate killing or attempted killing of a soldier—usually a superior—by another soldier. The term originated in Vietnam, where fragmentation grenades were often used for this purpose in order to make the killing or attempted killing appear to have been accidental or to have happened in combat with the enemy. Today, the term is used to refer to any deliberate killing of fellow servicemembers.
2. "One over the world" is a military term meaning that the intelligence picture is too broad for use by front-line commanders, who need details that are not provided by Air Force assets.
3. The YO-3 Quiet Star was an airplane built by Lockheed on the Schweizer glider design, capable of carrying two, with an engine, for night reconnaissance missions. It was so quiet that it could fly at 1500 feet and not be heard. It was reported that it could fly at 200 feet and only be as loud as a bird in flight. Eleven were built, nine deployed. Only one exists today, in the Vietnam Helicopters Museum in Concord, California.

2. PAVN Planning Guidance for MR-II

1. General Hoang Minh Thao died in September 2008 and is buried in Hanoi. "Hoàng Minh Thảo," Wikipedia, October 22, 2023, translated by Google Translate, https://vi.wikipedia.org/wiki/Hoàng_Minh_Thảo.

3. Discussions

1. Lewis Sorley, "Courage and Blood: South Vietnam's Repulse of the 1972 Easter Invasion," *US Army War College Quarterly: Parameters* 29, no. 2 (1999).

5. Rules of Engagement

1. Lieutenant General John Vogt was the Director of the Joint Staff. Major General Winton Marshall was Vice Commander, 7th Air Force. Admiral Thomas H. Moorer was Chairman of the Joint Chiefs of Staff.
2. "John D. Lavelle," Wikipedia, accessed September 26, 2023, https://en.wikipedia.org/wiki/John_D._Lavelle.
3. SIGINT is an abbreviation for signals intelligence.

7. Falsified Report

1. Franks ended up reporting the incident, and later similar incidents, not up the chain of command but directly to Senator Harold Hughes, informing him that air strikes were taking place outside the "rules of engagement." Hughes, a member of the Senate Armed Services Committee, sent a copy of the letter to the Air Force Chief of Staff. After an investigation, Lavelle was recalled to Washington, where he was relieved of his command, reduced in rank to major general, and forced to retire. When President Nixon found out about Lavelle's relief and retirement, he was furious. Laird admitted several years later that Lavelle had not in fact known about the falsified reports but had instructed his subordinates in accordance with Laird's and Nixon's instructions. Neither Laird nor Nixon came to Lavelle's defense during the investigation.

8. John Paul Vann

1. An Article 32 investigation is similar to a grand jury investigation, conducted by one officer who presents the facts to the convening court-martial authority.
2. Neil Sheehan, A Bright Shining Lie: John Paul Vann and America in Vietnam (New York: Vintage, 1989), 486.

9. Welcome to MR-II

1. General George E. Wear graduated USMA in 1944 and was wounded in the Battle of the Bulge. He commanded a brigade in the 25th Division in Vietnam and returned to Vietnam to serve as the deputy SRAG commander in 1971.
2. Re-blued was a common term used to indicate that someone was being briefed on the latest developments in an organization and was generally brought back to that organization for a period of time for these updates. Mr. Vann was back in Washington for six weeks in the beginning of 1972.

3. General Ngo Dzu, pronounced Duz, died in 1977 in California after escaping from Vietnam in 1975.

11. Operations Brief

1. I still have mine from my days on active duty.
2. There are discrepancies in three of my sources over which Border Ranger units were at Ben Het. One source says the 71st, another source says the 85th and another says the 73rd.
3. The pilot for the rescue operation, Major William E. Adams, Commander, A Company, 227th Assault Helicopter Battalion, was posthumously awarded the Medal of Honor for his actions.

12. Recap

1. Vann commanded a Ranger company for three months early in the Korean War and a heavy mortar company in Germany in the mid-1950s.

13. The Interview

1. An excellent account of the Battle of Ap Bac may be found in Neil Sheehan's book *A Bright Shining Lie: John Paul Vann and America in Vietnam.*
2. Neil Sheehan, A Bright Shining Lie: John Paul Vann and America in Vietnam (New York: Vintage, 1989), 331.

14. Defensive Plan, MR-II

1. US corps were designated by Roman numerals and still are today. I Corps is pronounced Eye Corps. All the others are pronounced according to their number—Two Corps, Three Corps, etc.

16. General Hoang Minh Thao

1. Colonel Giap Van Curong was the original commander. Surprisingly, he was an admiral and became the first admiral of the PAVN Navy in 1974.

17. Canary Sings

1. The Vietnamese term for a defector is *hoi chanh*. American soldiers reversed the words and called a defector a *chu hoi*.

18. Missing but Not Forgotten

1. I felt it was necessary to reaffirm that Captain Nguyen Duc Phuc is the name indicated in the accident report. Many ARVN infantry battalions were commanded by captains, unlike US infantry battalions. In many cases, the ARVN infantry battalion was no larger than a US infantry company.
2. Specialist Fourth Class Edward Puck Kow Wong Jr. was never recovered and is listed as MIA today. He was nineteen and from Oakland, California. CWO Woods flew over the area for two days, searching for Wong, but enemy activity was too intense to put troops on the ground.

20. Prepare for Insertion

1. BUFF is an acronym for Big, Ugly Fat Fellow, commonly referring to B-52 bombers.

28. Charlie Heats Up

1. QSY was a term used to indicate that the speaker was changing frequency on his radio.
2. Although no Russian officers were ever captured, Chinese advisors were captured over the years. Communication intercepts identified Russian advisors with NVA artillery units in 1972 and later.
3. Major John J. Duffy, *The Battle for "Charlie"* (self-pub., CreateSpace, 2014), 18.

29. Realization Sets In

1. Pronounced "lurp," LRPs were "long-range patrol" rations. They consisted of freeze-dried dehydrated food that required hot water to prepare but in desperate times could be eaten unprepared and were designed to replace the Meal, Ready to Eat "C" rations due to the heavy weight of the "C" rations. LRPs were issued only to Special Forces and ARVN airborne units.
2. The three planes in the strike each carried a total of 108 bombs, consisting of a mixture of 500- and 750-pound bombs.

31. Dak Pek Is the First to Fight

1. BDA stands for Battle Damage Assessment. Four-deuce mortars are 4.2-inch mortars, which were the largest mortars in the US inventory at the time.

32. LZ English Falls

1. Dale Andradé, Trial by Fire: The 1972 Easter Offensive, America's Last Vietnam Battle (New York: Hippocrene Books, 1995), 257.
2. Kit Carson Scouts was the unofficial name given to those former NVA/VC soldiers that had defected to the ARVN/US side and now were acting as scouts for the friendly units.

35. FSB Delta Falls

1. LP stands for listening post. These were usually positioned forward of the perimeter by 300 meters to hear enemy forces approaching the firebase.
2. Dale Andradé, Trial by Fire: The 1972 Easter Offensive, America's Last Vietnam Battle (New York: Hippocrene Books, 1995), 265.
3. General Wear arrived in the Philippines but was told of the situation in Tan Canh and got on the first plane to return to Vietnam. When he arrived in Saigon, General Weyand, Deputy Commander MACV, met him at the plane and told him that a replacement had already flown to Pleiku and he was to get back on the plane. He never returned to Vietnam.

38. Tan Canh Falls

1. Thomas P. McKenna, *Kontum: The Battle to Save South Vietnam* (Lexington: University Press of Kentucky, 2011), 221.
2. Captain Dobbins escaped and evaded for several hours before a helicopter spotted him and picked him up. Captain Yonan was captured and listed as a POW by the North Vietnamese. However, when the POWs were returned, he was not among them and the North Vietnamese had no explanation for this. He is listed as MIA today. It was reported that Colonel Dat was killed walking across the airfield.

39. Escape and Evade

1. Peter pilot was a slang term used for copilot.
2. For three days, Specialist Franklin Zollicoffer survived in intense pain. On the third day after the crash, he drew his .45-caliber pistol and asked the others to put him out of his misery. He had previously been a Baptist minister and couldn't do it himself. Everyone refused. He became angry and said he would crawl to the river and drown. He made it halfway when he expired. He was buried with Warrant Officer Wade Ellen in the same grave.

41. Dak To II

1. Lieutenant Colonel Brownlee was listed as MIA. His body has never been recovered. Two POW sources stated that Lieutenant Colonel Brownlee committed suicide with his sidearm rather than be captured when confronted by NVA soldiers.

43. Priorities

1. General Wear recovered and retired in 1974. In 2018, he passed at the age of 99. "George Wear Obituary," *Washington Post*, November 19, 2018, https://www.legacy.com/us/obituaries/washingtonpost/name/george-wear-obituary?id=1754193.
2. CORDS is an acronym for Civil Operations and Revolutionary Development Support Program.

49. TOW to the Fight

1. Oher sources, as indicated earlier, claimed that this equipment was destroyed by air strikes on the day that the 34th and 35th Ranger Battalions abandoned FSB Lam Son on Highway 14 in the vicinity of Vo Dinh.

55. All Hell Comes

1. Major Chuyen was captured and executed despite his cowardly act of running early in the fight.

57. Helicopter Support

1. A major fear of all crew members was not the possibility of being shot—it was the possibility of being burned alive.
2. Captain Bill Reeder was captured and with his wounds marched north to North Vietnam. He was repatriated at the end of the war.

59. Helicopter vs. Tank

1. One other source says the crew chief's name was Blackwell but gave no first name or rank.
2. Nickname for a white phosphorous grenade.

60. Hospital Move

1. Dr. Pat Smith's two boys were adopted Montagnard children whose mother was killed by the VC. She retired in 1997 in Lake Cushman, Washington, and died in December 2005 at the age of 78. Christine Clarridge, "Dr. Smith Provided Care, Compassion to Vietnam," *Seattle Times*, January 1, 2005, https://www.seattletimes.com/seattle-news/dr-smith-provided-care-compassion-to-vietnam/.

62. Relief in Place

1. Major Lovings was a graduate of the Citadel and served four tours in Vietnam with the 101st Airborne Division as well as his tour as an advisor. He retired in 1980 as a lieutenant colonel. Lieutenant Colonel Wade Lovings passed at the age of eighty-two in 2020.

66. Attack Continues

1. Colonel R. M. Rhotenberry was from San Antonio, Texas, and fought in Korea as well as serving four previous tours in Vietnam before joining the II SRAG. He died in 1995 and was buried in Arlington National Cemetery.

75. ARVN Offense

1. Thieu ta' is Vietnamese for Major. Pronounced "Too Dat."

76. The Final Days Begin

1. Lieutenant Colonel Norbert Gannon served three tours in Vietnam. He was Special Forces and Ranger-qualified. He retired as a colonel and rests in Arlington National Cemetery as of 2010. Audio Taped Interviews, *Battle of Kontum* website, https://thebattleofkontum.com/audio/index.html#11.
2. Thomas P. McKenna, *Kontum: The Battle to Save South Vietnam* (Lexington: University Press of Kentucky, 2011), 436.

79. Reinforcements

1. The C-130s employed an all-weather airdrop system, which used an onboard computer that selected the time to drop the loads without the need to slow the aircraft down or the use of visual references. Thomas P. McKenna, *Kontum: The Battle to Save South Vietnam* (Lexington: University Press of Kentucky, 2011), 465.

81. By the Hand of God

1. An NVA mortar round landed in the partially destroyed ammo dump from action on 27 May. It set off a massive explosion of ordnance that had not detonated from the previous days. This blast stopped the enemy attack. Dale Andradé, *Trial by Fire: The 1972 Easter Offensive, America's Last Vietnam Battle* (New York: Hippocrene Books, 1995), 354.

1. TF Smith

1. The average family income in 1950 was $3,300 or $275/month.
2. Image: Roy E. Appleman, *South to the Naktong, North to the Yalu: June–November 1950* (Washington, D.C.: Center of Military History, United States Army, 1992), 60.

9 781960 249135